CLAY AND THE IMMORTAL MEMORY

CLAY AND THE IMMORTAL MEMORY

BY

PHILIP K ALLAN

ISBN-13: 9798391106968

Cover design by Christine Horner from original art by Colin M Baxter
Edited by Dr Catherine Hanley

Dedication

To Christiane, with all my love

A friend, confidant, and godmother like no other

Acknowledgements

My Alexander Clay books start with a passion for the age of sail, which was first awakened when I discovered the works of C S Forester and Douglas Reeman as a child, before later graduating to the novels of Patrick O'Brian. That interest was given some academic rigor when I studied the 18th century navy under Patricia Crimmin as part of my history degree at London University.

Many years later, I decided to leave my career in the motor industry to see if I could survive as a writer. I received the unconditional support and cheerful encouragement of my darling wife and two wonderful daughters. I first test my work to see if I have hit the mark with my family, especially my wife Jan, whose input is invaluable.

One of the pleasures of my new career is the generous support and encouragement I received from my fellow writers. In theory we are in competition, but you would never know it. When I have needed help, advice and support, I have received it from Bernard Cornwell, David Donachie, Ian Drury, Helen Hollick, Marc Liebman and Jeffrey K Walker. I have received particular help from my good friends Alaric Bond, creator of the Fighting Sail series of books and Chris Durbin, author of the Carlisle & Holbrooke Naval Adventures. I would also like to mention Robin Brodhurst, who kindly helped me with the technical aspects of the Battle of the North Atlantic for my WW2 novel *Sea of Wolves* and sadly passed away earlier this year.

The production of *Clay and the Immortal Memory* was the work of several hands. In particular I would like to thank Dr Cath Hanley for her excellent and thoughtful editing; Christine Horner from The Book Cover Whisperer for her design and the talented marine artist Colin M Baxter for yet another beautiful piece of cover art. Readers interested in exploring Colin's work further can find his details at the back of this volume.

I will always be in debt to Michael James and the team at Penmore Press, for having enough faith in me to publish my first seven novels.

Cast of Main Characters

The Crew of the Frigate *Griffin*

Alexander Clay – Captain RN

George Taylor – First lieutenant
John Blake – Second lieutenant
Edward Preston – Third lieutenant
Jacob Armstrong – Sailing master
Richard Corbett – Surgeon
Charles Faulkner – Purser

Nathaniel Hutchinson – Boatswain

Able Sedgwick – Captain's coxswain

Sean O'Malley – Able seaman
Adam Trevan – Able seaman
Samuel Evans – Seaman

The Crew of the *Redoutable*

Jean JE Lucas – Captain

Camille Dupotet – First lieutenant
Francois Brissot – Third lieutenant
Pierre Morin – Fourth lieutenant

Yves Dorre – Captain of marines
Marcel Paillard – Surgeon

Jean-George Tournier – Boatswain

Robert Guillemard – Marine private

In Paris

Napoleon Bonaparte – Emperor of France
Louis Alexandre Berthier – Minister of War
Denis Decrès – Admiral and Minister of the Navy
José Miguel de Carvajal-Vargas – Spanish ambassador

Others

Pierre-Charles de Villeneuve – Vice admiral commanding the Franco-Spanish Combined Fleet
Honoré Ganteaume – Vice admiral commanding the French Atlantic Fleet

Lord Horatio Nelson – Vice admiral commanding the British Mediterranean Fleet
Thomas Masterman Hardy – Captain of the *Victory*

Contents

Prologue

The westerly gale had blown itself out during the night, but there was enough blustery wind to stir up an unpleasant swell in the sheltered waters of Boulogne harbour. The lines of invasion barges gathered there knocked and fretted against each other, while outside the heavy boom protecting the entrance lay the English Channel, a shifting green carpet flecked with veins of white. Just beyond long cannon shot lay a Royal Navy sloop assigned to keep watch on the port, pitching and rolling under reefed topsails. Lining one side of the inlet were blocks of patient infantrymen drawn up in full campaign dress, each one next to a large, flat-bottomed boat.

Napoleon Bonaparte, newly crowned emperor of France, stood looking out over the harbour, a hand thrust into the front of his coat as if in a sling. He turned to the man beside him. 'When will you give the order to begin?'

Admiral Eustache Bruix watched the wind flapping the tails of the soldiers' greatcoats and ruffling the plumes on the officers' hats, and shook his head. 'Not this morning, sire,' he said. 'I am sorry to disappoint you, but it is too rough. The craft only have a moderate freeboard, and fully laden they are certain to capsize …' He trailed into silence as he observed Napoleon's frown grow deeper, and his cheeks begin to flush.

'Still too rough?' queried Marshal Berthier, from the new emperor's other side. 'But we have been waiting for hours, for goodness' sake! When do you believe the weather will be right? This afternoon?'

'Perhaps, although the tide will no longer serve,' said Bruix. 'Maybe something might be attempted tomorrow?'

'*Putain*!' exclaimed Napoleon. 'All I want is a demonstration of how the embarkation will work! Is that too much to ask? I will never understand you admirals! When I order one of my generals to march, he does so, without hesitation, through the midst of an enemy army if he must. But when I order one of my fleets to put to sea, all I hear is excuses! The wind is too strong, or not strong enough, or just right, but from the wrong direction! Did Alexander the Great allow such trifles to detain him when he conquered the world?'

'He did not, sire,' conceded Bruix. 'Although I don't believe he was required to cross any seas. But I can assure you that your soldiers understand very well how to get in and out of these boats. They have practised little else these last few months.'

'Then show me!'

'But if I order the demonstration to proceed, perhaps half these men drawn up here are sure to drown,' protested the admiral.

'Let them,' growled the emperor. 'I have plenty more.'

Bruix noticed several soldiers in the nearest formation exchanging startled looks. 'I don't think that would be entirely wise, sire,' he cautioned. 'Word of any accident will spread through the *Armée de l'Angleterre*. When the time comes for the men to embark in earnest, we might have difficulty persuading them to enter the boats.'

'Hah!' snorted Berthier. 'And when is that likely to be? Your boats can't even cross a sheltered creek! How will they ever cross the Channel and reach England?'

'They work well enough when the sea is calm,'

explained Bruix. 'I have made the calculations with some care. To row the whole army across, together with their horses and guns, will take repeated trips over three days and nights. Three calm days and nights, that is.'

'Only three days,' said Napoleon, his good humour reviving at the prospect. 'And then we defeat the English once and for all. Surely there must often be such periods of fair weather? In the summer, for example?'

'There is another requirement, of course, sire,' said the admiral. 'The most important one. The Channel must be both calm and also empty of Royal Navy ships.'

'What ships?' scoffed Berthier. 'That little one waiting outside? Surely the frigates you have in the outer basin will suffice to drive her away?'

'That is true, but she serves only as a picket. The moment we start to cross in earnest, she will send up a signal to alert the enemy. There are powerful squadrons in Dover and Folkestone just over there, with more waiting in the Downs, not to mention the Channel Fleet.'

'Only God can grant us calm weather,' cautioned the emperor, 'but I, Napoleon, can give you a fleet of ships to drive the enemy away. How many do you require, Admiral?'

'Forty to fifty ships of the line. That should suffice to hold the English off.'

'I know we are building them as swiftly as we are able, but do we have so many yet?' asked Berthier.

'Not on our own,' said Bruix. 'But we do when combined with the Spanish fleet.'

'Then I have good tidings for you, Admiral,' said Napoleon. 'Foreign Minister Talleyrand and I have concluded a secret agreement with Spain for her to join the war soon. You shall have your fleet. Just make sure that your little boats are ready when they come sailing up the Channel, driving the remnants of the English navy before them.'

'When will that be, sire?' asked Bruix. 'Surely it will take many months to gather such an armada together, and if I know the Spanish, they will be found ill prepared. I don't believe they could be ready before the onset of winter.'

'Then let us put our plans in place to invade next summer, when they are ready,' said Napoleon. '1805 will be our year of victory, gentlemen. When I shall ride through the streets of London at the head of my guard. I have waited many long years to witness the English broken and defeated. I can be patient a little longer.'

1804

Clay and the Immortal Memory

Chapter 1
The China Fleet

Vice Admiral Peter Rainer had always been overweight, but ten years commanding his majesty's ships in the East Indies had seen him balloon in size. His natural fondness for sugar was all too easily indulged by the tempting variety of sweetmeats available in the East. A regime of vigorous exercise might have addressed matters, but he preferred to smoke a pipe of the local hashish during his leisure hours. Yet those who regarded his pendulous jowls and bulging waistcoat as a sign of indolence were mistaken. The eyes that lay behind his silver-rimmed spectacles had a shrewd, calculating air.

They rested today on the rather slighter frame of his clerk, who sat perched on the edge of his seat with a pile of open letters before him. The two men were in the main cabin of his flagship, HMS *Trident*. Five bells in the forenoon watch had just struck, and the temperature here in southern India was already uncomfortably warm even though it was only April. The onshore breeze that flowed in through an open gunport did little to help.

A bead of sweat made its way down the side of Rainer's face and he scratched irritably at his periwig. 'Pray, what is the next matter requiring my attention, Mr Bayley?' he asked.

'A letter from the dockyard superintendent in Bombay that accompanied his monthly returns, sir.' The official passed the document across. 'After the usual courtesies, he reports that termites have destroyed much of his store of spars. He recommends the digging of a mast pond next to number two dock, so that they may be stored underwater in future. A rather indifferent diagram of his project is attached.'

'Destroyed by insects, or sold on to John Company merchant ships for a handsome profit?' queried the admiral, glancing up from the letter.

'I believe the creatures to be genuine, sir,' said Bayley. 'Mr Bradshaw is as willing to enjoy the perquisites of his position as the next man, but I hold that he also understands the need to keep within reasonable bounds.'

Doubtless with a small cut of any profits included for you, thought Rainer, taking in the expensive cut of his clerk's coat, and the heavy gold links of his watch chain. He made a mental note to get a trusted agent in Bombay to quietly investigate the matter, and returned the letter. 'Very well, get Bradshaw to submit an estimate for the work in proper form,' he ordered. 'What's next?'

'A dispatch from …' began the clerk, when a commotion sounded through the open skylight above them. Rapid footfalls followed on the companionway outside, ending with a thunderous knocking at the door.

'A moment, if you please, Mr Bayley,' said Rainer, holding up a hand. 'Do come in.'

A breathless midshipman sprang into the cabin. 'Mr Rogers' compliments, sir, and Fort St George has just signalled,' he blurted out. 'Fleet in sight!'

'A fleet!' exclaimed the admiral, rising with surprising speed from behind his desk. 'Damnation! And all my ships spread to the four winds! What has been reported from the masthead?'

'Nothing as yet, sir, but it can surely only be a matter of time.'

Rainer considered matters as the youth shifted from foot to foot with barely concealed excitement. Then he crossed to peer through the stern windows. Outside the fierce sun beat down on the shipping moored between him and the shore. There was a wide collection of vessels, from a stately East Indiaman that was almost a match for the *Trident* in size, all the way down to Arab trading dhows barely larger than the flagship's longboat. Directly opposite him was a beach of white sand, lined with fishing boats and fringed by drooping palm trees. A little further up the coast was the squat mass of Fort St George behind its lofty walls of red sandstone, and then the main settlement of Madras.

'A *hostile* fleet, Mr Paine?' asked the admiral, turning from the view.

'Oh, I imagine so, sir,' enthused the midshipman. 'Should it prove to be Admiral Linois squadron, is there to be a battle with the French?'

'Certainly, if that is who is approaching, and yet I note a distinct want of clamour outside,' observed Rainer, indicating the peaceful view. 'No signal guns firing the alarm, no files of sepoys rushing to form up along the shore, no ships making haste to depart?'

'Are they not, sir?' said the youngster, peering past him, a little crestfallen.

'Hmm, perhaps you and I had best go on deck and speak with Lieutenant Rogers to confirm the precise nature of this report,' said the admiral, collecting his hat from its place by the cabin door. 'And it will go very ill with you, young man, if I find I have been deceived. We will resume our work presently, Mr Bayley.'

'Aye aye, sir.'

When they reached the quarterdeck the officer of the watch coloured with embarrassment. 'No, no, that wasn't the message at all!' he exclaimed. 'The signal was that the *China* Fleet was in sight, sir. Their topsails are even now visible from the masthead. I can only apologise for Mr Paine's inability to follow the simplest of instructions.' He turned a terrible eye on the now quaking midshipman. 'We shall presently see if the boatswain's cane can help him better attend to his duty in future.'

'Ah, that is much more welcome intelligence,' said Rainer. 'I have barely slept since Captain Clay wrote to say he believed the French meant to ambush them. This year's fleet is worth over eight million in sterling, Lieutenant. It would not have been Mr Paine alone in a deal of trouble if Linois had seized it.'

'Captain Clay may be with the convoy, sir,' said Rogers. 'The masthead reported a frigate to windward of them that might be the *Griffin*.'

Rainer called for his telescope and stayed on deck to watch the long-awaited convoy arrive. At first he could only see a crowd of topgallant sails, squares of white lifting clear from the blue line of the sea, but as they came over the horizon they resolved themselves into individual ships. There was a row of East Indiamen under towering columns of sails. To leeward of them was a second, more motley group of a dozen smaller merchant ships, boasting a variety of different rigs, while to windward were two warships, a small brig flying the same red and white gridiron colours as the East Indiamen and a large frigate with a Royal Navy ensign.

'It was twelve John Company ships that left for Canton, was it not?' the admiral asked.

'Yes, sir. I count sixteen returning, but that's not unusual,' said Rogers. 'There are often a few that join at the rendezvous in the Pearl River. Some of these ones have been in action. Do you mark the shot holes in the topsails of the leader?'

'I do,' said Rainer, examining the ship. 'That captain is a saucy fellow, is he not? Flying a broad pennant as if he was Nelson himself in his pomp. Why, he has even painted his strakes buff, just like a king's ship, for all love!'

'As has the one behind, I believe, sir.'

'So he has,' said the admiral. He turned his attention to the frigate. Here the evidence of battle damage was more obvious as the warship grew nearer. He could see plenty of spliced rigging and damaged sails. A silver jet of pumped water being thrown to one side spoke of more unseen damage beneath the waterline.

As he watched, signal flags broke out at her masthead, and beside him a midshipman scrambled for his slate. 'The frigate is making the correct recognition signal, sir,' he reported, touching his hat. 'She is the *Griffin*, thirty-eight. Captain Alexander Clay commanding.'

'Acknowledge and ask Captain Clay to come on board and report when convenient, together with the senior Company officer present,' ordered Rainer.

'Aye aye, sir. That will be Captain Nathaniel Dance of the *Earl Camden*,' said Rogers. 'He is commodore of this year's China Fleet.'

'Very good, Lieutenant,' said the admiral. 'Kindly have them shown below when they come on board.'

'Aye aye, sir.'

Rainer had almost concluded his work with the clerk when the squeal of boatswain's pipes and the stamp of marine boots from further forward told him his visitors had arrived.

Bayley quietly gathered up his paperwork and withdrew, trading places with a white-gloved steward. The servant had just taken his station by the bulkhead when two officers were shown in.

The first wore the full-dress uniform of a senior naval captain. He was mid-thirties in age with curly brown hair and pale grey eyes. He was a tall man and ducked his head beneath the cabin's deck beams with the ease of long experience. His companion was a shorter, solid-looking man in his early fifties, dressed in the elaborate uniform of an Honourable East India Company captain, its glittering braid comfortably out-matching that of a mere admiral. His silver hair contrasted markedly with a deeply tanned face that spoke of long years spent in the tropics.

'Captain Clay, my dear sir,' enthused Rainer, grasping the proffered hand. 'And you too, Captain Dance. Well met, gentlemen, well met! Be seated, I pray. Marshal, some Madeira for my guests.'

'That would be most welcome, sir,' said Clay, taking a seat.

'Bringing the trade this far as proved to be thirsty work, sir,' supplemented Dance.

'I confess I am mighty relieved to see you both,' said the admiral. 'When I received your dispatch, Captain Clay, I feared the worst. I sent all of my ships to search for you, but I despaired of finding you before the French did. But look now!' He waved an arm towards the stern windows, where the anchorage was crowded with all the new arrivals. 'I collect that you have managed to evade Admiral Linois, after all.'

'By no means, sir,' said Dance. 'His entire force was waiting for us in the Straits of Malacca.'

'What! His whole squadron? All present?'

'A seventy-four, two frigates and a corvette, sir,' said Clay.

'But … but then you have me all aback!' exclaimed Rainer. 'How the deuce do you come to be here at all, a little battered I note, but yet still intact?'

'In truth, I wonder at it myself,' chuckled Dance. 'It was a close-run thing, let me tell you. What I can certainly report is that we should never have come through the encounter at all were it not for Captain Clay here and the exemplary conduct of his men. It is a conclusion I shall share with the governor, and include in my official dispatch to the Company.'

'I am delighted to hear it, but I am none the wiser as to how the feat was achieved. Perhaps you could enlighten me, Clay?'

'After I attacked that shipyard in Travancore, I was troubled by the ease of the victory, sir. Linois could have frustrated my attack, yet apart from a modest shore party, there was no sign of him. I concluded that he must be after prey of a different sort, and the China Fleet was the obvious prize. I sent word to you via Lieutenant Hummer in the *Curlew*, but time was short, so I went myself without delay. Hummer was unsure of the exact route they would take from Canton, but assured me that they would have to pass through the Straits of Malacca, so it was to there that I hastened.'

'A shrewd move,' said Rainer. 'But would the French not also know the trade had to pass that way?'

'Indeed, sir, and so it proved. We arrived first and were able to meet with the merchantmen a few days ahead of Linois's squadron.'

'Word that war was renewed with France had not reached us in China when we left, so you can well imagine my distress at finding I was hunted by such a formidable foe,' added Dance, gulping down the rest of his drink at the thought.

'Quite so,' said Rainer, beckoning forward his steward to refill the glasses. 'So what did you do?'

'Lieutenant Hummer had thought there would be only twelve East Indiamen in the fleet, not the sixteen that we encountered, sir,' explained Clay. 'I understand there were additional vessels already in Chinese waters, but it struck me that if twelve was the generally expected number, Linois too may have had the same intelligence. In which case he might interpret the four additions as a powerful escort. He would not be the first to mistake an East Indiaman for a warship.'

'I have heard of that happening, from afar or in indifferent visibility,' agreed Rainer.

'To make the deception more certain, I persuaded Captain Dance here to repaint four of his ships in navy fashion and to fly blue ensigns, sir,' explained Clay. 'Then we formed them in a separate squadron with my *Griffin*, and came on bold when Linois appeared.'

'Did you, by Jove! And did it answer? Surely the deceit became obvious once the merchantmen were obliged to open fire?'

'It was the *Griffin* that did much of the fighting, and she was roughly handled in consequence, sir. But in truth the French never pressed matters, and Captain Dance and his ships showed enough pluck to see us through. Perhaps the French were shy of losing too many spars so far from home.'

'I dare say,' mused Rainer, visions of termites munching through masts briefly flitting through his mind. 'But your action does seem to have been a splendid affair. Do you have the particulars for me?'

Clay slipped a hand into his coat and passed across a bulky-looking document. 'It is all set out in my report, sir.'

'Capital. I shall send a note across to Government House. Lord William will be much relieved by the fleet's safe arrival. No governor wants his tenure to commence amid censure and calamity. I daresay his lordship may even wish to thank you in person. What is the state of your ships, Dance?'

'A little modest damage, here and there, but nothing more than that. A week will answer to mend all, and then the China Fleet must resume its journey. In matters of trade, promptness is profit.'

'If you say so, but that will answer well, for I expect the *Albion* and *Sceptre* to arrive any day now. Two seventy-fours should serve to convoy you safely through to St Helena, should they not? Two genuine seventy-fours, that is?'

'Very droll, Rainer,' chuckled Dance, close to the end of his third glass. 'I am much obliged to you.'

'That is settled, then,' said Rainer, turning towards Clay. 'Now, Captain, let us consider your immediate future. Thanks to your timely attack, our prestige in Travancore is largely restored, and now that I have been reinforced from home, I am instructed to let you return hence. But will the *Griffin* be able to attempt such a journey? I could not help but notice your pumps at work as you approached.'

'She is in need of some attention, I fear, sir. We went toe to toe with Linois's *Marengo*, and thirty-six-pound cannon balls are most unwelcome visitors. She was holed thrice between wind and water. I should say she will need a month in the dockyard to repair her.'

'More like two, if I know the facilities here in Madras,' grumbled the admiral. 'It is April already, but I would hope to get you away before May is long out. Indeed we must, before the season of rains is upon us – the monsoon, as it is named in these parts. I will order the *Griffin* warped over to the dockyard directly. And I daresay you and your people will not mind some shore leave in India? There is some capital sport to be had in the area, should hunting be your diversion?'

'It is not, but I daresay my officers may wish to partake, sir,' said Clay. 'May I remind you that there is Mr Vansittart to consider? I still have him on board, and now that his mission here is complete, he is anxious to return to London. I can't imagine him wanting to spend two months in Madras, irrespective of the quality of the hunting.'

'Ah yes, our well-connected diplomat,' said Rainer. 'Perhaps he could be accommodated in the *Earl Camden*? I'm sure he will not object to swapping the crowded wardroom of a frigate for a cabin on an East Indiaman.'

'It would be my pleasure to conduct him home,' said Dance, bowing in his seat. 'My ships are anxious to bring their cargos there. A minute wasted is a penny lost, as they say.'

'Then all is settled,' said the admiral. 'Vansittart can return home amid the tea, silk and porcelain of China, which I think will suit him very well, while you will be obliged to stay here a while longer, Clay.'

'I shall be content to see a little of the country before returning home, sir. But I confess that I am anxious to return. During the peace I longed to be at sea again, and yet now I have been away for the better part of a year, I find I miss my family exceedingly.'

*****

Lieutenant Francois Brissot let the tailor settle his new coat on to his shoulders, and turned towards the full-length mirror that stood in the corner of the shop. He was an upright young man of medium build, and the French naval uniform suited his frame well. He ran his dark eyes over the rich blue cloth, and reached up to push away a curl of black hair that had fallen across his forehead.

Over his shoulder he could see the play of emotions on his uncle's face as he stood watching. 'How do I look?' he asked, turning towards him.

'Your father would have been very proud of you,' said the older man, dabbing at his eyes while his wife patted his arm.

'Monsieur is joining the fleet soon?' asked the tailor, brushing at a loose thread.

'Next month,' replied Brissot. 'I am to be third lieutenant on the *Redoutable*, seventy-four. She lies at Toulon at present.'

'A ship of the line, no less,' said the tailor, reconsidering the value of his client. 'Will you be wanting a new waistcoat to go with the coat? I have some fine white cloth newly arrived from Lyon?'

'No, I think not. I am well supplied in that respect.'

'But stay a moment,' said the tailor. 'Monsieur said his ship was the *Redoutable*? Why, she was mentioned just yesterday in *Le Moniteur*. Recently returned from the Caribbean and carrying some of General Rochambeau's men home in triumph, I believe.'

'Believe what you like, but you will find only lies printed in that rag,' scoffed the uncle. 'That Corsican popinjay sent an army of twenty thousand to recover Saint Domingue from the blacks. Now a few thousand diseased scarecrows return, leaving the slaves still firmly in control of the island. Where, pray, is the triumph in that?'

'Have a care, my dear,' urged his wife. 'You never know who may be listening.'

'Let them!' said the older man, shaking off her hand.

'What do I care for informers! My brother and I did not shed our blood for the Revolution only to be silenced now, Marie. *Liberté, Egalité, Fraternité* is what we fought for. Pray tell me what part do expeditions to reimpose slavery have in that?'

'But surely the Revolution is over, monsieur,' said the tailor. 'Times have changed. We have an emperor now. I supported your brother back then, who was a fine man, but we must look to his son. Is he not ready to serve his country in, I blush to say it, a very finely cut coat?'

All eyes in the room turned on the young lieutenant, who coloured a little under their gaze.

'Always remember what your father died for, Francois. The nation's liberty above all else,' said his uncle.

'Would papa have approved what I do?' asked the young officer.

'Very much so,' said his uncle, coming over. 'He was also a true patriot who much preferred the navy to the army. I remember him saying that a ship cannot be used to suppress the will of the people, only a regiment can do that.'

'Good, then I am ready to go and join my ship, with your blessing, uncle.'

'Indeed you are, monsieur,' said the tailor, butting in to the touching scene. 'Once my modest bill has been settled, of course.'

*****

The *Griffin*'s barge was uncomfortably crowded as it left the frigate's side. In the stern sheets Clay sat squashed in one corner, trying to prevent his long legs from entangling with those of the other passengers. Next to him was George Taylor, his iron-haired first lieutenant, sitting stiffly upright in his full-dress uniform. Opposite them sat the dapper figure of the Honourable Nicholas Vansittart, fortunately a much smaller man than the two officers, in a black evening dress over a white waistcoat embroidered with bees. Manning the tiller was Able Sedgwick, Clay's coxswain, steering the boat through the crowded anchorage while trying to compress his bulky frame to leave as much of the space as he could to his betters.

'Goodness!' exclaimed Taylor, mopping at his brow with a handkerchief. 'An hour from sundown, and still hotter than Hades, sir. And this is what passes for spring in Madras.'

'Lord Bentinck was telling me that with the approach of summer his entire administration up sticks and head for some place in the hills, just to get any work done,' said Vansittart, leaning over the side to trail his fingers in the water.

'Have a care, sir,' cautioned Sedgwick. 'This here anchorage be stiff with sharks. A knot of them were milling over the galley slops earlier. Hefty buggers an' all.'

The diplomat hastily withdrew his hand. 'No matter,' he sniffed. 'The water is warm as blood, in any event.' He felt the prickle of sweat against his collar, and cast an envious glance at the boat crew as they worked the oars in their loose trousers and open shirts.

'It is very kind of his lordship to hold this dinner in our honour, sir,' said the first lieutenant.

'John Company can be very generous when they choose, Mr Taylor,' said Vansittart. 'They are rich as Croesus in his pomp, and that was a singular service the *Griffin* rendered.'

'Lord Bentinck is new to the governorship, is he not, sir?' asked Clay.

'Quite so,' confirmed Vansittart. 'Only a few months in post, and still finding his feet. Which means the poor man is plagued by every petitioner and crackpot in Madras, all pressing their favoured scheme. When I went to pay my respects to him the other day, he had just ejected some jumped-up clerk who wanted us to found a colony on the Malay peninsula. Raffles, I think was the cove's name.'

'It may have some merit, sir,' said Clay.

'In peacetime, perhaps, but we still have to beat Boney, which at present is a most uncertain prospect. Lord only knows what is going on at home.'

Clay sat back against the side of the boat as it glided across the water. The wind had dropped away with the approach of night, leaving the sea a mirror in which the ships sat deep upon their reflections. Ahead was the shore, dotted with points of lamplight. The jetty they were heading towards was brightly lit against the looming walls of Fort St George. It was a scene of beauty, despite the heat, but Vansittart's mention of home had stirred a longing to return. The first mail he had received since he left Plymouth had been waiting for the *Griffin* at Madras, letters posted almost ten months earlier by his wife, in a spring that had long vanished. Lydia's strong, flowing signature had been supplemented by a spidery 'Francis' from his son and an anonymous smear of ink, beneath which Lydia had added 'Miss Elizabeth Clay, her mark.'

'Easy there!' ordered Sedgwick. 'In oars, starboards. Handsomely, now!'

Returning from thoughts of home, Clay found they had arrived at the shore. The quayside was thronged with onlookers, drawn like moths towards the guttering torches that ringed the jetty. A line of sepoys held them back to allow the guests to disembark. 'I ain't seen crowds like this since Garrick last played King Lear,' muttered Vansittart, eyeing the multitude with alarm.

Rainer's barge was just ahead of them, the boat tipping perilously over as the admiral shifted his bulk to step out. Behind Clay were more boats arriving to deliver the captains of the four East Indiamen who had helped the *Griffin* hold off the French attack.

'Ah, there you are, Clay,' said Rainer, grasping his hand as he came ashore, his spectacles glinting in the light. 'Ready for the revelry? A selection of the great and the good of Madras society are to be present. I hear even the bishop has been invited.'

'Goodness, what a press, sir,' exclaimed Clay, surveying the crowd of faces, ten deep behind the cordon of soldiers. Moving among them were hawkers, calling out to draw attention to the trays of delicacies hung around their necks.

'It always seems deuced crowded in India, you know,' explained the admiral. 'Even for those accustomed to the lower deck of a king's ship. You should find it more agreeable once we are in the residency grounds.'

'That is a relief, sir. Mr Vansittart you know, of course, but may I present my first lieutenant, Mr George Taylor.'

'Honoured to make your acquaintance, Lieutenant,' said Rainer, taking the officer's hand. 'And here come the rest of the party. Come on, Dance, briskly now. Let us not keep his lordship waiting.'

The admiral led the way through the crowd, which parted before his swaying presence. Close by was a set of ornate gates in a high wall. The sepoys on guard saluted smartly in response to a barked command, and a sergeant with bristling whiskers led them through into the grounds beyond.

As the noise of the crowd outside receded, Clay found that he had entered another world. The hard stone of the quayside was replaced by a curving driveway of gravel between beds of flowering tropical plants. Other paths led off to left and right to vanish amid the stands of banana palms and graceful tamarind trees. The evening air was heavy with the perfume of flowers, the call of birds and the hum of insects.

'A veritable paradise, is it not?' said Rainer. 'Seventy-five acres of grounds in total, I believe. Of course it takes an army of gardeners to maintain, but as you have seen, in India there is no shortage of hands to do the labour. The residency is just a little further.'

The driveway curved on among the trees and then opened up before a sprawling building of white stone. The facade was imposing, with a broad flight of steps leading up to a portico. Running around the building was a deep veranda, lined with a stone balustrade. Lamplight glowed out from all the windows. More sepoy guards saluted as they approached and climbed the stairs. At the front door they were met by Indian attendants dressed in matching scarlet coats and black and gold turbans. The guests quickly found themselves relieved of their hats, and were then ushered through into the building.

Clay's overwhelming impression was of opulent wealth. A sea of polished marble floor stretched away before him. Gilded columns rose to support an elaborate plaster ceiling that was dominated by the relief of a huge peacock, its tail spread wide. Corridors led off into the building, while directly ahead was another staircase, richly carpeted.

'This way, sahibs,' urged an attendant at Rainer's elbow, indicating a pair of double doors to one side from which the chatter of voices came. The admiral led the way into a larger room in which about thirty people stood in groups sipping at glasses of wine and conversing with each other. The men were either in military uniform or crow-black evening wear, the women in muslin dresses of every colour. Obvious among them was the bishop, an elderly clergyman with a fine spread of purple showing beneath his coat. Deeper into the room was a long table set for a substantial dinner of multiple courses.

The walls of this room were lined with the portraits of previous governors set before Indian scenes. Clay looked at the nearest example, where the subject seemed curiously unconcerned by a ferocious battle being fought just behind his right shoulder between red-coated sepoys and a horde of native soldiers.

Beneath the picture stood a fresh-faced young man in conversation with two older men in Company uniforms. He seemed to be barely out of his twenties, but as Rainer led his party into the room, he raised his voice to call for attention and the party fell silent. 'My guests have arrived, ladies and gentlemen,' he announced. 'Pray show your appreciation for the defenders of the China Fleet.'

The party burst into polite applause, mixed with cries of hurrah from some of the more enthusiastic gentlemen. Clay and the four East Indiaman captains smiled and nodded in appreciation as they were led across towards the young man.

'Governor, may I present some of the heroes of the hour?' said Rainer. 'Captain Dance and his fellow commanders you know, of course, but this is Captain Alexander Clay, commander of the *Griffin*, and Mr George Taylor, her first lieutenant.'

'Delighted to make your acquaintance, gentlemen,' said Lord Bentinck, seizing both men's hands in turn. 'Upon my word, that was devilishly well played, deceiving old Linois like that. You bowled him quite the spinning lob, what?'

'I beg pardon, my lord?' queried Clay.

In answer the governor mimed throwing a ball

underarm, snapping his wrist as he did so. 'I was famed for that delivery when I played for my old regiment.'

The various naval officers looked from one to another in hope of an explanation.

'I believe his lordship may have a fondness for cricket,' offered Vansittart.

'Wonderful diversion, especially out here,' enthused the governor. 'We play in the cantonments over at St Thomas's Mount and have aroused considerable interest among the locals. Are you a player yourself, Captain?'

'Alas no, my lord. I joined the navy before I was old enough to play, and there is little space for such sport on board a king's ship.'

'And he will have little time to acquire the accomplishment, my lord,' added Rainer. 'Captain Clay has much work ahead to restore his frigate, prior to his return home.'

'Pity, but you naval coves are always in such a perishing hurry,' said Bentinck. 'Let me introduce you to the party before you vanish once more.'

Armed with a drink, Clay found himself presented to a variety of Company officials, soldiers and their wives. The men all had florid faces from a combination of the heat and the wine they were drinking thirstily. The women were more sensibly dressed in light fabrics, and armed with fluttering fans.

'Does one ever become accustomed to this heat?' Clay asked a Company officer called Palmer, whose face was a match for his crimson tunic.

'In time, one does, Captain,' he replied. 'With some changes to accommodate the conditions. I start the business of the day long before dawn, for example, when it is more tolerable. And we rarely dress in European fashion if we can avoid it.'

'You do not? What do you wear, then?'

'Why, local mufti. Loose garbs designed for the climate. It is only his lordship who insists on his officials wearing broadcloth in his presence, heaven help us.'

'With good reason,' said his wife. 'Consider where such lapses in standards can lead if unchecked. If only half the rumours are true regarding Major Kirkpatrick, it will be a scandal of the first order.'

'Did I hear the word scandal?' asked Vansittart, materialising at Clay's shoulder. 'Pray tell more, Mrs Palmer. I find myself far removed from the gossip of London and in need of nourishment.'

'Much of this is conjecture,' cautioned her husband. 'It concerns our Resident at the court of Hyderabad.'

'Hyderabad,' mused Clay. 'That is one of the native states, is it not? Some way inland from here?'

'Quite so,' said Palmer. 'Major Kirkpatrick represents the Company there.'

'I comprehend perfectly,' said Vansittart. 'What then is the nature of these rumours concerning the major?'

'Why, that he has turned Turk!' said Mrs Palmer. 'Gone wholly native, the rogue!'

'As I said, many of us find that adopting aspects of the local culture makes life more tolerable,' explained Palmer. 'But Kirkpatrick seems to have gone rather further than simply wearing local garb. Harrison, over there, visited him last summer and found he had grown a fine set of mustachios, and had hennaed his hands, just like a Mughal. Stranger still, he served not a drop of wine at dinner.'

'Eccentric, perhaps, but hardly scandalous,' said Vansittart, a little disappointed.

'But worse was to follow,' said Mrs Palmer, dropping her voice and leaning close. 'If the latest intelligence is to be believed, he has abandoned the ways of his race altogether, and become a thorough Mohammedan. He has even taken some local princess as his wife.'

'The whole affair is a damned poor show,' fumed Palmer. 'How can he truly represent the Company's interest if he is in bed with the locals. Literally, it would seem.'

'Can't your Mohammedan have as many wives as fancy takes him?' offered a young Company officer, with a wistful look in his eye.

'I don't see the call for that,' said Vansittart. 'Keeping one wife in frocks and bonnets through the season damned near bankrupts me as it is.'

Perhaps attracted by the sound of laughter, Lord Bentinck approached the group, accompanied by the bishop. 'Admiral Rainer informs me that you will be leaving us soon, sir?'

'Indeed,' said Vansittart. 'I will not wait for Captain Clay's ship to be restored, but will return home with the China Fleet, now that my mission to the Malabar Coast is complete. The maharaja of Travancore has been sharply reminded of his obligations to us, and I believe his chief minister has been cured of his partiality for the French.'

'I trust they will now receive our Christian forgiveness, Mr Vansittart,' said the bishop.

'Indeed so, your grace,' replied the diplomat. 'I am always happy to forgive my enemies. Once they are hanged,' he added.

The governor filled the pause that followed by turning to Clay. 'Before we sit down to dinner, I wanted to give you some welcome news. The council met earlier to discuss your prompt action to save the China trade from ruin. We agreed a formal vote of thanks to you, and a purse of six thousand guineas to indicate our appreciation.'

'I don't know what to say, my lord,' said Clay. 'That is very generous, and quite unlooked for.'

'John Company knows how to honour those who defend its interests, Captain,' said Bentinck. 'What will you do with your reward?'

'I shall consider it as prize money for the ship, and distribute it among my people accordingly,' said Clay, after a moment's thought. 'It is as much their victory as mine.'

'Well said, sir,' beamed Taylor, swiftly calculating his portion.

'Upon my word, the men's share will make their time here in Madras memorable,' chuckled Vansittart. 'The local grog shops and bawdy houses had best be ready, what?'

Chapter 2
Departures

The coach rounded the shoulder of Mont Faron and began a long descent through pine-covered slopes towards the port of Toulon. As the road turned across the hillside, the sea appeared through the trees, a glittering expanse of blue that stretched away to the far horizon. At sight of it, Lieutenant Brissot leant across the thin civilian snoring gently beside him to drink in the view. A moment later the coach lurched over a bump in the road, tipping the young officer forward on to his fellow passenger's lap.

The man woke with a start. 'Really, monsieur,' he exclaimed. 'Must you lie across me in such a fashion?'

'My apologies, sir, but I have never been to Toulon before, and I am most anxious to see my new ship,' explained Brissot. 'Perhaps if we were to exchange places?'

The civilian glared at him for a moment, but there was no denying the look of appeal in the soft brown eyes before him. 'Oh, very well, if you must.'

The coach was almost full, and there were protests from the other occupants as they shuffled around the interior, but eventually he was able to drop into the window seat just as the trees fell away and the port opened up below him.

Toulon sprawled around a wide harbour, an undulating mass of terracotta roofs divided into a grid of streets and confined within solid fortifications of grey stone. Dotted among the roofs were larger whitewashed churches and the occasional open square. But of more interest to Brissot was the port. He could clearly see the dockyard with its distinctive long ropery building. There seemed plenty of activity here. There were tall stacks of cut timber, white in the sunshine, and coils of smoke rising into the clear air from the fires used to melt tar. The dockyard waterfront was lined by slipways, all occupied by warships in various stages of construction.

Moored close to the dockyard were several lines of ships, most with their masts struck down on deck and white awnings spread against the sun. Ship's boats moved between them, their oars puddling the surface like the legs of aquatic insects. Sitting apart from them was a two-decked ship of the line with all its masts in place and its yards crossed. Brissot even fancied there were sails closely furled on her yards, to judge from their thickened appearance. Alongside the ship was a lighter full of casks. As he watched, a scrap of cloth waved amid the cargo and a barrel rose ponderously up through the air. The young officer felt a prickle of excitement. She must be preparing for sea, he concluded. Could she be the *Redoubtable*?

The road wound down around another bend and trees once more cut off the view, but in his mind's eye he held the image of the ship. She was certainly a seventy-four, but then so were most of the warships in the inner harbour. Please let that be my ship, he urged. He had spent much of the last war on board a frigate in Brest, unable to leave thanks to the blockading British fleet waiting just outside the harbour. He remembered the hours of tedious drill, the ill-tempered fights among the bored crew, and his longing for the silver sea that lay beyond the harbour entrance.

Now the coach emerged from the woods and ran out into the open. Lines of grape vines and small fields of vegetables appeared on either side, being tended by old men and women in black shawls despite the warm sun. No young men, reflected Brissot. They would all be in the army or navy now that the country was back on a war footing.

The sound of the road beneath the wheels changed as the coach rattled over a causeway that crossed a deep, stone-lined ditch. Lines of grey fortifications ran away on either side, patrolled by soldiers in shakos. Then the coach slowed and bumped over a heavy wooden drawbridge and through a gateway into the city of Toulon.

Buildings crowded close about the coach on either side, their whitewashed exteriors bright in the sunlight. An arcade ran along the side of the road, lined with windows and doorways that opened into the building's shadowy interiors. Images rattled past the coach window, vanishing almost before he had registered them. A saddle maker in a bright red waistcoat polishing gleaming leather with a soft cloth. A companionable circle of women in bonnets embroidering crisp white lace. Then the buildings drew back as they passed a square with a teeming market full of piled fruit and vegetables. A few blocks later the coach pulled around to the right and through another much narrower arch into the stable yard of an inn. With a final lurch and rattle it came to a halt.

Brissot stepped from the carriage and stretched his stiff limbs, while the inn staff passed down the luggage strapped to the roof. He soon found that his new naval uniform drew several ostlers to him looking for custom.

'Is yours the sea chest, monsieur?' asked a slightly built youth. 'To the docks, is it?'

'If the puppy can find them,' growled another lad, with all the authority of his two extra years. 'What ship was it, monsieur?'

Brissot ignored them both and picked out a man further back with a hand cart beside him. A gold ring hung from one ear and the rounded end of a wooden leg protruded from his trousers. ‘You there,’ he called. ‘What is your name?’

‘Flament, sir,’ said the veteran stumping over. ‘Quartermaster of the old *Nestor* before a ball took off my foot.’

‘Good to meet you, Flament. Would you take my dunnage down to the quayside for me?’

‘Yes, sir,’ said the sailor, swinging the chest on to the cart with ease, and setting off in the direction of the sea. ‘Which ship would it be?’

‘The *Redoutable*. Do you know much about her?’

‘A handsome-looking seventy-four, she is, sir,’ said Flament. ‘Although her backstays are set up tauter than fiddle strings, if I might be so bold. Them Brest-built two-deckers handle a deal easier with a bit of give in the masts, but I daresay I don’t need to tell you that.’

‘Eh … no, indeed,’ said the lieutenant, his pulse quickening once more. ‘So her masts are set up, you say? Does that mean she is due to sail soon?’

‘I should think so, sir. She’s been taking on board all manner of supplies this past week. Word is they’re for the garrison in Corfu. Mind, she’ll have to slip past the English first. They say that devil Nelson commands the blockade. Ah, there she is now.’

They had reached the end of the road and the harbour opened up before them. Flament immediately plunged across the busy quayside towards the steps that led down to the water. Brissot followed behind more calmly, all the time gazing across at his new ship.

The *Redoutable* was big for a seventy-four, he decided, taking in her soaring masts. Her long hull was cut by twin yellow strakes of a shade so rich it was almost orange. Gilding sparkled around her stern while beneath her long thrusting bowsprit was the figurehead of a woman painted ghostly white. She had a round buckler on one arm and held a sword in front of her, pointing the way ahead. All the ports were open to let in air, and her guns were run out to give her crew more living space. Those on her lower deck were heavy thirty-six-pounders, with smaller eighteen-pounders on the deck above.

'Sculls or oars, sir?' asked Flament, who was waiting patiently at the top of the stairs.

A single boatman with a pair of sculls would be fine for such a short crossing, but on the other hand arriving in a larger boat might impress his new captain. 'Oars, I think,' he decided.

'Right you are, sir.' The ostler let out a piercing whistle to attract the attention of two boatmen waiting at the bottom of the steps while Brissot fished out some change for him.

'*Merci*, monsieur,' said the sailor, pocketing the money and indicating the sea chest to the two men who came running up from their boat. 'Marcel here will charge you a fair price. Good winds and following seas, sir.'

'Thank you, Flament,' said Brissot.

Once he was settled in the stern sheets of the boat with his chest at his feet, they set off out into the harbour. With each of the boat's two oars manned they skimmed quickly across the surface of the water, the bow oar periodically glancing over his shoulder and varying the strength of his pull to keep them heading towards the *Redoutable*. Brissot felt a knot of anticipation growing in the pit of his stomach as the ship grew, until it filled his vision. The breeze brought him the smell of tarred rope warmed by the sun, mixed with poorly washed humanity. He could see faces looking out from the open ports at the approaching boat. A pair of sailors in boatswain's chairs turned around from their work repainting her side. More faces appeared at the quarterdeck rail, and a smartly dressed midshipman hailed the boat.

At a curt nod from their passenger, the bow oar replied. 'Lieutenant Brissot of the *Redoutable* asking for permission to come aboard.'

'Starboard side, if you please, sir,' replied the youngster. 'There is a whip ready for your dunnage.'

'Easy there, Pierre,' growled the bow oar, pulling the boat around under the stern. 'Now pull again!'

Soon they were approaching the column of slats build into the ship's side leading up to the entrance port. Brissot waited for a passing wave to raise the boat a little and scrambled his way aloft. Once he had cleared the first few rungs the seventy-four's pronounced tumble home made his climb progressively easier. He even had time to settle his hat and hitch his sword straight before he stepped through the entry port.

His initial impression was that he was on the main deck of a newly commissioned flagship. Immaculately scrubbed planking, dazzling white in the sunlight, stretched away from him. The ropes and lines along the ship's side were coiled with a precision he had seldom encountered. At the base of the main mast in front of him was a rack of boarding pikes, each steel head glittering like silver, a match for the buttons on the coat of the fresh-faced young midshipman who was there to greet him.

'Welcome aboard, sir,' said the youngster, touching the brim of his hat. 'My name is Pascal.'

Brissot returned the salute. 'Would you tell the captain that Lieutenant Brissot has come on board to report for duty, if you please, Monsieur Pascal,' he said.

'Captain Lucas is ashore, sir,' replied the midshipman. 'Monsieur Dupotet is our first lieutenant.' A bark of anger came from somewhere aft, making the youngster flinch. 'If you follow me, I'll take you to him.'

The young officer led the new arrival up the ladderway to the *Redoubtable*'s long quarterdeck, where a tall, thin lieutenant, his face flushed with anger, was bellowing at another midshipman standing a few feet from him. 'What have your men been doing this watch?' he demanded.

'Polishing the brass, sir,' offered the trembling youth.

'Polishing the brass?' queried the lieutenant. 'Really? Then why did I find two – not one, but two – finger marks on the bell?'

'I don't know, sir,' came the reply, barely above a whisper.

'Not good enough,' snapped the officer. 'How do you expect us to beat the English if we can't even keep the ship clean? You can reflect on that from the masthead. Off you go, and don't come down before six bells.'

'Yes, sir.'

'I'm surrounded by fools,' muttered the officer, turning to face the new arrival. Brissot found himself being inspected with care by a pair of dark eyes set either side of a sharp, aquiline nose. They travelled all the way down to his shoes before returning to his face. 'And who do we have here?' he asked.

'Lieutenant Francois Brissot, reporting for duty, sir.'

'You're late, monsieur. I expected you yesterday.'

'My coach was delayed north of Aix when one of the horses lost a shoe, sir,' said Brissot. 'I came aboard as soon as I arrived in Toulon.'

'Hmm, well, at least you understand how an officer should dress,' he conceded, indicating Brissot's new coat. He extended a hand. 'My name is Lieutenant Camille Dupotet.'

'Pleased to meet you, sir.'

'Your name seemed familiar to me when the captain told me that you had been posted to this ship. Have we met before, perchance?'

'I don't believe so, unless you too have served in the Brest fleet, sir?'

'Never,' said Dupotet. 'No matter. Monsieur Pascal here will show you to your quarters and introduce you to your servant. Then make haste to return, so I can explain your duties. There is much to do if we are to be ready to depart on Friday.'

'We are leaving Toulon, sir,' said Brissot. 'How splendid!'

'The captain is collecting our final instructions, so be swift. There is not a moment to spare.'

*****

To the north of Fort St George lay Madras proper, a sprawling network of narrow lanes and winding alleys known locally as Black Town. Within the confines of its encircling wall was a mass of teeming life. Silk-clad merchants rubbed shoulders with naked fakirs with strands of matted hair trailing down their spindly backs. Women in saris balancing brass pots on their heads swayed past hump-backed cattle resting in the shade. The entreaties of beggars competed with the cries of the traders in the spice bazaar, where piles of knobbly ginger roots lay beside hills of brilliant yellow turmeric. All the world's races seemed there, from florid Europeans, through Arab traders to dark-skinned Tamils with brilliant smiles.

It was small wonder, then, that a party of three sailors from the *Griffin* attracted little attention as they moved through the throng, in spite of their long pigtails and tattooed arms. In a quiet street they entered a modest hostelry and found a table where they could take their ease.

'A baker's dozen of Yellow Georges,' breathed Sam Evans, who was comfortably the largest of the three. He juggled his bulging purse in one hand to emphasise the point. 'I ain't seen so much bleeding chink since I was last milling in the ring.'

''Tis a rare fecking sight, to be sure, brother,' said Sean O'Malley, patting his own bulging coat pocket. 'No more than we deserve, in truth, given what we done for that John Company fleet.'

'Steady there, lads,' said Adam Trevan, his blond pigtail swishing in alarm as he looked around them. 'There be no call for showing your chink to the world, unless you wants every cut-purse and beggar in the parish hard about us.'

'So, how we going to spend it?' asked Evans. 'We ain't got long afore we sail, now the barky's set to rights.'

'Grog and wenches,' said O'Malley firmly, draining his cup and waving over the serving boy for a refill. 'Nice an' traditional, like. Back home thirteen guineas would have bought half the doxies in Dublin, so Lord only knows what it'll buy out here. Babylon will not be in it, I'm thinking.'

'Aye, that of course,' agreed Evans, 'But not even I could drink more than a guinea's worth of this gut-rot.'

'You could always keep some for them back home. I'll be saving most of mine for Molly an' the nippers,' observed Trevan.

'Nah, ain't a soul with any call on me there,' said Evans. 'But I were thinking of something else we could do? If we was back in London we might go to Vauxhall, or see a cock-fight, maybe. Ain't there no stuff like that hereabouts?'

'Dawson in the afterguard saw one of them serpents

being charmed,' said Trevan. 'Great big one an' all, in a basket, like. He near jumped out of his skin when this lascar blew on his fife an' the beast came a rearin' up.'

'If it's rearing snakes you're after, best come with me to the fecking bawdy house,' leered O'Malley.

'Excuse me, kind sirs, but are you coming from the *Griffin* boat?' asked a voice from the table next to theirs. Sitting there was a smartly dressed Indian man in a saffron yellow turban. He had kindly eyes and a well-trimmed beard threaded with grey.

'What would that be to you?' demanded O'Malley. 'An' how the feck do you know the name of our barky?'

'It is marked most clearly on the band of your hat, my friend,' said the stranger. 'As for what it is to me, my master is a merchant who had a modest interest in the fate of this year's China Fleet. He had only a little cargo on board, you understand, but its loss would have been unfortunate. He was not invited to meet your illustrious captain to thank him in person.'

'I shouldn't go worrying on his account,' said O'Malley. 'Pipe did handsomely enough, what with his captain's share of John Company's purse.'

'Pipe?' queried the stranger. 'I was thinking his name was Clay?'

''Tis just what we calls him,' explained Trevan. 'Clay Pipe, see,' he offered, removing a smouldering example from his mouth.

'Ah … I see. But I am grateful to be meeting with you, so as to thank you for your service to my master in person.' He rose from his table, touched his face with his hand in an elegant gesture and bowed low. 'My name is Abdul Khan, from Hyderabad,' he continued. 'Might I be knowing your names?'

Clay and the Immortal Memory

The sailors held out their hands a little sheepishly to Khan, who shook each one gravely in turn. 'Adam, like the first man Allah was creating, praise be upon him. Sam, you are truly the mightiest person I am ever setting eyes upon. Sean O'Malley, I am sorry to have been troubling you with my questions. Can you forgive me?'

'No call to speak of it, to be sure,' muttered the Irishman. 'Will you be after sitting with us?'

'If you are quite sure?' asked Khan, hovering beside the table. Trevan shuffled along the bench and the man perched on the end he had vacated. 'No arrack, I thank you. It is forbidden for me, but perhaps a little tea.' He waved over one of the serving boys and then paused as a thought came to him. 'I was not listening on purpose earlier, but did I hear you speak of desiring to see the snake being charmed?'

'Aye, that you did,' said Evans. 'I wouldn't mind copping a look.'

Khan spoke rapidly to the boy, who ran out of the door and down the street. 'I know the very person to perform for you,' he explained. 'The boy will be fetching him now.'

The sailors did not have long to wait before the youngster returned, accompanied by a bare-footed man carrying a heavy round basket. He placed it on the floor, squatted down beside it and drew out what looked like a thick, short recorder with a bulbous end close to the mouthpiece. Other patrons gathered in a circle to watch the performance and faces appeared in the shop's open window. Khan gave the snake charmer a few coins, and he pulled back the lid of the basket and began to play.

Almost immediately not one but two cobras reared up, their hoods unfurled and their black eyes glittering. Both were big animals, their heads held at least two feet aloft, but this still left plenty of scaly body coiled within the basket. The charmer swayed and rocked on his heels, all the while filling the air with a flow of reedy notes.

'Ain't that a rare sight,' said Evans, leaning forward to have a closer look. Both the snakes switched towards this new movement and one lashed at him with an angry hiss.

'Have a care, my friend,' said Khan, as Evans pulled back. 'The bite of the cobra is quite deadly. I have seen it kill a cow in moments.'

Eventually the snakes began to tire of being charmed. They dropped back upon their coils, despite their owner's cuffs to the side of the basket. When the larger cobra made an ill-tempered dart at his hand, he let out a final wail from his pipe and dropped the lid back into place. He gathered up the basket and those who had been watching returned to their tables.

'Thankee kindly for that,' said Evans. 'Bleeding dancing serpents! Not sure what folk back home would make of such a sight.'

'You are most welcome, Sam,' said Khan.

'So what manner of merchandise be your master a-dealing in, Mr Khan?' asked Trevan.

'Are you knowing much about Hyderabad, Adam?'

'Not a thing, bar it being your home,' said the Cornishman.

'It is far from the sea, so perhaps it is not so strange for a sailor not to be hearing of it,' explained Khan. 'But the great and the wealthy are knowing of it, for Hyderabad is being the capital of the Decan, and the Decan has the richest mines in all the world. As for my master, he is the biggest gem merchant in Hyderabad.' He drew out a soft leather pouch from his belt and placed a single greyish lump of what looked like glass on the table, about the size of a small bird's egg.

Clay and the Immortal Memory

O'Malley poked at the stone with a finger. 'What the feck is that?'

'That, my friend, is an uncut diamond,' said Khan. 'It is not much to look at, is it? But in the hand of a skilled jeweller, it is becoming a gift fit for a king!'

'How much be it worth?' asked Trevan.

'As every merchant knows, that is depending,' explained Khan. 'In my home, where such trifles are common, along with rubies and sapphires, perhaps three of four of your guinea pieces. But in Paris, London or Amsterdam, it will be fetching two hundred most easily.'

A fit of coughing erupted from O'Malley. 'Did yous say two hundred?' he spluttered.

'Oh yes,' said Khan, his face grim. 'At least, but the difference is most extreme at the moment, thanks to your East India Company, to the ruin of my poor master. During the peace the price paid here was being much better. Gem dealers from all of Europe were fighting for our business, but now your navy is sweeping their ships from the sea. The only fleets trading in these waters are those of the East India Company, who can name their price. It is very sad, for now they are making all the profit, and my master so little. But no matter. What can be done but wait for the peace to return, Allah willing.' The merchant returned the diamond to the pouch with a sigh, and rose from the table. 'But my troubles need not concern you, kind sirs. I must be on my way. Good day to you.'

Khan was halfway to the door when O'Malley called him back. 'Stay, a while, feller,' he urged. 'I'm after having a notion.'

'Steady there, Sean,' cautioned Trevan. 'I've seen that look in your eyes before. This ain't one of your daft fancies, like spending all our back pay buying up them parrots in

Bristol?'

'Or digging up half of bleeding St Lucia after pirate gold,' added Evans, folding his arms. 'Your schemes make the bleeding South Sea Bubble look solid.'

'Lads, you're not thinking this through,' insisted the Irishman, his eyes alight with avarice as he turned towards the merchant. 'Mr Khan, your problem is you can only trade with John Company, and them bastards are tighter than a miser's purse string.'

'Indeed.'

'An' that's all on account of theirs being the only fecking ships heading home, right?'

'Regrettably so, my friend.'

'But that isn't right,' said O'Malley. 'Our barky is away this very week! She's all fixed up lovely, and wants only a lick of paint and a hold full of vittles. What if we was to buy some of them fecking sparklers?'

Khan shook his head at this. 'I am admiring your spirit, Sean, but my master will not offer credit to sailors, excuse me for saying it, that are soon to depart, and I doubt that you are having the means to pay him.'

'But we *has* got the fecking chink! Right here, in gold. Thirty-nine Yellow Georges between the three of us.'

'I thought you was all for spending it on grog and wenches?' queried Evans.

'An' I has to bring mine back to my Molly,' protested Trevan.

'Think about it, lads,' urged the Irishman. 'Why is it always the Grunters or John Company as gets all the loot? It's the chance of our lives! We could take a dozen of them uncut rocks home easy as kiss your hand, and shift them for a fecking fortune! Why, they'd be worth … eh … em.'

'More than two thousand guineas,' supplemented Khan.

'Two fecking thousand!' repeated O'Malley. 'You can buy your Molly a carriage and four if you want, Adam. And you can have your own tavern, Sam.'

Evans and Trevan exchanged glances.

'That does sound grand,' offered Evans.

'Can we go meet with your man?' asked O'Malley to Khan.

'We did tell Able as how we'd wait for him here,' cautioned Trevan.

'Able?' queried Khan.

'Captain's coxswain of the *Griffin*,' explained Evans. 'Maybe you'll have clapped eyes on him steering the barge when Pipe comes ashore?'

'Yes, the large African sailor,' said the merchant. 'I have seen him. But in any case, my master would not wish to be seen trading directly. Your East Indian Company will be very angry if they are thinking he sells gems to any but them.' Khan sat for a moment and considered matters, while the anxious sailors watched on. Then his face cleared. 'Would you permit me to speak with him on your behalf? Perhaps, if he is in a good mood, I might persuade him, in this one case, to sell some stones. I will be sure to tell him you are from the *Griffin*, which will please him.'

'An' yous can return here with the fecking gems, an' our fortunes are made!' exclaimed the Irishman, plunging a hand into his pocket.

Trevan grabbed his arm to stop him pulling out his money. 'There be no call for offering up your gold just yet, Sean lad. Mr Khan will be back soon enough with word if the bargain be struck.'

'Aye, my chink stays put 'til I sees the goods,' growled

Evans. 'No offence, Mr Khan.'

'I understand, my friends,' said the merchant, rising again. 'You are wise in such matters, I see. You have thirty-nine of these guinea pieces, if I am correct? Good, that should be sufficient to buy twelve gems of the size I showed you. Wait here and I shall return.'

The time the merchant was away passed quickly as the sailors mapped out how their lives would be transformed by their newfound wealth.

'I likes the sound of owning me own tavern,' said Evans, leaning back against the wall and placing his hands behind his head. 'The Roving Sportsman, I shall call it. There'll be prize fighting bouts in the yard most nights, an' a place to train in an old barn. Lovely! How about you, Sean?'

'Oh, a plot of land for me, Sam. With a house. Turf burning on the hearth and a fair colleen drawing ale from a keg in the corner. Every fecking Irishman wants his own piece of dirt, with no rent to pay and no bailiff to doff your hat to. That would be just grand.'

'A bigger cottage for my Molly, up the hill from the sea, with an orchard, maybe,' said Trevan, a look of longing in his eye.

'An' to think we was after fecking spending the lot on grog and whores,' said O'Malley, shaking his head at the lunacy of the idea.

'In all fairness, that were always your notion, Sean,' said Trevan. 'But it be Able as I'm sorry for. Missing out on such a prize.'

'Too bleeding late for him, any road,' said Evans. 'Here comes Abdul, now.'

'Is the bargain fecking struck?' blurted O'Malley, the moment the merchant reached the table.

'It is and it is not,' said the merchant. He held up his hands as the sailor's faces fell. 'All is not lost, my friends. My master dares not be seen dealing with you directly, but I have a proposal, if you are willing. Give me your money, and I will sit outside on the seat that is just beyond that window. You will be able to see me from here. Then my master will come and sit beside me. We will be exchanging gems for money, in a quiet way, and so the transaction is being done.'

'That there window?' queried Evans, indicating the one that opened on to the bustling street.

'Yes. There is a bench set against the wall.'

'I says we fecking does it!' said O'Malley, already counting out his money. The other two sailors produced their purses with more reluctance.

'Meaning no offence by it, Mr Khan, but I ain't a bloke to get on the wrong side of, if you catches me drift,' warned Evans, adding his guineas to the growing pile.

'I can tell my master you are changing your mind?'

'No fecking call for that,' said O'Malley. 'Are yous in too, Adam?'

'Aye, I suppose I is.'

Khan swept the pile of gold into a cloth bag and hefted it for a moment in one hand. 'Please to be patient, my friends. My master is very nervous of his being seen, and does this only as a favour to you. If he sees you in the street approaching him, he will be turning away.'

'We'll sit here nice and still, to be sure,' said O'Malley. 'Finishing our drinks, like.'

'An' keeping a weather eye through yon window,' added Evans.

'Very well, my friends. Let us make you wealthy men!'

The merchant left through the door, and a few moments

later the back of his yellow turban appeared in the window as he took his place on the bench. The sailors tried to talk among themselves, but anticipation made them mute as they watched for signs of their friend's employer. Trevan puffed anxiously on his pipe. O'Malley drank thirstily, while Evans sat with his eyes never leaving the man outside.

After a few minutes the solid figure of Able Sedgwick came through the door, looking around the interior for them. 'There you be, lads,' he said, coming over with a smile. 'Sorry I be late. I had to drop the barky's mail off with the port admiral.'

'Hush your noise, there!' hissed O'Malley. 'An' sit yourself down, before you go and fecking ruin it all.'

'Ruin what?' queried the coxswain, taking a place at the table.

'The old feller out there is about to make our bleeding fortunes,' breathed Evans, indicating the open window.

'What old feller?'

'Are you fecking blind?' said O'Malley. 'Your man with the yellow cloth about his pate. He's a gem trader, so he is.'

'I'm not following, lads,' said Sedgwick. 'I can see that bloke, right enough, but he's no greybeard. Why he ain't much above a nipper. I walked past him coming in.'

The sailors stared open-mouthed at their friend for a moment, and then stampeded for the door. When Sedgwick reached the street, Evans already had a gangly youth pinned up against the wall, a yellow turban askew on his head.

'I do not know him, sahib!' wailed the terrified boy, holding up a copper coin to ward off the giant Londoner. 'He is giving me half anna to be wearing the turban. He is saying if I sit here very still, when he returns, he is giving me another.'

'So where the feck did he go?' demanded O'Malley.

The boy pointed a trembling finger down the street, towards a busy thoroughfare crowded with people. 'Th … that way. But was s … s … some time ago, sahib.'

'I'll pull that bugger's bleeding head off,' roared Evans, abandoning the boy and setting off down the street with the others at his heels.

The sailors searched Black Town for the rest of that day, but found no trace of Abdul Khan from Hyderabad. Nor anyone who had even heard of him, for that matter. As the shadows lengthened, they returned to the *Griffin*, considerably poorer but perhaps also a little wiser.

Chapter 3
Night

On a warm summer's night in 1804, the clock in the cathedral tower of Notre Dame in Toulon struck midnight. A moment later the sound was echoed from the other churches in the city and by the bells on the ships moored in the harbour. It was dark, with the moon yet to rise and the stars veiled by broken cloud. An onshore breeze had been blowing for most of the evening, but as the land cooled it had faded. Now it had been replaced by a wind flowing down from the mountains to the north, laced with the smell of pine trees and wild thyme. It pressed against the side of the *Redoutable*, swinging her around and making her mooring lines creak gently in protest.

Captain Lucas watched the lights of the city dance in the water while the deck beneath his feet vibrated as all hands were called. When the planking was still once more, he crossed to take his place by the ship's wheel. The light from the binnacle underlit the sharp features of his first lieutenant and the gnarled hands of the quartermaster where they rested on the spokes. At least those two are experienced seaman, unlike the rest of the crew, he reflected.

'It is time, Monsieur Dupotet,' he said. 'Set the fore topsail and let slip the mooring lines.'

'Yes, sir,' said the first lieutenant, turning to bellow instructions forward. In the light of the shuttered lanterns down on the main deck, Lucas watched the shadowy figures of his crew, many turning this way and that, unsure of where they should go. Even without the evidence of his eyes, the sound of the ship spoke of confusion. Hesitant footfalls instead of the disciplined rush of well-trained sailors. Volleys of curses and blows from the petty officers as they drove the men to their stations. It seemed an age before the big sail began to appear, a ghostly grey triangle in the night as one side dropped from the yard well before the other.

'Damn these peasants!' yelled Dupotet, one hand cupped beside his mouth, the other gripping the rail. 'Let loose the windward side, for the love of God!'

The triangle became a square at last and the ship began to slip sternwards through the water as the wind pressed the topsail back against the mast.

'Wheel hard over!' ordered Lucas. 'I'll have that sail braced around and drawing, if you please, Monsieur Dupotet.'

'Yes, sir.'

It took twelve long minutes before the sail was set properly, by which time the first lieutenant's voice was growing hoarse. The *Redoubtable* had slipped a long way to leeward, but was at least now moving forward towards the harbour entrance. Lucas stared ahead with concern. The exit to Toulon was difficult, even in broad daylight. Curved headlands encroached on either side, the one to the east ending with a big circular fort at its tip. As the ship came closer to it, a line of white appeared where the sea washed among the rocks that lay below the ramparts. Lucas quickly calculated their progress, balancing the ship's forward momentum towards the open sea with the drift to leeway that was bringing her ever closer to the rocks. He decided the ship would never clear the headland on her current course. He considered going about, but quickly abandoned the thought. A raw crew who took so long to set a single sail would take an age to perform such a manoeuvre in the dark, and any delay might be fatal. 'I'll have the main topsail set,' he ordered, struggling to keep his voice calm. 'Swiftly now.'

'Yes, sir,' said Dupotet.

More confusion and yelling from the deck below him, but this time among the competing orders Lucas picked out one voice he was unfamiliar with, calm but firm, giving clear, simple instructions. That must be the lieutenant who had joined the ship a few days back. He watched as the new sail was sheeted home above him. With its extra thrust the sound of the bow cutting through the waves rose to a pleasant chuckle. She cleared the fortress with no more than twenty metres to spare. Lucas caught a glimpse of startled gunners, their faces orange in the light of the battle lanterns set between their cannons, staring and pointing as the huge ship swept past. Lucas let out a sigh of relief as the shore line retreated from the seventy-four and she headed out into open water.

'I apologise for the tardiness of the crew, sir,' said Dupotet. 'I had little idea how poor their training was. I will see the amount of sail drill is increased, at once.'

'What can you expect, Camille?' asked his captain. 'Six hundred and fifty men on board but barely seventy are prime seaman. The emperor keeps building more ships, but where are the men to sail them?'

'I will drive them hard, sir,' said the first lieutenant. 'By the time we reach Corfu they will no longer disgrace you. I promise.'

'That is a noble objective, Camille,' said Lucas. 'Let us hope you are given that opportunity, for we still need to slip past the enemy.' He picked up the speaking trumpet from its place beside the wheel and stepped back a few paces. 'Masthead!' he bellowed. 'Any sail in the offing?'

'No, sir,' came the reply. 'None that I can see.'

'An hour before the moon rises,' said Lucas, tilting his pocket watch towards the light of the binnacle. 'We must use that time to our advantage. I'll have the head sails set, if you please, Monsieur Dupotet.'

'Yes, sir.'

'Quartermaster! Come around two points. Bring us in close to the shore. Three hundred metres out, no more.'

'Three hundred. Yes, sir.'

'Douse all the lights! I don't want so much as a candle showing.'

As the mountains of Provence loomed closer, the wind dropped. The *Redoutable* sailed on, her darkened hull and few grey sails barely visible against the mass of forested hills behind her. A trace of silver wake in the starlight lay on the black water to show where she made her way steadily eastwards. Her captain watched the lights of Toulon vanish, one by one, as they rounded Cape Giens, until the big ship was all alone in the night.

*****

Lieutenant Warren of the Royal Navy frigate *Active* heartily disliked the midwatch. He had come on duty at midnight, just after the final rubber of whist had been completed in the frigate's wardroom. He could still taste the glass of port he had drained before leaving to relieve the ship's sailing master on deck. All his fellow officers would be asleep, he mused, his own eyelids drooping with weariness. This was the graveyard watch, with the ship under easy sail and Captain Mowbray's standing orders not to disturb the watch below unless in an emergency. He decided to pace the windward side of the quarterdeck in the hope of pushing back the sleep he felt creeping up on him.

It was a warm night, with a gentle breeze blowing down from the mountains to the north. On the deck beneath him the crew sat around in small groups, talking quietly. From the forecastle ahead came a burst of laughter, quickly silenced by McGregor, the boatswain's mate, in his gravelly lowland accent. The *Active* was one of a pair of ships patrolling the approaches to Toulon. The other frigate, the *Phoebe*, would be somewhere to the west.

After a period of steady walking Warren's head was feeling clearer. He came across to the wheel and checked the ship's course and progress. From the belfry two strokes rang out. The midshipman of the watch stepped forward to collect the minute glass and log line from their place beside the binnacle and summoned one of the afterguard to him.

Warren listened to the familiar calls of 'turn' and 'nip' as the *Active*'s speed was measured behind him.

'Three knots, sir,' reported the youngster, appearing out of the dark.

'Very good, Mr Norbury. Record it on the log board, if you please.'

'Aye aye, sir.'

Away to the east a tiny sliver of moon appeared, just clearing the horizon and sending a few beams of silver through a gap in the clouds. Warren's eyes had fully adjusted now, and he watched as the light played across the waves, before the moon was masked once more.

'Deck there!' came a hail from aloft, followed by a pause.

'Masthead!' called Warren. 'What can you see, Cooper?'

'I ain't certain, in truth, sir. But I maybe thought I saw a bit of topsail, away to the north ag'in the loom of the land. Only it be gone now.'

'Aloft with you, Mr Norbury,' ordered the lieutenant. 'Take a night glass and tell me what you can see.'

'Aye aye, sir.'

Warren took another telescope and searched to the north. The land appeared as a pool of darkness against a backdrop of grey clouds and the odd star. No, not completely dark, thought Warren. Through his night glass he could make out the occasional tiny point of light escaping from cottages and crofts on the hillside. Off to his right was a little constellation close to the water. That would be the fishing village at the base of Cape Giens. He searched the coastline with care, but could see no trace of any ship. 'Mr Norbury!' he called. 'Have you found anything?'

'No, sir. Nothing as yet.'

'Keep looking,' ordered the lieutenant. 'This wind is fair for a blockade runner leaving Toulon.'

Warren resumed his own search but all he could see was the black coast and a little starlight on the water. He was about to close the telescope when he chanced to be looking at a point of light close to the water's edge just as it vanished. Probably a fire in a hearth being dowsed or a lamp blown out, he told himself, but then it reappeared again. 'Curious,' he muttered, shifting his gaze to a fresh point of light further along the shore. After a while this one too disappeared and returned. He called to the second midshipman of the watch. 'Mr Graham, my compliments to the captain, and would you ask him to join me on deck. Tell him that I believe a vessel showing no lights is passing to the north of us.'

'Aye aye, sir.'

For a man awoken in the middle of the night, Captain Richard Mowbray looked surprisingly alert as he hurried up on deck, his nightshirt flapping around his bare ankles and his close-cropped head devoid of its normal periwig. 'What's all this about a ship, Mr Warren?'

'She's moving slowly between us and the coast, sir,' explained the lieutenant. 'A little moonlight broke through some moments ago and the lookout reported a sail, although he was most uncertain. But if you direct you gaze to the north, you will observe that something large is passing in front of the lights on shore, moving eastwards. It will presently mask that village there.' He handed across the night glass and pointed towards the base of Cape Giens.

'Blacker than the Earl of Hell's hat,' muttered the captain, as he accepted the telescope and focused on the place Warren had indicated.

After a few moments of patient watching he stood a little more upright. 'By Jove, I think you may be right. Is Captain Capel in sight?'

'Not from the deck, sir,' replied Warren. 'Masthead there! Any sign of the *Phoebe*?'

'Aye, sir. I caught a glimpse of her topgallants when I came on watch,' replied Cooper. 'Away off to the sou'west, she be.'

'Have us close to within night signalling distance, Mr Warren, as quick as you are able. We must alert the inshore squadron directly. I shall go below and shift into some clothes.'

'Aye aye, sir.'

*****

The night remained dark until an hour before dawn.

Then the clouds began to thin and break overhead, revealing the new moon that had risen above the eastern horizon. Splinters of light stole through the gaps to play across the surface of the water, frosting the sails and rigging of the *Redoutable* in silver.

Moments later there was a cry from the French ship's masthead. 'Sail! There's a sail!'

Dupotet snatched up a speaking trumpet and pointed it aloft. 'Masthead there! Make your report properly, damn you! Or I'll have you scrubbing the heads for the rest of the voyage!'

'Sorry, sir. Deck there! Sail in sight, two points off the stern. Eight kilometres away and coming up right quick.'

Lucas rushed up on to the poop deck and crossed to the stern rail. Even without his night glass he could see the ship, a large frigate, her towering masts crowded with sails that glowed in the moonlight. She was overhauling them fast, to judge by the creaming wave beneath her bowsprit. As he opened his telescope to study her she passed out of the moonlight, becoming a shadowy, spectral version of herself.

'English, from her rig, sir,' said Dupotet, who had followed him up on to the poop. 'She looks big. A thirty-six or even a thirty-eight gunner. But still no match for us.'

'On her own, perhaps, but it is who she may be leading towards us that worries me, Camille,' said Lucas. Beside him was one of the big stern lanterns, extinguished when he ordered the ship darkened. 'They must be able to see like cats to have spotted us,' he added.

His eyes strayed to his first lieutenant while he pondered what to do. Carry on in the hope of shaking off any pursuit, or should he run back to the safety of Toulon, before it was too late? His orders were very clear that he should not imperil his precious ship in carrying out his mission, but had he already travelled too far to return now?

Dupotet shifted uncomfortably under the remorseless gaze, bringing his captain's attention back to the present. 'I must consider our position,' he said at last. 'Send one of the midshipmen aloft to search the southern horizon.'

'Yes, sir,' said Dupotet, touching his hat and running down the ladderway back to the quarterdeck. 'Monsieur Pascal! A word with you. Swiftly now, and bring the best spyglass.'

Lucas followed his first lieutenant more slowly, deep in thought. When he reached the wheel, he consulted the log board and calculated the ship's progress. Then he looked across at the frigate, still sailing hard and appreciably nearer. As he watched, her crew began taking in canvas with a speed he could only envy, until she had reduced her sail to match what his own ship carried. Then she took up station directly to windward. Of course, thought Lucas, the perfect position. Comfortably out of range of the *Redoutable*'s powerful broadside, but close enough to keep the French ship under observation. Every so often the frigate's fore topsail flapped and billowed as her crew released the wind to check her speed to that of the slower seventy-four. There was a bright glow on her forecastle, then a rocket shot upwards, trailing a long arc of yellow sparks. It exploded in crimson light high overhead.

As the fiery glow on the underside of the clouds faded, Lucas decided what he would do. 'No need to wait for the masthead to report, Monsieur Dupotet,' he said. 'Wear the ship around, and set a course for Toulon, if you please.'

'Back to Toulon, sir?' queried the lieutenant, and then. 'Yes, sir. All hands! All hands to wear ship! Lively now!'

More confusion beneath him as the men were driven to their stations. On the forecastle he watched a petty officer lining up his men and placing the rope they were to haul into their hands. With a start he realised he could see the sailors as individuals rather than anonymous dark shadows, even at the far end of his ship. Beyond the bowsprit the first light of dawn was colouring the far horizon in pearl. Above his head the black ensign resolved itself into broad bands of blue, white and blood red.

'Hard to starboard!' yelled the first lieutenant. The big ship began to lumber into a long curving turn downwind. Orders were yelled, many laden with obscenities as the yards jerked and creaked around. Once again Lucas picked out the voice of the new lieutenant, noting the oasis of calm that seemed to surround him. He could see him now in the growing light, a pleasant-looking young man in a well-tailored coat. He was in among his men, cajoling here, encouraging there. When the last sail was drawing, the seventy-four had reversed her course, with the stiff breeze flowing in from just ahead of her starboard beam and the dawn light behind her. Waves buffeted against her side, rolling her over.

The moment the seventy-four began her manoeuvre, the British frigate had tacked about, choosing to turn through the wind rather than laboriously wearing around. It was a much quicker, although it came with the risk of the ship being caught in irons if not well handled. She lay ahead of him in the grey light, her long single gundeck picked out by a yellow strake that ran the length of her hull. A backed topsail held her steady as she waited. Once the *Redoutable* settled on to her new course she too got under way. Now she was like a pilot boat, leading them home. Through his telescope he could just pick out the arc of white letters painted across her stern counter. *Active*, he read. She was certainly that. A line of coloured flags broke out at the top of her main mast.

'Masthead there!' roared Lucas. 'What can you see to the south?'

'Nothing as yet, sir.'

'Look properly, Monsieur Pascal!' yelled Dupotet. 'That frigate must be signalling to someone!'

Lucas watched the midshipman as he sat over sixty metres above the deck. He was perched on the thin royal yard as it drew dizzying circles through the air with each roll of the ship. One arm was tightly wrapped around the mast beside him while he struggled to control the telescope in his other. Then the lookout standing on the far side of the mast crouched down towards him, pointing further along the horizon. A long pause followed as the youngster focused on the spot.

'Deck there! Two ships, three points ahead of the larboard beam! I can just see their topgallants over the horizon!'

'Nothing in sight from the deck, sir,' added the first lieutenant.

'Nothing yet, you mean, Monsieur Dupotet,' said the captain, his face grim. 'Masthead there! Are they making directly for us?'

Another long pause. 'I don't think so, sir. They look to have changed course. Perhaps they want to cut us off from Toulon?'

'Of course they do,' muttered Lucas. 'Set the topgallants, Monsieur Dupotet. Stay sails as well, if she will bear them. The race is on. Thank the lord we went about when we did.'

'Yes, sir. All hands! All hands to set sail!'

Lucas watched the ship's topmen making their way aloft towards the distant topgallant yards, up shrouds as steep as a ladder. The few experienced hands led the way, rushing ahead, while the others followed in their wake, driven ever higher by the blows and rope-ends of the petty officers. These were the youngest and fittest men from those drafted on board, but none were blue-water sailors and many had never been higher than the top of a haystack before they joined the ship. The *Redoutable* was rolling extravagantly to each wave, causing the men to wail and cling on as the shrouds tilted towards the vertical, and they felt the suck of the growing void beneath them. One paused to be sick, the vomit borne away in tendrils on the wind, before being forced to resume his climb. Lucas looked away, hardening his heart. His ship would encounter far worse conditions than a stiff Mediterranean breeze in midsummer, and would need experienced hands to cope. The men were learning more out here than they had done through a month of harbour drills.

The frigate was setting more sail too, leaning further over as she gathered speed to stay ahead of the hulking seventy-four. As he watched, her sharp bow buried into a wave, sending a curtain of spray sparkling downwind in the first rays of the rising sun. He turned his attention to the two ships on the horizon. He could see their topgallants from the deck now, squares of pink in the dawn light, just lifting into view. From the sails' size he decided they must be ships of the line. One was a little larger than the other, and he searched his memory for the names of the Royal Navy ships in the blockading force. The bigger one could be one of several seventy-fours – the *Superb*, the *Renown* or perhaps the *Donegal*. That would make the smaller ship a sixty-four, almost certainly the *Monmouth*. Two ships of the line and a frigate, all with veteran Royal Navy crews. More than enough to beat the *Redoutable*, with her green crew, into a dismasted hulk. 'Isn't that fore topgallant drawing yet, Monsieur Dupotet?' he demanded.

'Just sheeting it home now, sir!'

'Too slow! Do you want them to catch us?'

'Deck there!' came a cry from the masthead. 'One of the

ships is signalling!'

Lucas snapped open his telescope and focused on the distant pair. He could just make out a coloured thread of bunting flying from the foremast of the larger one. Then he shifted his gaze to the frigate ahead. A lone coloured flag rose up the mast in response to the signal. 'Monsieur Dupotet! I'll wager a dozen golden Napoleons that frigate has just been ordered to try and slow us down. The moment you have that sail set I want the ship cleared for action.'

'Yes, sir.'

'And put a good officer in charge of the bow chasers. Lieutenant Brissot would be perfect.'

'He is very new to the ship, sir,' cautioned the first lieutenant.

'As are most of the crew, Camille. But I like the look of him. He carries himself confidently in front of the men.'

'Yes, sir. Pass the word for Monsieur Brissot, there!'

Lucas crossed to the weather rail and hooked an arm through the mizzen shrouds to steady himself. He first looked towards the two ships trying to cut him off. The angle of their sails had changed so that they appeared as narrow crescents. They must have gone about on to the other tack as they struggled to claw their way northward against a wind that was dead foul for them. Good, he decided. The *Redoutable* should be safely back at her moorings long before they could reach him, unless he should be badly damaged aloft, of course. He turned his attention to the *Active* ahead. Red-jacketed marines were making their way up the shrouds to take up positions aloft. As he watched, a heavy chain sling was swayed up to the mizzen crosstree to secure one of the yards against damage. Then the appearance of the frigate changed as her gunports swung open and her main guns were run out. Eighteen-pounders, he decided. No match for the mighty thirty-sixes on his ship's lower deck, but quite heavy enough to damage his rigging, if skilfully handled.

Beneath him men were assembling around the cannons that lined the sides of the upper gundeck. A petty officer came along, tossing a lighted slow match into the tub that stood beside each cannon. The crew closest to him gathered to peer at theirs, coiled and smouldering, as if it was a venomous snake, and Lucas realised that through all the drills they had done in Toulon the match had never been lit before. A file of marines came clumping towards him, their sergeant dropping them off in pairs along the gangway to man the rail. Lucas moved back to his place beside the wheel as they approached. His servant appeared with his sword, stooping to buckle it about his waist. He felt the worn grip in his hand as he settled it into place.

His first lieutenant came up and saluted smartly. 'The ship is ready, sir,' he reported.

'A full three minutes after it should have been,' observed Lucas.

'Some of the men were unsure of their stations, sir.'

'From now on we will practise clearing for action every evening,' ordered the captain.

'Yes, sir.'

'Deck there!' yelled the masthead lookout. 'The enemy is changing course!'

Lucas looked ahead to where the *Active* was coming around, her profile lengthening as she brought her whole broadside to bear. She vanished behind a billowing wall of smoke, pierced by glowing fire. There was a crash from somewhere on the forecastle and a mizzen shroud parted with a sound like a pistol shot. Moments later a large block clattered down through the rigging to crash on to the quarterdeck, dragging a tail of severed line behind it. Looking upwards, Lucas could see a round shot hole torn in one of the topsails. 'And so it begins,' he said. 'Run out the guns, if you please, Monsieur Dupotet, and tell young Brissot that he can open fire.'

'Yes sir.'

Chapter 4
Chase

Lieutenant Brissot climbed up on to the forecastle of the *Redoutable* and took in a scene of disarray. A shot from the *Active* had just struck the solid base of the bowsprit, leaving a pale gash and sending a spray of wood splinters across the deck. Two sailors were down, one crying in pain and clutching a bloody arm to his chest, and the other lay crumpled in a heap, ominously silent. The other sailors were either crowding around the casualties or pointing with alarm towards the British frigate as she turned away to resumed her original course. A billowing cloud of gun smoke drifted past from her opening broadside.

He paused for a moment, forcing down a rising sense of fear, and composed his face into one of calm. Deep breaths, Francois, he urged himself, clasping his hands behind his back. Then he stepped forward. 'Who is in charge here?'

'I am, sir.' A short, barrel-chested young officer with a strong Breton accent emerged from among those around the casualties. 'Midshipman Quellec is my name.'

'Very well, Monsieur Quellec. Choose four of your men to take those casualties down to the surgeon. The rest will return to their posts immediately.'

'Yes, sir.'

While the sailors dispersed, Brissot looked over the guns on the forecastle. There were four in total. He dismissed the pair of big carronades immediately. Not only were they pointing out to the sides, but they were only short-range weapons. The British frigate would never risk coming that close to the *Redoutable*. Of more promise was the pair of long eight-pounders with gleaming brass barrels that pointed directly forward, one either side of the bowsprit. Neither was ready for action yet. 'Gun captains of these two chasers, come to me,' he demanded. Two sailors stepped from among the crowd and approached the lieutenant. 'Have either of you seen action?' he asked.

One raised a hand, while the other shifted uncomfortably. 'Du Chemin, sir. I was loader on the *Joubert*. She was a privateer out of Nantes.'

'A loader?' repeated the lieutenant. 'I see. And you? Martin, isn't it? Have you at least seen a gun fired?'

'Only for a salute, sir,' said the sailor, a gangly man with a mop of ginger hair. 'The first lieutenant doesn't hold with live firing. Something to do with the paint work.'

The bow thudded into a fresh wave at that moment, sending a curtain of spray off to windward.

'We shall have plenty of water to wash away any smoke stains today,' said Brissot. 'You have both gone through all the drill steps before, I don't doubt. Get your crews in order. Swiftly now. Guns loaded and run up, and let's give that damned frigate some of her own medicine.'

The gun captains returned to their pieces with renewed enthusiasm, and began preparing for action, while Brissot stood further back. 'More water in that bucket, Du Chemin,' he ordered. 'You can take it from the starboard side carronade. Hold an arm aloft when you believe your gun is ready.'

At that moment Midshipman Quellec appeared at his elbow. 'The captain says you can open fire when you are able, sir.'

Brissot took in the progress being made rigging the two guns. 'Give the captain my respects, and we will be ready in five minutes.'

'Yes, sir.'

Despite his lack of experience, it was the red-head whose arm shot up first. Brissot stepped across to the eight-pounder and ran his eye over the gun. 'Have you ever harnessed a cart, Martin?' he asked.

'A cart? Why yes, sir.'

'And what is the last thing you must check before you set off?' continued the lieutenant.

'Eh … mmm …' mused the gun captain, before his face cleared. 'You check that the traces are free of the horses' legs.'

'Very good,' said Brissot, pointing to where the gun tackle was strewn across the deck. 'If a loop of that gets around one of the men's legs the recoil of the cannon will snap it like a twig. Always lay the gun ropes out straight and neat. Get it sorted. Quickly.'

'Yes, sir.'

Brissot stepped across to the larboard side eight-pounder, just as Du Chemin's hand shot up. A glance at the gun showed that it was ready to fire.

'Quoin out another turn,' he ordered, peering along the barrel. 'And ease her a little to the right.'

'Yes sir,' said the former privateer, making the adjustment while one of the crew levered the cannon around.

'Open fire, then,' ordered Brissot.

The gun captain blew life into the glowing linstock in his hand, and then waited for the roll of the ship. 'Stand clear!' he warned, before thrusting it down on the touch hole.

A splutter of yellow sparks, and the eight-pounder roared back inboard. Brissot jumped clear of the smoke and watched the tall plume of spray as the ball plunged into the sea well short of the target. He turned back to the gun to find the crew looking to him for instructions. 'Don't just stand there waiting!' he roared. 'Reload the damned thing! You there with the rammer! You should be swabbing her out the moment the recoil stops. And loader, where is the next charge?' He watched them jump into action and then turned to Du Chemin. 'The shot was on line, but you need to anticipate the firing delay. Bring the linstock down a little sooner in the roll. Understood?'

'Yes, sir.'

'And keep the men at it. You're the gun captain. Lead them.'

'I will, sir.'

Brissot stepped across to the other gun, which was now ready to fire, and crouched down to check the aim. The gun had been lain with care, squarely pointing at the main mast of the frigate. 'Excellent Martin,' he said, straightening up. 'Kindly open fire.'

A gust of wind rolled the seventy-four over, just as Martin brought down the linstock, sending his shot high and wide. Brissot watched the distant splash, far beyond the *Active*. As if in response, her rudder went over and she came up into the wind again, her guns banging out in a long, rolling chain as each one bore. Shots howled overhead, slicing through the French ship's rigging, and more cut lines came hissing down on to the deck. Several of the gun crews ducked as a ball passed close overhead.

'Keep at it, men!' urged Brissot. 'Load and run up! The surest way to put them off their aim is to pay them back in kind. Fire as soon as you can.'

'Yes sir.'

'Midshipman Quellec! Go and find the boatswain, and

ask him to send a party to make repairs to the foremast rigging, if you please.'

'Yes, sir.'

*****

Captain Lucas stood on his quarterdeck, thoughtfully patting one hand with the telescope he held in the other. The eight-pounders in the bow were firing steadily now, even hitting the *Active* from time to time as their gun captains' aim improved. He could see Lieutenant Brissot gesturing as he urged them on to greater efforts. He returned the telescope to his eye and studied the frigate. One of her stern windows had been knocked in, and there was a shot hole in her mizzen topsail, but otherwise she seemed unscathed. And she continued to play her part well. Every so often she came up into the wind to let fly with a broadside, always aiming high. Then, just as quickly, she turned away, pulling ahead until she had gained enough sea room to repeat the manoeuvre.

He looked up at his rigging and cursed. Everywhere he could see cut ropes hanging down like jungle creepers and tattered shot holes in the sails. The boatswain and his mates were working aloft with the few skilled hands the ship possessed, splicing and repairing, but theirs was a losing cause. No vital spars had been damaged yet, but surely that was only a matter of time.

He turned his attention to the two other Royal Navy ships. They were appreciably closer now, with topsails visible beneath their topgallants, sailing to cut him off. As things stood, he was still confident he would make Toulon before them. Unless the wind should ease, or change direction, he reminded himself. Or worse still, what if that dammed frigate should knock down a yard. He looked at the *Active* once more, gauging when her next attack would come. She would need to draw further ahead. Twelve minutes, he decided. Not much time to make his preparations.

He closed his telescope with a snap. 'Monsieur Dupotet, a word with you, if you please.'

'Yes, sir,' said the first lieutenant, coming over.

'I want the larboard side battery made ready to fire a broadside. Use the best gun-layers we have and double shot all the cannon.'

'Double-shotted guns,' repeated the officer. 'Very well.'

'Then I need all the sheets and braces manned and ready for a quick manoeuvre,' continued the captain.

'To wear ship, sir?'

'I said quick, Camille,' said the captain. 'We will have to turn through the wind if we are going to catch this one out. You need to have everything ready in twelve minutes.'

'Twelve minutes? Yes, sir,' said Dupotet, dashing away shouting orders.

Lucas moved to the side until he had an uninterrupted view of his opponent. She was standing away from him, a foaming wake churning behind her. To the north of her was the coast of Provence, black pine-covered hills with blue mountains beyond them, while far ahead the bulk of Cape Carqueiranne was appearing through the morning haze. The approach to Toulon would be just beyond.

One of the bow chasers banged out, raising a column of water close alongside the *Active*. Respectable practice, given how much the forecastle was rolling.

'The ship is ready, sir,' gasped his breathless first lieutenant. 'And Midshipman Pascal reports that the other two ships are hull up over the horizon.'

Lucas looked to where the young officer sat perched on the royal yard. The sail below him had an ugly gash where a shot from the frigate had narrowly missed one of his dangling feet. 'He knows how to do his duty, even under fire,' he mused. 'Perhaps something can be made of the boy.'

'Perhaps it can, sir.'

'Very well, wait for my signal, and come up into the wind upon that instant,' ordered the captain.

'Yes, sir.'

Lucas returned to examining the frigate. Her broad stern appeared in his telescope, with its arc of letters and row of window lights. He ignored the elaborate gilding and focused lower, where her rudder dipped into the turbulence of her wake. Nothing. He continued to watch. Come on, he urged, surely you are far enough ahead now. And then the rudder began to swing across as her helm went over. 'Now, Monsieur Dupotet!' he roared. 'Wheel hard over!'

The lithe frigate had swept up into the wind, her head sails flapping and her long side beginning to appear once more, but this time the *Redoutable* followed her about. The French ship's turn was much more laboured, her deep, heavy hull gripping the sea. Now all her sails were flapping in protest, the noise deafening. Dupotet was yelling himself hoarse as he bellowed instructions through the speaking trumpet towards the crew gathered in the waist. Lucas ignored him and focused on his opponent. 'Ready, larboard side guns!' he yelled.

The big seventy-four turned more and more slowly, creaking up into the wind, but still her guns wouldn't bear. Below him the crews on the upper gundeck were hauling their pieces around until the barrels were jammed diagonally in the ports as they tried to reach the frigate. 'Come on!' urged the captain. 'Get this damned ship around!'

'The enemy's falling off, sir!' yelled one of the afterguard. 'The cowardly dogs don't fancy it!'

A glance told Lucas that the man was right. The *Active*'s yards were swinging back as she reversed her turn to resume her original course. Another few degrees, and he might still have her under his guns before she could sail out of range. But the deck beneath his feet had a strange, lifeless feel to it. 'Monsieur Dupotet!' he yelled. 'Get the ship through the wind, for the love of God!'

'She won't turn any further, sir,' reported the lieutenant, gesturing aloft with his speaking trumpet. Overhead all her sails were pressed back against the masts while her head sails continued to flap with a sound like distant thunder.

'She's dead in the water, sir,' called the helmsman, spinning the wheel first one way and then back again to demonstrate his point. 'I've no way to steer by.'

'In irons!' roared Lucas, his face scarlet with rage. 'My ship is in irons! Where did you learn your seamanship, lieutenant? On a bloody farm?'

'She … she has never liked passing through the wind, sir,' explained Dupotet, his expression set.

'And have you ever thought to investigate why, eh? As any half-competent first lieutenant should?'

Before the officer could answer, a hail came from the masthead, high pitched with anxiety. 'Sir! Sir!'

'What is it, Monsieur Pascal?' called the captain.

'The enemy, sir! Off the larboard quarter! They are coming around!'

Both men spun to see that the *Active* had continued her turn away from them, extending it into a long circle until she was sailing back up towards their stern. For the first time in the engagement Lucas felt fear grip him, tinged with admiration at the way his opponent was handling his ship. The course the frigate was on would avoid the *Redoutable*'s dangerous broadsides, yet still bring her to a position where all her cannon could fire through his poorly protected stern and down the entire length of his ship.

'*Mon dieu*!' exclaimed Dupotet. 'They mean to rake us!'

'Of course they do.' said Lucas, his face grim. 'While we are completely helpless.' He turned to bark an order at one of the midshipmen standing by the wheel. 'You, boy! To the forecastle! Tell Brissot to back the head sails off to starboard. He will have to force them out there. Run!'

The youngster took a moment to absorb the message, and then was off.

'Afterguard!' continued the captain. 'I'll have the mizzen driver hauled out to larboard. Make haste!'

'Yes, sir.'

'Helmsman! Put your wheel over!'

'Hard over it is, sir.'

'And what shall I do, sir?' asked his first lieutenant, a point of stillness among all the activity set off by his captain.

'Get the yards braced around, Camille,' said his captain, grabbing his arm and guiding him towards the rail at the front of the quarterdeck. 'Ready to catch the wind again the moment we are able.'

'Yes, sir,' said Dupotet, raising his speaking trumpet to his lips once more.

Beyond his first lieutenant, Lucas could see Brissot on the forecastle. His hat was off, and he was swinging it through the air as he urged his men to bodily heave the seventy-four's huge jib against the force of the wind. He had taken the crews from the bow chasers and combined them with the other sailors into a long line of men, all leaning far back as they hauled in pulses to the timing he set.

Behind Lucas the driver flapped and shivered as it was forced outwards by the straining afterguard. The jib should push the bow in one direction, he reflected, while the driver would push the stern the other way, twisting the big ship around until her sails could catch the breeze once more. But fully laden, with a deep keel the reached down almost eight metres, she seemed as immovable as a mountain.

He turned his attention to the frigate. She was beating up towards the *Redoutable*, her yards braced around, her hull heeling over as she clawed her way forward. A cloud of spray rose up as her bow shouldered into a wave, before streaming away downwind. Along her side was a long row of cannon, loaded and ready. It would be ten minutes at the most before she would in a position to fire, he decided. He must have his ship back under way by then. 'Isn't that driver out yet?' he bellowed towards the afterguard.

'Almost, sir!' replied the petty officer in charge. 'Pull, you bastards! Pull!'

Up on the forecastle the jib had been belayed into place, inverted oddly towards him and trembling like the skin of a nervous stallion. Brissot's weary men were lining up to haul the next headsail out, but the officer himself was talking animatedly to a midshipman, gesturing towards the rigging, and then pointing back towards the quarterdeck. The midshipman touched his hat and came running along the gangway while Brissot returned to his men.

'What is it, Monsieur Quellec?' said Lucas, as the Breton arrived before him.

'Lieutenant Brissot's compliments, sir, and he believes

that if the backstays were slackened off, the ship might turn more readily.'

'Not this again!' exclaimed Dupotet, turning from his place at the rail. 'Has he been talking to Tournier?'

'Tournier?' queried the captain. 'Are you telling me that the boatswain thinks the backstays are too taut?'

'He talks of little else, but the man learned his seamanship on a Marseille polacre. He would have this ship looking like a fishing smack rigged by a drunkard, if I let him have his way.'

'Find the boatswain now, Monsieur Quellec,' ordered Lucas, 'as swiftly as you are able, and tell him to immediately slacken off the backstays.'

'Yes sir,' said the midshipman.

'Tournier was appointed boatswain of this ship when she was no more than a keel and a pile of timber, Lieutenant,' said the captain, the flush of anger returning to his face. 'He knows every plank and spar. I suggest you defer to him in matters of seamanship from now on. I would sooner command a fighting ship with slack stays than a tautly rigged wreck. Is that clear?'

'Yes, sir.'

'Now get those yards braced around and ready.'

Lucas strode across to stand behind the ship's compass and took a bearing on the long bowsprit. Still the deck had a lifeless feel beneath his feet, as if the ship was no more than a drifting log. 'Any sign of her turning yet, helmsman?' he demanded.

'Still in irons, sir,' said the sailor.

Lucas looked over at the British frigate, growing larger all the time, and cursed to himself. With a final heave the driver was pulled stiffly into place by the gasping afterguard. He returned to the binnacle, trying to detect the slightest tremor.

Up on the forecastle he could see Tournier with Brissot, one on each side of the ship, as they directed the men. The boatswain's bald pate gleamed in the sunlight in marked contrast to the younger man's dark curls. With a loud creaking the thick black ropes that held the soaring foremast aloft slackened a little, the ruler-straight line softening into a gentle, barely perceptible curve. When all was secure, they both charged on towards him, leading their working parties to the main mast's back stays.

Lucas returned his attention to the frigate, and he was shocked to see how close she was. Her figurehead seemed to be looking towards him from beneath her bowsprit, the dark eyes on the painted face cruel. She was comfortably within cannon range, and she began to come around. Her side lengthened into a long yellow strake, studded with cannon and her white Royal Navy ensign streaming in the wind.

'Sir! Sir!' called out the helmsman. 'I think she's starting to respond!'

Lucas was over by the wheel in a few quick strides, crouching down to look across the compass. There was no doubt about it, the bearing had changed by two degrees. Slowly, almost imperceptibly, his ship was inching her way around.

'Stand by to get her under way!' he roared. 'Make fast those backstays. Headsails, there! Are you ready, Monsieur Dupotet?'

'Yes, sir,' said the first lieutenant, his voice neutral and his face blank.

The *Redoutable* still seemed dead beneath his feet. Then a helpful wave crashed against her starboard bow, nudging her round a little, and the turn accelerated, until her captain no longer needed the compass to detect it. On the forecastle Brissot gradually released the headsails, flapping wildly at first before stiffening into a more familiar curve as the wind began to fill them. The deck beneath Lucas's feet came alive at last, heeling a little under the wind's pressure.

Then the *Active* fired her broadside.

If the British ship had aimed high again, sending her fire blasting through the *Redoutable*'s battered rigging, the French would have been in serious trouble. Any more damage aloft while she was midway through such a difficult manoeuvre would have almost certainly seen her back in irons, or even dismasted. But all the training and instincts of her Royal Navy crew came to the rescue of the seventy-four. With such a tempting target on offer, her gun crews fired on the down roll, sending their shot crashing into the *Redoutable*'s stern instead.

The roar of the guns was deafening. Fragments of gilded wood and splintered glass flew up over the poop deck in a glittering cloud. Lucas felt the deck beneath him jar and tremble as ball after ball crashed home. A screeching clang sounded as one of the *Redoutable*'s cannon was struck. As the last echo of the broadside came rolling back to him from the nearby hills of Provence, the cries of the wounded below decks began. Lucas hardened his heart to the sound. 'Sheet home the headsails! Brace those yards around! Haul in the driver.'

Lucas felt his ship coming to life, in spite of all the damage she had suffered. Flapping canvas cracked into place as the wind moved steadily around from ahead, to off the bow and then further aft. The dead slap of waves against her hull was replaced by the gurgle and surge of a bow wave forming.

'What course, sir?' asked the helmsman as the ship gathered way. Lucas glanced across at the *Active*, almost stationary as she tacked slowly around to resume her pursuit of her battered opponent. Almost stationary, he repeated to himself, his pulse quickening as the idea came to him. 'The damned hubris of those bloody English!' he exclaimed.

'Sir?' queried his first lieutenant.

'Look at them,' demanded the captain, pointing. 'Manoeuvring within half cannon shot of us, the dogs! They think they have us beat! That we will just turn tail and run for home. Well, I intend to teach them a sharp lesson. No one underestimates Jean Lucas. The larboard side guns are still double-shotted and run out, are they not Monsieur Dupotet?'

'They are, sir,' said the first lieutenant. 'The crews will have suffered from that broadside, of course.'

'No matter. There will be enough still manned. Away below with you. Draw on the starboard guns for crew if you must. I want them ready to fire. Now!'

'Yes, sir.'

'Helmsman, keep her turning!'

'Hold the turn. Yes, sir.'

The *Redoubtable* gathered speed as she came about, rounding on her tormentor. Lucas thought he could see signs of consternation on board the frigate as the long side of the big warship turned towards them.

'Midships! Keep her there! Stand by larboard side!'

'Yes, sir!'

'Just a moment more,' muttered Lucas. 'For the gun captains to settle.' He looked over the ship's side. One of the lower deck guns was missing, the empty port as obvious as a gap in an otherwise perfect smile, but the rest of the cannons were all run out. He watched as the barrel directly beneath him inched around and then was still. 'Fire!' he yelled.

The *Redoutable* heeled over as her ponderous broadside roared out. A billowing curtain of smoke rolled up, obscuring the *Active* altogether. Her captain waited for his ship to emerge from the cloud she had created, while around him the crews of the quarterdeck eight-pounders rushed to reload. It had been a poorly aimed broadside, he concluded, as he surveyed the damage to the frigate. With so few skilled gunners on board, more than half the shots had missed, but one ball at least had been aimed true. The towering symmetry of his opponent's masts had been ruined. Her foretopmast hung down, a mass of broken yards and flapping canvas. A cheer went up from his crew at the sight.

Lucas's blood was up, and for a moment he considered bearing down on his disabled opponent to finish her off at a range where even his raw gunners couldn't miss, but then he recalled the two other British ships sailing to cut him off from Toulon. He could see them, above the horizon and pressing on with every sail set.

'Secure the guns,' he ordered. 'Set a course to clear Cape Carqueiranne. Time for us to return home.'

Chapter 5
Summer

Over two months had passed since the *Griffin* had left Madras, and she was still in the heart of the Indian Ocean. From a distance she seemed a thing of beauty, with her sails tall pyramids of white against the endless blue. But closer too, her progress was laboured and slow, as she beat her way forward, day after day, against a strengthening wind that blew dead foul for her journey towards the Cape of Good Hope, and her way back to Europe.

Lieutenant Edward Preston was officer of the watch as it approached noon one day. He was a handsome young man with a friendly, open face, but four hours on deck in the heat of the tropics was starting to trouble him. His dark hair was limp with sweat, his shirt prickled uncomfortably against his skin, and the stump of his missing left arm itched unbearably. He had positioned himself with care in the centre of a triangle of shade cast on the quarterdeck by the frigate's mizzen topsail. Beyond this oasis the planking stretched away from him, bleached white by the fierce sun.

'This darned heat is turning the deck seams to molasses,' protested Jacob Armstrong, the *Griffin*'s American sailing master as he came up on deck. For once he had abandoned his customary periwig, and his hat sat deep on his bald head.

Preston sniffed the air, noticing for the first time the

resinous scent of melting tar mixing with the more familiar smell of woodsmoke from the galley chimney as the crew's dinner was cooked.

He turned to the curly-haired midshipman beside him. 'Kindly have the pump rigged, Mr Todd, and organise a party to swab the decks to keep them cool.'

'Aye aye, sir,' said the youngster, reluctantly leaving the patch of shade.

'My, how that kid has grown,' commented the American. 'Almost as tall as you, Edward. He was the smallest boy on the ship when he joined. How old is he now?'

'Sixteen or seventeen, I believe. What brings you up from the cool depths, Jacob? Is it noon already?'

'It will be directly,' said Armstrong, hefting his sextant in one hand. He looked around to assess the strength of the light, and swung an extra smoked glass plate into position. 'With the sun almost directly overhead, it will be a deuced awkward altitude to take, so I thought I would come up and do it myself, if you have no objections?'

'None at all,' smiled Preston.

For a man with such big fingers, the veteran sailing master operated the sextant with a delicacy and precision that came from long years of practice. Preston watched him work with admiration tinged with sadness. It was four years since he had lost his arm in a desperate action off the coast of Brittany. He had been certain that he would die as he lay writhing in pain, stretched out in the gloom of the cockpit, the sound of battle continuing overhead. His dreams were still filled with images from that long night. The wet leather of the gag that choked him. The iron-grip of the lob-lolly boys holding him down, and lamplight glittering like fire from the polished steel of the surgeon's saw. But he had lived, and when he had pleaded with

Clay not to be left on the beach, he had promised his captain that he would be able to perform all his duties with one arm. It was a promise that he had kept. In his own jerky fashion, he could climb to the masthead when required. He had led his men in a successful boarding action, heart in mouth as he launched himself across the wide gap between ships, ignoring the hulls grinding together beneath him. He had even learned how to focus a telescope one-handed by using a mizzen ratline to support the end. The only duty that was beyond him was taking a noon sighting with a sextant. But his promise to Clay remained unbroken, because each time he was on watch during the forenoon, one or other of his fellow officers would appear with a fresh excuse as to why they had come to make the observation for him.

Armstrong still had his sextant to his eye when eight bells rang out, and the frigate came to life. The watch below streamed up the ladderways to take the place of those on deck. Preston's good friend Lieutenant John Blake came to relieve him, while Clay appeared from his cabin with Napoleon, the ship's pet mongoose, scampering at his heels. The creature had been asleep in his favourite place, the sunniest window seat in the great cabin, but was now hungry. He was off to beg for titbits from the lower deck, before descending into the hold in hope of a rat.

'Good afternoon, gentlemen,' said the captain, in response to the salutes of the officers.

Armstrong clamped his sextant and lowered it from his eye to read the result from the scale. He shook his head as he came across.

'What progress have we made, Jacob?' asked Preston.

'Very indifferent, I fear,' he replied chalking the position on the slate that hung by the wheel and holding it out to Clay.

'So little?' queried the captain.

'We should have left India a full month sooner than we did, sir,' explained the sailing master. 'The monsoon winds are blowing now, and will only strengthen for the next few months. Even the sea currents hereabouts are against us.'

'We could hardly leave before the ship was repaired,' said Blake. He indicated the Indian sailors dotted among the men coming on watch. 'And we had to recruit replacements for those who perished when we fought with the French.'

'Nevertheless, we cannot proceed as we are doing, gentlemen,' said Clay. 'Our fresh water will not last indefinitely, and now that the Dutch control the Cape once more, we will be unable to replenish it until we touch St Helena.'

'I cannot fathom why we gave such a valuable place back to the Butter-boxes,' said Armstrong.

'What is your plan, sir?' asked Blake.

'In truth it is Jacob's plan. He holds we must turn more southerly in the hope of picking up the trades.'

'Will that not bring us closer to the islands the French hold, sir?' asked Preston. 'Isle de France and Reunion?'

'It will, but that is a risk that we can no longer avoid,' said Clay. 'Kindly plot a new course for us, Mr Armstrong. Mr Blake, have the ship put about, if you please. And let us hope that Admiral Linois and his fleet are not at home when we pass their gate, gentlemen.'

*****

The wind blowing over Toulon would have served the *Griffin* very well, coming down from the north and carrying with it all the raw heat of a French summer. Even out on the water of the inner harbour, where the *Redoutable* lay at her temporary mooring, it was oppressively hot.

Brissot sat in the wardroom dressed in a linen shirt that was open sufficiently to reveal a few wisps of dark chest hair, yet he still found it hard to concentrate on his book. A small pleasure boat sailed past the stern, the gay chatter of those on board coming clear to him through the splintered ruin of the wardroom's window lights. The temporary square of canvas tacked across them did little either to shut out the noise or to conceal the damage caused by the *Active*'s broadside.

'Fortunately, the ship will be handed over to the dockyard for repairs tomorrow,' said Dupotet, coming into the wardroom at that moment and noticing where the younger man had been looking.

'That is welcome tidings, sir, although how will they find the workmen with all the new ships they have under construction?'

'With grave difficulty,' confirmed the first lieutenant. 'I doubt we will have our ship back for several months. Still, some leave will be welcome.' He picked up the book Brissot had been reading and examined the spine. 'Apian's *History of the Punic Wars*. Goodness, don't you find it too damned hot for history? I will pass out soon if I don't shift this coat.' He shrugged himself free of the garment, his face growing blotchy and red with the effort, and passed it to the wardroom steward. 'A glass of pinard, if you please, Barbier, and perhaps one for you, Francois?'

'Not for me, I thank you, sir,' said Brissot. 'I will wait for the wine the captain will serve later. He has asked me to dine with him.'

'Has he, indeed,' said the first lieutenant, taking a seat

at the wardroom table and drinking thirstily from the glass the steward placed beside him. 'Ah, that is better!' he sighed. 'And has he extended this invitation more widely? To the rest of the wardroom, for example.'

'Not that I am aware of, sir.'

'So, just the two of you,' said Dupotet, regarding his fellow officer across the rim of his wine glass, his eyes growing hard. 'I wonder why?'

Brissot shrugged his shoulders, but the stare persisted. To escape it, he turned to the steward. 'Perhaps I will have some wine, Barbier, and the first lieutenant's glass needs refilling.'

'Are any of the other officers in their cabins?' asked Dupotet, indicating the doors that lined both sides of the room.

'No, sir,' said the steward. 'The master and second lieutenant are ashore; the surgeon is in the sickbay and Monsieur Morin is on watch.'

'Good. Kindly leave the bottle and go, Barbier. I wish to speak with Monsieur Brissot alone.'

'Yes, sir.'

The sound of another boat passing astern of the *Redoutable* came from beyond the canvas screen; a ship's launch, to judge from the regular creak and splash of the oars and the crisp commands from its coxswain. Dupotet ignored it and continued to hold his fellow officer's gaze, his stare unwavering.

Brissot shifted uncomfortably in his chair. 'What was it that you wished to discuss, sir?' he asked.

'Loyalty,' said Dupotet.

'Loyalty? I'm not sure that I understand you, sir.'

'As senior lieutenant, I expect complete loyalty from all of this ship's officers, and I want you to remember that when you sit down for your cosy little repast.'

'But surely my loyalty to this ship is beyond question, sir,' said Brissot, a frown appearing on his face.

'And what of your loyalty to me, as your superior officer?'

'Naturally, you have it.'

'So why did you see fit to undermine me by questioning the way I had rigged the masts in front of the captain?'

'When?' queried Brissot, genuinely puzzled.

'When we fought that bloody frigate last week,' said Dupotet. 'You sent word to the captain that the backstays were too taut and should be slackened off.'

'But … but they *were* too taut, sir! The *Redoutable* was in grave danger. It was my loyalty to the ship that made me act as I did.'

'And you never considered that it might reflect badly on me?'

'In truth, no. The thought never crossed my mind, sir. My only concern was for the ship, and the perilous position she was in. And how would I have known that you were responsible for their set-up?'

'Because I am responsible for every aspect of the running of the ship,' said the first lieutenant, jabbing a finger down on the table to emphasise his point. 'When you criticise me, you shake the confidence of the captain in me, and encourage others to question my authority. Like that bloody fool of a boatswain, Tournier. And once that begins, where will we be then, eh?'

'I'm truly sorry for any offence I may have caused, sir, but that was never my intention. I only wanted the ship out of irons.'

'Welcome as your apology is, how do you propose to mend your ways in future?'

'Perhaps I should bring any concerns I have to you first.'

Dupotet held Brissot's gaze for a moment longer, and then reached for the bottle to refill the glasses. 'I'm glad that we understand each other, Francois,' he said, forcing his mouth into a smile. 'Kindly bear in mind what we have agreed when you see the captain later. And remember, nothing ever happens on this ship that I don't know about.'

*****

Two weeks later, Clay was more content as he stood on his quarterdeck. The moment he had abandoned the *Griffin*'s battle against the constant flow of the monsoon and yielded to the wind's pressure, the ship's progress had been transformed. For the first week she had the wind on her beam, sailing away to the south east for mile after mile. The direction his ship was taking was further east than he wanted, but Armstrong had assured him that soon they would break free from the grip of the monsoon altogether.

The change had come three days back. At first the wind had died altogether, leaving the frigate slowly turning on her own reflection in the glassy water. Then the following day it had returned, fitfully at first, but growing steadily more reliable as the south east trade wind started to blow. Now she was running due west, her wake a creaming line of white across the deep blue ocean, towards the Cape and the Atlantic beyond. Then Clay gulped nervously, as he reminded himself that the ship was also running towards the main French naval base on Isle de France.

But on a day like today, with a clean wind flapping at his coat, it was hard not to be content with life. It was early morning, and he was taking his daily walk along the weather gangway of the frigate before it became too hot. The wind was blowing so constant and true that the ship needed little intervention from those on watch, so Taylor was taking the opportunity to drill the crew. The first lieutenant was up on the forecastle, speaking trumpet in hand, bellowing instructions to a party of men high in the mast above him.

'You can bring her down now, Mr Todd!' he shouted. 'Handsomely, this time!' Clay paused to watch as the foretopgallant yard made its jerky progress towards the deck.

'That was tolerably done, George,' said his captain, coming across once the yard was down. 'Mostly with the new hands, I collect.'

'Yes sir. Some of the younger ones I hope to make into topmen one day. They have much to learn, but I might yet live long enough to witness them bring a little credit on the ship. Every man jack claimed to be an experienced sailor when they signed on at Madras, if you'll believe it.'

Clay smiled at this, and patted his first lieutenant on the arm. 'I have witnessed you make able seamen from the most unpromising of recruits, so I daresay you will succeed with these Mohammedans too.'

'That I shall, sir. Indeed, some of them are not without talent.' He pointed towards a ring of men sitting on the deck, each with a length of line coiled on his lap. In the centre of the group was Ezekiel Davis, the oldest member of the crew. He was a wizened veteran with only a thin grey rat's tail of hair left of the thick plait he had once sported. Davis was widely held to be an expert on knots and splices, not least by himself, and Nathaniel Hutchinson, the ship's boatswain, frequently used him to train the more promising members of the crew.

Davis had just demonstrated how to long-splice a

severed rope by first plucking the cut ends into strands, and then weaving them together with fingers that were still surprisingly nimble. 'Now you has a try, shipmates,' he said, passing the newly spliced rope around the group.

'Mark the Saleem brothers, sir,' whispered Taylor. 'They are the two lascars closest to the grating.' The new recruits squatted on their heels among the cross-legged sailors. Their lithe fingers twisted and tucked the strands together at a speed that far exceeded their fumbling colleagues. With shy hesitancy they both held out their completed work.

'Well, I never did!' exclaimed Davis, turning one of the ropes in one hand while he scratched at his bald pate with the other. 'An' you two ain't never spliced a line afore?'

'No, Sahib,' replied one, his head bobbing from side to side with pleasure. 'But my brother and I are knotting carpets in our uncle's shop since we were little boys. It is not so very different.'

Clay turned to comment to Taylor, when a hail came from the masthead. 'Deck there! Sail in sight!'

'Where away?' queried Clay, stepping back along the gangway until he could see the masthead lookout, standing on the thin royal yard far, far above him.

'Two points off the starboard bow. sir!'

'Best get that topgallant yard back in place, Mr Taylor.'

'Aye aye, sir.'

Clay returned to the quarterdeck, passing Midshipman Russell, the oldest of the midshipmen, as he bounded towards the mainmast chains, telescope in hand, and ran up the shrouds with ape-like speed.

Armstrong was officer of the watch, and was sweeping the horizon when Clay joined him at the rail. 'Anything in sight, Jacob?' he asked.

'Nothing yet, sir, but perhaps Mr Russell will be able to tell us more.'

Clay looked towards the masthead where the young man was settling himself on the crosstree, and following the direction in which the lookout above him was pointing.

'She's making sail, sir!' reported Russell. 'Just clear of the horizon, and turning this way. She has the look of a warship, to my eye.'

'Like enough she is,' said Armstrong. 'Coming to see if she has found a plump East Indiaman.'

'I daresay that is true. Hold our course for now.'

'Aye aye, sir.'

'Deck there!' yelled Russell. 'Dawson here thinks she may be that big French frigate we tangled with at the turn of the year. The *Belle-Poule*.'

'Forty guns, and the best handled of the Frog ships we milled with that day, sir,' added the ship's master. 'I think I may just be able to see her topgallants.'

'Forty guns?' queried Taylor, coming up to join them. 'Shall I have the ship cleared for action?'

'Not yet,' said Clay, peering through his own telescope. 'Something seems amiss. If Dawson can mark them as the *Belle-Poule*, I have no doubt they will have recognised us. Yet they come on very bold against an evenly matched ship. Not the French way, is it?'

'Deck there! I believe I can see a brace of other ships astern of the *Belle-Poule*. One on either beam.'

'That makes a deal more sense,' said Clay. He came across to stand behind the ship's compass in its binnacle, assessing the wind direction and his ship's best point of sailing. 'Come around to larboard and make our course southwest-by-south, if you please, Mr Armstrong, and I'll have the topgallants set.'

'Aye aye, sir.'

Broad reaching was the *Griffin*'s best point of sailing, and when the extra canvas was sheeted home, she began to fly. Soon she was crashing through the waves amid plumes of spray, her deck heeling over as she thrashed along. Clay gripped one of the mizzen stays for balance and felt the humming tension in the rope against his hand.

'Off the decks there, you lubbers!' roared a petty officer in response to a wail in Urdu from some of the newer recruits, caught out by the change in the ship's motion. 'Puke over the lee rail, if you must!'

Clay returned his attention to those chasing him. All three ships were over the horizon now, and on a course that was bringing them ever closer. The *Belle-Poule* was the easiest one to identify, with her heavy yards and bulky hull. Close behind her was a second frigate. She was a little smaller, but shared the same round bow and tall foremast that marked her out as a French-built ship. He was certain she was Linois's other frigate, the thirty-six-gun *Sémillante*. But try as he might, he could not identify the third ship in the squadron. 'What do you make of that smaller frigate, Mr Taylor?' he asked. 'I am sure the others are our friends from the Straits of Malacca, but I cannot place her at all.'

'She doesn't look French to me, sir,' said Taylor. 'And she doesn't have enough gold leaf and gingerbread for a Don ship. From her rig I would have said she was one of ours, only her hull is a touch slab-sided.'

'I reckon she's a Hollander, sir,' said Armstrong. 'Out of Batavia or the Cape. Good fighters, the Butter-boxes, and excellent sailors to a man.'

'Odds of three to one, then,' said Clay. 'Too rich for my

taste. If we carry on as we are, will they intercept us, Jacob?'

'I believe not, sir. I took a bearing earlier and by my reckoning they will cross our wake six miles behind us.'

'And then it will be a stern chase,' said Clay. 'I doubt if they have the beating of the *Griffin*. Once they realise that, I daresay they will haul their wind presently and leave us in the hope of easier prey.'

Clay stayed on deck for the next few hours, and things developed much as he had predicted. The *Griffin* drove on southwards and a little bit west, while her three pursuers formed into a ragged line behind her, neither gaining on her, nor falling back. So long as all stayed as it was, his ship was safe, even if she was being driven far further south than he would have liked. He could sense from the creaking of the hull and the shriek of wind through the rigging that his ship was sailing close to her limit. He found himself anxiously looking aloft to check that all was well. The thin topgallant yards above him were bending in the wind. If anything carried away, their pursuers would fall on them like hounds on a fox that had gone lame. He would dearly have liked to order Taylor to check the rigging, but he knew that hell would ice over before his first lieutenant was found wanting in his duty.

'I shall go below, Mr Armstrong,' he said. 'Kindly see that I am called the moment the weather changes, or if the enemy should start to gain on us.'

'Aye aye, sir.'

Down in his cabin his steward, Harte, had the table laid for his lunch. Clay hung his coat and hat on the bulkhead, and took his place.

'Glass of bishop, sir?' said Harte, approaching with the decanter. 'Mutton pie again, I'm afraid. I've spiced it up with a deal of cloves, and Mr Faulkner tells me it weren't above six months in the barrel, which is a comfort.'

'That sounds delicious,' said Clay, with a forced smile. Like the rest of the ship's company, he had grown tired of endless mutton some time ago. Apart from a little goat, it was almost the only meat available in India, where cows were sacred to much of the population and pork unclean for the rest. As Clay toyed with his food, he found his attention wandering towards the run of window lights that stretched across the back of the cabin. Beyond the glass was the frigate's wake, churning up from below, and then the three pursuing ships, filling the rest of his vision as they battled along.

He raised his glass towards the portrait of his wife, Lydia, which hung on the bulkhead opposite. 'No matter, my dear,' he assured her. 'They will tire of this pursuit presently, and then I shall resume my way home. I daresay they will have gone before it grows dark.'

But he was wrong. They were still there when he had dinner that night with Taylor, their sails glowing coral in the light of the setting sun. And they were still there when he breakfasted in the morning with the officers who had come off watch. Day after day they followed the *Griffin*, driving her further and further to the south.

Chapter 6
Autumn

It took three months for the *Redoutable* to return from the Toulon dockyard, fully repaired after her battle with the *Active*. The heat of summer had passed, and on the slopes above the town the grape harvest was being gathered by stooping figures with wicker baskets on their backs. Grey clouds drifted in from the Mediterranean, bringing with them a shower of rain that dappled the surface of the inner harbour and pattered on the deckhead above where Captain Lucas sat. The sound made him rise from his desk and cross to the stern. He ran a hand over the new frame of the window, freshly painted in dove grey, and looked out.

Two newly built ships of the line had joined the moored fleet since he had last looked out of this window, on that hot summer evening when he had dined with young Brissot. The next day they had handed their ship over and all gone on leave. He was pleased to see his country was at last taking seriously the effort required to challenge the Royal Navy, but his pleasure was tinged with unease. Where will the crews come from to man them all, he wondered. France's merchant ships were once more blockaded in port, unable to stir without being set upon by an enemy that awaited them just beyond the horizon. No maritime commerce meant no new sailors learning their craft out at sea for the navy to draw on. And experienced sailors were the foundations of a navy.

Clay and the Immortal Memory

From behind Lucas came the toll of the ship's bell, prompting him to turn away from the view. 'Thibault!' he called towards his day cabin.

'Yes sir,' said a portly, balding man, stepping through the door. He wore a green moleskin waistcoat above his britches and a leather apron around his middle.

'How long have you been at sea with me?' asked his captain.

'Almost ten years, sir.'

'Ten years! And still you dress like an Auvergne tavernkeeper.'

'If it is a sailor you want to cook for you, I will happily step aside, sir,' sniffed Thibault. 'Captain Letellier of the *Formidable* seeks a new steward, and has offered me an extra livre a week to join his ship. You'll recall the praise he heaped on my grilled flounder with capers and *beurre-noisette* last time he dined here. Shall I send word I am available?'

'Certainly not,' said Lucas. 'Letellier needs no more excuse to over-indulge, and I have no trained sailors to spare. Besides, I need you here. I will be inviting my fighting officers to dine with me tonight. We have much to discuss.'

'Dinner for six, sir,' mused Thibault, rubbing his chin. 'The first of this season's truffles have arrived, and I managed to buy a basket of live rabbits at the market this morning, along with some excellent cheese from Savoy …'

'I am sure the meal will be splendid, as always,' said his captain, his mouth salivating at the prospect. 'Kindly make the necessary preparations, if you please.'

'Of course, sir.'

Thibault's reputation as a cook was well deserved, and it was an expectant group of ship's officers who gathered around their captain's table later. The sun had set, and the candles and lamps in the cabin were echoed by the lights of Toulon, winking in the dark water beyond the stern windows.

In addition to his four naval lieutenants there was also Captain Yves Dorre, who had recently taken command of the seventy-four's contingent of marines. 'Wonderful rabbit, sir,' he enthused, sucking the flesh from a last, tiny bone, before wiping his mouth on a napkin tucked into his stock. 'I have rarely tasted better. Your cook is a man of genius.'

'He is, but please say it softly,' said Lucas. 'His opinion of his own abilities needs no enhancing from us.'

'Ha! Have no fear on my part, sir,' said Dorre, placing a finger beside his bulbous nose. 'Your secret is safe with me.'

'Thibault, kindly bring more wine,' ordered their host. 'Monsieur Dupotet's glass is empty, as is Monsieur Brissot's. Then you can serve the cheese.'

'Ah, perfect,' said the marine officer, his eye's alight at the prospect. 'I always say that a meal without cheese, is like a beautiful woman with only one eye.'

When the laughter died, Lucas cleared his throat to gain their attention. 'It has been a most pleasurable evening, gentlemen, but while we enjoy our cheese, I have some matters I would like to discuss that have arisen while we were on leave. The Mediterranean Fleet is to have a new commander. He will arrive shortly from Paris to take up his post.'

'Not before time, sir,' said Morin, the most junior of the ship's lieutenants. 'Admiral Latouche Tréville is an excellent officer. I served with him back in ninety-eight.'

'I agree,' said their captain. 'Regrettably he is also in no position to serve France further. He is a very sick man whose life is despaired of. No, it is Admiral Villeneuve who is to lead us.'

'Villeneuve?' spluttered Dorre, choking on his wine.

'Isn't he the fellow who cut and ran at the battle of the Nile?'

'He is, and in doing so he saved the last few ships of the fleet from that disaster,' said Lucas.

'Along with his skin,' whispered Morin, leaning towards Brissot.

'I don't believe we should judge a brother officer harshly for choosing to withdraw when placed in a false position,' continued the captain. 'The battle was irretrievably lost. No, I am more interested in what his arrival means. The emperor has appointed a young, ambitious admiral to the fleet. Something is afoot, gentlemen.'

'About time we came out and confronted the English, sir,' exclaimed Dorre, hammering the table with his hand and making the candles flicker. The others gave muted smiles of approval.

'Quite, which brings me on to the second matter I wished to discuss,' said Lucas. 'I have been considering it while I was away. Do we believe that our ship is ready to face the enemy? And pray answer truthfully.'

'The ship is as smartly run as I am able, sir,' said Dupotet, sitting upright and straightening his cutlery.

'I don't doubt it for a moment, Camille,' said his captain, placing a hand on his first lieutenant's sleeve, 'and yet when we last put to sea, we were roughly handled by a ship of less than half our size.'

'The men were very inexperienced then, sir,' said Morin. 'With more sail and gun drill they will perform better.'

'Sail training while at anchor, and play-acting at firing the guns,' said Lucas. 'This is how we have prepared for battle since the Revolution. And how has it worked for us, gentlemen? Meanwhile our enemy is at sea, month after month, sailing in all weather and able to discharge his cannons in earnest. How do you suppose we will fare against one of their ships of equal force? Manned by such experienced veterans?' He looked around the table, reading the anxiety in his officers' eyes and softened his tone. 'I do not question your courage, gentlemen. I know that you will all do your duty, and that our men will fight bravely. But in the end, courage alone will not prevail against an enemy that fires faster, lays his cannons better, and can out-sail us. So I ask again, how can we prepare ourselves to meet our enemy at least on equal terms?'

It grew quiet in the cabin. Dorre pushed away his plate, his appetite gone. The other officers sipped at their wine, avoiding each other's eyes. Lucas looked around the group, and noticed the frown on his third lieutenant's face. 'Monsieur Brissot,' he said. 'You seem thoughtful. I would welcome any ideas you may wish to share.'

The young officer rolled the stem of his glass between his fingers for a moment before replying. 'I agree with you, sir. To simply repeat the mistakes of the past would be folly. And perhaps there is another way. It seems to me that our nation does have one very strong asset in this war that might help us.'

'And what is that, pray?'

'An all-conquering army.'

'Ah soldiers, sweeping the enemy before them with *les armes blanche*,' said Dorre, brandishing his cheese knife so that the blade glittered in the candle light. 'Cold steel has long been the natural weapon of a Frenchman.'

'I'm not sure I understand how the army can possibly help …' began Dupotet, but his captain held up his hand.

'Let us hear our friend out. Do please carry on, Lieutenant.'

'I recently finished an account of the Punic Wars, sir,' said Brissot. 'In it I found some striking parallels between our situation and that of the Roman Republic. Just as we have our army divisions, they had their legions, who could defeat all-comers on land. But in fighting Carthage, they found themselves locked in a war with a predominately naval power. And like us, they were confident of defeating their foe, if only they could cross the sea to come at them. So they too expanded their navy, building ever more warships. But they found that the Carthaginians were much more skilled in the ways of the sea, and when they fought them on the water, they lost.'

'That is our situation exactly!' exclaimed Morin. 'So what did the Romans do?'

'They resolved to turn sea fights into land battles by employing a device named a corvus,' explained Brissot. 'It was some manner of movable bridge with a spike which held the enemy fast when it was dropped across on to their deck. Then Roman legionnaires could use it to board their enemies and defeat them.'

'Interesting as all this is, I'm not sure that I follow,' said Dupotet. 'Are you suggesting that we build one of these bridges?'

'No, I am not, sir. But I believe it is the principle that is important,' said Brissot, leaning forward in his seat. 'The Romans found that by simply copying the Carthaginian way of fighting, they lost, so they resolved to change the very nature of the battle to one that favoured them. Look, when a French fleet encounters an English opponent, what happens? After a period of manoeuvring, the ships range up beside each other and hammer away with their cannons until the matter is resolved, yes?'

Brissot looked around the table, and received nods of agreement. 'Both sides have a few sharp shooters up in their rigging, and more soldiers lining the sides, but it is the guns that win the day. And because the English fire quicker and straighter, they inevitably emerge victorious, agreed?'

'Yes, regrettably,' said his captain. 'And how would you change matters?'

'Bring the battle to a close before the enemy's guns can win it for them. Have many more sharpshooters than we have today, sailors as well as marines, and train them to be the best. So that they can clear the upper deck of an opponent with a hail of musketry. We may not be able to fire our cannon in these confined waters, but we can certainly practise with small-arms. Then train the rest of the crew to board an enemy quickly. French ships always try and keep their distance from an English one. We should do the opposite. Range alongside, clear their deck with our volleys, and then board them.'

'It is certainly bold,' mused Morin, 'but will it answer?'

'Oh, undoubtedly,' enthused Dorre, grinning broadly at the prospect. 'Imagine the look on their faces as we pour across into their ships like buccaneers! I love it!'

'I would urge caution, sir,' said Dupotet. 'Warfare is a deal more complex than it was in the time of the Romans, or indeed the pirates.'

'True, but I do like its originality,' said Lucas. 'It might only succeed once, after which the enemy will be alert to the danger, but perhaps once will be enough. Surprise is, after all, the greater part of victory, is it not? I shall ask you, Monsieur Brissot, and you as well, Captain Dorre, since you seem so taken with the idea, to work together. Find me a way of defeating an opponent by small-arms and boarding.'

'Yes, sir,' said Brissot, wondering what he had let himself in for. He was conscious that across the table from him were two contrasting faces. Dorre was rubbing his hands at such an important role for his men, while the first lieutenant's dark eyes bored into him, his expression full of disapproval.

*****

Clay sat at his desk with the ship's log propped up beside him, referring to it from time to time as he worked on a letter to his wife. His pen scratched away, covering the paper with line after line in his spidery hand. He reached the end of the page, held it up to his face and blew gently on it. While he waited for the ink to dry fully his eyes strayed to the stern windows. The sea beyond had lost its rich tropical blue and now had a grey sheen to it. The frigate was heeled over, sailing as close to the wind as it could, making it seem that the horizon was at a slope, and his cabin and the pursuing ships upright.

'How long have you been chasing me, I wonder,' he mused out loud, flipping through the pages of the log book. 'It must be a week at least.' To his surprise, he found it was eleven days. Days in which the wind had moved around until it blew from the north west, which meant that the *Griffin* was barely making any progress towards home at all. The temperature too had dropped steadily to that of a temperate summer. He compared the ship's position now with when they had first spotted their pursuers. Near to eight hundred nautical miles travelled, he concluded, almost all to the south.

A knock interrupted his thoughts. Clay added the sheet to the pile of similar ones on his desk, returned them to a drawer and called, 'come in!'

The door opened and Napoleon scampered in, his claws clicking on the deck as he ran beneath the desk and bounded up on to his favourite seat cushion beneath the stern windows. He was followed by Clay's steward. 'I has Mr Faulkner here wanting a word with you, sir.'

'Then let him in, Harte,' said his captain. 'And light along a pot of coffee for us both, if you please.'

'Aye aye, sir.'

Harte withdrew, to be replaced by the ship's purser, an aristocratic-looking man whose shock of auburn hair was turning silver above his temples.

'Do take a seat, Charles, I beg,' said Clay.

'Thank you very much, sir,' said the officer, carefully parting the tails of his coat as he sat down. He nodded towards the stern windows. 'I see the hounds are still hot upon our trail.'

'They are indeed, and damnedably vexing it is too,' said Clay. 'They force us ever further from our route home. Already we are so far south that the wind barely serves. Many more days of this pursuit, and we shall pass into the Horse Latitudes. Mr Armstrong tells me the winds there are very indifferent and fluky.'

'Perhaps that region will provide us with the opportunity to lose them at last?' suggested Faulkner.

'Amen to that,' exclaimed Clay. 'For another ten degrees further and we enter the forties, where the sea is boisterous, and the wind blows both very strong and wholly foul for a ship heading west. If we are compelled to sail in those waters it will be quicker to return home via Botany Bay and the Horn, than attempt to fight against it.'

'Coffee hot from the galley, sirs,' announced Harte, backing through the door with a tray in his hands. 'Though how I ain't lost the lot on the way back with the barky heeled over is a miracle.'

'Why have they not closed with us, sir?' asked Faulkner, stirring sugar into his drink.

'I don't suppose they have the bottom for it,' said Clay. 'Or they are waiting for something to carry away aloft on the

Griffin, so they can fall on us when we are in a false position.' He pointed towards the ships. 'Do you mark the largest of them, off to leeward?'

'Is that the one named after a chicken?'

'Indeed so, the *Belle-Poule*. She is much the same size and speed as us, so cannot close. The other two, the *Sémillante* and the Dutch one, could, but I suppose are shy of doing so without their larger consort. Remember, just as we recognise them, I have no doubt they mark us as the ship that handled them very roughly at the start of the year.'

'And so the stalemate continues, sir,' said the purser, 'except it cannot do so for ever. I fear we have an issue with our fresh water.'

'Our water!' exclaimed Clay. 'How so?'

Faulkner pulled a leather notebook from his pocket. 'We left Madras with six months' supply, ample to see us through to St Helena beyond the cape, where we can replenish it. Our passage this far has been slow, meaning we have used the better part of half.'

'But we still have water for three more months?'

'Alas not, sir. Some of the hogsheads in the aft of the hold have become contaminated with sea water. I sampled them earlier and it is very brackish.'

'So how much do we have untainted?'

'Eleven weeks and four days at normal allocation, sir,' said Faulkner, consulting his notes.

'And at two thirds allocation?'

'Fifteen weeks and three days, sir.'

Clay looked across at the three ships bounding along in his wake. Surely, they could not maintain this endless chase much longer? Yet even if they gave up now, it might be days before he could work his ship northward, back to regions where the winds were kinder. He knew what the prudent thing to do was, but he also knew that the full water allocation was barely adequate for men doing hard physical labour on a diet of salt meat and dried biscuit. 'Let us keep the ration as it is for one week more, and then cut it.' he ordered. 'If we must fight our way past the enemy, it will be harder to do with thirsty men. But empty the scuttlebutts and halve the amount the cooks and officers' stewards can draw. Meanwhile, I will consider how to bring matters to a head. Enjoy your coffee while you can, Charles. I shan't be wasting fresh water on such beverages after today.'

*****

Lieutenant Brissot and Captain Dorre had chosen a day of filthy weather for their visit to the citadel at Toulon. A cold wind tugged and flapped at their boat cloaks as they were rowed across the choppy grey water of the harbour. Once ashore, they splashed their way along the cobbled quayside towards the massive grey fortress, heads down as dead leaves and discarded rubbish swirled around their feet. Even when they arrived, they were compelled to stand waiting in an inner courtyard with rain drumming on their hats while a bored soldier went in search of Dorre's cousin.

'My dear Yves!' exclaimed their host, jumping to his feet when his bedraggled guests were eventually shown in. 'Why you are quite sodden! Has your ship foundered, or did you fall overboard? Come and stand by the fire, I pray, before you both take a chill. Orderly! Another log for the fire, and hot wine for my cousin and Lieutenant … er … Lieutenant ...'

'Lieutenant Brissot, third of the *Redoutable*,' said Dorre, coming to his rescue. 'May I present Major Fortin of the artillery.'

'A pleasure to meet you, sir,' said Brissot, peeling off a wet glove to accept the proffered hand. The major was a small man with a balding pate, a dark moustache and a kindly face full of concern.

'Likewise, monsieur,' replied Fortin. 'Now surrender your outer garments, I pray. We shall have them placed before the guardroom fire directly, which is far superior to my little blaze. Ah, here comes the wine.'

The orderly collected their hats and cloaks, and Fortin seated them by the fire with a glass of hot wine. Soon Brissot felt the chill recede as he sat back and let the two cousins chat amicably about the latest news of their family.

'Are you both a little restored?' asked the major at last. 'Good. I always imagined that Toulon would be a most agreeable posting, but it can be full of surprises. Wait until the spring, Lieutenant Brissot, when the icy *Mistral* blows down from the north, to pluck the tiles from the roofs and the blossom from the trees. Shall we proceed to the armoury?'

Fortin led them out of his office and along a corridor to where a stone-flagged passageway led off it at a downwards angle. The walls and ceiling were made from large blocks of well-dressed stone and the occasional lantern supplied an amber light. Brissot could feel the weight of the fortress growing above him as they went deeper.

'Vauban knew how to build a redoubt,' enthused Dorre, slapping his hand against the wall, 'Look at the quality of this masonry.'

'He did indeed,' smiled Fortin. 'This was the magazine for the original citadel until the fortifications were expanded after the siege in ninety-three. Another was built, more conveniently situated to serve the guns. We now use this one to store weapons.' He turned towards Brissot. 'My cousin has told me a little of your idea to try and turn a sea battle into a land one, which I find most interesting. I have some suggestions that may prove helpful. Ah, here we are.'

At the bottom of the corridor was a low vaulted space. Arched openings in front and to the sides led into dimly lit storage rooms. In one Brissot could make out the start of a rack of closely spaced muskets running away into the dark, and another was lined with crates and boxes stacked chest-high. In the middle of the chamber was a sturdy table with a shallow wooden case and several short-looking muskets on it. A pair of soldiers in the blue and white uniform of the artillery stood close by.

'I wondered if these might be of interest,' said the major, picking up the muskets and handing one to each of them.

Brissot took the weapon and held it towards the light of the nearest lantern. The butt and firing mechanism seemed that of a conventional musket. Next he examined the muzzle, and saw the start of grooves cut into the inside of the barrel. Pushing his finger in, he could feel them gently twisting away from him.

'These are rifled,' said Dorre, bringing his up to his shoulder and taking aim back up the passageway at an imaginary foe.

'Quite so,' said their host. 'Sixty of them were ordered as a trial for the 9th *Chasseurs à Pied*. They were part of the garrison here at the time. They proved to be much slower to reload than a musket, but a good deal more accurate. A musket can barely hit a thing beyond a hundred paces, but in the hands of a marksman, these rifles can down a man four hundred metres away.'

'Why did the *Chasseurs* not want them, then?' asked Brissot.

'It was all a matter of logistics. The ball they fire is slightly different in size to that of standard-issue muskets and carbines. Keeping one regiment in the field supplied with different ammunition to all the others was deemed too complicated. But it struck me this would be less of an issue on board a ship that carries all it requires within it.'

'That is true,' said Dorre. 'I hold these may answer very well, Francois.'

'Agreed,' said Brissot. 'We will recommend them to Captain Lucas, Major.'

'The second thing I wish to show you lies within this box,' said Fortin, indicating the wooden case. 'Would you open it for me please, Corporal?'

'Yes, sir,' replied one of the soldiers. He picked up a crowbar and levered open the lid. Inside were rows of iron spheres, each nestling in a sheet of greased paper, like fruit on display in a market.

Fortin pulled one out, hefted it for a moment, and passed it across to Brissot. 'What do you make of that, Lieutenant?'

The iron ball was a little smaller than a round for a six-pounder cannon, and Brissot was expecting to feel a solid mass of that weight in his hand, but to his surprise it was much lighter. Intrigued, he rolled it around and found an opening with a raised rim, like that of a wine bottle. 'It's hollow,' he said, knocking the rough surface with his knuckle. 'I would almost have thought it a shell for a howitzer, only it is much too small for that. What is it, pray?'

'It is a grenade,' said the major. 'The weapon that gave grenadiers their name, although no French soldier has carried one in the field since the time of Louis XIV. A well-handled musket is so much more effective than such primitive weapons.'

'And how does it function?' asked Dorre. 'I have never witnessed one used in action.'

'The inner part is filled with powder and a short fuse leads out through the centre of the plug that seals the opening,' explained Fortin. 'When an enemy is at hand, the fuse is lit, left to burn down until a finger's width remains, when the grenade is hurled towards the foe. All being well, it explodes in his midst, spreading fragments of casing and general consternation in equal proportion. As I said, they are no longer used in the field, but we still maintain a stock of them in our strong places. We find them useful in sieges. They can be thrown down from the walls on to an enemy gathered below, which was what made me think of your ships, cousin. From the height of your masts, could a few sailors not send a rain of such grenades on to the deck of a ship alongside?'

'They could indeed, Major,' said Brissot, with a thoughtful expression. 'They could indeed.'

*****

Clay came on deck at dusk, and noticed the change in the weather immediately. After the stuffy warmth of his cabin, the air was refreshing. The wind had grown light, a cold breath against his face and was just strong enough to send the frigate ghosting forwards with every sail set. Around the *Griffin* the sea had an oily look, slopping against the side of the hull, while overhead the sky was hidden by grey clouds, and the horizon was lost in mist.

He walked across to the binnacle and studied the traverse board.

'Good evening, sir,' said Preston, coming across to join him. He was wearing a pea jacket with an empty sleeve thrust deep into a pocket. The garment was heavily creased from the long months it had lain folded in his sea chest.

'Good evening to you, Edward,' said his captain. 'How have we fared this watch?'

'Poorly, sir. What wind there is has backed round to the south west, I am afraid. With the set of the current, we will be making very indifferent progress.'

'I am glad to see the rats have left your dunnage be,' said his captain, indicating the coat.

'What rats, sir? Any Napoleon has spared lie hiding in the ballast and dare not show their faces. But I am grateful to find it intact. How it has grown chill! Some of the whalers in the crew think there might be ice mountains about, drifted up from the south.'

'Good,' said his captain. 'We can send across and replenish our water. Strange to tell, this is the antipodean spring, Edward. Or would be if this murk would clear away. What of the enemy?'

'Following astern, like so many footpads on the trail of a promising victim.'

Clay nodded at this, pulled out his telescope and focused it behind the *Griffin.* A week had passed since he had reduced the water ration, and still they pursued him. They had dropped back a little in the light airs, straggled across several miles of sea. His grip tightened on the telescope, and he bit his lip in frustration. Were they going to chase him all the way to the damned pole? The time was fast approaching when he would have to turn and face them, whatever the odds. As it grew darker the ships began to recede into the grey twilight. Then navigation lights appeared in their rigging, silver points in the gloom. Each ship also had a single blue lamp at the masthead.

'Beg pardon, sir,' said a voice beside him. 'Can I be a

coming at that there light?'

Clay looked around to see a sailor beside him, a glowing spill cupped in his hands. 'Carry on, Chapman,' he said, stepping aside to allow him to access the frigate's stern lantern. Behind him another sailor was lighting the lamps in the binnacle, while overhead a lantern was hauled up to the *Griffin*'s masthead. Clay considered it for a moment, trying to bring something to mind. Then he remembered, and the germ of an idea started to form in his mind.

'Mr Preston,' he called. 'I daresay we set the same navigation lights each night?'

'Yes, sir,' said the officer. 'In accordance with your standing orders.'

'Quite so,' said Clay. 'And the enemy, they set theirs at this time in like fashion, I collect?'

'Yes, sir. Of course, they have more need of them, sailing in company, than we do. To avoid running aboard each other.'

'Indeed,' said Clay. 'Would you be so good as to redeploy the masthead light for me? I will have it hung under the mizzen top tonight, if you please. At the stern end, where the enemy can see it clearly. Let that be its station for the next few nights.'

'Aye aye, sir.'

Clay next turned to the midshipman standing by the wheel. 'Mr Sweeney, pray tell, what kind of moon shall we be enjoying tonight?'

'Eh, not very much of one, I imagine, sir.'

'A seaman should always know the state of the moon, Mr Sweeney, especially when the enemy is at hand. You have an almanac, do you not? Pray spare a moment to glance in it on occasion. Mr Preston, can you enlighten Mr Sweeney, please?'

Clay and the Immortal Memory

'It will be a waning crescent in its second from last phase, sir,' said Preston. 'Rising just after three bells.'

'Which means we will have what the day after tomorrow, Mr Sweeney?'

The youngster's face frowned for a moment, and then cleared. 'Why, no moon at all, sir!'

'And a black night, if these clouds should persist,' added Clay. 'We must use it wisely. Kindly pass the word for Mr Taylor, if you please, and ask the carpenter and boatswain to join us. I have just recalled something I learned of while dining at Lord Keith's during the peace, that may serve us too.'

'Aye aye, sir.'

Chapter 7
Winter

A cold wind blew from the north-east across Toulon harbour, bringing the chill of winter with it. It made the *Redoubtable* tug at her moorings, and the men waiting on her deck hunch a little deeper into their coats. They were standing in a line that snaked along the portside gangway and up the foremast shrouds to end just beneath the foretop. This was a large square platform at the top of the thick lower section of the seventy-four's massive foremast, and was crowded with men.

'Next, if you please, Sergeant,' said Dorre, his face raw with the cold, despite the greatcoat he wore.

'Yes, sir. You there! Up you come!'

The topmost sailor of those waiting on the shrouds clambered up through the lubber hole and on to the platform. He gave his name to Midshipman Pascal, who was sitting with his back against the mast and trying to control a large notebook that rustled in the breeze. 'Gaspard, sir. From the afterguard, larboard watch.'

'Gaspard ... larboard ... watch,' repeated Pascal, the tip of his tongue appearing as he wrote.

'Very good,' said Dorre. 'Now, Gaspard, pray come over here. Do you mark that boat down there, with a target at its heart?' He pointed to where an old lighter borrowed from the shipyard was moored fifty metres out. Lashed to a post was a canvas tube stuffed with straw, about the size and shape of a man. The dark wood around the target was peppered with bright scars from close misses, but some shots had found the target, leaving little tuffs of pulled straw.

'Aye, I see it sir,' said the sailor.

'Excellent. I want you to take this rifle, and see if you can hit it.'

Dorre raised a spy glass to his eye and focused on the lighter, while Gaspard accepted a weapon proffered by one of the marines on the platform and brought it up to his shoulder.

'You might want to cock that first, lad,' growled the sergeant.

'Oh, of course,' said the sailor, pulling the flint back with a solid click. A moment later the rifle fired and grey powder smoke rolled across the platform.

'I didn't see a hit,' reported Dorre.

'That would be because it struck the water midway between the lighter and the *Bucentaure*, sir,' said the sergeant, recovering the rifle and passing it to one of the marines to reload. 'Probably best if we don't go hitting the flagship.'

'Quite so,' agreed his captain. 'You can resume your duties, Gaspard. Down by the larboard shrouds, if you please.'

'Yes, sir,' said the sailor, vanishing from sight.

'I doubt if that one could hit a barn with a shovel, Sergeant. Let us hope that the next shows more promise.'

'Can't … barn … shovel,' repeated Pascal, scribbling furiously.

'Up you come, there,' ordered the sergeant. 'Ah, one of ours, sir. Just transferred in from the army, 16th Line Regiment.'

Dorre watched the man clamber up from below. He was thin and gangly, and not long out of adolescence, to judge by the wisp of moustache growing on his upper lip. He came to attention before his commanding officer.

'What's your name, soldier?' asked Dorre.

'Private Robert Guillemard, sir.'

'Very well. I would like you to take this rifle and see if you can hit that target down there.'

The man accepted the weapon, and looked at the lighter floating on the water beneath him. He moved slightly to one side to clear the topmast shrouds from his view, made an adjustment to the back sight, cocked the rifle and brought it up to his shoulder in a single smooth motion. 'Ready, sir.'

Dorre brought his spy glass up to his eye. 'Carry on.'

There was a short pause before the shot banged out. Dorre saw the bullet strike the target, roughly where the knees would be if it really had been a man. 'A hit,' he reported. 'A trifle low, but definitely a hit.'

'This downwards angle takes a little getting used to, sir,' explained the soldier. 'And the platform is swaying in the breeze. My next shot would have been better.'

'Another rifle, if you please, Sergeant.'

'Yes, sir.'

There was the same careful pause, and then the rifle banged out once more. This time the shot went straight into the middle of the target.

Dorre lowered his spy glass. 'Where did you learn to shoot like that, Guillemard? Not square-bashing in the 16th, I'll warrant.'

'No, sir. I used to go hunting with my father in Sainte-Baume Forest. I have hunted deer, duck and rabbits since I was a boy.'

'Very good. That will do for now. Down you go, Private.'

'Yes sir.'

'I believe we may have found another of our marksman,

Sergeant.'

'We just might, an' all, sir. Shall I send up the next?'

'If you please.'

'Guillemard … private … marksman …' intoned the midshipman.

*****

The *Griffin*'s twenty-four-foot cutter was the least popular of the frigate's boats. She had been painted blue some years ago, but was still universally known as the red cutter on account of her previous colour scheme, sailors being a retentive breed as a whole. She was the oldest of the boats, and had seen plenty of service. Her keel was hogged, she had a slow leak in her stern that no one could find and an annoying tendency to ship water over her bow in the mildest of swells. Which all made her the obvious boat for Lieutenant Taylor to select for the special service required of her.

She had been lifted from her position on the skid beams and now hung in the air above the quarterdeck, where an anxious working party awaited her arrival.

'Walk away a pace, starboards,' ordered Hutchinson, his grey pigtail bobbing with agitation as the boat swung in the wind. 'Hold her steady, blast you! Easy there! Lower away both! Handsomely!'

The boat came slowly down, stubborn and wayward to the last, until she rested on the deck. Once the tackles had been cleared away the boatswain came across to join Taylor, where he stood with the ship's carpenter, his working party close behind.

'We shall need that mast you fashioned from the old fore topgallant yard stepped, Mr Kennedy,' said the first lieutenant, the officers at the centre of a ring of onlooking sailors.

The Irish carpenter looked at the long thin spar, twice the height of the boat's normal mast, and sucked at his teeth. 'She will need a deal of shingle ballast, sir,' he concluded. 'I'm after thinking three hundredweight, sir. Maybes even a touch more. Any less, and she'll capsize like a coracle in a storm, afore you knows it.'

'That much, Chips?' queried Hutchinson. 'We'll need to stow it with care, sir. Else it could shift in the swell, and then she'll look all to cock.'

'I'd be after stowing it in sacks,' commented O'Malley to Trevan, in a conversational tone behind the boatswain's shoulder. 'That'd keep them little stones in place.'

'Damn your impertinence, O'Malley!' roared Taylor, rounding on the sailor. 'Presuming to join in the discourse of your betters! Stand back there, I say. The lot of you!'

The officers waited while the sailors sheepishly withdrew a few paces, before resuming their discussion.

'O'Malley's forwardness aside, sir, sacks ain't a bad notion, if we're to use loose ballast from the hold,' said the boatswain. 'Plenty of empty ones in the bread room. We could fill 'em up and stow them between the cutter's frames.'

'She will ride deep with such a load,' observed Taylor. 'How will we keep her afloat?'

'I've some empty kegs from the cooper, sir,' said Kennedy. 'I can lash them to the thwarts, so I can. That'll make her a deal more stable.'

'They will certainly help,' said Taylor, 'but what if she ships too much water? She will surely founder.'

'Aye, an' that red bugger's always been a wet boat, sir,' added the boatswain. 'Too much briny, an' she'll sink like an anvil.'

'I could be after making a deck for her, sir,' offered the carpenter. 'Cover her over and seal her up, tight as a drum.'

'Nah, Chips,' said his fellow warrant officer. 'That'll just make her even heavier.'

Over Kennedy's shoulder Taylor could see O'Malley looking significantly aloft. He followed his gaze to where it rested on the bulging mizzen topsail above their heads. 'I agree, Mr Hutchinson. A wooden deck would be too heavy, but perhaps the sailmaker could fashion a canvas boat cover? Will that serve? If it is securely lashed into place?'

'I daresay that it would, sir,' said the boatswain, brightening. 'I'll have him working on it directly while Chips and I get this mast up and rigged.'

'And you both have the captain's requirements clear in your mind?'

'That I do, sir,' confirmed Kennedy. 'Don't you fret, Mr Taylor. We'll have her ready in good time for sundown.'

'Very well then. Carry on.'

*****

'I must protest, sir,' exclaimed Dupotet, coming into the cabin of the *Redoutable*.

Lucas stifled the sigh that rose to his lips, and instead transformed it into a smile of welcome. He laid down his pen and rose from behind his desk. 'Do please take a seat, Camille. A glass of wine, perhaps? Before you deliver your protest?'

'Not for me, thank you, sir. I am altogether too agitated.'

'I see,' said his captain. 'Well at least sit down and tell me what is troubling you. This time.'

The first lieutenant gestured towards the cabin window,

where the terracotta roofs of Toulon gleamed in the thin winter sun after a passing rain shower. 'Today being a calm day, I wished to put the men through some additional sail drill, sir. They are somewhat improved from when we last ventured out, but there is still much more work to be done.'

'An admirable plan, Camille,' said Lucas. 'Where does the problem lie?'

'Lieutenant Brissot and that oaf Dorre have half the crew engaged in their latest act of foolishness. Do you know that they are throwing little canvas bags of sand down from the tops and trying to land them in some lighters moored alongside?'

'Naturally they are, Camille,' said his captain. 'We would be very unpopular if they were throwing live grenades into the harbour. As it happens, they have my permission to be doing this, and it is I who neglected to inform you, for which you have my apology. But you say they are performing this exercise with half the crew? Could you not perform your sail drill with the other half?'

'Yes, of course, sir. And I will be doing so shortly. But don't you see that all this is making the *Redoutable* a laughing stock in the fleet? While they practise with their great guns, we toss bags of sand over the side!'

'I must say, it is refreshing to find you an advocate of gun drill, Camille. Not so very long ago you abhorred the damage it did to your spotless decks,' smiled Lucas. 'And we will soon be doing plenty of training with our cannons too, you have my word. But we will also continue with our small-arms drill. I really think that young Brissot may be on to something. Come, have a glass with me, and let me explain how I see things. Thibault! Bring some wine. And some of that dried sausage you barbarians make in the Auvergne.'

The steward acknowledged the order with little more than a grunt from the direction of the day cabin, but soon came in with the wine and a plate of thinly sliced sausage, burgundy-coloured and flecked with black.

'Smoked boar and truffle, and quite delicious,' said Lucas, popping one of the discs into his mouth and closing his eyes with pleasure while Thibault poured the wine.

'Your health, sir,' said Dupotet, raising his glass.

'And yours, Camille. Now, imagine these pieces of sausage are ships.' The captain leant forward and arranged the slices into two rows. 'Our fleet is this line, and the enemy are those. With the sail drill, which we will not neglect, we manoeuvre into a position parallel with our opponents. But we know that the Royal Navy will not be content to exchange fire at range, especially not if they are led by that madman Nelson.'

'Are not all the English mad, sir?'

'True, but few are as demented as he is. Look how he threw himself at the Spanish at St Vincent, or how he destroyed our fleet in Egypt.' With a few deft pokes with his finger, the enemy line slid menacingly across the plate to close with their opponents. 'And now we find ourselves in the sort of close quarters fight where their superior rate of fire guarantees them victory.'

'Which is why we must train more, sir,' said Dupotet. 'To fire faster, or to be able to avoid their manoeuvres.'

'Or, we spring our surprise,' said Lucas, his eyes alight. 'We welcome them closing the range. Indeed we throw grappling hooks across to bring them alongside. Grenades pour down, exploding on deck among their crew. Our marksman cut down all their officers, so the survivors are leaderless. And while the bulk of their crew still serve their useless guns, deep within the ship, our men have been quietly forming up on deck, seizing pikes and swords as they come, to sweep across and capture our opponent before they realise the danger. Imagine that, Camille! Isn't such a victory worth a few sour comments?'

'What does the admiral think of your plan, sir?'

'Ah, the great Pierre-Charles de Villeneuve. I fear he is not the man of decision I hoped for. He both approves of our plan, and yet is most uncertain about it. He found it interesting, and urged me to carry on; yet saw no reason for the fleet to adopt it more widely.'

'Perhaps his caution is merited, sir.'

'Why so?'

'What do we truly know of the man behind these ideas? Young Brissot has barely served six months on the *Redoutable*, yet seems to be trusted more than me or any of the other officers.'

'Camille, do I detect a little jealousy?' said his captain, regarding his first lieutenant over the top of his wine glass. 'I will freely admit I like him. He is a fine officer who handles his men well. But if he now occupies a position of some favour, it is only because he chose to put himself forward. When I asked my officers for ideas, in this very cabin, his was the only credible proposal. And Dorre speaks highly of him.'

'That old soak,' scoffed Dupotet. 'But what do we know of his motives, sir? In persuading you to adopt such strange tactics.'

'His motives? You think they are not the same as yours and mine? The greater glory of France?'

'It took me some time to place him, sir. When he joined I thought his name was familiar. Are you aware that he is the son of a notorious revolutionary? In the wardroom I have even heard him openly question why France has need of an emperor.'

'Is he now? That is interesting, although we all

supported the Revolution once. That is why we are still alive today, Camille. But I will think about what you have said, and will keep an eye on young Brissot.'

*****

Captain Alain Bruilhac, the veteran commander of the French heavy frigate *Belle-Poule*, had just started on dinner when there was a thunderous knocking at his cabin door. 'Let him in,' he growled to his steward, through a mouthful of sea pie.

A young midshipman marched in, saluted smartly and began speaking in response to his captain's raised eyebrow. 'Lieutenant Harang's compliments, and he believes we are gaining on the enemy, sir.'

Bruilhac took a sip of his wine, wiped his mouth on his napkin, and glanced towards the stern windows. Outside a grey dusk was gathering, save in the west, where the sky was still light. 'Really?' he queried. 'Has there been some change in the weather?'

'No, sir. Still a light wind from the north-west and a little swell.'

'Very well. Tell Monsieur Harang that I will come directly.'

'Yes, sir.'

Bruilhac dropped his napkin beside his plate, shrugged on the coat that his steward held out for him and with a last look of regret towards his dinner, made for the door. On deck the cool of evening was settling around him. Ahead was the British frigate still sailing away from him, but several cables closer than before. 'When did we first start to gain on her?' he asked, studying the enemy through his telescope.

'From about six bells, sir,' said Harang. 'At first I thought they might just be shaking out a reef, but when we continued to close, I thought it best to send for you.'

'You did quite right,' said his captain, looking around him. A mile off to windward he could see the silhouette of the *Sémillante*, against the setting sun, while the smaller Dutch frigate *Utrecht* was little more than a dark blur away to the east.

'I see the Dutch are keeping station badly again tonight,' he growled. 'Although Motard on the *Sémillante*, is hardly doing much better. Signal them to form up astern, please.'

'Yes, sir.'

In the short time that he had been on deck, the evening had grown darker. The sun vanished altogether, and the *Griffin* ahead became little more than a pale, ghostly blur in the gloom. 'Give me a night glass, someone,' he ordered, snapping his fingers towards the midshipman next to the binnacle.

'Here you are, sir,' said the youngster, passing it across.

'*Sémillante* acknowledges, sir,' reported Harang. 'I had best get our navigation lamps lit, so she can mark where we are.'

'Of course. And the Dutchman?'

'No response yet, sir, but I may have missed her signal in this gloom.'

'Send up a rocket to warn her, although she will take an age to beat up towards us,' grumbled the captain. The masthead lamp appeared above them, washing the *Belle-Poule*'s deck in chill blue light, while nearer at hand a warm glow came from the compass binnacle. Bruilhac watched as a petty officer opened the lamp box to light a spill, his face lit in yellow for a moment. He took it across in his cupped hands to the signal midshipman. A brief splutter, and then the rocket shot off, high above them, trailing a curve of sparks. As it burst above them the *Griffin* reappeared, sailing away from them, with one of her ship's boats trailing behind her.

'Was she towing a boat earlier, Monsieur Harang?' he asked.

'I can't remember, sir. Do you think it is important? We often tow our boats, to make more room on deck, or to stop their planking from drying out.'

'Perhaps not, but a ship that expects action sometimes does so, to remove a source of dangerous splinters. Perhaps she is less innocent than she seems,' said Bruilhac, resuming his vigil. But even with a night glass he could barely see his quarry. Her wake was the slightest of grey pencil strokes on the dark sea. And then two points of light appeared, a brighter one closest to the sea, and another at about the hight of the mizzen top.

'Same as last night, sir,' reported Harang. 'I can't make much else out, but we are still closing.'

'We are indeed,' said his captain. 'Too quickly. Have the topgallants taken in. This one is a dangerous bastard. I want the *Sémillante*, at least, with me when we bring her to battle.'

'Yes, sir.'

The last of the day had gone now, and night lay all about the pair of French frigates. The clouds overhead were as dark as the flat sea, as they crept towards the *Griffin*, her twin lamps flickering off the water behind her.

'Have the ship cleared for action, Monsieur Harang,' ordered Bruilhac. 'Battle lanterns on the gundeck, but shutter them until I give the order. I'll have no light showing on deck, either. Douse our navigation lamps and the binnacle. Hail the *Sémillante* and tell her to do the same.'

'Yes, sir. But how will the *Utrecht* find us?'

'By our gunfire,' growled his captain. 'And send a

reliable man with keen eyes into the bow.'

The frigate was in total darkness, as if the impenetrable night had stolen on board. Only the creak of the rigging and the hiss of passing water gave any hint that Bruilhac was at sea at all. He could sense the crew around him as they coughed and shifted at their stations. His whole world had narrowed to the two points of light ahead, slowly growing all the time. Nearer and nearer came the French ships, panthers in the dark, stalking their prey.

'Open the battle lanterns, Monsieur Harang,' he ordered. 'Give the gun crews some light, but don't run out yet.'

A faint glow picked out the lower rigging of the *Belle-Poule*, seeping up from the main deck below, and by contrast the night became darker still. Behind them the *Sémillante* could just be faintly seen, following close behind as they glided onwards.

'Courses in!' ordered the captain. 'Bring her to the wind, helmsman.'

'Yes, sir.'

The lamps on the *Griffin* were barely a hundred metres away now, as the *Belle-Poule* turned until every gun would bear.

'Up ports and run out!'

Squares of orange appeared along the side of the frigate and her eighteen-pounders emerged rumbling from her side. The crews around Bruilhac were training their cannon with care towards the steady lights beside them.

Bruilhac paused for a moment, knowing in his heart that something was amiss. Too easy, he thought. Much too easy. 'Open fire!' he ordered.

Night vanished as long tongues of flame leapt out from the side of his ship, painfully brilliant after so many hours searching the darkness, and he knew at last what was what was wrong. The twin lamps vanished in an instant, and then there was nothing. No cries of confusion from a surprised enemy. No ship rearing up alongside. No return broadside, crashing home on his own ship. Nothing.

The *Sémillante* fired her own ponderous broadside at that moment, and as the light sped away it revealed an empty ocean of dark water. The only thing visible among the smoke of the broadsides was a shattered ship's cutter, listing badly, with trailing wreckage beside it.

'But … but where is the enemy?' exclaimed Harang.

Bruilhac looked at the boat, with its canvas cover and long mast, now cut through at the base. 'They will be long gone, Monsieur Harang,' he said, gripping the rail to control his anger. 'Laughing to themselves at how easily they made fools of us, damn them!'

*****

It was just as dark on the gundeck of the *Griffin* that night. The ship had been cleared for action while it was still light, and the gun crews sat around their pieces, equipment worn smooth by long familiarity littering the deck. The only light came from the smouldering ends of slow match in their tubs, glowing like so many eyes in the dark, there as a backup in case a cannon's flintlock firing mechanism should fail to spark. But although the men could see little, they had sailed for long enough to be able to judge the frigate's progress with their other senses. From the gentle send and tilt of the deck they knew that they were broad reaching to the south, leading the two French frigates on into the gathering gloom. The note of the wind through the shrouds and the gentle brush of the sea against her side told them that they had slowed a little, to let their enemy draw close.

The crew of the eighteen-pounder next to the main mast were in the best position to judge her progress, in the centre of the ship and beneath the officers on the quarterdeck.

'Pipe be leaving it tight to spark up them lanterns on the boat,' grumbled Trevan, the gun's loader, his head thrust out of the port. 'It be darker than a Newgate lockup already.'

'Kindly have the lamps lit, and let slip the red cutter, Mr Taylor,' came the quiet voice of Clay from the darkness above them, as if he had heard the Cornishman's suggestion.

'Aye aye, sir.'

'Move yer arse, Adam, and let the rest of us have a fecking peek,' complained O'Malley, the gun's captain.

Trevan moved reluctantly away, and the others crowded around the open gunport.

'Cutter be adrift, sir,' came the growling bass of John Powell, the frigate's heavily scarred boatswain's mate.

'Good. Bring her around on the other tack, Mr Taylor. Quietly now.'

'Aye aye, sir.'

Feet pattered across the deck above them and the yards creaked around to the accompaniment of hissed orders. The hull beneath them heeled over as the *Griffin* changed direction.

'Where did you learn your seamanship, on a Portuguese bum boat?' hissed the voice of Hutchinson from the forecastle, his normally thunderous tone muted to a strangled whisper. 'Take another turn and a half on them headsail sheets.'

The frigate settled on her new course, close hauled and heading to the north east. Suddenly there was something moving in the night. The sailors watched as the red cutter drifted down the portside. Her hull was low in the water and the sides were lined with small barrels. She was being propelled by a square sail set on a willowy-thin mast, impossibly tall, stepped in the middle of the little boat. A large lantern blazed out from part way up the mast, while a smaller lamp hung from the top. The gun crew looked at the odd craft they had spent the afternoon creating as it sailed away, following the *Griffin*'s original course.

'If that fools the bleeding Frogs, I'll dine on me hat,' declared Evans. 'The cutter and a brace of burners ain't going to pass for the barky, even if it is uncommon dark.'

'That be 'cause you knows it's only our old sculler,' said Trevan. 'It be like watching a conjurer at the fair. If you knows how the trick be done, it don't answer. But them as don't be still taken all aback. See them Frogs are looking for the old *Griffin*, and ain't taken their peeps off her this night. It'll work, you mark my words.'

'Adam has the truth of it, Sam,' added O'Malley. 'Why, we never took our eyes off that fecker Khan back in Madras, all the time the cutpurse were stealing away with our chink.'

'Aye, but that was 'cause one turban looks much like another. But a cutter ain't the same as a bleeding frigate,' said Evans. 'One bleeding look at that there boat, an' they'll hoot with laughter at us trying to fool them with such gammon.'

'Oh, 'tis not gammon, Sam,' said O'Malley, with authority. 'I was sharing a twist of backy with that Harte, last night. He was laying up the cabin table when Pipe was telling Old Man Taylor how he came by the notion. See, he was scoffing at Admiral Keith's table, a while back, with a load of Grunters, one of whom was that mad Scottish lord. The feller as captured a Don frigate with naught but a sloop. Back in the year one.'

'You talking of Lord Cochrane?' suggested Trevan.

'Him as captured the *El Gamo*?'

'That's the fecker! So, your man Cochrane was after bragging about all the high jinks he'd been up to, and how he was near to being caught by a brace of Frog ships a deal bigger than his. Only he gave them the slip, on account of running until it was night, an' then setting a hogshead adrift showing a light on a spar. The Frogs swallowed it easy as kiss me hand, closed with your keg, an' Cochrane lived to fight again. And our Pipe, being a proper deep one, stowed the notion away in that pate of his.'

The gun crew digested this, while the *Griffin* sailed onwards through the night, further and further from the little boat and her twinkling lanterns.

It was several hours later, when most of the sailors were dozing by their guns, that the roar of the *Belle-Poule*'s distant broadside woke them. Trevan was back at the port in an instant, with the others crowding close, just in time to see the *Sémillante* firing her cannon. The golden flash was like a distant sunrise against the clouds, gone almost before it could be registered. In that moment, the sailors all saw the dark silhouette of the Dutch frigate hastening away from them towards the other two ships. She was several miles to leeward and the gap between them was growing all the time.

'Bleeding hell,' breathed Evans. 'Pipe's only gone an' done it. We've given the bastards the slip.'

'So, how's it to be, Big Sam?' asked Trevan, placing an arm around his friend. 'Broiled or roasted, like?'

'Eh? What you on about, Adam?'

'This 'ere hat of yours. How does you want it served?'

Clay and the Immortal Memory

1805

Clay and the Immortal Memory

Chapter 8
New Year

The map room at the Tuileries Palace in Paris was full of golden candlelight. During the day, light flooded into the room through a row of tall windows along one wall, but the short winter afternoon had ended some hours earlier. José Miguel de Carvajal-Vargas pulled his elaborately braided coat closer as the hateful wind rattled sleet against the dark glass, and thought how warm it was on his estate in distant Andalusia.

'My thanks for joining us this evening, your excellency,' said Napoleon. 'I look forward to spending more time in your company, now that Spain is our ally once again.'

The ambassador bowed in his chair towards the three Frenchmen in the room, the plentiful orders on his chest clattering together as he did so. 'It is indeed fortunate that Spain has such a powerful friend. My king is still in shock at the unprovoked attack the British made on our treasure fleet.'

'What happened, exactly?' asked Rear Admiral Denis Decrès, France's Minister of the Navy.

'Piracy, señor, pure and simple!' exclaimed the diplomat. 'Four of our frigates left Montevideo, loaded with bullion. As they approached Cadiz, they found a Royal Navy squadron waiting for them, demanding that they surrender. Naturally they refused, whereupon our ships were brutally attacked. One was sunk and the others captured. We lost a whole year's production from our mines in Peru! Over four million dollars in silver and tens of thousands in gold ingots! The enemy claim the money will be returned one day, but it has left my country's finances in a most precarious state.'

'We find their navy often behave little better than corsairs,' agreed Napoleon. 'Yet even for a nation as perfidious as the English, such a bold action does seem out of character. I wonder if they might have learned of our secret treaty. Did they know that it obliged Spain to declare war the moment the treasure had been landed?' The emperor's dark eyes narrowed into a frown as he regarded his new ally.

'Your majesty,' spluttered de Carvajal-Vargas, rising from his chair. 'I must protest! What are you implying?'

'Oh, do sit down, Ambassador,' said Marshal Berthier, the Minister of War. 'You are among friends, so let us speak frankly. We all know that Godoy is a seasoned gossip, and the Spanish court leaks secrets like water through a sieve.'

'No matter,' said Napoleon. 'The attack has brought Spain into the war, at last. Let us speak no more of the past. Instead, I want to plan our revenge for your country's humiliation. Shall we move to the map?'

The men rose from their chairs and followed Napoleon across to a table placed beneath the spreading arms of a chandelier. Lying on it was a huge map of the Atlantic, including the western half of Europe on one side and the eastern side of North America on the other.

'We have long been preparing to invade Britain, Ambassador,' said Berthier, picking up a wooden pointer and indicating the narrow strip of sea between France and the British coast. 'Encamped around Boulogne is most of our army, together with an invasion flotilla of two thousand boats. All they need to cross is three days of calm weather and control of the English Channel.'

'Is that all?' smiled the Spaniard. 'And how will you gain such control, opposed by their Royal Navy?'

'France alone does not have the naval strength to defeat the enemy, and nor does Spain,' explained Decrès. 'But what if we should combine our fleets?'

'That is easy to say, but our navies are divided between many ports, some in the Atlantic, some in the Mediterranean, señor, with the Royal Navy waiting outside each.'

'The emperor has devised a plan,' said Berthier.

'We will use the same principles I use on land to crush an enemy,' said Napoleon, leaning across the map. He balled a fist and brought it down to emphasise each point. 'Speed.' Thump. 'Surprise.' Thump. 'And unity of strength at the vital moment. Show him how it will work, Decrès.'

The Minister of the Navy accepted the pointer from Berthier and let the tip rest on Toulon, in southern France. 'It shall begin here,' he explained. 'Where Admiral Villeneuve commands our Mediterranean Fleet. Lord Nelson has withdrawn his ships to a bay in Sardinia for the winter, leaving only a few frigates watching the port. Villeneuve took his ships to sea in January for some training, and brushed them aside with ease. He will break out again, with his eleven ships of the line, avoiding Nelson, and sailing for the Atlantic.' The pointer slid across the map towards Gibraltar.

'One moment, señor, if you please,' said the ambassador. 'You speak of evading Lord Nelson as if it were a trifling matter, yet is he not the most feared of our enemies? The Buonaparte of the seas?'

'The what?' queried the emperor. '*Non non*! Please do not compare that man with me. He has enjoyed a little good fortune, that is all. How many battles has he won, eh? Two?

Three? I have fought countless times, and never drunk the bitter dregs of defeat. Never!'

'Also, he holds King Ferdinand at Naples in high regard,' explained Berthier, once the ambassador had absorbed the imperial outburst. 'The king made him a duke after his victory at the Nile, and it was at Ferdinand's court that he met his mistress, the Hamilton woman. We shall use this to distract him. We shall get our troops in southern Italy to make trouble for Ferdinand, just when the fleet sails. Nelson will certainly link the two, and move to protect Naples, leaving the way to the Atlantic unguarded.'

'Having entered the Atlantic,' resumed Decrès, sliding his pointer past Gibraltar and coming to rest on Cadiz, 'Admiral Villeneuve will arrive before your chief naval base, where your fleet will be waiting. They sortie as soon as Villeneuve arrives, and the combined fleet will drive off the Royal Navy squadron outside.'

'And then they sail for the Channel, señor?' asked the Spaniard.

'No!' interjected Napoleon. 'You are forgetting my second principle. Surprise! An immediate assault on the Channel is exactly what the enemy will be expecting.'

'Standing orders for all Royal Navy admirals, if uncertain what an enemy intends, are to fall back and protect the Channel,' explained Decrès. 'It is where the squadron outside Cadiz will certainly go. So our combined fleet will instead sail into the Atlantic, and make for …' This time the pointer proved to be too short, and the admiral had to walk around the table. 'Make for our base at Martinique. Meanwhile, our Atlantic fleet will escape from Brest, collect our squadrons at Rochefort and your Spanish ships based at Ferrol, and sail to join Villeneuve in the Caribbean.'

'Imagine the English, when our fleets all vanish, like mist before sunlight,' urged Napoleon, his eyes alight at the prospect. 'Their ships will gather to defend their shores, but no threat will appear. Where is the enemy, they will ask, as the days go by? Have they made fools of us? Are they seizing all our islands in the Caribbean? Or sailing to conquer our lands in India? Have they returned to the Mediterranean in overwhelming numbers? Fear and doubt will grip them, and then they will start to spread their strength in all directions. That will be the moment when we strike! Continue, Decrès.'

'Once the fleets have combined, they will return to Europe in overwhelming numbers, and will sail into the Channel, driving all before them.'

Only the gutter of candles could be heard in the room after the Minister for the Navy finished speaking. All eyes were on the Spanish ambassador as he stood looking at the map, taking in the plan. 'It is certainly bold,' he said, at last. 'When do you propose to start?'

'Admiral Villeneuve is ready to sail the moment I give the word,' said Napoleon, 'but Decrès here advises that we wait until the end of March, when the danger of winter storms is over.'

'March?' exclaimed the diplomat. 'This March? But our navy will never be ready! Remember we have been at peace until a few weeks ago. Ships must be brought into service, stores gathered, officers recalled, sailors recruited. All this cannot be done instantly.'

'Do I need to remind your excellency that your king signed a solemn treaty with me promising that thirty-three ships of the line would be made available to fight?' said Napoleon.

'And he will fulfil that promise, your majesty, but it will take time. And money that the English now have.'

'What can you commit to provide?' asked Berthier.

'I would need to consult with Madrid, but I am certain only a part of our fleet could be made available. But can you not delay your departure to later in the year?'

'He who hesitates in war, is lost,' said Napoleon, wagging a finger at the ambassador.

'Then I will urge my government to have as much of our fleet prepared as possible,' said de Carvajal-Vargas. 'I should be in a position to supply you with numbers once I have heard from them.'

'Very well, Ambassador,' said Napoleon. 'I look forward to hearing from you. Decrès will show you out.'

The Spaniard bowed and was escorted from the room by the Minster of the Navy, down a long corridor with a polished wooden floor and soldiers on guard lining the walls. When they reached the palace entrance the two men waited together while the ambassador's carriage was called.

'Tell me, now that we are alone, what you truly think of the emperor's plan?' asked Decrès.

'I think that it shows all the ambition and boldness for which he is famed.'

'It is certainly unique,' agreed his host.

'Not to a Spaniard,' said the ambassador.

'Your excellency?'

'Assemble a huge fleet and sail it into the English Channel so that an army waiting in Flanders can cross the narrow seas? Phillip II would recognise it instantly. It is precisely what our Great Armada tried in 1588. Let us hope that Napoleon's Armada doesn't suffer the same fate. Ah, my carriage. Good evening to you, Minister. I shall pray for all the good fortune that our enterprise will require.'

*****

Two months after giving her pursuers the slip, the *Griffin* finally rounded the Cape and entered the Atlantic. There she picked up the south-east trade wind and her anxious crew, on a reduced water ration for many weeks, spread every sail she could carry to catch its steady thrust. Each mast was full from the deck to the masthead and the frigate responded as if she too was eager to return home. With her hold half empty, and a wide strip of gleaming copper showing along her hull, she flew over the sea, shouldering the long rollers aside and trailing a streak of wake behind her like the tail of a comet.

On the leeside of her quarterdeck two of her officers were enjoying the exhilarating progress. Blake sat on one of the carronade slides, a sketch book flapping on his knees as he tried to capture the profusion of sail. Beside him stood Preston, leaning against the mizzen shrouds.

'We make fine progress, do we not, John,' commented Preston, his voice croaky with thirst. 'She touched twelve knots at the last cast of the log.'

'Small wonder, with every man jack trimming the sails to urge another yard of pace,' said his friend. He pointed with his stick of charcoal to where some of the afterguard were surreptitiously tweaking the mizzen topsail sheets a half-inch tauter behind their petty officer's back.

'Even a wise old cove like Hutchinson has been affected,' said Preston. 'I heard him speaking with Mr Taylor of the possibility of trying a moonraker, if the wind should ease.'

'A what-raker?'

'A moonraker. I now know it to be an extra sail added to the very summit of a mast. Until I heard them discussing it in earnest, I had thought it a mythical thing beloved of old seadogs, like mermaids and Krakens and the like.'

'More moonshine than moonraker, eh,' chuckled Blake, his laugh turning to a dry cough.

'Very droll, brother,' said Preston. 'But I share their desire to press on. Ahead lies the island of St Helena, full of tumbling streams of crystal-clear water. I for one plan to drink and drink until I can hold no more when we make landfall.' The young officers gazed out over the rolling ocean.

'*Water, water, everywhere, nor any drop to drink,*' commented Blake.

'Lord Byron?'

'Coleridge. The captain has a copy of *Lyrical Ballads* given him by his sister, and he was good enough to lend it to me. For some reason the line struck a chord.'

'I wonder why,' smiled his friend.

'Deck there! Sail ho!' yelled the masthead lookout. 'Sail a point off the larboard bow!'

'Take my compliments to the captain, Mr Todd, and tell him a sail is in sight,' said Armstrong to one of the midshipmen of the watch.

'Aye aye, sir.'

Blake closed his sketch book, got to his feet and the two men crossed to join the American at the rail. 'Anything in sight, Jacob?'

'I reckon so,' said Armstrong, passing across his telescope. 'A topsail proud of the horizon, just beyond the larboard cathead.'

The blue sky overhead faded to white as it touched the dark bar of ocean. Blake focused with care and slowly tracked until he found the sail, a shell-white fragment of something more solid. As he watched, it broadened into a square. 'She's turning to run from us,' he reported.

'Small wonder, Mr Blake,' said Clay, appearing at his elbow. 'Any ship sailing alone out here is sure to be wary, but she will need to be swift indeed to outpace the *Griffin* in a hurry. Kindly alter our course to close with her, if you please, Mr Armstrong.'

'Aye aye, sir.'

As the day wore on, mile by mile, the *Griffin* steadily overhauled the other ship. Soon she was hull up over the horizon and clearly visible to the officers of the frigate as they lined the quarterdeck rail.

'Three masted,' decided Blake, as the profile of the ship changed a little. 'With a dozen gunports per side.'

'But not a man o' war, from the look of her,' added Armstrong. 'Might she be a privateer, or even a slaver, with Africa just over the horizon?'

'Not a very swift one if she is, Jacob,' said Taylor. 'Why, we're hauling her in hand over fist. Ah, a flag at last.'

'Spanish colours, I believe,' said Blake.

Clay watched the red and yellow ensign break out, a point of gorgeous colour against the white of her sails. She was big, perhaps two thirds the size of the *Griffin*. Her dark hull rode deep in the waves and she was broad of beam for her length. He lowered his telescope and turned to his officers.

'I hold she is a merchantman, gentlemen,' he said. 'Those gun ports are more to deter pirates than to give battle in earnest. She is on the wrong side of the ocean if South America was her destination. Would her course have been right for the Cape when you first saw her, Jacob?'

'It would indeed, sir,' confirmed the sailing master.

'Very well. Mr Taylor, would you clear away one of the bow guns and have the launch crew drawn up on the main deck.

They had best be armed.'

'Armed, sir?' queried the first lieutenant. 'You do recall that Spain is neutral?'

'Was neutral, Mr Taylor, when we left India,' corrected Clay. 'But word takes at least six months to reach there from Europe, and we have been at sea for many months more. I don't know if we are at war with Spain, but I fancy the master of that ship over there does. Our colours have been plain for him to see for some time, yet he has not resumed his original course and runs from us as if we were the very devil.'

'Aye aye, sir.'

Before long Clay could read the ship's name, *Fortuna*, painted in white letters across her stern. His attention was caught by movement beside her wheel. A young man in a plain blue coat was standing there, looking back at the frigate as she loomed closer. He turned as a woman in a dark dress and bonnet appeared, gesturing first towards the *Griffin*, and then forwards. An elderly man in a deep crimson coat joined the group, wringing his hands in frustration. Moments later the man in the blue coat raised a speaking trumpet to his lips. Clay was too far away to hear anything, but moving his telescope further forward he saw that some of the crew were rigging a whip from the main yard, while another party were removing a grating. 'Signal her to haul her wind, Mr Armstrong,' he ordered. 'They look to be preparing to ditch their cargo to escape us, although they have left it much too late for that to answer.'

'Aye aye, sir.'

The signal broke out overhead, but still the *Fortuna* sailed on. As Clay watched, a large crate was swung up from the hold and tipped over the side. 'Give her a gun, Mr Taylor!' he ordered. 'Across her bow, if you please.'

'Aye aye, sir.'

The splash of the next crate striking the water coincided with the deep boom of the *Griffin*'s forwardmost eighteen-pounder, and an altogether more threatening splash, just ahead of the Spanish ship. The conversation around the wheel became even more animated, ending with the man in the blue coat turning his back on the couple to give orders. Behind him the elderly man placed an arm around the woman and something white fluttered between them. The *Fortuna* came creaking around until she lay up into the wind, with all her sails volleying and flapping. The red and gold flag came jerkily down towards the deck. The woman was now in the arms of the man in crimson, who was patting her back.

'Heave to just to windward of her, if you please Mr Armstrong.'

'Aye aye, sir,' said the ship's master. 'Steer a point to starboard, helm.'

'Launch crew away!' roared Clay, the moment the frigate came to a halt. 'Take possession of her, Mr Preston. And send her master over when you have her secured.'

'Aye aye, sir,' said the lieutenant.

Clay watched the boat row across the narrow gap between the two ships, rising and falling in the long Atlantic swell. As it came alongside, he saw Preston get up from his place in the stern sheets and make his way to the centre of the boat. He paused to give instructions to the crew, and then stood on the thwarts. Two sailors steadied him as he waited for a wave to lift the boat up the *Fortuna*'s side. When it came, Preston leapt for the main chains, his lone arm held aloft. His hand locked on to a shroud, and with a convulsive jerk of his body he managed to get first one and then his second foot up on to the channel before hauling himself upright. He straightened his hat, and stepped down on to the deck of the merchantman and vanished from sight.

'How in all creation does he do that, sir?' marvelled Armstrong, as the launch crew followed their leader up and over the side.

'It is truly wonderous, Jacob,' agreed Clay. 'When he first returned from his injury, I did try to spare him from such duties, but he would not have it and I don't hold the ship to be any the poorer for his presence. Edward with but one arm is worth more than many an able-bodied officer I have encountered.'

A few minutes later Preston was at the quarterdeck rail hailing his captain through a speaking trumpet. 'She is the *Fortuna* from Cadiz, bound for Manilla with a general cargo, sir. My men are just checking that now. So far they have found furniture, several cases of musical instruments and some bales of cloth.'

'Very good, Mr Preston. Are you sending her master across?'

'Directly, sir. The ship's owner is also on board, and wishes to come. And his wife is most insistent on accompanying him too, if you have no objection?'

'Really?' queried Clay. 'Three of them? Oh … very well, Mr Preston, but pray no more visitors or you shall require the longboat. If you find they have children with them, kindly keep them aboard the prize.'

'Aye aye, sir. I had best have a bosun's chair rigged for the lady.'

As soon as the party from the *Fortuna* were brought up on to the quarterdeck and spotted Clay, the elderly man in the crimson coat came bustling forward. 'Señor, I must protest!' he cried, in good, if heavily accented English. 'By what right do you stop my ship?'

'And who, pray, are you, sir?' said Clay.

'My name is Don Rafael Sorondo, owner of the *Fortuna*. And I demand to know …'

'And these others?'

'My wife and Captain Ruiz de Contreras, master of the ship. But I must insist …'

'Dona Sorondo, Captain, welcome on board,' said Clay, bowing to each in turn with old-world courtesy. 'My name is Captain Alexander Clay of his majesty's frigate *Griffin.*' He then turned to the owner. 'Now, sir, what is the nature of your protest?'

'Why, that you have seized the ship of a neutral state, in violation of all rules of war, señor!'

'I see,' said Clay, holding his face impassive. 'Your desire to evade your current predicament is quite understandable, Don Rafael, but it will not answer. This ship fell in with an outward-bound East Indiaman three days ago who brought word that hostilities have been declared between our two nations.'

Don Rafael exchanged glances with his wife, who shrugged her shoulders in response. 'You cannot blame my husband for trying, Captain,' she said. 'We only learned of the war when we stopped at Recife. When we saw you were on a course from the Cape we hoped that the news might not have reached you.'

'War!' exclaimed Don Rafael. 'It will be the ruin of us all! Before the last one the House of Sorondo was one of the wealthiest merchant families in Cadiz, with over a dozen ships. Now that I have lost the *Fortuna,* I have only one elderly brig left.'

'It is indeed unfortunate, sir,' said Clay. 'But only ruin can be expected while your king persists in supporting France against my country.'

'Our king is an imbecile!' hissed Dona Sorondo, her bonnet trembling with the strength of her emotions. 'It is that devil Godoy who rules Spain, and he has long been in the pocket of the French.'

'I do sympathise with your distress, señora,' said Clay. 'At least permit me to ensure your swift return to your friends and family. We are bound for St Helena, where plenty of neutral shipping touches. I am sure you could arrange a passage home from there. Alternatively, you could stay on board the *Fortuna*. I shall be sending it under a prize crew to Gibraltar, from where it is but a short journey to Cadiz. Which would you prefer?'

'I would be most grateful if we might stay on the *Fortuna*, Captain,' said Don Rafael. 'For what it is worth you have my word that we will not attempt to retake the ship. Not that my wife and I could pose much threat to your men. And you have my thanks for your courtesy.'

'Let it be so,' said Clay. 'Now, I would be obliged if you would tell me more of your cargo.'

'The *Fortuna* carries no bullion or treasure, Captain,' smiled Dona Sorondo. 'Trade goods and wine for the most part, and a large supply of Papal indulgences for the church. Sorry to disappoint you.'

'I was more interested in how you were furnished in the matter of fresh water, señora?'

'We have plenty,' said her husband. 'We stopped in the Azores to refill, and were carrying enough to make the Philippines without any need for touching land.'

'Glory hallelujah with trumpets!' exclaimed Clay. 'Mr Taylor, have the pumps rigged and the prize warped alongside. I'll have enough water pumped across for all to drink their fill and to see us through to St Helena, if you please.'

'Aye aye, sir.'

*****

As darkness fell over Toulon, the lights of the city appeared in the gloom, shining out all along the waterfront. The warm, amber glow was echoed aboard the row of warships moored in the harbour, as lamp and candlelight spilt out through stern windows and open gunports.

On the *Redoubtable* a weary group of officers gathered for their well-earned dinner at the end of a day spent preparing their ship for sea. They had been driving the crew hard over the course of the last week, as the fleet prepared to set sail. They emerged from the cabins that lined the sides of the wardroom, one by one, to take their places at the table until only one chair was vacant.

'Ah good, we are all here,' said Dupotet, the last to emerge and quite the most immaculately turned out, as he took his place at the head of the table. 'You can bring through the food now, Barbier,' he added, towards the pantry.

Along both sides of the table the ship's boys who stood behind each chair leant forward to shake out napkins and serve wine and bread to their respective officers.

'Mutton stew, messieurs,' announced the wardroom steward, appearing with a large, battered pewter tureen. 'Although there are many more vegetables than mutton, I'm afraid, with every purser in the fleet competing for livestock as soon as it appears.'

'No matter,' said Dorre, rubbing his hands. 'With sufficient herbs and garlic, I am certain that it will be quite delicious. Goodness knows how long it will be until we next have access to fresh provisions.'

Clay and the Immortal Memory

'Do we know when we are to sail?' asked Morin, accepting a steaming plate.

'The moment the wind serves,' said the first lieutenant. 'As of now, we are on notice for an immediate departure.'

'I hear that even the admiral has been obliged to put his mistress ashore,' said Dorre. 'For my part, I cannot wait to come to grips with the enemy.'

'Then you may be disappointed,' said Dupotet. 'The captain tells me we are instructed to avoid battle and head for the Atlantic as swiftly as we are able. It is all part of a grand manoeuvre designed by the emperor himself, if the rumours are to be believed.'

'Pity,' said Dorre, through a mouthful of stew. 'A battle would have been good. My men are more than ready.'

'I am sure they are,' said the first lieutenant, 'should the English challenge us to a duck shoot.'

There was laughter around the table at this, and Brissot found all eyes on him. His face coloured as he turned towards the head of the table. 'If you truly find the ship's new battle tactics so objectionable, sir, you should address your remarks to the captain. Dorre and I have simply been following his orders, as good officers should.'

Dupotet sipped at his wine as he regarded the younger man. 'Monsieur Brissot is being too modest. Only following the captain's instructions? We have all witnessed how you have steadily worked your way into his favour.' His voice changed to imitate the clipped tones of Lucas. 'Doesn't Monsieur Brissot handle the men well? Put Monsieur Brissot in charge of the bow chasers. What a bold idea, to fight like Romans.'

'Steady, sir,' cautioned Dorre. 'I believe we all have much to thank Francois for, as will be shown when we eventually go into battle.'

'Unless we are obliged to fight with cannon, when our want of training with them could ruin us all,' said Dupotet. 'I have already spent time as a prisoner of the English, and have no desire to repeat the experience.'

'But Francois is correct, sir,' said the marine commander. 'We were all there when he offered his suggestion, and had the opportunity to give our views. It was the captain who chose this path, and it is to him you should address your concerns. Come, let us not fall out on the eve of battle, for that way lies certain defeat. And let us not allow this noble stew to grow cold.'

'A glass of wine with you, sir,' said Brissot, holding his own towards the head of the table.

'I will gladly drink a glass with you,' said Dupotet. 'Why don't we drink to the health of the emperor?'

'I would sooner drink to all of the country, rather than only one citizen,' said Brissot. '*Vive la France*!'

'*Vive la France*!' echoed the others, emptying their glasses.

Dupotet followed suit, but his eyes never left Brissot. 'I am intrigued by your reluctance to drink to the health of the emperor, Francois,' he persisted, when it was quiet once more. 'Surely he is the embodiment of France?'

'In truth, I wonder what need we have for an emperor, sir.'

'Because we have an empire, thanks to his conquests, and empires require emperors,' said the first lieutenant. 'How would you have France ruled? By a committee of revolutionaries? We all know how that ended last time.'

'You seem to view Napoleon's coronation as a temporary affair, sir,' said Brissot. 'A simple administrative post to which he has been elevated. But I fear that now he has sat on a throne and felt the weight of a crown upon his head, he will find that it suits him very well. Did we have a revolution to free ourselves of the tyranny of a king, only to replace it with that of an emperor?'

'The *Ancien Régime* may have had its faults, but they were nothing when compared with the excesses of the Revolution,' said Dupotet, colouring. 'The emperor ended that chaos, giving our nation law and order at home and respect abroad.'

'But at what cost to France, sir,' began Brissot, growing passionate in his turn.

'Gentlemen, enough!' cried Dorre, bringing his fist down on the table with a thump. 'Let us not have politics in the wardroom, I pray. No good will come of such discussions, and agitation is so perilous for the digestion. Come, let us eat, drink and be friends, while we still may. Goodness only knows what tomorrow will bring.'

There was a general rumble of agreement at this around the table, and Brissot smiled an apology.

Dupotet kept his peace, but his dark eyes were still full of anger.

Chapter 9
The Mediterranean Fleet

Vice Admiral Lord Horatio Nelson sat at a circular rosewood table in the great cabin of the *Victory*. It was early spring in Sardinia, and the slopes of the island were flushed with green. They made a pleasant contrast with the blue waters of Palma Bay and the yellow and black hulls of the warships moored there. Sunshine streamed through the glass and fell on to his coat. Its warmth helped to ease the ache in the stump of his right arm, but the brightness was painful for his injured eye. He closed it against the light, and enjoyed the warmth for a little longer.

'Shall I fetch your eye patch, my lord?' asked John Scott, his secretary, 'or would you prefer me to have the windows screened?'

'My eye patch, if you please, John,' said the admiral. 'It has been such a long winter; it would be a pity to shut out the sun just as it has resolved to shine once more. The flowers will be blooming at Merton. I trust my Emma will be enjoying them.'

'Here you are, my lord,' said his secretary, stepping behind his chair to tie the patch into place.

Nelson straightened it a little with his left hand, and returned his attention to the paperwork strewn across the table. 'My thanks, John. Now, what must we attend to next?'

'A dispatch from Mr Elliot, our ambassador in Naples,

my lord, where I fear the enemy are up to mischief again,' said Scott, selecting a letter. 'He writes to inform your lordship that King Ferdinand has received a protest from France's military governor in southern Italy. General St Cyr considers the presence of our mission there to be an act hostile to France, and demands that it should be expelled. King Ferdinand is minded to refuse such an impertinent request, but wishes to know your mind on the matter.'

'His majesty is right to be cautious,' said Nelson. 'St Cyr may only have a division in southern Italy, but they are all veterans. When the French last attacked Naples, back in ninety-eight, Ferdinand's troops performed disgracefully. Bolted like hares after a single volley. I had to bring the whole royal family off in the *Vanguard*.'

'Perhaps something similar is being planned, my lord,' said Scott, plunging through a stack of newspapers on the deck beside him. 'A notice I saw in the latest *Moniteur Universal* comes to mind. Where was it? Ah! I have it.' He folded open the copy, and tapped one of the articles. 'The author condemns King Ferdinand for his misrule … the most corrupt Bourbon still with a throne … prisons groaning with jailed opponents … an afront to moral sensibilities, and so forth. Is it not precisely how Napoleon prepares public opinion for his next outrage?'

'Very like,' agreed Nelson. 'Trust a Frenchman as you would the devil, John. Let us compose a suitable reply to Mr Elliot. Pray take this down … Now what is the matter?'

'A ship has just appeared, my lord,' said the secretary, pointing towards the window. 'Rounding the headland.'

The admiral rose from his place and stepped across to the window lights. The upper masts of a frigate, crowded with sail, were visible rising above the long finger of land that formed the northern entrance to the bay.

'It's the *Active*,' pronounced the admiral, his voice tightening with excitement.

As they watched, the frigate rounded the tower at the end of the spit of land, her dark hull with its yellow strake a match for the other ships in the anchorage. From her mizzen halliard a line of signal flags broke out.

'Would you like me to fetch a spyglass, my lord?' asked Scott.

'No thank you, John. We can trust Hardy to have matters in hand,' said Nelson, resuming his place at the table and forcing himself to appear calm.

But Scott knew his master too well, and noticed the fixed look in his eye and the way his hand tweaked at the front of his coat. 'She is making her turn into the anchorage, sir, reducing sail as she does so,' he commented, continuing to watch the ship.

'I dare say that she is,' said the admiral, picking up the copy of the *Le Moniteur* and pretending to read it.

'She is tasked with watching the French fleet in Toulon, is she not, my lord?' he persisted.

'That is so, along with the *Phoebe*. Come in!' This in response to a knock at the cabin door.

A midshipman with dark curly hair walked across to the table and stood to attention. 'Captain Hardy's compliments to your lordship, and the *Active* is just entering the anchorage. She has signalled to say that the French fleet has left Toulon. The captain says he took the liberty of asking her commander to come across to report in person.'

'I can see her barge being lowered, my lord,' supplemented his secretary.

'Thank you, Mr Smith, for your most welcome message,' said Nelson, smiling at the midshipman. 'Kindly ask

Captain Hardy to send a general signal to the fleet to prepare for immediate departure.'

'Aye aye, my lord.'

'Pray God this sortie is in earnest , John,' said Nelson, letting the newspaper fall on to the table. 'The last time Villeneuve came out he drilled his ships for a while, and then returned to port.'

'Amen to that, my lord.'

Through the open window came the sound of a hail from the quarterdeck above them. 'Boat ahoy!' called one of the midshipmen of the watch.

'*Active*,' came the coxswain's reply, followed by 'Larboard side.'

'Their captain wants no ceremony as he comes aboard, my lord,' said the secretary. 'He must be in a hurry to see you.'

'Naturally,' said Nelson, removing the eye patch and concealing it under the papers on the table. 'Would you draw that curtain, if you please.'

Now they could hear the boat passing beneath the stern – the splash and pull of oars working together and the low growl of orders from the coxswain. A few minutes' pause and then Thomas Hardy, the *Victory*'s big captain, strode into the cabin, ducking his balding head low under the deck beams. 'I have Mowbray with me, my lord,' he announced.

The commander of the *Active* emerged from behind his fellow captain's considerable frame.

'Well met, Richard,' said Nelson, jumping up and grasping the officer's hand. 'What word of the French?'

'They are out, my lord. Eleven ships of the line and eight frigates left Toulon at noon on the thirtieth of March. And this time I believe they have some object in mind. They are coming on much bolder than before, standing to the south. I left the *Phoebe* to follow them and came to find you.'

'You could not have brought me more welcome tidings,' said Nelson, beaming at the news. 'Now we need only come up with them, and pray that God will grant us a great and glorious victory. When will the fleet be ready to sail, Thomas?'

'Within the hour, my lord,' reported Hardy. 'What course should we set? Westwards to cut them off from the Atlantic?'

'I think not, my friend, for I believe I know exactly where the enemy are bound. It all fits into place. They are heading for Naples, to finish with King Ferdinand once and for all. We shall hunt for them to the east.'

'Aye aye, my lord.'

*****

The *Redoutable* was standing to the south of Toulon under topsails, one of a long line of warships. Most were seventy-fours, like her, but four were big eighty-gunners, wide as first rates with twenty-four-pounders on the upper of their two gundecks. Far ahead of the fleet were six frigates, just within signalling distance, fanned out and scouting for any enemy that might appear from over the horizon. Astern were another two frigates, holding at bay the lone British ship that had been stubbornly following them since they had left Toulon.

Lucas felt competing emotions as he stood on his quarterdeck in the late afternoon sunshine, his hands clasped behind his back. On the one hand he revelled in being at sea again. The deck beneath his feet, so flat and dead during all those months in harbour, was alive once more, rising and falling to each wave that swept past. The rigging hummed and sang as the keen wind blew through it. A newly released prisoner must feel like this, he decided. He would have beamed with the joy of it, were it not for the nagging doubt that every French captain felt out of sight of land. Were Nelson and his Mediterranean Fleet sailing to intercept him and about to appear over the horizon? Or were they already waiting somewhere ahead, ready to pounce? There had been two enemy frigates tailing them when they first left harbour, but one had now sailed away and had not been seen since.

He looked along the line of warships, and suddenly they seemed less impressive. For one thing they were straggling badly, with ships bunching together in some places and pulling apart in others. It was only to be expected, of course. The eleven ships all had different sailing qualities, and such a long period moored in harbour was poor preparation for manoeuvring as a unit. But he also knew that an enemy would quickly exploit any gaps to break the fleet up. 'Monsieur Morin,' he called. 'Why are we overhauling the *Formidable*?'

'I have detailed a party to man the foretopsail sheets and spill wind to slow us, sir,' said the officer of the watch.

'Then they are either neglecting, or do not comprehend, their duty,' said his captain. 'I expect you as officer of the watch to make sure that they understand the importance of what they do. You have five minutes to return this ship to its correct position, and to make sure it stays there. One cable length directly astern, if you please.' He pulled out his watch and flipped open the cover to emphasise his point.

'Yes, sir,' said Morin.

Lucas watched him hurry towards the forecastle. On his way, Morin had to go around the sailmaker and his mates, who were sitting cross-legged on the deck, cutting and stitching canvas. Intrigued, the captain walked forward to see what they were doing. 'Pray continue with your work, Monsieur Touffet,' he urged, as the sailmaker started to get up. 'I only came across because I wasn't aware that we had damaged a sail, so soon in the voyage.'

'Nor have we, sir,' said Touffet, holding up what looked like a canvas bucket. 'We are making containers for Lieutenant Brissot. They are for swaying grenades up to the fighting tops just before we go into action. Each one holds a dozen.'

'They look good,' said Lucas, examining a completed example. The canvas was double thickness, and the seams and top had been reinforced with rope. 'I can see these will answer very well. Monsieur Brissot seems to have thought of everything. Please carry on.'

'Yes sir.'

By the time Lucas returned to the quarterdeck, the officer of the watch was back. He touched his hat as his captain approached. 'The ship is in its correct station, and Midshipman Pascal now understands his duties, sir.'

'I am pleased to hear it, Monsieur Morin,' said Lucas. Looking forward he could see the young officer was carefully monitoring the stern of the ship ahead. As he watched Pascal turned to wave his arm to the party manning the windward sheet, who spilt some air.

'It seems strange to be in a fleet without any three-deckers, sir,' said the lieutenant. 'The enemy have several, I understand.'

'The *L'Orient* used to be our flagship,' said Lucas. 'She was a sight to behold with her hundred and twenty guns. Worth any two of the enemies. It was terrible when she blew up and sank at the Battle of the Nile. But have no fear, when the Spanish join with us they will bring plenty of three-deckers with them.'

'Flagship is signalling, sir,' announced one of the

midshipmen, busily chalking down numbers on his slate as they were read to him. The signal took some time to send, with hoist following hoist. Eventually the midshipman came across and handed over his slate. The completed message filled most of it.

Lucas read through it several times, before handing it back. 'Thank you, Monsieur Quellec,' he said. 'Please acknowledge.'

'Yes sir.'

'Will it work, I wonder,' mused the captain, when the midshipman had gone.

'Will what work, sir?' asked Morin.

'Admiral Villeneuve has an interesting plan to shake off the annoying frigate following us. We are to show no lights tonight and carry on as we are until the stroke of midnight. Then we must all change course together to due west, without any prearranged signal. The two frigates astern will continue on their current course, and it is to be hoped that the English will follow them and not us.'

'It certainly has the advantage of simplicity, sir,' commented the officer of the watch. He gestured away to the north-east. 'And these clouds have been building all day. It is likely to be a dark night.'

'Perhaps too dark, for the station keeping we have been managing so far,' said Lucas. 'We will need to have our very best lookouts posted to avoid any collisions.'

'Yes sir,' said Morin. 'What will become of the frigates, sir?'

'If it works, they are to lead the enemy in a merry dance until we are long gone, when they will return to Toulon. If it works. But consider, the *Redoubtable* alone couldn't evade a single frigate last year on a blacker night than we have in prospect, so I doubt if this will succeed.'

But Lucas was wrong. When the first silver light of dawn stole into the sky it found the French Mediterranean Fleet in a messy cluster, but quite alone. They made haste to reconstitute their formation and set all sail for Gibraltar and the wide Atlantic beyond.

*****

Several months had passed since the *Griffin* had captured the *Fortuna*. Leaving her prize to follow in her wake, she headed north, day after day, with only a brief stop to replenish her stores at St Helena. Even the notorious Doldrums around the equator had proved kind to the returning ship, with barely a day spent becalmed before they picked up the first cool breath of the north-east trades. By mid-April the frigate was level with north Africa, driven forward by a crew eager to return home after almost two years away.

'I'll be back in Polwith afore long,' said Sedgwick, stood up on the forecastle, the wind flapping at his open shirt. Beneath him the sharp bow was slicing through another long, sleek Atlantic roller, reducing it to dazzling white foam that tumbled back along the sides of the hull.

'Funny to hear you talk of Cornwall as home, Able' commented Trevan, looking up from the piece of elm he was shaping. He pointed with his knife. 'Not Africa, nor the Carabee?'

'Never Barbados, Adam. And them cursed slavers left naught but cinders to mark my first home. No, Polwith it is, where my Ann waits.'

'Aye, that be a grand thought,' agreed Trevan. 'I can't wait to see my Molly, and little Kate will be a nipper now, in need of this.' He held up the piece of wood, already showing the shape of the doll it would become.

'Ain't it grand when mates share tales of domestic fecking bliss,' said O'Malley, folding his arms. 'A shared room in a Plymouth boarding house is the best Sam and I can expect.'

'But you lads will have two years' pay a waiting for 'ee,' said Trevan. 'Our wives will have spent most of ours by now.'

'An' there'll be prize money from that *Fortuna*,' added Sedgwick.

'There never were so ill-named a prize,' grumbled Evans. 'Fortune, my arse. Half the bleeding cargo were them bales of papist rags. I thought they might be worth some'it when we first slit them open. Then Lopez in the starboard watch read a couple out. Indulgences, for scoffing meat on a Friday, or humping a wench. Bleeding useless, the lot of them.'

'I might have taken the fornication ones,' said O'Malley, 'only there weren't near enough, at all.'

'Shame there weren't one for coaxing your mates into giving all their chink to a sharp,' observed Evans. 'Coz that pope of yours'll forgive you a sight sooner than I bleeding will.'

'Hush, Sam,' said the Irishman. 'Are you after mentioning that every fecking morn from here 'til doomsday?'

'Deck there!' yelled the lookout. 'Sail ho! Two points off the larboard bow!'

Sedgwick climbed partway up the fore shrouds, but Trevan and O'Malley, topmen both, were much swifter than him as they scampered up for a better look, only pausing when level with her foretop.

'Man o' war, from the look of her tops'uls,' commented Trevan, shading his eyes with one hand, the other nonchalantly resting on a shroud, despite the lively motion of the ship.

'Not one of ours,' supplemented O'Malley. 'Clean

canvas and a foreign rig. She's a blockade runner, for sure. Let see what Goldilocks makes of her.'

The others turned to watch as Midshipman Todd reached the top of the main mast, his blond hair spilling from beneath his hat. He settled himself into position beside the lookout and focused his telescope on the horizon ahead. 'She's a frigate, sir,' he announced. 'French from the look of her.'

'We're after knowing that already, nipper,' commented the Irishman.

'Deck there!' The midshipman paused for a moment, his glass still to his eye.

'What do you see, Mr Todd?' prompted the voice of Clay from the quarterdeck.

'I think I can see more sails beyond her. Four or five ships, for certain, perhaps more.'

'I best be clearing away my Kate's toy,' said Trevan, jumping for the back stay and sliding down it.

'Mr Taylor!' ordered the voice of Clay. 'Have the ship put on the larboard tack, if you please. Let us take a closer look. Mr Russell, kindly join Mr Todd with a notebook and record all you see of the enemy.'

'Aye aye, sir.'

'All hands!' bellowed Taylor from astern. 'All hands to make sail!'

'What the feck is a fleet doing out here?' said O'Malley as he joined the others back on the forecastle.

'I don't know, Sean,' said Sedgwick as the sailors started to run to their places. 'But it ain't good. I'm thinking.'

*****

All day the enemy fleet sailed steadily westwards,

seemingly unconcerned by the *Griffin* as she kept pace with them, several miles to the south of the nearest of the screening frigates. Now the sun was setting, turning to an orb of molten gold as it neared the horizon, and still the ships sailed on, following the sun into the west. Clay watched their sails glow rose before fading into grey with the dying of the light. Lamps appeared, hung from mastheads or shining out of cabin windows, until the fleet was transformed into a spreading constellation across the darkening sea.

'Mr Taylor, Mr Russell and the ship's master are gathered in the coach, sir,' reported the officer of the watch from beside him.

'Thank you, Edward,' said Clay, closing his telescope. 'Keep an eye on the enemy, if you please, and call me the moment anything should change.'

'Aye aye, sir.'

Clay crossed the quarterdeck and disappeared down the ladderway. The marine sentry guarding his cabin door came to attention, and then leant over to open it for him. Clay smiled his thanks and ducked his head low as he stepped inside. The coach was a smaller space off the main cabin where much of the ship's navigation took place. An oil lamp burned overhead and several candles were lit on the table where the three officers were gathered. On it was spread a large chart of the North Atlantic. Lining the bulkheads were boxes of other charts, below shelves of sailing guides and almanacs, while gleaming beside the door were the frigate's marine chronometers.

'Pray resume your places, gentlemen,' said Clay as they rose from their seats. He passed his hat to his steward and took the vacant chair. 'Some refreshment? A glass of wine, perhaps? Could you bring some, Harte.'

'Aye aye, sir.'

'Now, Mr Russell, what have you observed of the enemy from the masthead?' asked his captain.

'I counted seventeen of the line, sir,' said the midshipman, consulting his notes. 'The greater part of them were French, and the other six were Spanish.'

'How are they served in the matter of frigates?' asked Armstrong.

'They have six, sir. All of them large. Four scouting ahead and one off to either flank.'

'What size are their ships of force?' asked Clay.

'All third rates, sir. Five of them are uncommonly large. Eighty-gunners, I should say. One of those was the flagship.'

'No three-decked warships among the French part of the fleet?' repeated Clay. 'Are you quite certain?'

'Yes, sir. Quite sure.'

'Is that significant, sir?' asked Taylor.

'It may serve to help us narrow down which of the enemy's fleets we are dealing with,' explained the captain. 'You will recall the many weary months we spent off Brest observing the size and preparedness of the French Atlantic Fleet, back on the old *Titan*?'

'Reporting daily to our masters in the inshore squadron,' said Taylor, 'and to the empty horizon during the Great Mutiny of ninety-seven.'

'Why in all creation would you do that?' asked Armstrong.

'To fool the Frogs into thinking that a fleet still lay in wait out at sea,' said the first lieutenant. 'It was the captain's notion,'

'And a smart one at that,' chuckled the American. 'I'll be damned!'

'But if I may return to those times, the Brest fleet was

well served in the matter of first rates?' continued Clay.

'They were indeed, sir. They had three or four.'

'Then I believe we can say with some certainty that the French portion of this fleet has not come from there,' said Clay. 'No admiral would sail out so boldly leaving his most powerful ships back in port.'

'That would make sense, sir,' said Armstrong.

'Which means we are dealing with either the Rochefort squadron,' said Clay, pointing to the port on the Bay of Biscay, 'although I doubt if they could muster such numbers, or more likely their Mediterranean Fleet. Do you concur?'

'Agreed, sir,' said Taylor.

'Very well,' said Clay. 'So we have a considerable fleet that has sailed from the Mediterranean out into the middle of the Atlantic. My question is, what are they about and, more significantly, what mischief do they have in prospect?'

'If I may, sir,' said Armstrong, moving the candlestick to better illuminate the chart. 'I had a clear sight of the sun this noon, and I was able to correct our chronometers at St Helena, so I'm passing sure of our position. The pencil cross there is where we first fell in with the enemy, and the line is their track this day.'

'Not much to go on, Jacob,' said Taylor, squinting at the little mark.

'Perhaps not,' conceded the American. 'Until we extend the line.' He reached behind him for his longest ruler and laid it across the chart. One end was close to Cadiz, and the mouth of the Mediterranean, the other pointed towards the island of Martinique in the Caribbean. 'It would seem to confirm where they have come from, and perhaps indicate where they may be bound.'

'They could be maintaining this course while we are in

sight, and will change it once they are free of us,' warned Taylor.

'Maybe, but I believe you are on to something, Jacob,' said Clay. 'Let us assume the French have broken out from Toulon, avoiding our fleet somehow, and are headed west. They probably picked up the Spanish ships at Cadiz, which speaks of a degree of coordination. And the guard ships at Gibraltar would not have been able to prevent such a large fleet from passing.'

'That all seems clear, sir,' said Taylor. 'But why send a huge fleet to the Caribbean?'

'I do not know,' mused Clay. 'Yet here they are, out in the Atlantic and heading west.'

'With what object, sir?' asked Taylor.

'There are none to warrant such a force in the Americas, that at least is certain,' said the sailing master.

Clay stared at the chart, trying to penetrate the mind of his opponent, but nothing came to him. One of the candles was starting to gutter and smoke, making his eyes water and he could feel the heat from the oil lamp just above his head. 'It is indeed a mystery,' he concluded, massaging his temples. 'I find it very close in here. I will go on deck presently. Fresh air generally helps me to think. But the key decision we must take is what we should do now? Sail ahead to Barbados to warn the Leeward Island squadron of the danger approaching?'

'I say no, sir,' said Armstrong. 'They have too little strength to oppose such a gathering, warned or not. We should seek out our own forces in Europe that might be able to help them. Sir John Orde is nearest. He commands the ships blockading Cadiz.'

'Have a care, sir,' cautioned the first lieutenant. 'We have no knowledge as to the objective of this fleet. Jacob's ruler is all very well, but extending the track of a few hours sailing to a destination on the far side of the ocean is a jump into the dark. A powerful enemy fleet is at large, and we are the only friendly ship that has it under observation. If we leave it now, we may never find it again, or learn its true purpose.'

'With respect, George, it may only be the *Griffin* that has stumbled upon it, in which case it is doubly important we should act,' urged the American. 'Surely it is our duty to report it? Darn it, what is a frigate for, if not to act as the eyes of the fleet?'

'Should we stay with the enemy or go and fetch help,' said Clay, smiling grimly. 'We will be in the wrong, whatever path we choose, I daresay. But I truly cannot think in here. Thank you for your counsel, gentlemen. I shall go on deck and consider matters before deciding what is for the best.'

*****

The *Griffin* had a crew of two hundred and fifty souls, most of whom lived on the lower deck. It was a space that was less than a hundred and fifty feet long and under forty feet at its widest point. Day or night, no sailor was ever more than a few feet from his fellows. Even the officers in their cabins were only separated from each other by the thinnest of bulkheads. As a result, there were few secrets on board and most of the crew took a lively interest in the doings of both the ship and their neighbours. Small wonder, then, that ever since the huge Franco-Spanish fleet had spread across the horizon, they had been openly speculating about what it might portend. Harte, with his privileged access to their captain's quarters, found himself especially popular after the group of officers in the coach broke up. He was met with an unusual number of cheerful greetings and friendly banter as he made his way forward through the ship. He was bound for the galley, the only place in a wooden ship where smoking was permitted, for his customary evening pipe. When he arrived, he found a large crowd of sailors gathered there already.

'Ah, there you are, shipmate,' declared O'Malley, patting the stool beside him. 'I've been after saving your favourite place.'

'Much obliged, Sean,' said the steward, sitting down. He took out a short pipe and began patting at his coat pockets.

'Have a twist of mine,' suggested Trevan, from his other side, producing his tobacco pouch with a smile.

'Thankee kindly,' said Harte, helping himself to a generous amount.

'Flame here, if you please, Mr Walker,' growled Josh Black, the big captain of the foretop, towards the cook tending the galley fire.

All the sailors watched in silence as Harte puffed his pipe into life, shook out the spill and dropped it with a hiss into the leather bucket left there for the purpose. He sat back with a sigh of contentment. 'Been quite the day, eh lads?'

'Ain't that the bleeding truth,' agreed Evans. 'I ain't clapped me eyes on such a deal of warships since Copenhagen back in the year one.'

'Got the bleeding Grunters proper riled, an' all,' commented Black. 'I heard that Pipe and the rest were close as thieves in the coach earlier, chewing upon matters.'

The sailors looked expectantly towards the steward. He innocently emitted a languid trail of smoke, his gaze resting on the painted deck beam overhead, a smile twitching at the corner of his mouth.

'I daresay they'll have been a pondering what all these

here Frogs and Dons be about, Mr Black,' prompted Evans, still looking at Harte.

'Heading for the Carabee, from the course they be on,' added Trevan, but still Harte was mute.

'Oh, for the love of God!' exclaimed O'Malley, rounding on the steward. 'There's no call for being so close! Sat there like fecking Solomon in his pomp! Will yous tell us what's going on, or am I after pitching your arse off that stool as I kept for you special?'

'Perhaps I may have overheard a bit of talk,' conceded Harte. 'Not that I was eavesdropping, mind, but while serving them grog and tending to the candles and the like.'

'Lughole pressed tight as a limpet to the bulkhead, more like,' muttered Evans.

'Sure, you weren't spying at all,' said the Irishman. 'An' what was they after saying?'

'Pipe was grilling Rusty about the number of first rates he'd seen,' continued the steward. 'Seems as the Frogs ain't got none in the Mediterranean, like.'

'That be so, after that great ark of theirs blew up at the Nile,' commented Trevan to nods from the crew, many of whom had been present at that battle.

'That *L'Orient*, weren't it?' suggested a voice.

'An' where do they reckon the buggers be heading?' asked Black.

'Carabee, according to the Yank,' said Harte. 'But Pipe be trying to figure what to do for the best. Do he leave them and head off to warn the fleet? Do he sail on ahead to warn that they be a coming or do he hang on their coat tails 'til he truly knows what they be about. He's pacing up and down the quarterdeck right now, fit to wear through the planking, while he makes up his mind.'

'Them be the choices, right enough,' said Trevan. 'But I'll be blown if I knows which one be right. An' the navy don't take kindly to them as makes the wrong call.'

'Poor bugger,' commented Evans. 'Who'd be a bleeding captain.'

Sedgwick had been leaning against the frigate's fore bits next to Josh Black, listening to the sailors' talk. Now he joined the discussion with a shake of his head. 'Plain as day what he should be about,' he declared.

'Oh, aye?' queried Harte, pointing his pipe stem towards the coxswain. 'An' what be that?'

'He has to warn the fleet back home and proper sharp, afore it's too late.'

'How you be figuring out that, Able?' asked Trevan.

'They may be Carabee bound, but that ain't what they be about,' said the big coxswain. 'Frogs ain't got above a brace of little islands now, much the size of the one I lived on. Look at this here fleet. Why, there must be the best part of fifteen thousand souls aboard! How they going to supply that lot with all the vittles they be needing, not to mention rope and spars for all them ships? It don't make no sense.'

'So why are they fecking heading there in the first place?' exclaimed O'Malley.

'To meet up with others as has broken out too. Once they got a right big fleet together, all in one place like, they'll be heading straight back,' said the big coxswain. 'You mark my words. Ain't Boney been planning to cross the Channel for years? I reckon he's finally minded to try. An' if we don't get word back in time, it might just succeed.'

The sailors fell silent as they considered this, but struggle as they might, none could find fault in his reasoning.

'You be a proper deep one, Able,' concluded Black,

slapping the coxswain on the back.

'Shouldn't we be a telling Pipe all of this?' asked Trevan.

But before the coxswain could answer, the sound of a boatswain's call twittered along the deck. 'All hands! All hands to make sail!'

'No need, Adam,' said Sedgwick, as they joined the rush towards the ladderway. 'He be mindful of what them Frogs are about. Ain't much as sneaks past our Pipe.'

Chapter 10
The Pieces on the Board

It was an hour after dawn but tendrils of sea mist still lay across the grey surface of the Rade de Brest among the lines of moored warships. On board the 120-gun *Impérial*, the routine of the day was well underway. Across the flagship's upper deck bare-footed sailors were busy scrubbing the planking clean with sea water pumped up from over the side, while a grey trail of wood smoke drifting up from the galley chimney promised a hot breakfast to follow.

Midshipman Chauvet was doing his best to avoid getting his shoes and stockings splashed by those at work on the quarterdeck, when one of his signal party recalled him to his duties with a cough and a glance towards the shore. He looked past the stone houses and church spires of Brest to where the black arms of the semaphore tower up on Kerouhant Hill had jerked into an upright position. 'We are about to get a signal from Paris, sir,' he reported.

'Remarkable, isn't it,' commented the lieutenant of the watch, coming across. 'There are over sixty of those towers, stretched in a line between here and the capital. They say it takes little more than ten minutes for a message from the Naval Ministry to arrive. Why, a courier would take days upon such a journey.'

'If you say so, sir,' said Chauvet, focusing his telescope on the semaphore. 'Are you ready, Pluchet?'

'Yes, sir,' confirmed the sailor beside him, chalk poised above the signal slate.

The arms began to whirl and twist, freezing in position for a moment before moving again to create a fresh shape against the pale sky. At each pause the midshipman announced a number.

'It's quite long, sir,' observed Chauvet, once the message was complete. He held up the slate, now covered in dense lines of numerals. 'I had best get it down to the admiral's clerk.'

'Indeed,' said the lieutenant. 'Off you go, then.'

It took another half an hour for the message to be deciphered, by which time Vice Admiral Honoré Ganteaume was enjoying his second cup of coffee at his desk in the *Impérial*'s great cabin. The signal's arrival supplied the commander with a fresh reason to delay tackling all the paperwork that accompanied command of a fleet of over twenty ships of the line.

'A fresh semaphore message from Paris, sir,' said his flag captain, coming in through the door. 'Word has arrived from Spain that Admiral Villeneuve joined with the Spanish squadron at Cadiz last month, and that they are at sea, bound for the rendezvous. The emperor wishes to know why we have not left Brest yet.'

Ganteaume put down his cup and accepted the message. He read its contents and laid it to one side. 'You know, Daniel, the port of Brest is both brilliantly served, and yet also quite blighted by its situation.'

'Admiral?'

'On the one hand, it boasts as fine a natural harbour as one could wish for, protected from the elements by surrounding hills, with only one narrow, formidably defended entrance through which an enemy must pass to threaten us.'

'That is so, sir. But in what way is it blighted?'

'The entrance faces due west, straight into the prevailing wind, which means that for nine days in ten we are trapped here like turds in a chamber pot. I have tried numerous times to demonstrate to the emperor that we cannot simply leave whenever we wish, but explaining winds and tides to a soldier is a wearying business. To his way of thinking, our fleets are just pieces on a chessboard, to be moved as the whim takes him.'

'We were able to leave last month, sir.'

'We were indeed,' said the admiral. 'And found Lord Gardner with twenty-four ships of the line just beyond the Black Rocks blocking our path. The emperor is most particular in his orders. I am not just to leave port, but I am also instructed to do so without fighting the enemy. Exactly how I am meant to achieve such a thing, he doesn't bother to explain.'

'The glass is falling at present,' observed his flag captain. 'Perhaps the wind will back around sufficiently for us to try to leave once more?'

'Perhaps it may,' said Ganteaume. 'And perhaps we shall find the English waiting again, to check our move once more. But I agree, it must be tried. Very well, inform the emperor that, weather permitting, we will attempt to sortie again tomorrow.'

'Yes, sir.'

*****

Once Clay had decided to turn the *Griffin* about and bring word of the fleet he had found back to Europe, he found the weather just as persistent an opponent as the squadron that had chased him in the Indian Ocean. The same north-east trade winds that were bearing Villeneuve's fleet across the Atlantic blew dead foul for his return in the opposite direction. It took over two weeks of steady beating northwards before they encountered the first breath of a westerly just south of the Azores. They crowded on all sail and headed towards Cadiz, but it was not before early May that the frigate was nearing land once more.

All those on board could sense the approaching continent, as only sailors can. The send and roll of the waves seemed to shorten beneath their feet as they neared the ocean's edge. The bold white columns of marching clouds became more broken and diffuse. Then the sky above the frigate, empty of life for so long, began to fill with straggling lines of hunting sea birds. A trading brig briefly appeared on the horizon before hastening to make sail as the *Griffin* sped closer, but Clay had no time for chasing prizes. So it was that the quarterdeck and forecastle had filled with expectant crew when seven bells struck in the forenoon watch.

'Lands is being ahoy!' cried the younger of the Saleem brothers, from the masthead.

'Where away?' queried Preston, who was officer of the watch.

'Two pointings back from left of front, Sahib!'

'Land in sight, two points off the larboard bow, sir,' translated Preston, in response to his captain's raised eyebrow. 'The form of Saleem's reporting leaves a little to be desired, but he attends to his duties well and is blessed with uncommon good vision.'

'It will be Cape St Vincent, sir, or I'm a Dutchman,' said Armstrong, heading for the mainmast shrouds with a telescope in his hand. When he returned, he had a beaming smile. 'Just as I said, sir, and as handsome a landfall as you could wish for, given we last touched at St Helena an age ago.'

'You are indeed a fine navigator, Jacob,' said Clay. 'Which is why I have every confidence that you can now bring us swiftly to Cadiz. It lies but ninety-odd miles to the east, does it not?'

'A trifle over a hundred miles, but I can lay off the course now, sir.'

'Can you also keep us out of sight of land until our final approach?' continued Clay. 'I do not wish to give the enemy any knowledge of our presence. Oh, and if we could appear from the west, ideally at dusk, with the setting sun behind us?'

'Eh ... well now ... I daresay it could be done, sir,' said Armstrong, pulling thoughtfully at his chin. 'It will call for a darn fine piece of seamanship. If you will excuse me, I had best return aloft to take a proper bearing on that cape.'

'Pray carry on,' said his captain.

'Aye aye, sir.'

'Do you not expect to find Orde's squadron off Cadiz, sir?' asked Taylor, as the two officers watched the American make his ponderous way back up the shrouds once more.

'In truth I am not sure what we shall find, George,' said Clay. 'That fleet we met with may have swept his squadron aside, or even defeated them in battle. We are but a single ship a long way from home, with little knowledge of what we may encounter. I wish to take every precaution approaching the Dons' most important naval base.'

With Armstrong conning the frigate, Clay stayed on deck, enjoying the spring sunshine and quietly watching the rhythm of the ship around him. There was the outbreak of nervous clucking from the frigate's four remaining hens as Napoleon paused to stare longingly at them in their coop. Then one of the midshipmen stepped forward to turn the half-hour glass, while his colleague scampered off to take a cast of the log. As noon approached, Faulkner, the ship's purser, approached Taylor with a routine question, to which he received the customary nod of approval.

The moment eight bells rang out from the forecastle, the boatswain's calls began to twitter through the ship. 'Up spirits!' roared Hutchinson from the main deck. 'Rum from the king, God bless him!'

All thoughts of landfalls or Spanish naval bases vanished like mist as the crew raced to form up in their divisions to receive their tots of lemon juice and grog. Meanwhile the *Griffin* sailed on, entering the funnel of sea that led towards the Straits of Gibraltar and the Mediterranean. Out of sight to the north was the southern coast of first Portugal and then Spain, while beyond the horizon to the south was the Barbary Coast of north Africa. As she advanced the density of shipping steadily increased, parting before her like fish at the approach of a shark. There were delicate Arab trading dhows, with triangular lateen sails; brightly painted fishing boats with patched canvas from the Algarve; sturdy trading brigs from northern Europe; but no other warships. As the sun dipped towards the western horizon the distant mountains of southern Spain appeared ahead.

'Bring her a touch more to windward,' ordered Armstrong.

'Touch to the wind aye, sir,' repeated the helmsman.

'No sign of Orde's squadron, sir,' commented Taylor. 'Nor any friendly ships, for that matter.'

'So it would seem,' said Clay, as more of the Spanish coast appeared, glowing yellow in the light of the setting sun above a sea of delicate blue. To one side of the bowsprit a few points of reflected light marked the approaching city. 'Kindly send Mr Russell to the fore masthead with a good glass, if you please, Mr Taylor.'

'Aye aye, sir.'

Clay placed his telescope under his arm and strode forward along the gangway and up on to the forecastle. Many of the watch below had gathered there to enjoy the evening and observe the approaching coast.

'That Cadiz be very like to an island, with only this here thin spit of land betwixt it and the shore,' explained Trevan to the older Saleem brother. 'Inside of it be a fair-sized bay where any number of ships can ride at anchor.'

'Make way for the captain, there!' barked Sedgwick, as he spotted Clay's approach. 'Off to the lee side now, lads.'

The sailors retreated, knuckling their foreheads towards Clay as they did so. 'Thank you, men,' he said, taking his place at the rail. Overhead broken cloud was advancing behind the *Griffin*, but the setting sun had dropped beneath it, and was shining from directly behind, sending a long shadow of the foremast out ahead of him. Armstrong had timed their arrival to perfection. Cadiz and the bay beyond were brightly lit, but there was a reasonable chance that the frigate would pass unnoticed, lying as she did in the eye of the sun. Through his telescope he looked briefly over the city, with its formidable walls dropping directly into the Atlantic. The whitewashed houses beyond were blushing in the evening light, while looming over them was the massive block and round domes of the cathedral. He could see some shipping in the bay behind the city, but could make little out from where he stood. 'Mr Russell,' he called. 'What can you see of the enemy?'

'Plenty of ships in the outer harbour sir, but almost all of it is trade,' replied the midshipman from his perch high above. 'Only two men of war. One is a big frigate with yards crossed, the other is a seventy-four, but she has no upper masts set up. More ships in the inner harbour, including some first rates, but none ready to sail. Most are riding so high in the water I doubt they even have their guns on board.'

'Very good. Make a note of all you can while the light holds, and report to me on the quarterdeck.'

'Aye aye, sir.'

The sun had vanished from the sky, leaving a brilliant stain of vermillion astern, by the time Russell came down to make his report. 'Six of the line, two of which are first rates, and four smaller warships in the inner harbour, sir,' he said. 'None ready for sea, and the lone frigate and seventy-four in the outer harbour.'

'Thank you, Mr Russell,' said Clay.

'Nothing in Cadiz to trouble us, sir,' observed Taylor.

'No, that horse has bolted,' said Clay. 'At least we know where the Dons we observed in the Atlantic are like to have come from. But I do find the lack of any of our own ships blockading Cadiz strange. Let us press on to Gibraltar. We have still to pass on word of the enemy, even if it is some weeks old.'

'A course to Gibraltar is it, sir?' asked Armstrong. 'Doubtless arriving from the south, five minutes after dawn, so the newly risen sun shows our sails off with advantage?'

'Just as quickly as may be arranged, Jacob,' laughed Clay.

'Aye aye, sir.'

As night fell over southern Spain, and the lights of Cadiz shone out, the *Griffin* turned away and headed south east. The wind grew lighter, while overhead stars appeared in the dark pools of sky between shores of cloud. Although the distance wasn't huge, it took the frigate most of the night to work her way past Cape Trafalgar and Tarifa point, and around into the straits. So it was at dawn that they approached Gibraltar. The rock loomed up in the grey light, lying across their path like some huge sphinx. Straggling around its feet and up the lower slopes was the town, the first trails of smoke rising in the air as it slowly came to life. Along the shore were the walls and batteries that defended the fortress from the sea.

'Deck there!' called the lookout. 'I reckon I can see a right deal of masts in the harbour.'

'What manner of shipping, Dawson?' queried Lieutenant Blake.

'Warships, for the most part, sir. Frigates right through to a brace of first rates. One looks like the old *Victory*, with an admiral's duster at the fore peak.'

Blake turned to the two midshipmen of the watch standing by the wheel. 'Mr Sweeny, my compliments to the gunner, and tell him that a salute will be required for a vice admiral within the hour.'

'Aye aye, sir.'

'Mr Todd, my compliments to the captain, and tell him that the Mediterranean Fleet is in port. Make haste, now.'

'Aye aye, sir.'

*****

The terrace of the *Lion d'Or* in Port Royal, Martinique, was crowded with naval officers. Most wore the blue and white of the French navy, but some sported the more elaborate uniform of Spain, with blood red waistcoats and gold lace glinting in the tropical sun. It was fortunate that the party of three from the *Redoutable* had arrived at the tavern early enough to secure one of the better tables, placed in the feathery shade of a palm tree and with a fine view over the town and the grey-walled fortress that protected it.

'What a beautiful island,' declared Dorre. 'One starts to wonder why we didn't break out of Toulon sooner, my friends.'

'The view is certainly diverting,' said Brissot, indicating the brilliant blue waters of the bay beneath them, now crowded with French and Spanish warships. The water softened to the palest turquoise where it met the curve of the white sand beach below the town. Behind them the slopes of the Gros Morne were a chequerboard of cane fields, while further back loomed Mount Pelée, a languid trail of smoke rising from the volcano's crater.

'How long are we to be here, do you suppose?' asked Morin.

'Long enough to give that sluggard Admiral Ganteaume time to escape from Brest and join us with the Atlantic Fleet,' explained the marine. 'The pieces are moving on the board, my friends. The admiral has instructions to wait here in Martinique for him. They could arrive any day, like those two seventy-fours from Rochefort that came in yesterday.'

'I would not be so confident, Yves,' cautioned Brissot. 'You forget I served with the Atlantic Fleet. The enemy guard Brest closer than a miser does his hoard.'

'I trust we will not be idle here for too long,' said Morin. 'The ship's supplies are already getting low, and agreeable as this island is, it cannot provide more than a fraction of what we need, let alone what Admiral Ganteaume will require. I already have two men in my division showing early signs of the scurvy.'

'Then we had best get some more fruit juice onboard,' said Dorre, turning towards the interior of the inn. '*Patron*! Another jug of your rum punch, if you please.'

'If we are compelled to wait here, we should at least try

and achieve something,' said Brissot.

'What does monsieur have in mind?' asked Dorre, with a wink towards Morin.

'What about that little island the enemy have occupied?' suggested Brissot. 'That pillar rising from the sea we passed on our way into the bay.'

'Diamond Rock?' suggested Morin.

'The very one,' said Brissot. 'I may mention it to the captain. The English have occupied it for over a year, and the guns they have placed up there are an infernal nuisance to every ship that tries to approach Martinique. Why, they even fired on us as we passed!'

''Tis not just their guns, I hear,' said Morin. 'The garrison are driving the governor to distraction. Apparently, they have defeated every attempt of his to storm the place, and have taken to launching raids on the island at night. A few months back Paris sent a colonel of engineers out to assist with the rock's fall, but the only person captured was the good colonel himself, when a party of marines from the rock attacked the house he was staying in at night and took him prisoner.'

'You do have to admire the English,' chuckled Dorre. 'I daresay we could help reduce this place. Or better still, we could enjoy the pleasures Martinique has to offer, eh? We have worked damned hard to train up the men this last year. Surely, we have earned the right to do something more diverting? I know an officer in the garrison, who tell me there is good shooting to be had in the forests beyond that volcano. What do you say to a few days' sport, gentlemen?'

'I would like that very much,' said Morin.

'I doubt very much if our first lieutenant will grant me the shore leave,' said Brissot. 'He was most grudging about me joining you today. It is a mystery why that man has such a strong dislike for me.'

'Is it really so mysterious?' asked Dorre. 'Have you ever asked him?'

'I did on one occasion, and received a lecture on the importance of loyalty, by which he meant loyalty to himself. And he makes little secret of his dislike for the regard in which the captain holds me.'

'His jealously is understandable,' said the older man. 'What first lieutenant would not resent a newly arrived junior who is clearly his superior both in wit and ability? But his dislike of you runs deeper than that, I fancy. Do you know anything of his background?'

'Little, in truth,' said Brissot. 'His people are from the Bourgogne, are they not?'

'That's correct,' said Dorre. 'Pierre here comes from there.'

'I am not intimately acquainted with the Dupotets,' said Morin. 'But I know something of them. They were petty nobility in the Dijon area. Nothing too grand, you understand, but they were proud of their place in society. The family lived in an inherited house on a few feudal dues, and there was an uncle in the church. But like many in their situation, they lost everything during the Revolution. The father tried to organise some local royalist resistance, and was sent to the scaffold for his efforts, while the uncle died in prison, leaving the family destitute. The mother passed away soon after and the orphaned son was obliged to make his own way in the world.'

'Small wonder that our first lieutenant so admires Napoleon,' commented Dorre, 'and why he welcomes the return to stability he represents.'

'And what has all this to do with me?' asked Brissot.

His two friends exchanged glances. 'Are you not the son

of Jacques Brissot? The revolutionary leader?' asked Morin.

'Yes, but I barely knew him,' said the lieutenant. 'He went to the guillotine when I was a child. Why, he was probably a victim of the same crazed zealots who executed Dupotet's family! And my father was no killer, but a democrat, who believed in universal rights.'

'I suspect it is a distinction that is too fine for our first lieutenant,' said Dorre, spreading his hands. 'Your father was one of those who led the revolution that killed his.'

'I think I need to speak with him about this,' said Brissot.

'I'm not sure what that would achieve, my friend,' counselled Dorre. 'But you might start by trying to avoid criticising the emperor at every turn. Now, what is going on?'

The officers turned to see excited arms being pointed toward the south. A Spanish officer who had produced a small telescope from his coat pocket found himself crowded by his fellows, all anxious to use it.

'A ship!' exclaimed one man in the uniform of a surgeon.

Brissot rose from his place and shaded his eyes with the flat of his hand. The white sails of a large warship had appeared above the verdant green of Cape Salomon. As he watched they flapped in the breeze and her yards slowly swung across as she turned in towards the bay. 'A big two-decker,' he suggested. 'Spanish from the look of her.'

'Another eighty-gunner from her beam,' added Morin.

'She is the *San Rafael*,' announced the Spanish officer with the telescope. 'Sister to our *Argonauta*. She was delayed leaving Cadiz with the rest of our ships.'

'And so, little by little, the pieces move across the board,' said Dorre. 'We have twenty ships of the line now, with perhaps the same again enroute. I start to believe that this invasion scheme of the emperor's might actually work.'

Chapter 11
Diamond Rock

When Brissot had gone to Lucas with his suggestion that the fleet should mount an attack on Diamond Rock, his captain had taken the idea straight to Admiral Villeneuve. It would only require modest resources, two or three ships at most, with the bulk of the assault force to come from the island's garrison. It would also provide Lucas the chance to give his men a taste of real action after all their long months of training. Besides, how much resistance could a hundred-odd Royal Navy sailors and marines offer the might of the *Redoutable*? But now that he could see the fortified rock coming closer, he was starting to wonder what he had taken on.

His ship was cleared for action, leading another seventy-four, the *Pluton*, the heavy frigate *Sirène*, and a gaggle of smaller craft provided by the governor towards their objective. Lucas surveyed Diamond Rock through his telescope. It rose from the blue water like a thick pillar, almost two hundred metres tall and two kilometres out to sea from the coast of Martinique. The precipitous sides were composed of a mixture of sheer cliffs, or broad patches of straggly vegetation dotted with trees where the slope lessened enough for them to cling. In among the greenery, he could just make out the dark mouths of several large caves.

But the rock also showed signs of its occupation. There was a naval launch dragged up on the little beach at the column's foot, and a steep track winding its way upwards where the sand ended. Above the boat, Lucas could see a line of breastworks made from rocks and felled tree trunks, and glimpse the occasional flash of colour from the scarlet-coated marines who manned it. Near the cave mouths were lines of washing fluttering between the trees, while close to the top of the rock he could see the muzzles of several large artillery pieces poking out from behind revetments. Above them streamed a union flag on a pole. As he watched, a gush of smoke masked one of the cannons and moments later a column of water rose from the surface of the sea, startling white against the blue, a hundred metres ahead of the *Redoutable*'s bow. The boom of the cannon sent a cloud of sea birds swirling up into the sky.

'*Sacré bleu*!' exclaimed Dupotet. 'What sort of gun are they firing there? Why, we must be over four kilometres away, yet they can almost reach us?'

'Standard naval eighteen- and twenty-four-pounders, according to the governor,' replied his captain. 'But small wonder they have such a prodigious range. Why, they are sited almost three times as high as our masthead! We shall have to sail a good deal closer before we can reply, and yet if we come too near, we shall not be able to elevate our cannon sufficiently to reach them. I start to understand how the English have been able to hold out for so long.'

Another shot boomed out, but this time it was more wayward, falling off to one side.

'The governor told me he tried to storm the place last year with soldiers approaching in boats at night,' continued Lucas. 'But the wind got up, and dawn found them well short of the beach. Three were sunk outright before the rest could get away.'

As the range came down, the splashes grew steadily closer.

'*Pluton*'s been hit, sir,' reported one of the afterguard, shortly before a tall splash reared up just beside the *Redoutable*, close enough to wet the curved side of her hull.

'They make good practice, sir,' commented Dupotet.

'What I want to know is how the devil they got such huge guns up there,' said his captain with a shake of his head. 'Not to mention all the shot and powder they require. And the food and water for the crews. Can you imagine the effort! Incredible!'

There was a sound of ripping canvas overhead, and the mizzen forestay broke with a crack.

'Monsieur Tournier!' yelled the first lieutenant. 'Send a party of men aft to repair that, if you please.'

'Yes, sir!'

Diamond Rock was growing all the time, taller and taller as the ships approached. Lucas carefully judged the distance, but decided the range was still too great. His guns might reach the column's base, but not the upper slopes where the garrison were. He looked astern at the *Pluton*, just in time to see a fresh shot hole appear in her fore topsail, one of several. 'They are warming to their task, Camille,' he commented. 'Signal to the governor's little armada to stand off for now. None of them have the scantlings to resist an eighteen-pounder ball arriving from such a height. Why, it would probably drop clean through the bottom of those little schooners.'

'Yes, sir.'

It was fortunate that the British only had three guns that could bear on the approaching warships, for, as the range continued to shorten, they began hitting the *Redoubtable* regularly. Soon most of the sails had holes in them, and more sailors were busy splicing severed lines in the rigging. Lucas lowered his telescope as a crash sounded from the bow, followed by a cry of pain. A few moments later two sailors appeared from under the forecastle carrying a shipmate between them. One of his legs was dark with blood from a nasty looking splinter wound.

Lucas forced his face into the calm detachment expected of a captain and returned his attention to the rock ahead. She was not as close as he would like, but he decided that at least some gun smoke might protect his ship from the steady pounding she was taking. 'Starboard guns, out quoins,' he ordered. 'Maximum elevation, if you please.'

'Yes, sir,' said Dupotet.

Lucas watched the quarterdeck crews pull the wedges free and the breeches of their eight-pounders sank deep into the gun carriages. A shot crashed against the side of the ship before plunging into the sea. He glanced over the rail and saw the bright scar of white oak where the ball had struck a glancing blow.

'You may open fire when the guns bear, Monsieur Dupotet,' said Lucas. 'On the up roll, if you please.'

'Yes, sir,' said the first lieutenant.

The broadside roared out, heeling the *Redoutable* over and blotting out Diamond Rock behind a wall of smoke. It was more ragged than Lucas would have liked, with some excitable gun captains firing the moment they heard the order, the steadier ones remembering to wait for the hull to start rising as a wave passed beneath them.

Beside him on the quarterdeck the petty officer in charge of the nearest division of guns was taking his crews through each stage of reloading. 'Stop your vents! Wet swab out the barrel. All the way in, Faucher! Better. All clear? Right, fresh charges now!'

When the fog of gun smoke rolled aside, he searched the target for damage. There was a little scarring on a cliff face, and some broken vegetation floating on the sea beside the beach, but otherwise Diamond Rock showed no sign of harm. One of the guns close to her summit banged out, and a moment later a section of quarterdeck rail disintegrated in a shower of splinters, fortunately without hurting anyone. Behind him the *Pluton* erupted in fire and smoke and he watched the broadside strike home. Numerous spouts of water appeared all around the target, more balls fluttering through the trees, dislodging a brief avalanche of stones from close to the summit.

'General signal, Monsieur Pascal,' barked Lucas. 'Anchor when convenient. Monsieur Dupotet, kindly have the boatswain drop anchor. He will need to fit a spring to keep the target under our guns.'

'Yes, sir.'

Soon the three warships were clustered in a crescent around the rocky pillar, pounding it with almost a hundred heavy naval guns. The space between the ships and their target filled with dense clouds of smoke, forcing the gun captains to fire blind, but with the ships at anchor they knew they only had to run their guns up straight to be sure of hitting something. Broadside followed crashing broadside, the noise deafening. To Lucas it seemed impossible that anything might survive such punishment, but in the brief lulls between French ships firing, the enemy guns banged out in response, their shots crashing home or splashing into the sea alongside.

When an hour of steady pummelling had passed, Lucas closed his watch, and turned to the midshipman beside him. 'General signal, if you please, Monsieur Pascal. Launch assault.'

Clay and the Immortal Memory

*****

'Longboat crew, to me!' shouted Brissot from close to the entry port.

'Launch crew, over here,' cried Morin, like a rival stall holder in a bustling market. Bare-footed sailors pattered across the deck to form up behind the two lieutenants, their footfalls in contrast to the heavy boots of Dorre's marines.

Brissot followed his crew down into the longboat and made his way towards the stern sheets. Thick clouds of gun smoke lay across the surface of the sea, through which emerged the boats from the governor's flotilla, each one packed with cross-belted soldiers, all heading towards Diamond Rock. He took his seat beside Midshipman Quellec, who had the tiller, and watched as the first of the blue-coated marines began making their plodding way down the ship's side to fill the middle of the boat. In front of him the sailor manning the stroke oar spat noisily on the palms of his hands.

'You don't normally sit there, Lubin,' said Brissot. 'Where is Du Chemin?'

'He's down with the Grey Killer, sir,' explained the sailor. 'The surgeon has him in the sick bay. Poor man's weak as a kitten.'

'More damned scurvy,' muttered the lieutenant. 'But you seem well enough?'

'I started to feel sick, sir, so I bought a couple of limes from one of the bumboats in the harbour. Strange taste, but I felt much better.'

'Limes, you say,' said Brissot. 'Who told you to do that?'

'During the peace, I got some work on a Danish trading

brig that came into L'Orient, sir,' said the sailor. 'The first mate had served in the English navy in the last war. He said they give all the crew a tot of lemon or lime juice each day, and none of them ever got the Grey Killer.'

'The soldiers are all on board, sir,' said Quellec beside him. 'Here comes Captain Dorre, now.'

Brissot looked up to see the marine officer making his unsteady way towards him down the packed boat, using the shoulders of the seated men for support. 'Goodness, but I'm getting too old for small boat work,' he exclaimed, flopping down in the stern and hauling out a coloured handkerchief to mop his brow. 'Or too fat, perhaps. You may proceed, young man.'

'Push off, starboard side!' ordered the midshipman, in response to a nod from Brissot. 'Out oars! And pull!'

The heavily laden boat got slowly under way, the oars foaming through the water at first. Brissot glanced behind him to check that Morin in the launch was following. They were initially sheltered by the bulk of the big seventy-four, but as they gathered speed they rounded the bow and headed towards the rock. Beside him the *Redoutable*'s guns rumbled out once more, and then erupted as they fired a final broadside. The sound was stunning out on the open water, the shock wave booming off the surface of the sea. Scalding heat from the tongues of flame washed across Brissot for an instant and were gone, leaving the boat lost in a thick brown fog.

'Keep pulling!' yelled the lieutenant, as the stroke faltered, his voice strange and distant. Then his ears cleared and the sound of battle roared back. From somewhere behind him he heard the piercing note of a whistle, followed by 'Ceasefire! Ceasefire!' Ahead was only choking smoke, full of the cries of coxswains urging their rowers to pull harder, and the occasional bang of the enemy's guns. Then the longboat emerged into open water, and the hot tropical sun beat down on him once more.

In front of him towered Diamond Rock, partly swathed in smoke that clung like mist amid the vegetation tumbling down the steep slopes. Ahead were half a dozen boats of various sizes from the flotilla. Off to one side were more ship's launches from the *Pluton* and one from the *Sirène*, all packed with marines like his own. A gush of smoke appeared close to the summit of the rock, and a column of water rose up beside one of the boats, causing it to slew around before resuming its forward progress. Then another spout climbed skywards just ahead of them.

'Cover your locks!' roared Dorre, as sea water cascaded down over the men in the boat. 'Sergeant, see the men dry their pieces.'

'Yes, sir.'

'Tricky place to storm, ain't it?' observed Dorre, shaking water from out of the crown of his hat. 'I start to understand why it has resisted the best efforts of the governor for so long.'

'Let us hope our barrage has dealt with most of the defenders,' said Brissot.

'Hmm … it don't seem to have slowed their gunners any.'

Another gush and bang from the summit, and this time a ball struck one of the smaller boats, sending fragments of planking cartwheeling across the surface of the water. Its stern rose dripping from the sea as the bow vanished, accompanied by a despairing wail from those on board.

'Pull harder, men,' yelled Quellec. 'Unless you want to join them with the sharks!'

Soon they were passing the shattered hull. Two of the

crew were clinging to the stern, another to a fragment of painted side. Others thrashed around amid the floating debris and bobbing corpses. One of the flotilla's boats was hauling bedraggled survivors on board.

'Shall I stop, sir?' asked the midshipman.

Brissot shook his head. 'We have no room,' he said, hardening his heart to the pitiful cries. 'And another stationary boat will make too good a target for their gunners.'

They sped on, the men at the oars starting to grunt with the effort of rowing fast in the heat.

'Come on, lads,' urged Brissot. 'A few strokes more, and we'll be too close to be troubled by those guns. They won't be able to depress far enough.'

Closer and closer they came, until Diamond Rock filled Brissot's vision, towering up like a mountain. Small-arms fire replaced the big naval guns, which returned to pounding the warships further out. Brissot watched as a few puffs of smoke appeared high up on the rock, raising splashes of water around the leading boat as it neared the beach. As the bow grounded in the shallows, the crew tumbled out, the soldiers wading ashore with their muskets held above their heads. They began to fan out across the sand. From higher up the slope the sound of a ragged volley echoed off the cliffs. Several of the soldiers fell, and the rest wavered, but under the urging of an officer, his sword twinkling in the sun, they pressed on towards the forbidding slope ahead.

More and more boats were arriving, each one discharging a fresh wave of attackers, until the stretch of sand was full of milling figures. It was an almost perfect target for the defenders above them. Dorre banged his fist against the side of the boat in frustration as they watched soldiers falling under the steady rain of fire. 'What are they thinking?' he raved.

'There is no cover! Advance off the bloody beach, for the love of God! Get me ashore, Francois. Now!'

'Easier said than done,' said Brissot, searching for a way ahead. 'The shore line is choked with boats. Ah, there! Off to the left, Monsieur Quellec,' he ordered. 'Come in close under that cliff.'

The crack of small-arms fire became louder as they neared the shore. The precipitous slope above them blotted out the sun and they entered a pool of shade. The longboat knocked and pushed its way in among the other boats clustered in the shallows, Morin's launch following them through.

'Marines out,' ordered Dorre, stepping over the side and into the water. 'Sergeant, draw the men up under that cliff, while I see what the hell is happening.'

'Monsieur Quellec, keep the men with the boat,' ordered Brissot, joining the marines in the shallows.

'Yes, sir.'

Dorre waited for him and then strode across the beach. It was at most thirty metres wide, and was scattered with dead and wounded soldiers. At the back were a few stunted trees and then a scrub covered slope, angled like the roof of a house. Along the bottom was a thick line of French soldiers, most of whom were busily reloading their muskets, or peering upwards in search of a target. From higher up the slope came the steady bang of returning fire. As the officers from the *Redoutable* arrived, a man in front of them spun away, clutching at his shoulder. Behind the soldiers was a steadily growing tideline of dead and injured.

'Who is in charge here?' demanded the marine captain.

A scared-looking officer with a silver gorget at his neck looked around and saluted stiffly. 'It was Major Renard, but he was killed earlier, sir.'

'Very well, Lieutenant,' said Dorre. 'I shall take command. What is the situation?'

'The enemy is up there, behind that wall of rocks and felled trees,' said the officer, pointing to a solid-looking barricade fifty metres above them. Brissot saw the head and chest of a scarlet-coated marine briefly emerge. He took aim, fired his musket and ducked back into cover to reload. Moments later another marine appeared a few metres away from the first. His shot was rewarded with a cry of pain from further along the beach.

'I see,' said Dorre, pulling at his moustache. 'And how does one come at them?'

'The only way appears to be over there, sir,' said the officer, pointing to a thin path that led upwards, crossing the slope in a series of zig zags.

'But … but … that is little better than a goat track!' exclaimed Dorre.

'I know, sir. Major Renard was trying to lead the way up it when he died. What should we do?'

'Your men are making precious little progress against such a well-protected enemy, other than to provide him with an excellent target,' said Dorre. 'I have a number of marksmen armed with rifles with me. A skirmish line of them should be able to persuade the enemy to keep his head down, after which we can advance up the track. But first we need to get your men into cover where you can reorder them.'

'What cover, sir?' queried the lieutenant, looking around at the flat expanse behind them. Sand spat up as a musket ball thudded into the beach between them.

'There is your cover!' exclaimed Brissot, pointing behind him. 'The ships' boats! We can drag them up the beach and make a barricade of our own.'

'Excellent!' said Dorre. 'Your men can assist, Lieutenant, while I position my skirmish line.'

With a little direction and some organisation, morale began to lift on the beach. There was no shortage of willing hands ready to manhandle the heavy boats, despite the steady toll of casualties still falling to musket fire from above. When each boat was in position, Brissot had it rolled up on to its side and supported there by oars driven deep into the sand. Soon most of the soldiers and boat crews were crouched behind the strange barrier. The occasional musket ball pattered against the hulls, but none could penetrate their thick timbers.

'We can't leave all these wounded out in the open,' declared Brissot to Morin and another naval lieutenant from the *Pluton*. He pointed to the seventy-fours' big longboats, which had been left in the shallows as they were too heavy to haul up the beach. 'Can you two evacuate them back to the ships? I must rejoin Captain Dorre and his marines.'

'Yes, sir,' said Morin. 'It should be safe enough. Even the English will not fire on men doing such work.' He reached across and gripped Brissot's hand. 'Take care of yourself, Francois.'

Brissot ran in a crouch along the line of boats until he reached the end. He peered cautiously around it to locate Dorre. To his surprise the officer was standing in the open, in conversation with another marine captain, who was pointing at something further up the slope. Along the back of the beach a loose line of marines had replaced the dense row of soldiers, some busily working their long ramrods, others aiming upwards, waiting. He stood upright and stepped out from behind the boat as he realised that the enemy were barely firing.

'Ah, Monsieur Brissot,' said Dorre. 'May I introduce my fellow marine? Captain Griset of the *Pluton*.'

'What a splendid fortification you have created, Lieutenant,' said Griset, a darkly handsome officer with a thin moustache. 'I am most uncertain if we will ever persuade these useless colonial troops to come out from behind it, however.'

'Between us we have the men for the task,' said Dorre. 'It was only direction that was wanting. As you can see, a properly constituted skirmish line has done much to persuade the enemy to keep his head down.'

Brissot scanned the barricade above them, apparently now abandoned. Then he caught a slight movement as a musket appeared from behind a tree trunk. Immediately several shots rang out, sending chips of wood flying around the area, and the musket vanished.

'Those rifles of yours are damned useful,' commented his fellow marine. 'But I suspect the enemy is merely holding back until we attack in earnest, which we must next attempt. Shall my men advance up the track, while yours cover them? When we have stormed their position, we can cover your advance up to join us. Agreed?'

'A most excellent plan,' said Dorre.

'Do you want the troops behind the boats to join in?' asked Brissot. 'They could fire from where they are.'

'Heavens, no!' exclaimed Griset. 'The last thing my lads need is a wildly discharged volley in the back. Gentlemen, let us end this.' He touched his hat to them, and then strode away, bawling orders.

'Ready, men?' asked Dorre in a commanding voice. 'Make every shot count!'

Brissot watched as Griset swept out his sword, and led his men in a long file up the path. Initially there was no reaction, and then he heard shouted orders from above. A mixed line of marines and sailors appeared behind the barricade, levelling their muskets at the attackers, and both sides began exchanging fire once more. Two of Griset's men were quickly hit, one falling head over heels down the steep slope, crashing through the scrub until he fetched up against a tree with a sickening thud. But Dorre's marksmen quickly gained the upper hand. He saw several defenders hit, one left draped over the barricade, his scarlet coat a patch of colour against the vegetation. The attackers broke into a trot as the defenders' fire became ragged, a long line of blue-coated men snaking their way upwards. Three more fell, but the rest pressed on.

'Cease fire!' roared Dorre, as Griset's men reached the last turn in the path. The defenders now played their final card, some heaving rocks over the wall, the rest manning the barricade with a mixture of cutlasses and muskets. More of Griset's men were knocked off the path, but the others closed ranks to fill the gaps. Those still strung out on the track hastened upwards to join the rest of their unit. At a barked order from their commander, they levelled their muskets, fired a rolling volley, and charged.

Brissot tried to peer through the trees to see what was happening above him. He could hear that the fight was brutal, from the screech and clash of steel on steel, the cries of the wounded and the desperate tone of the yelled orders, but he could make out little else. Then the haze of musket smoke that clung among the scrubby bushes slowly thinned. He began to see a little detail. The twinkle of sunlight on steel. Two marines, one in red, the other blue, wrestling in a fierce embrace.

Beside him Dorre let out a grunt of satisfaction. 'The battle goes our way, I declare.'

'It does?' queried Brissot.

'Oh, indubitably,' confirmed the marine. 'An assault such as this can only end in two ways. The attack fails to breach the wall, in which case it will be a bloody failure; or it breaks through and their superior numbers overwhelm the defence. The fact that the fighting has endured so long must mean it is the latter. See, the English start to retreat.'

Brissot watched a pair of sailors climb up the slope above the barricade towards the nearest cave mouth, pulling a wounded comrade along behind them. More figures began to appear, scrambling up the path. They were followed by blue-coated soldiers hot on their heels.

'Sergeant!' yelled Dorre. 'Have the men fall in at the bottom of the path! We are going to advance!'

'Look by that cave over there,' said Brissot, pointing upwards. A flutter of something white had caught his eye against the dark entrance. A naval officer appeared, holding a makeshift flag. Then he noticed something else. 'Their guns have stopped firing, and that flag on the summit has been hauled down. I don't think your advance will be necessary.'

'On the contrary!' cried Dorre, hastening across the sand to where his men were gathering. 'I need to get up there now! Before that bastard from the *Pluton* takes all the damned credit!'

Chapter 12
Nelson

In the early morning light the Rock of Gibraltar cast a blue shadow across the warships moored at its feet. The *Griffin* had signalled that she had news of the enemy as she ghosted into the harbour, propelled by the last push of the Atlantic. She picked up a vacant buoy and began firing her salute. But the echo of the last gun had barely come back to her from the cliffs above, when a line of coloured flags rose quickly up the *Victory*'s mizzen mast.

'Our number, sir,' announced the signal midshipman. 'Captain to repair on board.'

'Barge away!' roared Taylor, to where Sedgwick already had his crew assembled on the main deck. They were smartly turned out in white shirts and straw hats decorated with ribbons of the same green as the oar blades and hull of their captain's barge.

'Thank you, Mr Taylor,' said Clay, who was freshly shaven and in his full-dress uniform, despite having only risen from bed a scant forty minutes earlier. He slipped a hand into his coat to check that his report was there. 'In my absence kindly see about revictualling the ship. I hope that our visit will not be a lengthy one.'

'Aye aye, sir.'

'Shove off in the bow!' ordered Sedgwick, the moment that his captain had settled on to the seat beside him. 'Take a stroke, starboards! And another! Now together!'

The boat set off through the fleet, threading its way between the looming warships. Despite the early hour, the harbour was already busy. Broad lighters, heaped with provisions, were creeping out from the victualling yard, manned by locals who propelled their craft standing with long handled sweeps. They passed a big water hoy warped alongside a seventy-four, the canvas hose that trailed through a lower gun port pulsing and jerking as fresh water was pumped across. Everywhere ships' boats were heading to and fro. Sedgwick was forced to stand up as he deftly piloted his way through the traffic towards the flagship.

They approached the three-decker from behind, her big stern curving out above them, a mass of windows and decoration picked out in a yellow that contrasted with her black timbers. A midshipman appeared over the taffrail and levelled a speaking trumpet towards them. 'Boat ahoy!' he yelled.

'*Griffin*!' replied Sedgwick, holding three fingers up to let the officer know a senior post captain was coming on board.

Now the barge was level with the first rate's side. All her gunports were open, and her cannon run out to maximise the available space on board. The lower tier of massive thirty-two-pounders were passing a few feet above Clay's head. From within came the sound of animated conversation and the scrape of spoon on bowl as the crew had their breakfast. Suddenly a sailor with a gold hoop in one ear thrust his head out of a porthole to spit into the sea, halting mid-hawk at finding himself in the presence of a captain. Clay stifled a smile as the man opted for a bout of theatrical coughing instead, before vanishing from sight.

'Easy all!' growled Sedgwick. 'In oars, larboards! Clap on in the bow!' With a final push on the tiller, he brought the barge alongside the *Victory*, level with the first rungs of the side ladder that led up the curved wall of oak, and Clay made his way through the boat until he stood below it.

Fortunately, the entry port with its elaborately decorated canopy was in the middle gundeck, barely further above the sea than that on the *Griffin*. Clay paused to settle his hat straight and hitch his sword clear of his legs and then jumped across. He scrambled up the first few steps, after which the tumble home of the side came to help him, so that he was able to duck through the port, hand raised in salute, with the dignity expected of a post captain. The marines slapped their muskets noisily as they presented arms, the boatswain's mates twittered on their calls, and at the end of the corridor of white-gloved ship's boys stood one of the few commanders in the service even taller than his visitor.

Captain Hardy gravely returned Clay's salute before extending his hand with a grin of recognition. 'Alexander, dear fellow,' he rumbled, enveloping his visitor's hand in his own. 'Now I know matters have become serious! How the devil are you?'

'You find me in tolerably good health, thank you, Tom,' said Clay. 'And yourself?'

'Oh, I'm fine, or would be if deck beams were a little higher, what?' he laughed, slapping the one that ran between their foreheads. 'But it is good to see you. Why, I haven't had the pleasure of your society since that damned close-run affair with the Danes back in the year one. I seem to remember you turned up on the eve of battle on that occasion too.'

'You are expecting a battle then?'

'The French are out,' said Hardy. 'The Dons too, and the admiral is champing at the bit to be up and at them, if only we knew where the blighters have gone. But to judge from your signal, you have some knowledge of that?'

'I know where they were three weeks ago, for I ran into them in the mid-Atlantic.'

'Then I had best take you to see his lordship without delay. Watch your head as we go.'

Nelson was sitting at the rosewood table once more with his secretary beside him, but he was on his feet the moment he saw Clay. 'Alexander, my dear friend, well met,' he enthused, gripping his visitor's hand. 'I thought that you might appear.'

'You did, my lord?' exclaimed Clay. 'I cannot think how. Surely no one in Europe knows of my return?'

Nelson chuckled at his reaction. 'That handsome little Spanish prize of yours came in yesterday. The *Fortuna*, wasn't it? I have allowed the owner and his wife to return to Cadiz as you requested and I daresay you will be pleased to have your prize crew returned?'

'Indeed I shall, my lord.'

'But I don't know yet how you come to be here,' continued the admiral. 'The last I heard was that you were away in the Indies, confounding the wicked French at every turn.'

'In truth I am but newly returned, my lord. I have been away two years wanting three days. The *Griffin* was dispatched to India at the end of the peace.'

'Two years, eh?' chuckled Hardy. 'That will explain why you are dark as a moor, what?'

'Yes, you certainly seem in rude health,' said Nelson.

'Thank you, my lord,' said Clay, thinking how sallow and thin the admiral looked.

'Now, pray take a seat, gentlemen,' said Nelson. 'Have you broken your fast, Alexander? Can I offer you refreshment? A dish of coffee, perhaps?'

'I have eaten, but coffee would be most welcome, my

lord. Mine ran out south of the equator. My return voyage was somewhat extended by the need to avoid a rather persistent frigate squadron who obliged me to sail far to the south.'

'Light along a pot for the captains, would you, Mr Scott? said Nelson to his secretary. 'And kindly clear away all these manifests.'

'Aye aye, my lord.'

'I have my report on my voyage home here, my lord,' said Clay, pulling the envelope from his coat pocket.

Nelson handed it to his secretary. 'I shall attend to that later. Now, pray tell me what news you have of the enemy. I am in a fever to learn more.'

'I encountered them three weeks back, close to twenty-nine degrees of longitude, due west of Santa Cruz in the Canaries,' explained Clay. 'I was on a northerly course when I met with a considerable fleet crossing my track. Seventeen of the line, we counted, all French bar six which were Spanish, and six frigates in addition.'

'That will be Admiral Villeneuve and the Toulon fleet for certain, my lord,' said Hardy. 'With whatever the Dons could scrape together at Cadiz to join them.'

'Mr Scott!' called Nelson. 'The chart of the Atlantic, if you please.'

'I have it here, my lord,' said the secretary, bringing it across and spreading it on the table.

A steward in white gloves with a silver coffee pot and porcelain cups on a tray appeared at Clay's elbow. He took one and drank thirstily, while Hardy leant forwards and pushed a large finger across the map.

'Twenty-nine degrees, you say,' he muttered, as his digit came to rest. 'That would place them … there. Mind, they could have covered a deal of ocean in three weeks.'

'What course where they on?' asked the admiral.

'I encountered them late morning and followed them through that day and into the night, my lord,' said Clay. 'Their course never deviated from west-south-west. Then we left and made haste to bring word of them. I had hoped to encounter Sir John Orde, but no one was off Cadiz, so I continued here with all dispatch.'

'I should not place over reliance on that old fool,' snorted Nelson.

'But would Sir John not have tried to stop Villeneuve's escape into the Atlantic?' asked Clay.

'No, he seems to have cut and run,' explained Hardy. 'His six of the line were revictualling here in Gibraltar when Villeneuve showed up. They hastened to sea briskly enough, but made no attempt to prevent a junction with the Dons. I daresay he will have fallen back on the Channel Fleet. In his defence, he would have been outnumbered three to one in any action.'

'And what of that?' scoffed Nelson. 'How would the Battle of Cape St Vincent have gone if I had cared about such niceties? Our country will sooner forgive an officer for attacking an enemy than for letting them alone, as Orde has done.'

'Quite so!' rumbled Hardy, banging his hand on the table and making the coffee cups rattle in their saucers.

'But it is not only Sir John who is at fault,' sighed the admiral. 'I too have been sadly amiss in my reckoning. I was quite convinced that Villeneuve had some more limited object in mind – a descent on Sicily, Naples or perhaps Malta, and I moved my fleet eastwards to thwart him. There I lay in wait for the best part of a month, but it seems my actions only served to open the door to the Atlantic for him. Perhaps Orde has the truth of it, and we should follow him north, to help protect Ireland and the Channel?'

'If I may, my lord, I say no,' said Clay. 'For I believe that something greater is afoot here.'

'What the deuce do you know, Alexander?' asked Hardy.

'Nothing for certain, but I don't understand why the French would have sailed so far into the Atlantic, if their object was Ireland? They were sailing in quite the wrong direction, away from Europe, when I encountered them. Their course was one for the Caribbean.'

'But that makes no sense,' protested Hardy. 'What is there in the West Indies for such an armada to achieve?'

'I was struggling to understand that too, and then it came to me,' said Clay. 'What if it is not just the Mediterranean Fleet that has broken out? What if the squadrons at Ferrol, Rochefort and Brest were attempting to leave as well? Such a plan would see various fleets escaping at different times and surely encountering a variety of weather. They would need somewhere they could rendezvous. Where one part could await the arrival of the rest in safety.'

'Such as one of their sugar islands!' exclaimed Hardy.

'Martinique has a fine harbour,' said Clay. 'As does Guadeloupe, to a lesser extent. And it would explain why Villeneuve was on that course.'

'But I return to the objective,' said Hardy. 'What task is there in the Caribbean for such a fleet to perform?'

'None,' said Nelson. 'Once combined with the others they will sail for the Channel to overwhelm those protecting it. Their object will be nothing less than the invasion of our nation. Has Napoleon not long prepared for it, with every creek and harbour on the Flanders coast choked with small craft, and his army encamped at Boulogne?'

'That is what I thought too, my lord,' said Clay.

'So what is to be our response, gentlemen?' said Nelson. 'The enemy has a month's lead on us, at least, if not more. Do we follow Sir John, and fall back on the Channel, or pursue our enemy?'

'Perhaps falling back is the safest course?' mused Hardy.

'Your pardon, Tom, but I say that would be a mistake,' said Clay. 'Our enemy has not yet succeeded in combining his forces, and the fleet at Brest will find it much harder to leave port than did Villeneuve. We have an enemy divided that we can defeat in detail. If we tamely withdraw as Sir John has done, we give him time to combine his forces. Defeat Villeneuve, and Napoleon's invasion is defeated with him.'

'A month is quite a lead,' mused Hardy.

'But all is not lost,' said Clay. 'Remember the Nile, my lord. How slow and lubberly the French were? No fleet that has spent so long at anchor could be otherwise, and the Dons will be worse, since they were so recently at peace. If you make haste, I have no doubt you can catch them.'

'When has the path of caution ever led to glory, eh?' said Nelson, his good eye alight at the prospect of action. 'I like your pluck, Alexander, I always have. You give me heart. And desperate affairs require desperate measures. Let us hunt Villeneuve down, gentlemen, and if we must cross the Atlantic to do it, so be it. Mr Scott! Signal the fleet to complete taking in stores as swiftly as possible. I shall hang out the Blue Peter at noon.'

'Aye aye, my lord.'

'And see that the *Griffin* is given priority,' he added.

'The *Griffin*, my lord?' queried Clay. 'I can surely wait

until you have sailed?'

'As ever, I am shockingly ill-served in the matter of frigates, Alexander, so your arrival here is like manna from heaven,' said Nelson. He extended his hand across the table and lightly touched Clay's. 'I know you will have been desperate to return to Mrs Clay and your children after such a long absence.' His eyes strayed to the portrait that hung on the bulkhead beside them. 'I too have not seen my Emma, or little Horatia, for almost as long. But I also know that the decisive moment in this war may be fast approaching. I feel it in my heart. And when it comes, I shall need all my band of brothers with me.'

'I understand, my lord,' said Clay. 'I won't say that I do not yearn for home, but I can hardly urge you to chase the French and not do so myself. What duty would you have me perform?'

'To be the eyes of my fleet,' said the admiral. 'Sail ahead and track down Villeneuve for me.'

'Very well, my lord,' said Clay rising to his feet. 'I had best attend to replenishing the *Griffin*.'

'Please do,' said Nelson. 'Mr Scott will send across your orders presently. And Alexander?'

'My lord?'

'Pray take the time to write to your wife before you go, and when you do, I'd be obliged if you would pass on my sincere apologies for preventing your return.'

'Aye aye, my lord.'

*****

It was early summer in Paris, and the gardens of the Tuileries Palace were at their best. Pale gravel paths made pleasing geometric patterns among flower beds packed with colour. Dotted across the garden were bronze statues, frozen into stillness with only the constantly playing fountain in the centre of the garden providing any movement.

But even the calm beauty before him could not soften the frown of annoyance creasing Napoleon's brow. He turned from the window to join the others grouped around the table in the middle of the map room. They were the same men who had met there in the winter to help plan the conquest of Britain. The Spanish ambassador, José Miguel de Carvajal-Vargas, seemed more content now that the weather resembled that of his native land. Marshal Berthier was his usual relaxed self, sitting back from the table with legs crossed, idly twisting at one of his many curls. It was only the portly Admiral Decrès who seemed nervous.

'So, has that sluggard Ganteaume left Brest yet?' Napoleon asked.

'Eh … not yet, sire,' said the admiral, shuffling the papers before him.

Napoleon approached the table, placed both hands on it and leant forwards to bring his face closer to that of his Minister of the Navy. 'Why not?' he demanded.

'The Atlantic Fleet did leave their moorings two days ago, following a promising storm, but found the enemy waiting for them once more with seventeen ships of the line,' explained Decrès. 'It is their fifth such attempt to break out. As he was unable to leave Brest without avoiding battle with the enemy, as stated in his orders, the admiral returned to port.'

'He has twenty-one ships of the line, does he not, as well as many smaller ones?' asked Berthier. 'Surely if the enemy has only seventeen, why can he not fight his way out?'

'Because he would lose,' growled the emperor. 'Our navy always loses, haven't you learned that yet?'

'The outcome would be uncertain,' said Decrès. 'But even if Admiral Ganteaume was to be victorious, his fleet would likely be so damaged, he would be compelled to return to Brest once more for repairs. That is why achieving a junction with Admiral Villeneuve before battle is so important. Combined, the two of them can defeat any Royal Navy force they encounter.'

'Can our Spanish friends not help?' asked Berthier, turning towards his neighbour.

'We are supplying as much assistance as the perilous state of my country's finances permit, señor,' explained the ambassador. 'But despite our penury, I understand that some of our finest ships are being prepared for war in our Atlantic ports, even as we sit here now.'

'How many ships?' demanded Napoleon.

'Six of the line.'

'Only six?' queried Berthier. 'It is hardly the thirty-odd promised in our treaty!'

'And quite inadequate to help drive away the enemy ships blockading Brest,' added Decrès.

'The support we offer cannot be measured by numbers alone, gentlemen,' said the Spaniard, drawing himself upright in his chair. 'Many are of a superior size, including our flagship, the most magnificent *Santissima Trinidad* of a hundred and thirty cannon.'

'Many of which are very small,' observed Decrès, holding up his little finger for comparison.

'And may I also remind you that this is in addition to the seven ships that are already serving alongside your Admiral Villeneuve, somewhere on the far side of the ocean,' added de Carvajal-Vargas.

'*Putain*!' exclaimed Napoleon. 'On the far side of the

ocean, waiting for Admiral Ganteaume, who cannot leave Brest! How I hate these damned ships! Manoeuvring armies is so much simpler!'

'Perhaps the answer is also simple, emperor,' suggested the Spaniard. 'If the mountain will not go to Mohammed …'

'Speak plain, ambassador,' said Napoleon. 'What are you suggesting?'

'Order our combined fleet to return. If Admiral Ganteaume cannot go to Admiral Villeneuve, then Villeneuve should return to join with him. Thus you still achieve your junction of fleets.'

'Could it work?' asked Napoleon.

'Perhaps,' mused Decrès. 'We would need to make sure that Admiral Ganteaume was ready to come out the moment that Villeneuve's ships were sighted. They could move out of the inner harbour at Brest and wait in Bertheaume Bay, where he will be less dependent on the right wind blowing. It is a dangerous anchorage in a westerly gale, but now that summer is at hand that danger may have passed.'

'How quickly could fresh orders be sent out to recall Admiral Villeneuve from Martinique?' asked Napoleon.

'A swift passage might take a month, longer if the wind is indifferent,' explained Decrès. 'The frigate *Didon* lies at Rochefort at the moment, and is a tolerably fast ship.'

'And what are his orders to be?' asked Berthier. 'A month for them to reach him, rather longer for him to return. Much may have changed here in that time. Do we order him to sail directly to Brest, not knowing what he may find when he arrives?'

'Might I make a suggestion, señors?' said de Carvajal-Vargas. 'Order Admiral Villeneuve first to Spain. He can resupply his fleet at Ferrol, be reinforced with the ships I mentioned, and avail himself of the latest reports of the enemy's dispositions before going into battle. Brest is no great distance from Ferrol.'

'An excellent suggestion, ambassador,' said Napoleon. 'Make it so, Admiral Decrès. Send fresh orders to Martinique immediately and I may yet be in London before the leaves fall.'

*****

The *Redoutabl*e was back in Martinique, moored among Villeneuve's other ships, all still waiting for the Brest fleet to join them. But Captain Lucas had no intention of letting her crew grow idle. He had decided to hold a complete dress rehearsal of the ship's new boarding tactics. At the appointed hour, he strode up the ladderway from his cabin and across to join his first lieutenant on the quarterdeck. 'Is the ship ready to begin the exercise, Camille?' he asked.

'Yes, sir,' said Dupotet, touching his hat.

Lucas pulled out his pocket watch. It had originally been his father's, made in the Paris workshop of Ferdinand Berthoud when the watchmaker was at the height of his powers. It was a thing of exquisite beauty resting heavy in the palm of his hand. The few rays of sunlight that filtered down through the mass of yards and ropes above him glittered off the tooled silver case, with its bearded Hercules wrestling a lion within a garland of delicate foliage. It was also the only timepiece on board the *Redoutable* that had a second hand. 'Thank you,' he said, clicking the knob of the winder so that the cover sprang open and making a mental note of the time. 'Kindly clear the ship for action.'

'Yes, sir.'

Down on the main deck the ship's marine drummer

began to beat out the *Pas de Charge*, and the ship burst into life around him. Much of what happened was familiar to him from his long years in the navy, such as the dull thump of wedges being knocked free to let the bulkheads in his great cabin be taken down beneath his feet. Or the cook and his mate carrying the smouldering fire box from the galley stove between them to be dumped over the side. But much was new, like the long lines of sharpshooters making their way up the shrouds, a mixture of both sailors and marines, in much larger numbers than was usual. Or the canvas bags, knobbly with grenades, that followed them aloft. Then there was the profusion of weaponry laid out by the armourer and his mates along the centre line of the main deck. He could see thickets of short, stout boarding pikes with glittering tips and racks of cutlasses and tomahawks above the open chests of pistols. And the grappling hooks with their coiled lines positioned along both gangways. With a final flourish, the drum fell silent and Dupotet came across, touching his hat to his captain. 'The ship is ready for battle, sir.'

Lucas glanced down at his watch once more. 'Almost eleven minutes, Lieutenant,' he said. 'Better, but still too long. I want it under ten minutes before we face the English.'

'Yes, sir.'

Lucas glanced at the rest of the fleet moored around them and selected the nearest ship. 'Let us imagine that Spanish seventy-four there, the *Firme*, is our opponent. Open fire with the great guns, if you please.'

'Yes, sir.'

Although it was only an exercise, Lucas wanted it to be as close to the real thing as could be achieved. He left the quarterdeck and walked down the ladderway into the heart of his ship to join the men. The relay of orders seemed to be going smoothly enough, as the lieutenant in charge of each gundeck had the target pointed out to them, and transferred extra men from the disengaged side to reinforce those in action. The loading and firing was done without ammunition, with the petty officer in charge of each section chanting out the stages of the process. It was slower than the rapid fire achieved by the best Royal Navy ships, where gun crews were trusted to work as swiftly as they were able, but was much safer. Down on the lower deck the men were already streaming with sweat in the warm tropical air as they hauled the enormous thirty-six-pounders backwards and forwards, doubled over under the low deck beams. A ship's boy wandered past him in the gloom, carrying an empty leather charge case up from the magazine.

'Monsieur Morin,' Lucas said sharply. 'Why is a charge being brought up to a gun that has yet to fire?'

'My apologies, sir,' said the lieutenant. 'Some of the boys are feeling ill.'

'Then they should be sent to the surgeon,' said the captain. 'But they cannot be allowed to do that. There are six kilos of powder in the charge for one of these guns. Six kilos! Imagine the effect down here if one spark was to touch that?' He gestured across the packed deck. 'That is why the boys must wait for their gun to be fired before they go to fetch the next charge. Please speak to your men.'

'Yes, sir.'

Lucas stayed for another few silent broadsides, the watch back in his hand to see how swift they were. It was slower than he had hoped for, but still a marked improvement over their first action with the British frigate outside of Toulon, all those months ago. He made his way up through his ship and back into the sun and air of the quarterdeck to rejoin his first lieutenant. 'Very well, Camille. The enemy has taken some damage, now. Imagine that we have edged to within musket range.'

'Yes, sir,' said Dupotet. He looked upwards towards the mizzen top above their heads. 'Monsieur Dorre! Kindly engage with your men!'

The sound of orders and squealing gun-trucks from below was joined by the click of flintlocks and the rattle of ramrods from above, as those aloft pantomimed their part. Lucas stepped across to the rail, watching the men taking careful aim down at the deck of the imaginary ship looming ever closer through the smoke alongside. He tried to picture the effect of that musket fire. Again, he glanced at his watch. Another ten minutes of this should be about right, he decided. He looked across the anchorage, taking in the bemused crews on board nearby ships as they watched what the crew of the *Redoutable* were up to. Then he noticed a frigate rounding the headland, a line of signal flags rising up her mizzen halliard. 'Monsieur Pascal,' he barked. 'You should be reading that for me, not staring aloft.'

'Sorry, sir,' said the midshipman, grabbing his telescope with a start. 'She is the *Didon,* forty guns, with dispatches for the admiral.'

'Thank you,' said Lucas, turning back towards Dupotet. 'Now we are alongside! Give the signal, if you please!'

'Yes, sir. Captain Dorre! The trumpet!' ordered the first lieutenant.

Down on the main deck a bugle began to bray, and the crew of the *Redoutable* burst into renewed activity. From the decks beneath came the bang of closing port lids as the guns were secured, followed by the thunder of running feet as their crews poured up the ladderways, pausing only to arm themselves on the main deck, before continuing up on to the starboard gangway. From above came dozens of canvas balls, each the size of a grenade. They plunged into the sea alongside over a wide area, but some at least would have burst on an enemy's deck. Now the bulk of the sharpshooters were coming down the shrouds, fixing bayonets as they ran to join the rest of the crew. Soon the angle of the deck took on a noticeable heel beneath his feet as almost her entire crew thronged one gangway, armed and ready to board, looking aft towards their captain.

'Extraordinary,' muttered Dupotet beside him.

'Six minutes and twenty seconds after the order was given, and we are in a position to send five hundred armed men pouring across on to an enemy's deck,' announced Lucas, snapping shut the cover of his watch. 'No Royal Navy ship could possibly resist such an assault. It has been a most satisfactory exercise. Kindly have the ship restored and the watch dismissed below.'

'Yes, sir.'

'And I would be honoured if the wardroom would join me for dinner tonight, Camille.'

'Thank you very much, sir.'

*****

Later that day, when the sun had set, Brissot was pulling on his best uniform coat. It was the one his uncle's tailor had made, and even after so many months it still fitted him well. He straightened his waistcoat and hastened to join his fellow officers for dinner. As he stepped out of his cabin, he found himself alone in the wardroom with his first lieutenant. 'Good evening, sir,' he said.

'Good evening,' said Dupotet, who was adjusting his neck cloth using his reflection in the dark stern window. He tucked it into place and turned towards his fellow officer. 'How do I look?'

'Very creditable, sir,' said Brissot.

'Very creditable,' repeated Dupotet. 'Yes, I suppose that is the correct way of describing it.'

'Sir?'

'I was thinking about the exercise this afternoon. As you know, I have had my doubts about such an odd manner of fighting, but I may have misjudged you and Dorre. Your combination of sharpshooters and boarders may surprise an enemy with its boldness, after all. At least on the first occasion.'

'Thank you, sir,' said Brissot. He was surprised by the change in Dupotet's manner, but quickly hastened to capitalise on the moment. 'I … eh … I have been reflecting on my own views, also. Regarding politics.'

'Oh? To what end? Are you become a Bonapartist then?'

'No, not yet, sir,' smiled Brissot. 'But while I am by no means reconciled to France with an emperor, I can understand the benefits of the stability he brings, especially at time of war.'

'A grudging admission, if ever I heard one,' said the first lieutenant. 'So you don't concede that the Revolution was a mistake?'

'Certainly not, sir. The monarchy was both unjust and incapable of reform. Two thirds of our nation's wealth was owned by either the church or the nobility, both of whom were exempt from tax, leaving only the poorest to pay. In our home village we had two neighbours. One was a cobbler, the other a tavern keeper. The cobbler had to pay tax, but the other had a deed of nobility, a scrap of paper issued to his great-grandfather who had been a local justice in the time of Louis XIII! Quite absurd! It was such injustice that spurred my father on.'

'Have a care, Lieutenant,' said Dupotet. 'My father was just such a petty nobleman.'

'And did he think the system fair, sir?'

'I cannot say. He went to the guillotine before he could share his views with me. In the orgy of blood-letting that accompanied your modest reforms to the taxation system.'

'As did my own father,' said Brissot. 'It would seem we have that in common, at least, sir.'

'Let us at least shake hands on that, and then we must join the captain.'

'Yes, sir.'

The two officers were shown through into the great cabin and joined the others at table, where a lively discussion was taking place over the exercise earlier in the day.

'The trumpet came as a surprise,' said Marcel Paillard, the ship's surgeon. 'It seemed very un-naval. I am more accustomed to bells and bosuns calls regulating our affairs. Why, I had no knowledge that we even had such an instrument on board.'

'They are issued to the larger marine detachments found on ships of the line,' explained Dorre. 'Presumably for when we are ashore, not that I have ever seen fit to make use of ours. But it came to mind again when young Francois and I were trying to come up with a signal that could be heard above the tumult of a fleet action. And if it reached into the depths of the hull where you were stationed with your saw, doctor, it may answer very well.'

'I found today's exercise most satisfactory, gentlemen,' said Lucas, to general approval. 'Our gunnery still needs work, but the speed that the boarders were armed and assembled was most impressive. Certainly, Captain Courrege of the *Aigle* thought so. He sent word across to me earlier asking how it was achieved.'

'Do you think we may see a fleet action soon, sir?' asked Morin.

'Patience, *mon brave*,' said Lucas. 'There are too few Royal Navy ships to challenge us in these waters, and we must not allow ourselves to be distracted. Remember that our true objective lies on the far side of the ocean, but I do have something to relate. The arrival of the *Didon* earlier cannot have escaped your attention? With dispatches for the admiral and some welcome mail for us all?'

'The crew have been speaking of little else, sir,' confirmed Brissot. 'The general view is that she has been sent ahead from the Brest fleet with word of their imminent arrival.'

'Then I am sorry to disappoint you, Francois,' continued the captain. 'It would seem that Admiral Ganteaume has been unable to leave Brest, thanks to the strength of the English Channel Fleet. So instead we will be sailing to break him out. The admiral sent fresh orders across to me earlier today. Gentlemen, our ship is ready for battle, and we sail at dawn.'

Chapter 13
Caribbean

The waters of Carlisle Bay were the same astonishing shade of blue that Clay remembered from the first time he had arrived in Barbados, almost ten years earlier. The Bridgetown quayside still bustled with life, lined with trading brigs and island schooners, and the long curving beach still lay beneath its fringe of waving palm trees. Clay was admiring the view through the stern windows of the seventy-four *Northumberland*, as he waited for his host, Rear Admiral Alexander Cochrane, commander of the Windward Islands station, to read through the dispatch he had brought from Nelson.

‘’Tis a most pleasing sight, is it not, Captain,’ said the admiral, in his gentle Scottish burr. He was a solidly built man with iron grey hair. ‘Is it your first time in Barbados?’

‘By no means, sir,’ said Clay, returning his attention to his host. ‘I first made landfall here nine years back, when it was the most welcome of sights. I was a lieutenant then, the senior surviving officer on the *Agrius*, which was barely afloat with the pumps going day and night. Four days earlier we had fought with and defeated the *Courageuse*, a decidedly superior frigate, in the hottest action I was ever in.’

‘I remember reading of it at the time. The loss of Captain Follett was much lamented in the service, but it won you your promotion, did it not?’

'Your predecessor, Admiral Caldwell, was good enough to give me my step up to master and commander and appointed me to the sloop *Rush*, sir. I went on to take part in the capture of St Lucia.'

'So you will know these waters well enough,' said Cochrane. 'I doubt if this wee island has changed much in that time. The production of sugar is still the obsession of most, just as it was then.'

'I had hoped to renew some acquaintances from my time here, sir,' said Clay. 'Mr George Robertson, for example, who owns a plantation over Melverton way. His daughter married my ship's surgeon.'

'Mad Robertson, you mean? The fellow who freed his slaves on a whim? I know of him, but I have not had the pleasure of meeting his son-in-law. Nor will you have the leisure for such pleasantries, if I know Admiral Nelson. I had the honour of serving with his lordship in the Mediterranean, when I was captain of the *Ajax*, and found him to be a most active commander. It comes as little surprise to find him rushing across the broad Atlantic to come at the enemy. When do you suppose he will arrive?'

'He is but a few days behind me. I left his fleet near Madeira three weeks back, sir,' said Clay. 'He wished me to find out if Admiral Villeneuve has been seen?'

'Oh aye, he's here right enough. He appeared last month at Martinique with a damned great armada of ships, much to our consternation. He was quiet at first, but recently has started making a nuisance of himself. His frigates prey on the local trade, and he captured our Diamond Rock after a fierce action.'

'*Diamond Rock*, sir?' queried Clay. 'I haven't heard of a ship of that name?'

'Sure you have,' said Cochrane. 'A very fine frigate.

Quite unsinkable, on account of her stone hull, and armed with two long eighteens and a twenty-four-pounder. Lieutenant Maurice had command of her.'

'A frigate made from *stone*?' queried Clay. 'I'm not sure I have the pleasure of understanding you, sir.'

Cochrane burst into laughter. 'My apologies, Captain, but I am making game of you. Diamond Rock is an island we occupied, not six miles from the entrance to Port Royal in Martinique. But for the garrison to be able to draw provision and be paid, the Navy Board insist they must be serving on a ship. So, we were obliged to create that fiction, and commission HMS *Diamond Rock* into the navy in due form. And now it has fallen, I daresay the garrison commander will have to stand trial for the loss of his "ship"!'

Clay joined in his laughter. Like all commanders, he was aware of the hide-bound workings of naval bureaucracy. 'But I am still unclear how it came to be occupied at all, sir?'

'That was Sam Hood's doing, who was in command of the blockade back in the year three,' said the admiral. 'No one lives on the rock, so he let his crews visit the place in quieter moments for recreation. His first lieutenant, a fellow called Maurice, was a keen mountaineer and fancied climbing to the top. When he arrived at the summit, he realised that a lookout posted up there had a commanding view for twenty leagues in any direction. And if he had the benefit of a simple mast, word of the enemy could be quickly signalled to our ships. Furthermore, a few guns sited so high up would wholly dominate the area, to the great annoyance of the French. No sooner had he reported back, than Hood decided to occupy the place, with Lieutenant Maurice in command. And a mighty thorn in the French side it has proved. They have easily repelled numerous attacks, succumbing only to the attentions of two seventy-fours. In truth they might have defeated this assault too, but with Villeneuve's cruisers in the area, we have been unable to resupply them for over a month. The garrison had exhausted their fresh water just before the French attacked, so would have been compelled to surrender in any event.'

'What a remarkable tale, sir,' said Clay. 'Perhaps we shall be in a position to reoccupy the place when his lordship arrives.'

'That would depend on what force he brings with him.'

'He has nine of the line, sir,' said Clay. 'He was obliged to detach some of his ships to protect a troop convoy bound for the Mediterranean, now that Cadiz is no longer blockaded. What of the enemy?'

'Villeneuve has twenty of the line, with more joining all the time. Long odds, even for Nelson.'

'He had hoped to combine with your squadron, sir.'

'So he writes in his dispatch,' said Cochrane, lifting up the letter Clay had brought. 'And nothing would please me more than to sail into battle with his lordship. Alas, Vice Admiral Dacres in Jamaica has beaten him to it. He is quite persuaded that such an enemy concentration must presage an attack on that island, and has stripped me of four of my ships of the line to reinforce his command, leaving me only two ships of force – the one we are on, and the old *Spartiate*. Nelson is welcome to her, but that hardly changes the odds.'

'Perhaps I should sail for Kingston, in the hope of persuading him to reinforce Nelson, sir?'

'That would be quite futile,' said Cochrane. 'Dacres will sit on my ships like a brooding hen while Villeneuve is still a threat to his precious island. Also he is senior to Nelson, so he is as like to take some of his command, once he learns of his presence. No, I would proceed to Martinique to keep close watch on Villeneuve, as his lordship recommends in his dispatch, so you can return in a few days to furnish him with the latest position when he arrives.'

'You are right, sir,' said Clay. 'His lordship asked me to be the eyes of his fleet. Could you instruct the dockyard to revictual my ship with all dispatch, so that I can depart before sunset?'

'Consider it done,' said the admiral, rising to his feet and extending his hand. 'Good luck, Captain. I hope when we next meet, you will have the leisure to dine with me and tell me the particulars of the *Agrius*'s fight. Percy Follett was a good friend of mine.'

'That would be most welcome,' said Clay, his grey eyes unreadable.

*****

As things transpired, it was only a few days before Clay returned from Martinique. By then Nelson had arrived, and he hastened across to the flagship to report. The scene in the great cabin of the *Victory* was oddly reminiscent of his last visit, with Nelson and Hardy sitting at the rosewood table, and the admiral's secretary hovering in attendance. Only the grey-haired Cochrane was out of place, as he stood by one of the open windows, looking over a Carlisle Bay now filled with warships.

'Alexander, well met!' exclaimed Nelson, jumping up from his place. 'What news do you bring of the enemy?'

'That they have gone from Martinique, my lord.'

'Gone?' queried Nelson, falling back into his chair. 'What, all of them?'

'I fear so, my lord,' said Clay. 'The anchorage at Port

Royal was quite empty, save for a few local craft.'

'By Jove, that Villeneuve fellow is more slippery than an eel!' exclaimed Hardy.

'Perhaps these are good tidings, my lord,' observed Cochrane, coming over to join them. 'They cannot have long gone, for my sloop *Kingfisher* reported them still there Friday last, and their departure may be of help. It would have been difficult to come at the enemy in Martinique. Port Royal is protected by a fair-sized fortress and a number of shore batteries. A sea fight will be an altogether more straightforward affair.'

'I have oft heard you say that a ship is a fool to take on a fort, my lord,' added Hardy.

'I have also always said it is the business of an English commander-in-chief to bring the enemy fleet to battle, yet in that regard I have been found sadly wanting these last few months, Tom,' said Nelson, his face despondent. 'Does anyone know where the devil they may have gone?'

'I have some notion, my lord,' said Clay. 'Off Martinique I stopped a passing schooner bound for Grenada. The master claimed to have witnessed the fleet's departure from Port Royal. He said they had sailed northward. I searched in that direction, towards the enemy's other possessions of Guadeloupe and Marie Galante, but without success, after which I made haste to come and find you here.'

'Northward, you say?' exclaimed Cochrane. 'Oh, but that is very bad! The West India convoy is at sea. It will have left Jamaica for Bristol ten days back, touching at Antigua to pick up the Leeward Islands trade before heading out into the Atlantic. It never carries less than a quarter million in cargo. Rum, sugar and logwood, for the most part.'

'What protection does it have, sir?' asked Hardy.

'Nothing above a brace of sloops,' said Cochrane. 'Just enough to repel the attentions of any privateers. Villeneuve's frigates alone would suffice to bag the lot.'

'Then our duty is clear,' said Nelson. 'We must sail for Antigua, and hope the convoy will detain the enemy long enough for us to come at them. Let the merchantmen be the bait within the trap, if you will. Admiral, with battle in prospect, I shall need whatever assistance you can provide.'

'The *Spartiate* is yours, my lord,' said Cochrane. 'And I will happily accompany you with my flagship to take part in any action, although I cannot long abandon my station here in the Windward Islands. I only wish Admiral Dacres had left me with more of my ships to assist you. The odds will still be very much in the enemy's favour, I fear.'

'I have yet to fight an action when that has not been the case, my old friend,' said Nelson. 'And consider the other factors in our favour. A fleet drawn from two nations can never have the same unity of purpose as us, certain of the justice of our cause and confident in the fighting spirit of our men.'

'Hear him!' said Hardy. 'The French are out! Let's be having the blighters!'

'And what part would you have me play, my lord?' asked Clay.

'Why, that of Uriah the Hittite, leading us into battle, Alex,' said Nelson. 'Position yourself ahead of my frigate screen when the fleet sails, and find Villeneuve for me. I shall do the rest.'

'Aye aye, my lord.'

*****

The *Redoubtable* was at sea once more, sailing

northwards, the rearmost ship of the fleet. Far ahead was a screen of frigates, halfway to the horizon, probing forwards like the antennae of some huge sea-creature. All around was deep blue sea beneath a sky dotted with puffs of white.

On her quarterdeck Brissot was officer of the watch. He breathed in the fresh sea air and smiled with pleasure at being back at sea once more. Most of his naval career had been spent blockaded in port, so for the last few months he had felt like a newly released prisoner, delighting in all he saw around him. The paintwork on the hulls of the ships was weathered and salt-stained. Their sails had faded from crisp white to ochre in the tropical sun, but all that was positive. The novice crews that had started out from Toulon and Cadiz had now experienced at least one oceanic voyage, with a return crossing in prospect. They were still far from being veterans, but that would come in time. Down on the main deck Captain Dorre was busy supervising bayonet drill with his men, the sharp blades twinkling in the sunshine as they were thrust deep into a line of straw-filled targets. From beneath his feet came the squeal and rumble of gun-trucks as Lieutenant Morin's division practised gunnery with a section of lower-deck cannons. The only worrying sign was the twenty or so of the crew suffering from scurvy. From where he stood, he could see them sitting in the shade of an awning up on the forecastle, in the hope that sea air might help them.

'Deck there!' yelled the lookout. 'Sail in sight! Off the larboard quarter!'

Brissot focused his telescope in that direction. The horizon passing to the west of the fleet was broken by a long row of Caribbean islands rising from the sea. Dominica was level with them at the moment, her lush green slopes made blue by the distance. Against her looming bulk a large, topsail schooner with lofty masts was sailing out into deeper water, standing towards the south. The stars and stripes fluttered from her mizzen.

'Where are your damned eyes, Gaspard,' he demanded. 'She must have been in sight for half an hour at least!'

'Sorry, sir,' said the lookout.

Brissot snapped his telescope shut, annoyed with his own daydreaming as much as with the sailor's inattention. 'Monsieur Pascal, report the sighting to the flag, if you please,' he ordered. 'Monsieur Quellec, kindly find the captain and inform him that an American merchant ship is in sight off the stern quarter.'

'Yes, sir.'

Lucas appeared on deck, accepted the telescope proffered by his officer of the watch, and looked across at the schooner. 'She is magnificent looking, is she not, Francois,' he said. 'Very fast from her lines. She would make a fine privateer. Have we reported her to the admiral?'

'Yes, sir.'

The captain turned to look across at the *Bucentaure* sailing along in the midst of the fleet, just as signal flags began to rise up her mizzen halliard.

'Our number, sir,' reported the signal midshipman. 'Investigate sighting and report.'

'Acknowledge please,' ordered Lucas. 'And have the ship put about. Sailing so close to our fleet, I'm sure she is an American, but it is possible she could be an English ship flying their flag.'

'Yes, sir.'

'All hands! All hands to make sail!'

Beneath their feet ports were hastily banged shut as Morin secured the guns on the lower deck. On the main deck

Dorre's marines were elbowed aside by the rush of sailors pouring up the ladderways in response to the boatswain's call. The wheel went over, the topsail yards were hauled creaking around, and the *Redoutable* turned on to a new course to intercept the schooner.

Lucas watched for any sign of nervousness among the American crew as the bulky seventy-four loomed ever closer, but all seemed well. By her wheel stood a man wearing a buff-coloured coat looking back towards him through his own telescope. 'Signal to them to heave to, please, Monsieur Brissot,' he ordered.

'Yes, sir.'

The schooner rounded up into the wind smartly enough with her topsails backed and her big fore and aft sails shivering. The French ship lumbered around rather more cumbersomely with her first lieutenant yelling angrily at the crew from the quarterdeck rail.

Lucas hailed the schooner through his speaking trumpet. 'What ship is that, please?'

The man in the buff coat replied. '*Star of Maryland*, out of Baltimore. I'm her owner. Nathaniel Goddard's the name.'

'And what are you doing in these waters, Monsieur Goddard?'

'Trading. I bring best Virginian leaf out and return with a mix of sugar, rum and molasses. But I could ask you the same question, Captain. Mighty surprised to see such a deal of Frenchmen. I heard the Brits had your fleet locked up good and proper over the pond, yet here you all are. Why, I can't remember ever seeing so many of you. Spanish ships too, by the look of things.'

'Perhaps our fortunes are changing,' said Lucas. 'And France still has possessions in these waters to protect.'

'Right,' said the American, lowering his speaking trumpet to pull at his chin for a moment. 'So you folks being here ain't connected with that Nelson fellow pitching up in Bridgetown?'

'What!' exclaimed Lucas. 'Did you say Admiral Nelson? He is here?'

'Just showed up as I was leaving Barbados,' said Goddard, pointing southwards. 'With a fair-sized fleet, too.'

'How big?'

Goddard looked across at the Franco-Spanish fleet. 'Can't say as I counted them, but they had a lot too. Certainly a dozen, maybe more. So is there going to be a battle?'

'I sincerely hope not,' said Lucas.

'Oh, that is a shame. I would have paid a good few dollars to have seen that. But I daresay you folks are more interested in going after their convoy.'

'Convoy? What convoy?'

The American laughed at this. 'You fellers really don't go in for scouting much, do you? Why, they'll be somewhere up ahead. They generally leave Antigua about now, making for home. Never less than a dozen ships, often more. Sail north north-east from here, and I daresay you'll find them.'

'Thank you, Captain. You have been most helpful,' said Lucas. 'Have a prosperous voyage.'

'Don't mention it,' said Goddard, touching the brim of his hat. 'Makes a nice change from being stopped by the Royal Navy every other day, and at least you don't parade my crew looking for deserters. Besides, my uncle was at Yorktown, and told me what your countrymen did for us that day. Happy to pay down the debt. God watch over you, especially if you fall in with that Admiral Nelson.'

'Get the ship back underway!' yelled Lucas. 'Quickly

now! Nelson, a matter of days away! Make all sail to close with the flagship. There is not a moment to lose!'

*****

'And you are quite sure that you have no knowledge of any French or Spanish warships in this area, Captain?' asked Clay, pointing his speaking trumpet towards the American ship that rocked and swayed just under the *Griffin*'s quarter. 'They would have sailed from Martinique not above two days back.'

'I've not seen hide nor hair of them, sir,' said the master of the schooner. 'Perhaps they headed south?'

'No, that cannot be, for I would have past them,' said Clay. 'It is strange that you did not fall in with them, what with Martinique being so close.'

Before the American could reply, Clay's attention was caught by another sailor laughing as he exchanged a joke with the helmsman. The ship's master turned towards the pair and barked an order, after which both men adopted fixed expressions, staring forward. 'Apologies for that, sir. You were saying?'

Clay's eyes narrowed with suspicion. 'I trust you are not seeking to make game of me, Captain? Should I send one of my officers across with an armed boarding party to continue this conversation?'

'If you wish to, sir,' said the American. 'I would endeavour to make him welcome. I can assure you that my licences to trade are in order, and I have some fine aged rum from Barbados in my cabin if he would care for a glass?'

Clay was sorely tempted to follow through on his threat, sure that he was being deceived, but already one of the other frigates in the screen, the *Amazon*, was well over the horizon.

The rest of Nelson's fleet would not be far behind, making all sail to come up with the enemy.

'That will not be necessary,' said Clay. 'Fortunately for you time does not permit any distraction from my purpose. Good day, captain.'

'And to you, sir,' replied the schooner's master.

Clay watched the American ship depart as the frigate got under way once more. He read the name painted in bold white letters across its counter, *Star of Maryland.*

'What did you make of that, sir?' asked Taylor. 'Have we missed Villeneuve once more?'

'By no means, George,' said Clay. 'Mr Goddard of Baltimore may be passing good at dissembling, but his crew are not. No, I believe we are very much on the right track.'

The frigate stood on once more towards the north, beating against the wind blowing in from the open Atlantic. Her round bow butted into each roller, shouldering through the sea and sending a dazzling foam of white boiling down the ship's side and into the long line of wake behind her. It was the sort of sailing Clay usually enjoyed the most, with the hull heeling over and every shroud humming in the wind, but today he was too anxious to find his elusive enemy at last. All day the *Griffin* battled on, hour after hour, without sight of Villeneuve's fleet, until he began to wonder if the captain of the schooner had been telling the truth. Perhaps he really had not seen the enemy, and the sailor had just been sharing an innocent joke with the helmsman? But at last, when the sun was beginning its long plunge down to the western horizon, there came a cry from the masthead.

'Deck there! Sail ho!'

'Where away, Dawson?' yelled Clay.

'Point off the bow, sir! Man o' war, from the look of

her.'

'Away with you, Mr Sweeney,' said Preston, who had the watch. 'Take a glass aloft, and tell us what you make of her.

'Aye aye, sir.'

Both officers watched the youngster fly up the rigging with a twinge of envy. Preston, because his lost arm that meant he could never again emulate such a breathless climb, and Clay because of the fear of heights he had long kept secret, that had meant his own time as a midshipman had been spent in dread of clambering aloft.

'Man of war for certain, sir!' reported Sweeney, sitting with his feet dangling in the air with one arm nonchalantly draped around the topgallant mast. 'A frigate, from the look of her.' There was a pause while Dawson bent towards him, pointing. 'And another sail, sir! Beyond the first. Could be another frigate!'

'Will you kindly signal the admiral via the *Amazon*, Mr Todd,' said Clay. 'Unidentified warships, numeral two, in sight bearing north-north-east.'

'Aye aye, sir.'

As they pressed on, the first of the two frigates slowly appeared above the horizon, her rear quarter towards the British ship. The very fact that she was not coming to investigate the *Griffin* told Clay she could not be Royal Navy.

'*Amazon* is signalling, sir,' announced Todd. 'It's an acknowledgement from the flag.'

'Thank you,' said Clay, wondering how far behind Nelson was. The length of time it had taken for his signal to be acknowledged suggested that it had been repeated by several ships, which meant he might be as much as fifty miles away. He looked towards the sun, estimating how much daylight remained. It would be long after dark before they could possibly arrive.

'Deck there!' called Sweeney. 'Chase is signalling, and I think I can see some more sails on the horizon.'

'A fleet?' questioned Clay.

'Hard to say, sir. Certainly several ships. They are only just visible beyond the second frigate.'

'Signal the sighting to the admiral, Mr Todd,' ordered Clay. 'Be sure to say that it is an unidentified fleet.'

'Aye aye, sir'

'Villeneuve at long last, sir?' suggested Preston.

'Maybe,' said his captain, looking towards the south where the *Amazon* followed them, her sails beautifully cross lit by the sun sinking towards the west. 'But she signalled the moment she sighted the *Amazon* appearing behind us. Look. Now she is making sail to get away.' As they watched a puff of grey smoke blossomed into life beside the French frigate, although they were too far away to hear the gun firing.

'Whatever that signal was about, they certainly want it attended to, sir,' said Preston.

Clay looked towards the mainmast shrouds, his desire to learn what was happening ahead almost overcoming his fear of the climb. Then his natural good sense reasserted itself. Sweeney and Dawson had much keener eyes than his.

'Masthead there!' he yelled. 'What do you make of those ships beyond the chase?'

'Maybe a dozen or so sails on the far horizon, sir,' said Sweeney. 'But it is hard to tell what they are.'

'Them frigates be making for them like the devil be astern, sir,' supplemented Dawson.

'I think I may be able to see some of the fleet, sir,' reported Preston, who had clambered up on the carriage of a quarterdeck carronade. 'Now, that is odd. What can that be?'

Clay sprang up beside him and extended his telescope. Ahead was the stern of the French frigate, heeling over with all sail set in her haste to get away. Beyond her was the second frigate and then, as the Griffin lifted to a wave, he saw a few tiny flashes of white, the upper sails of ships beyond the horizon. But it was the pale evening sky that caught his attention. Rising from where the concealed fleet lay was a faint line of grey, like a pencil stroke on a drawing. As the frigate sailed on it was joined by a second line.

'Mr Sweeney! Attend to the sky beyond the fleet! What do you see?'

'Faint lines in the sky, sir,' said the midshipman. 'Three of them, but they are hard to make out in this light. Might it be smoke?'

'Smoke? What are the French playing at?' asked Preston.

Clay watched as one of the lines thickened into a solid bar of black, and at last he understood what must be happening. The *Griffin*'s bold approach, her signals to the empty horizon, the appearance of a second warship and the French frigate's sudden flight. His mind told him what his eyes could not. He looked towards the west. The sun was touching the horizon, filling the sky with crimson fire and turning the frigate's sails to scoops of coral.

'Is the *Amazon* still in signalling range, Mr Todd?'

'I believe so, sir.'

'Send this to the admiral. Fleet ahead is West Indian convoy. Now in French hands.'

'Aye aye, sir.'

'Deck there!' called Sweeney. 'Definitely smoke, sir. One of the far ships at least has taken fire. And another now!'

As the sun vanished, the *Griffin* stood on across a sea of

palest blue towards the columns of swirling smoke on the horizon. Then, in tiny increments, the tropical night crept from out of the east, and sea and sky grew darker. The two French frigates had vanished into the gloom, as had the *Amazon* astern. As the fiery glow of the sun vanished it was replaced by a fresh stain of red in the sky to the north, getting steadily closer.

*****

The *Griffin* stole across the dark water beneath a sky stippled with stars. Only a single reefed topsail pushed her forward, allowing her longboat and launch out on either side to keep pace. On board, her guns were run out and manned as she entered the field of debris that was all that remained of the West Indian convoy.

Lines of wood smoke lay like river mist across the surface of the water, lit by the flicker of tiny flames that still licked across the tops of some of the large pieces of wreckage. Balks of timber and floating barrels knocked and clattered against the frigate's hull, or slopped and pulled in the gentle waves.

'Ahoy!' called Blake through a speaking trumpet. 'Anyone there?'

Clay watched as the launch backed water, to free an oar from a web of torn canvas and straggling rope just below the surface. To starboard one of the burning fragments had drifted close, golden firelight shimmering across the surface of the water, but Taylor had a party of men ready with spars to pole it away.

'Anyone ahoy!' yelled Blake again, and this time there came an answering hail from out of the darkness.

Clay peered in that direction and caught sight of the

splash of oars as a boat picked its way towards them. 'Heave to, if you please, Mr Armstrong.'

'Aye aye, sir.'

The boat came alongside, into the pool of light from the lanterns held out from the rail by some of the afterguard. It proved to be a large launch, with a mast stepped and provisions piled along the centre line. Thirty tired-looking sailors rested on their oars or peered upwards, blinking in the light. Then they came scrambling on board, helped by the crew of the frigate. They were followed more slowly by a grey-haired man in a blue coat who had been sitting in the stern sheets.

'Greetings, sir,' said Clay. 'Welcome aboard the *Griffin*. My name is Alexander Clay, commander of this ship.'

'And a gratifying sight you are too, Captain,' said the man, grasping his hand. 'William Ashmole, master of the *Shearwater* of Bristol. The finest brig on the Jamaica run, or she was before the damned French torched her down to the waterline.'

'Mr Blake, my compliments to the cook and kindly ask him to provide a hot meal for these men,' order Clay. 'And you can resume the search.'

'Beg pardon, Captain,' said Ashmole, 'but I doubt you'll find more out here than us. The French took the rest of the crews with them.'

'Indeed? I see there is more to tell of what has happened here,' said Clay. 'Would you care to come below with me, Mr Ashmole, and take some refreshment? Then perhaps you can tell me the particulars.'

Down in Clay's cabin Harte had lit most of the lamps, and was setting a place at Clay's table for the new arrival.

'Do please take a seat,' urged Clay. 'A glass of wine for you? And something to eat?'

'Wine will suffice for the present, I thank you, sir,' said Ashmole. 'In truth I have not long been adrift.' He pulled out the chair and then stopped, a puzzled look on his face. 'There would seem to be some dashed odd-looking ship's cat asleep here.'

'Ah, that will be our mongoose. We are but lately returned from the east, and he is held in high affection by my crew. Kindly remove him, Harte.'

'Come along, Nap,' said the steward, scooping up the docile creature in his arms. 'Back to the lower deck with you. The gentleman don't care for your hairs all over his britches.'

'Would you be so good as to relate what has happened to you and your ship?' asked Clay, once the two men were seated with glasses of wine.

'Our voyage began well enough,' explained Ashmole. 'We left Jamaica a fortnight back, in company with twenty others and a brace of king's ships for our protection; the sloop of war *Barbados*, and the armed schooner *Netley*. We touched at Antigua four days back, and were joined by the trade from the outer islands, after which we set off for home. Two days back we fell in with the largest damned fleet I ever clapped eyes on. Frenchmen as well as Dons, arriving one after another until the sea was thick with the blighters. Ships of the line, for the most part, along with a half dozen big frigates. I tell you; the Channel Fleet weren't in it!'

'I knew that damned Yank was playing me false!' exclaimed Clay.

'I beg pardon, Captain?'

'A Baltimore schooner I met with that claimed not to have seen the French,' explained Clay.

'Indeed? For my part I find my dealings with Americans tolerable enough. They are good seamen, as a rule, although I daresay that some of the older ones still hold a grudge over the war.'

'I must have had the misfortune to encounter one of those. No matter. So where did you meet with this fleet, exactly?'

'Nineteen degrees and twelve minutes north. Sixty degrees twenty-seven west by dead reckoning. They all came up from the south.'

'Thank you, Mr Ashmole,' said Clay, noting down the location. 'Pray continue.'

'As you can imagine, there was little that the escort could do in the face of such an armada but order us to scatter like hens before a fox, and then take flight themselves. A few of the swifter ships got clear, but the enemy captured the greater part of us, including my *Shearwater*. They put a prize crew on board and confined my men to the forecastle, although I was allowed the freedom of my cabin and the deck in exchange for my word not to engage in any mischief.'

'How did you find them?'

'Perfectly amiable,' said Ashmole. 'The midshipman in charge was no more than a youngster, but the crew were competent enough, for Frenchmen, although there was something about them that I found curious. We had a fair amount of fresh provender on board to see us through to Bristol, and they fell upon it.'

'They were hungry, then?'

'No, for they seemed well fed. This was more like men will do when they have a touch of the scurvy. The mind compels you to consume what the soul desires. I have seen it before, when I was first mate on a ship that was dismasted in a blow. Most of the men caught the scurvy and when we eventually made port, they acted much the same.'

'That is very interesting,' said Clay, making another note. 'Once you were taken, what happened next?'

'Their fleet headed on its way, leaving the prizes in the charge of two of their frigates.'

'And do you know where they were bound?'

'They were bending a course towards Europe when they left us,' said Ashmole. 'And I believe I may know their object. I have traded in these waters for many a long year, and to do so you need to acquire a facility with several foreign tongues, including French. From the talk I overheard between the midshipman and his petty officer they are seeking a rendezvous with their Brest fleet. Of course, that may have just been gunroom tittle-tattle.'

'Perhaps, but it is what we fear they are about,' said Clay, making another note. 'Might we come to the events of this day?'

'The morning passed quietly enough. I checked on my crew, and saw they had occasion to exercise and take the air. At midday I helped their midshipman with his noonday sighting. He seemed a little uncertain how an almanac worked, and even as a prisoner, I still preferred to make port in some degree of safety. One of their frigates was a few miles to the southward of us, the other further off. In the afternoon the more distant one must have spotted you, which caused a deal of consternation. There was much talk of Lord Nelson being in the offing. Then when a second ship was reported behind yours, the French resolved to destroy the convoy rather than to permit its recapture. Both frigates closed with us and launched all their boats to take off their men and the original crews, before setting a fire in each hold.'

'I guessed as much,' said Clay, nodding at this. 'So how did you and your men come to be set adrift?'

'By now I was on friendly terms with the lad in charge of the *Shearwater*. He was pleasant enough, no older than my boy at home, so I pleaded my case with him. I told him that my men and I had spent three years locked up at Valenciennes in the last war, and couldn't face the prospect of prison again, and that we would sooner take to the ship's launch and chance making our way back to Antigua. With his lieutenant bawling at him to make haste, he eventually agreed to let us go.'

'Goodness, that was bold!' exclaimed Clay. 'Antigua is a fair distance in an open boat.'

'In truth, I had hoped to come back on board the moment the French had fled, douse the flames and save my ship, but by then the blaze had reached the rum in the forward part of the hold and the old *Shearwater* was doomed.'

'A sad loss, for any captain,' said Clay, raising his glass in salute. 'I lost my previous command, also to fire.'

Both men drained their glasses, and there was a moment of quiet as Harte refilled them.

'The last report I had of Lord Nelson was that he was off Toulon,' resumed Ashmole. 'Can he truly be in these parts?'

'Indeed he is, just below the horizon, with the greater part of our Mediterranean Fleet,' said Clay. 'His lordship can be most determined when coming at the French is in prospect. He has chased them all the way here from Europe, and I daresay he will chase them all the way back again if he must. And God help Villeneuve if Nelson should prove the swifter.'

'Amen to that,' said Ashmole.

Chapter 14
Cadiz

A month after the destruction of the convoy, Villeneuve's fleet was out in the vastness of the Atlantic, heading back towards Europe. It was midsummer and they had still not encountered Nelson. But no sooner had one threat to the fleet receded than another, more sinister, had taken its place. On board the *Redoutable*, Brissot was making his way along the lower gundeck. With the ship at sea, the ports were bolted shut, so that little natural light or fresh air filtered down from the brightly lit world above. In the gloom, the watch below sat listlessly at tables placed between the guns. He had seldom seen the crew so quiet. There were none of the usual lively games of cards in progress. No sailors gathered to listen to a Breton piper or Gascon flautist perform for his messmates. Instead, he felt as if he had entered an enchanted world, where the men were held under some spell.

The forward part of the *Redoutable*'s lower gundeck was a sectioned-off area called the manger. It was usually reserved for the ship's livestock. But the half a dozen bullocks and two dozen sheep taken on board when they left Toulon had long since been butchered and consumed by her hungry crew, and no replacements had been available in Martinique to replace them. Now the space had been scrubbed clean and freshly painted, so that only a modest tang of farmyard remained, and it was being used as a temporary sickbay.

Despite the canvas wind chutes installed to bring some breeze down from the forecastle, it was a hot, airless place. To make matters worse, most of the patients were packed shoulder to shoulder in a layer of hammocks strung from the beams. The more advanced cases lay upon straw pallets on the deck beneath them.

Brissot gagged a little at the smell as he went beyond the canvas screen separating the sick bay from the rest of the ship. Immediately in front of him was one of the surgeon's assistants, dressed in a filthy apron, blood-letting the occupant of the nearest hammock. Brissot watched as he nicked an artery with the blade of a fleam stained dark from previous patients, releasing a stream of crimson down into a chamber pot placed on the deck. After a while the man tightened a band of canvas around his patient's upper arm to staunch the flow, wiped the wound with the sleeve of his shirt, and turned towards the officer. 'Can I help, sir?' he asked.

'Yes, I wish to check on the condition of some of the men of my division,' said Brissot, swallowing hard.

'Of course, sir. Would you like to come this way?' The man dropped the fleam into the pocket of his apron, tucked the chamber pot under one arm and led the way deeper into the sickbay. They passed patients in all the various stages of advanced scurvy. Some had kicked off their blankets in the heat, revealing pale skin marked with a mix of livid spots and dark bruises. One sailor they passed was sleeping with a mouth wide open to reveal gums swollen and brown.

'Here we are, sir,' said the assistant. 'Your lot are from this hammock to the bulkhead over there.'

'Thank you,' said Brissot, stepping up to the first patient in the line. 'Du Chemin, are you awake?'

The sailor opened his eyes to reveal whites the colour

of butter. 'Is that you, sir?' he croaked, his mouth gap-toothed and bloody.

'Yes,' confirmed the officer, leaning closer to hear. 'I've come to see how you are feeling?'

'Like shit, sir, beg pardon,' said the sailor. He moved around gingerly, one arm heavily strapped between wooden splints.

'What's the matter with your arm? When did you break it?'

'When I was a lad, sir. I was too slow witted when my uncle's fishing boat jibbed and the boom knocked me down the hatchway for a caution. I'd forgotten all about it, 'til the bone unknit once more. The doc says the Grey Killer can do that. Old scars open up fresh an' all, like poor Martin over there.' He indicated a man in nearby hammock, who had a blood-stained bandage wrapped around his fore-arm. 'A knife wound from a fight ten year back, that is, if you'll credit it.'

'And how are they treating you?'

'Taking our blood and giving us drafts of vinegar in its stead,' reported Du Chemin. 'Not that it seems to be helping any. They'll be moving me down to join those on the deck, before long. Then there's no hope after that.' He gripped his officer's arm. 'Will you see that they bury me ashore, sir? Not pitch me over the side for the fishes. When my time comes, like?'

'No need for that sort of talk,' said Brissot. 'I'm sure you'll be better soon.' He patted the sailor on his good hand with a smile of reassurance, and moved on towards the next hammock.

'Lieutenant, what an unexpected pleasure,' said a cultured voice from behind him. 'My assistant said you were visiting your men.' He turned to see a tall young man in the plain blue coat of a naval surgeon. He had appeared from behind the *Redoutable*'s bowsprit, the thick trunk of which ran diagonally down from the deck above.

'Monsieur Paillard,' said Brissot, taking the surgeon's proffered hand. 'I understand now why you haven't been able to join us in the wardroom of late. Is there any hope for them?'

'Would you care to step through to my dispensary?' said Paillard, holding a finger to his lips, before leading the way.

The two officers walked back along the gundeck and down the ladderway to the orlop. The dispensary was a tiny space towards the stern, its bulkheads lined with shelves. These were crammed with small boxes and squat glass bottles, each one with a label in the surgeon's handwriting. Beneath the shelves the deck was stacked with sturdy chests and big straw-covered demi-johns with ground-glass stoppers. Paillard indicated the only chair at the tiny desk to his visitor and pulled up a chest for himself to sit on. He pushed a pestle and mortar to one side and replaced it with a bottle and two glasses he produced from a drawer.

'Cognac, Francois?' he asked, uncorking the bottle. 'I know I certainly need one.'

'A small glass, please.'

'*Santé*,' said Paillard. He drained his quickly, and sloshed some more into his glass, while Brissot sipped at his.

'Ah, that is better,' said the surgeon. 'Sorry for bringing you away like that, but it is best not to converse openly in front of the men. One of the few tools I do have to combat this terrible malady is keeping my patients from despair.'

'I apologise for not warning you that I intended to visit.'

'No need for that. In truth I wish that more of the wardroom would take an interest in the men's welfare. The captain comes each day, of course, as does Morin, but our noble first lieutenant has yet to visit at all, and our second lieutenant only the once.'

'Monsieur Dupotet has much on his plate, at present, with so many sailors unable to work.'

The surgeon raised an eyebrow at this. 'Well, you have changed your tune! Have the two of you been reconciled?'

'More of a truce, really. And how is the war with scurvy going?'

'I am steadily losing it,' said Paillard. 'Most of the crew are showing some sign of the disease. You cannot have failed to spot the general lassitude affecting them. Of the more serious cases, twelve have died and I am currently treating another fifty-four.'

'And yet the officers seem unaffected,' mused Brissot.

'The officers are unaffected by it *yet,*' corrected the surgeon. 'That is often the way, thanks to the superior diet of the wardroom, but have no fear, our time will come, Francois. Dorre came to see me earlier complaining of fatigue and sore joints, which are the first signs of its onset.'

'And how are you treating the men, Marcel?' asked Brissot. 'Apart from offering them hope.'

'I follow the latest instruction from the School of Naval Medicine in Rochefort,' explained Paillard. 'Bleeding of the patients, to rebalance the grosser humours, and drafts of an acidic nature. Ideally that would be lemon juice, as the enemy uses, but in its absence, I am obliged to use vinegar in its place.'

'And do you find it to be efficacious?'

'Not in the slightest,' said Paillard. 'The physician of the fleet suggested increasing the acidity of the dose by adding elixir of vitriol to the vinegar, but I have observed no improvement.'

'Back in Martinique, when the first signs appeared, one

of my men tried drinking the juice of limes, and he still seems healthy.'

'That is interesting,' mused the surgeon. 'I suppose your lime is very like to a lemon in general form and appearance. It is a shame that I didn't acquire any when we were there, although I doubt that I would have found enough to treat all the sufferers we have. Most of the island's agriculture seems devoted to the production of sugar.'

'How does the rest of the fleet fare?' asked Brissot.

'We are rather more fortunate than most, thanks to our captain, and his insistence on cleanliness and fresh provisions for the crew,' explained Paillard. 'He is a keen student of naval exploration, and has read the observations of Vancouver, Baudin, Cook and de Bougainville. Do you know that Cook never lost a man to the scurvy in his three great voyages?'

'So why are we suffering an outbreak?'

'Because that tiny island we visited would have struggled to supply a handful of ships with fresh food, let alone a fleet this large,' said the surgeon. 'The purser tried his best, but what was available in the markets was all snapped up as soon as it appeared. No, the only solution is a swift return to Europe, where there is fresh provender to feed such a multitude, before we are reduced to a ghost fleet.'

'The rumour is that the emperor may have ordered us to Brest, to clear the English from before the port and release Admiral Ganteaume's ships from their blockade.'

'Out of the question!' said Paillard. 'We would take another month to reach Brittany, by which time those who are still alive will not have the strength left to run out the guns. It would be madness.'

'Have you told the captain this?

'Of course! We must make for a port with plentiful

provisions, where we can restore the health of the men! Ferrol in Spain I understand to be the nearest. Then we can fight the emperor's battle. It is imperative that he persuades the admiral of this.'

'Actually, we should sail for Cadiz,' mused Brissot.

'Is it nearer?

'No, but it is close to where the Spanish grow their lemons, and only a little further off than Ferrol. If we need to restore the men as soon as possible, it is to there that I would go.'

'Francois,' said Paillard, leaning across the little desk. 'I am just a doctor. You are a fighting officer, and one that the captain listens too and respects. Speak with him, I beg you. Before it is too late.'

*****

While Paillard and Brissot were discussing how best to restore the crew of the *Redoutable* to health, a few hundred miles away Clay was contemplating the simpler task of clambering up the side of the *Victory*. Last time he had come on board had been in the calm waters of Carlisle Bay, with the flagship resting at her moorings. But now they were far from land, and the big three-decker was rolling and plunging in a lively cross sea. Each wave passing under Clay's barge sent it several feet up her side, before dropping back down again into the following trough. And to add to the challenge of the task, a recent rain squall had thoroughly wetted the steps of the side ladder.

'Shall I hail for a bosun's chair, sir?' suggested his coxswain from the stern sheets.

'No need, Sedgwick,' said Clay, standing with one foot

on the thwarts. 'It is just a matter of awaiting the right moment.' The barge swooped up once more, and as it approached its zenith Clay launched himself across to the ship's side.

'Can I lend you a dry pair of britches, Alexander?' said Hardy, contemplating his fellow captain's attire, gold laced splendour from the waist up, a dripping morass below. 'Deuced tricky getting on board when the sea is running like this. It was fortunate that you had a good grip on the hand rails, or we might have lost you to the waves all together.'

'Indeed,' said Clay, his face flushed with embarrassment. 'Britches would be most welcome, Tom, along with a pair of stockings, if you can spare them.'

'My compliment to his lordship, and tell him Captain Clay and I will be with him directly,' said Hardy to one of his midshipmen.

'Aye aye, sir.'

'Come through to my cabin,' said Hardy, leading the way. 'We can't have you taking a chill.'

The marine sentry at the door wore the stone face of someone determined not to laugh, as he snapped to attention at their approach. 'Tyler!' yelled Hardy. 'A towel for Captain Clay, and come and help him shift out of his clothes.'

'Aye aye, sir.'

'We are much the same height, but I fear my coat may be a little large on you,' said Hardy.

'No matter, for it was only the tails that were thoroughly wetted.'

Tyler proved very efficient, quickly towelling Clay dry and dressing him with Hardy's rather baggier garments. He did his best to mop out Clay's shoes so that they only left modest footprints as he crossed the great cabin to join Nelson.

'My dear sir, are you quite restored?' asked the admiral,

all concern. 'Can I pass word for a hot brick? Or a warm beverage?'

'My thanks, your lordship, but Captain Hardy has furnished me with dry clothes which is all I require. It is hardly the first time I have been drenched in the service of my king, and I daresay it shan't be the last.'

'Indeed so,' said Nelson, waving across his steward with a decanter of Madeira.

'And I trust I find your lordship well?' asked Clay, accepting a glass. Sunbeams reflecting from off the sea outside played across the cabin ceiling, and in their light he thought the admiral looked pale and tired.

'I am as well as my shattered constitution permits, I thank you, but I must confess this interminable chase is weighing heavy on my spirits. But it is nothing that getting up with the French will not cure. Which is why I sent for you, Alexander. For a month we have searched, with our frigates spread wide, yet we have still seen no sign of them. How is it that they have managed to vanish once more, do you suppose?'

'Think back to the months before our victory at the Nile, my lord. We lost contact with the French then too, for weeks on end, and that was in the confined waters of the Mediterranean. Small wonder if it has happened in the Atlantic. We would have only had to choose a course a few degrees different from theirs to never cross paths with them.'

'Very like,' said Hardy. 'If I remember right back then, we even passed their fleet at night, without spotting them. We only found how close we had been from the captured logbooks on the prizes.'

'Very well,' said Nelson. 'So what would you gentlemen recommend we do? Change course in the hope of finding him?'

Both captains shook their heads at this. 'There is too much ocean to scour, my lord,' said Hardy. 'Better to arrive at his destination and force battle on him when he arrives. We can meet him outside Brest in company with the Channel Fleet.'

'I am not certain that is his destination, Tom,' said Clay.

'But dash it all, Alexander! Didn't that Ashmole chap report he had heard exactly that?' fumed Hardy.

'What he actually said was that that they were heading to Europe to seek a rendezvous with the Brest fleet,' said Clay. 'Such a union could occur anywhere.'

'True, but outside Brest would make sense,' persisted Hardy.

'Would it?' queried Clay. 'Where our Channel Fleet is on hand and certain to intervene? And then consider, why did Villeneuve leave Martinique and returned home?'

'Because he was frit, and didn't fancy fighting us,' growled Hardy.

'No, that can't be it,' said Clay. 'Remember I was several days ahead of you. When I arrived at Martinique, Villeneuve had already gone. But you were still at sea, two days out from Barbados. He left before word of your arrival could have possibly reached him, which can only mean he must have received fresh instructions from Paris.'

'And what do you deduce those instructions were?' asked Nelson.

'To return to Europe, clearly, my lord. And doubtless to rendezvous with the Brest fleet, but I doubt he was ordered to go directly there. Think of the time taken for such orders to reach Martinique from France, and for Villeneuve to recross the ocean. He would be arriving off Brest with instructions based on information that was three months out of date, at best. No one this side of Bedlam would send a fleet into action based on such poor intelligence.'

'I agree it would be bold, even rash,' said Nelson. 'But surely boldness is something we should expect of Boney?'

'Of Bonaparte, perhaps, but not of Villeneuve, my lord,' said Clay. 'The man who abandoned the fight at the Nile to save his command would not attempt something so reckless. Besides, his fleet will be in no condition to fight when it arrives at Brest. Remember that Captain Ashmole also reported the prize crew on the *Shearwater* were suffering from some of the early signs of the scurvy. We are a month on from then, and all of that time Villeneuve's fleet will have been at sea, with another month in prospect before they reach Brest.'

'And neither the French nor the Spanish issue their men with lemon juice as we do,' mused Hardy. 'You make a good case, Alexander.'

'So where do you think they will go?' asked Nelson.

'Somewhere they can resupply and restore the health of their crews and learn the latest position, my lord,' said Clay. 'Rochefort is too small for such a fleet, Ferrol in Spain would be a better choice. But if it was me, I would head for Cadiz. Not least because the Dons will have got more of their ships into service by now.'

'And if you are wrong, and they are bound for Brest?' asked Nelson.

'It matters not, my lord,' said Clay. 'They will be so riddled by the scurvy that the Channel Fleet will defeat them as easy as kiss my hand.'

'I am glad you came across, Alexander,' said Nelson. 'Even at the expense of a dunking. You cheer me with your spirit, and few of my captains have your facility to get to the nub of matters. I am convinced. Off you go to Cadiz. The fleet will head for Gibraltar first, for we too are in need of resupply, and then I shall join you there. Then we shall see what we shall see.'

'Pass the word for Captain Clay's barge,' roared Hardy towards the cabin door. 'And see that a boatswain's chair is rigged for him this time.'

*****

It was almost the end of August, and the sun was heavy and full as it beat down on the *Griffin*. All around her was the same vast disc of blue ocean that had been there for week after week, yet her crew could sense that land was growing close, as they approached the funnel of sea between Spain and Africa once more.

Dawson was the first to notice the change, as he clambered up the shrouds to replace the younger Saleem brother as lookout. He stood on the main topgallant yard, a dizzy hundred and seventy feet above the surface of the Atlantic, and sniffed at the air flowing past from the south east.

'Get a whiff of that, Saleem lad,' he said. 'That ain't yer regular sea air.'

The Indian sailor raised his nose to the breeze. 'No indeed not, shipmate. It is being musty and warm also.'

'Aye. That be desert air, straight from the wastes of Barbary. When it blows strong, I've heard tell of it smothering a ship in dust fine as snuff, even out at sea. I reckon we'll be a touching land afore long. Maybe this watch.'

Clay, far beneath the two sailors, was thinking back to the spring, when the ship had been bubbling over with excitement at the prospect of returning home. Then they had run into Villeneuve's fleet, and duty had compelled him to abandon thoughts of Lydia and the children waiting for him back in Lower Staverton. They had been in these same waters, searching for a British squadron to report their sighting to, and had eventually found Nelson's fleet at Gibraltar. If only he had known then that four months and two crossings of the Atlantic later he would still be no nearer home. Perhaps he might have used the little admiral's famous blind eye to ignore the enemy fleet, and carry on to Plymouth.

The day was beginning to take on a strange sense of déjà vu. The set of the waves beneath the *Griffin*'s hull were subtly changing once more as the sea bed rose beneath him, just as they had last time he was here. The sea birds were less numerous than in the spring, but every bit as raucous. And the dhows and distant trading brigs sped away from the frigate's path once more. And just as then, Armstrong appeared on deck with Taylor beside him, confident of another successful landfall.

'Will it be Cape St Vincent once more, Jacob?' he asked.

'Indeed, sir, unless I am sadly out in my reckoning,' confirmed the American. 'She should be appearing on our larboard bow presently.'

'What do you suppose we will find, sir?' asked Taylor.

'I wish I knew, George,' said Clay. 'Word of Villeneuve's fleet being out will have reached London, but I am uncertain as to what dispositions will have been made in consequence. But when we were last here the Dons were busy bringing more of their ships into commission at Cadiz, so we may find friends watching that port.'

'Deck there! Land ahoy!' bellowed Dawson. 'A point off the larboard bow.'

'Well done, Jacob. Mr Taylor, kindly bring us in towards Cadiz, if you please.'

'Aye aye, sir.'

The point of land grew steadily into the southern coast of Portugal. The distant hillsides were clothed in pine forests and the sea close to the shore was dotted with the triangular sails of little fishing boats. Then the coast swung to the south as hostile Spain replaced neutral Portugal. The hills here were bare, baked brown after months of hot Andalusian sun, and backed by distant mountains.

'Deck there! Sail ahoy!'

'Where away, Dawson?' called Clay.

'Right ahead, sir. Squadron of man o' war, I reckon. Standing towards us.'

'Take a glass aloft, Mr Russell, if you please. Let me know what you make of them.'

'Might they be Spanish, sir,' asked Taylor. 'This close to Cadiz?'

'They might, George, but I'd wager they are our blockading ships.'

With the *Griffin* and the squadron on converging courses it was not long before Russell was able to report on the approaching ships. 'Deck there!' he yelled. 'There's three of them, all ships of the line. Third rates and a three-decker. Ours, by the look of them. I think the three-decker has an admiral's duster at the forepeak.'

'I wonder which vice admiral it can be,' said Taylor. 'Sir John Orde, perhaps?'

'I sincerely hope not,' said Clay. 'Not only does he want the firmness the hour needs, but he is also senior to Nelson.'

The line of ships appeared over the horizon, the three-decker leading with the seventy-fours in an evenly spaced line behind. Just the precision of the formation was enough to tell Clay that these were veteran ships with well-drilled crews, and not hastily commissioned Spanish vessels. All had the same yellow and black sides as the *Griffin* and the same open bow. The lead ship even strongly reminded him of the *Victory*.

'The flagship is signalling, sir,' warned Russell from above.

'She is the *Royal Sovereign*, sir,' reported Midshipman Todd. 'First rate. Captain Edward Rotheram commanding. She is the flagship of Vice Admiral Cuthbert Collingwood. The other ships are the *Colossus* and the *Achille*.'

'Old Salt Junk and Sixpenny, himself,' whistled Taylor. 'At least he is comfortably junior to Nelson.'

'Why is he called that?' asked Armstrong.

'On account of the dreadful dinners he served to his guests when he was in the Channel Fleet,' said the first lieutenant. 'There was only ship's fare and gut-rot wine to be found at his table. Apparently, Mrs Collingwood spends his fortune faster than he can earn it.'

'But he is also a sound fighting man,' said Clay. 'And he and Nelson are well acquainted, having served together as junior officers. I'll take Old Salt Junk over Orde with pleasure.'

'Signal sir!' said Todd. 'Flag to *Griffin*. Captain to come on board and report.'

'Acknowledge, if you please. I had best go below and shift into my better coat. Kindly pass the word for my barge crew, Mr Taylor.'

'Aye aye, sir.'

When Clay came back on deck the frigate was hove to a cable's distance to windward of the line of warships and Sedgwick had his barge in the water. This time the sea was relatively calm, and Clay was able to scramble up the side of the *Royal Sovereign* with relative ease.

The great cabin of the big first rate was almost identical

in size to that of the *Victory*, but was much more austere. There were no gilt-framed pictures on the bulkheads to add a homely touch. The deck was uncovered planking and the furniture was solid and functional.

Collingwood was a middle-aged man with a slight stoop and lanky, fair hair thinning on top. He turned a pair of clear blue eyes on him as he rose from his desk to greet his visitor. 'Captain Clay, I don't believe I have had the pleasure.'

Before Clay could answer there was a furious barking from beneath the desk and a ragged-looking terrier came bolting out towards him.

'Have no fear of Mr Bounce,' said Collingwood. 'His bark is decidedly more impressive than his bite. Indeed, he abandons his master entirely at the first sound of gunfire, and hides in the deepest part of the hold. Do you have an animal companion yourself, Captain?'

'Not intentionally, sir, although I do seem to have been adopted by the crew's mascot. It is a mongoose acquired in India.'

'I find his presence comforting during the long months I am obliged to be at sea,' said the admiral, stooping to scratch Mr Bounce's ears. 'Would you care for a glass of wine?'

'Ah … only if you are having one, sir,' said Clay.

'It is a little early for me, in truth,' said Collingwood, returning to the far side of the desk. 'Pray be seated, Captain, and tell me what brings you to these waters.'

'Lord Nelson has sent me ahead of his fleet to seek out Admiral Villeneuve, sir. His lordship missed him in the Caribbean, and believes he has returned to European waters.'

'Nelson is not far behind you, I collect?'

'No more than two or three days, sir.'

'By Jove, but that is welcome intelligence!' exclaimed

Collingwood, 'for you have found your quarry. He is in Cadiz. But if you and his lordship have been on the far side of the ocean, I had best apprise you of what has been happening here.'

'If you would, sir.'

'As you can imagine, Villeneuve's little vanishing act in the spring caused general consternation,' said the admiral. 'Sir John Orde has been censured for letting the Frogs join up with the Spanish, but by falling back on the Channel Fleet, he at least gave us the ships to keep Admiral Ganteaume locked up, despite his repeated efforts to wriggle free from Brest. Then last month I was detached to watch Cadiz. Villeneuve cleaned the place out in the spring, but since then the Dons have brought more ships into commission, including the biggest one I ever clapped eyes on. Named the *Santissima Trinidad*, with four gundecks, if you'll credit it. I tell you, Noah and his ark ain't in it!'

'Goodness,' said Clay. 'How many guns does she carry?'

'A hundred and thirty, I believe, but many are small, and she sails like a hay wain,' said Collingwood. 'No match for my *Royal Sovereign*. Anyway, all was well until a week ago, when Villeneuve turned up with his whole damned fleet. There must be over thirty of the line in Cadiz now, with just the three of us out here to oppose them. Command of a powder hoy in hell would be safer.'

'Have they attempted to bring you to battle yet, sir?

'Twice, coming at me with a dozen ships. But I have modelled myself on Mr Bounce here. We give way while they charge at us, and yap at their heels when they return to port. It ain't much of a blockade, but with Nelson in the offing, and reinforcements I have been promised from home arriving presently, we should soon have their measure.'

'Provided Villeneuve doesn't leave port again before his lordship can reach us, sir.'

'Indeed,' said Collingwood. 'That would go very ill.'

Chapter 15
Blockade

The inside of the *Victory's* great cabin was ablaze with light. Oil lamps hung from the beams overhead, while candles flickered on the admiral's dining table. It had all its leaves in place to extend it to its maximum size. Nelson and Collingwood sat opposite each other with a large plan of battle spread between them. All the other seats were occupied by naval captains, with another dozen standing behind them, leaning forward to watch the slight, one-armed figure at the heart of the group.

'What did you observe when you closed with Cadiz this evening, Captain Blackwood?' asked Nelson.

'That the enemy were still in the outer harbour, your lordship,' he said, his Ulster accent making his report seem oddly harsh. 'Thirty-three of the line, so there was. All with masts set up and yards crossed, ready to depart.'

'Excellent, then we must be prepared for battle at a moment's notice, gentlemen.'

'Hear him!' said Captain Israel Pellew of the *Conqueror*, who was standing close to Clay. His voice had the same hint of West Country burr as his more famous brother Edward.

'You will have noted that I have kept the fleet out at sea to give the enemy no hint as to our increased numbers,' continued Nelson. 'That is also why I sent ahead to order that no salutes should be fired to greet my arrival. I want nothing to alarm the enemy. Captain Blackwood will pull his frigates back out of sight of Cadiz. Only Captain Clay with the *Griffin* is to be right in the offing, watching the enemy.'

Clay was conscious of faces turning towards him. Faces flushed with the admiral's wine, trying to pick him out from the crowd. Appraising faces of those who hadn't crossed paths with him. But also smiles of acknowledgement from those who had fought with him before, like Hardy, and Berry of the *Agamemnon*.

'What shall we do if they won't come out, my lord?' asked Captain Grindall of the *Prince*.

'Then we stay here, gentlemen, for as long as it takes,' said Nelson. 'I shall detach ships three at a time to revictual at Gibraltar in rotation, so supply will be no issue for us. But he will come out, for he must. The enemy has put enormous energy and resources into gathering this fleet together. Why will he leave it to rot at its moorings here?'

Pellew led another rumble of agreement at this. When it had passed, Nelson continued. 'Whenever possible, the fleet's station shall be fifty miles to windward of Cadiz, so that when Captain Clay alerts us that the enemy is coming out, we shall be in position to force an action. I intend that battle to be one of annihilation. If the greater part of the enemy are not sunk or captured by us, we shall have failed in our duty to our king. Pray attend to this plan and I shall show you how it is to be achieved.'

The ring of captains drew in a little closer, moving chairs and craning to see the sheet of paper the lay between the admirals.

'The enemy will be here, to leeward,' explained Nelson, indicating one side of the sheet. 'And we shall approach from over there, with the breeze at our backs. Because the prevailing wind in this season is westerly, I hope to catch the enemy between us and the coast of Spain, so they cannot avoid battle.'

'Just like at the Nile, my lord,' said Hardy, with a smile of satisfaction.

'Very like,' said Nelson. 'We will form up into two divisions. One under my command and one under Admiral Collingwood. Each will approach directly towards the enemy in line of battle. I shall head for the centre of the enemy fleet, and Admiral Collingwood's division will attack their rear. Once we have defeated those parts, we shall turn on their van.'

'When you say directly towards, you cannot surely mean bow on to them, my lord?' queried Grindall.

'I mean precisely that, Captain. Bow on, like spears thrusting towards the body of the enemy.'

'But all of their guns will be able to fire on us as we approach, and yet none of ours will be able to return the compliment,' added another voice.

'My *Victory* and Admiral Collingwood's *Royal Sovereign* will be at the head of each line,' explained Nelson. 'They will act as shields for those that follow, taking the brunt of the enemy's fire because they are the largest of our ships and best able to endure such punishment. A direct approach means that we come at the enemy as swiftly as possible, to bring on the sort of pell-mell battle where our superiority in gunnery and our dash will win the day. Time is everything, gentlemen. Five minutes may make the difference between victory and defeat.'

Clay marvelled at how Nelson was controlling the gathering, bending them to his will. He looked at the faces around him. Some were veterans of previous battles, who could appreciate the sense of what the admiral was saying. They knew from personal experience that at close range a Royal Navy crew firing as rapidly as they were able would overwhelm any less-experienced opponent. But at least half the captains had seen little or no real action. Most had spent long years in the Channel Fleet, endlessly waiting for a battle that never came. Yet he looked to have had won these over too, with a characteristic display of reckless bravery. Look at me, he seemed to be saying, small and crippled, yet ready to lead you into battle, taking the bulk of the risk on myself. All I ask is that you follow close in my wake.

Nelson left a long silence, for the duller members of the party to absorb what was being asked of them. When he spoke again, his voice was quieter, so they had to press even closer to hear his words. 'I will not be able to give you much in the way of instruction during the battle, gentlemen. Nor will Admiral Collingwood, for ours shall be the first ships among the enemy. Once you are up with us you must break formation and find an opponent as swiftly as you are able. I have no knowledge of the situation you shall find. But rest assured of this – no captain can do very wrong if he places his ship alongside that of an enemy. Are there any questions?'

'Not from me, my lord,' boomed Hardy from the end of the table. 'An excellent plan, if I may be so bold. I only pity my fellow captains who are not here among us, to share in our glory.'

That raised a ragged cheer from the group.

'No further observations?' asked Nelson, when there was quiet once more. 'Good. My secretary has detailed orders for you all which he will distribute on the way out. I have nothing further to add, save to urge you to trust to the Great Disposer of all events and the justice of our cause. Good night, gentlemen.'

As Clay joined the throng to shake their host's hand

before leaving, Nelson's steward appeared at his elbow. 'His lordship would be much obliged if you was to remain behind for a moment, sir. Perhaps you might like to sit over there? Can I bring you another drink?'

'No thank you,' said Clay.

It took a while for the last of the officers to leave, after which a tired-looking Nelson came across to join him. 'How do you think that went, Alexander?' he asked.

'I was most impressed, my lord. Not least by Captain Hardy's little speech.'

Nelson chuckled and he lent across to touch Clay's sleeve. 'Did it sound false?'

'A little too rehearsed for Tom, my lord. His style is more "up and at 'em" rather than such flowery words, but I think only I spotted the deceit and it had the desired effect. And I hold your plan to be an excellent one.'

'I am sorry for the need for such theatrics,' said Nelson. 'At the Nile, I had the pick of the service, my band of brothers, who I could rely on come what may. But this time I have a ragtag fleet formed from whatever the Admiralty has been able to sweep together and send me in haste. If I had the time to form an opinion of their character I would handle things differently, but we may be in battle with Villeneuve tomorrow.'

'You won them over, my lord, have no fear,' said Clay. 'They will follow you through hell now, if needs be. And I must thank you for the trust you have shown by giving the *Griffin* such an important role.'

Nelson waved dismissively at this. 'Blackwood will back you up, and relay your signals directly to me. Besides, I have another task that I need you to perform.'

Clay looked across at Nelson. His left eye was blank and lifeless as usual, but his right was full of determination.

'Another task, my lord?'

'It will be October soon, Alexander,' explained the admiral. 'The season of autumn gales, and this is a treacherous lee shore in a blow. I didn't speak of it in front of the others, for I want their minds focused only on battle. But if a storm should arrive, we may very well be driven far off station, letting the enemy escape to make for the Channel and the ruin of us all. Boney still wants to invade our homeland, and if we are to defeat his plan, we must bring his fleet to battle. The sooner the better.'

'But what if the enemy will not leave port, my lord?'

'You must make him do so, Alexander,' said Nelson, reaching across once more to touch Clay's sleeve. 'I do not choose to place the *Griffin* at the very forefront of my fleet because it is in some way a superior ship. I place her there because you command her, and you are the ablest of my officers. Fighting captains, like Blackwood and Hardy, I have aplenty, each one as brave as any Ajax or Achilles. But what I need is an Odysseus, who will produce some clever trick to tempt the Trojans out from behind their walls.'

'I ... I'm not sure how that might be achieved, my lord.'

'No, but you will find a way, I have no doubt.'

Nelson smiled at Clay, and then the eye that regarded him filled with sadness. 'Time is short in another way, my friend,' he said. 'My constitution is very poor. The physician of the fleet ordered me home to convalesce April last, but I chose to ignore his instruction. Many of my injuries are obvious – the eye and missing arm. Others are less so. Pain has been my constant companion for years; thanks to that blow I took to my head when we fought together at the Nile. Then there is the ague I caught as a young lieutenant in the Caribbean, that still returns to trouble me.'

'But you are still young, my lord,' protested Clay.

'Perhaps, but I am also weary, from all my years at sea and all my battles. My time is coming to an end, that I know. But I also know that I have one more task to do before I can rest. One last battle I must fight. I have long prepared for this moment. That battle plan has been among my papers ever since I was given command of the Mediterranean Fleet. I know that only I can deliver victory. And it must be such a great one that it brings Bonaparte to his marrow bones, and makes our country safe, once and for all. Your part is to get Villeneuve to come out. Do that, Alexander, and I shall do the rest.'

*****

Napoleon was pacing the floor of his office, one hand thrust deep between the buttons of his coat while he absorbed the news he had just heard. His Foreign Minister, Charles Maurice de Talleyrand, watched him patiently from one of the gilt-framed chairs, brushing some imagined dust from the sleeve of his elegantly-tailored coat.

'And you are quite certain of this?' demanded the emperor, still striding back and forth.

'Naturally, sire,' said Talleyrand. 'I do not make a habit of troubling you with rumour and gossip. This comes from my most reliable source in Vienna. Madame X has never been wrong before.'

'*Putain*!' muttered Napoleon. 'Why has this happened now?'

Just then came a knock on the door, and a smartly dressed orderly entered.

'Imbecile!' roared the emperor. 'I gave clear instructions that I was not to be disturbed!'

'Pardon me, sire,' said the quaking officer. 'But you also said that you wanted to be informed the moment word came of Admiral Villeneuve. The Minister of the Navy is outside …'

'At last!' said Napoleon, his face clearing. 'Well, send him in! Don't keep him waiting!'

If Admiral Decrès was bringing good news, he was hiding his elation well. He came in and bowed his head stiffly first to Napoleon and then to Talleyrand.

'Minister, you come at a most opportune time,' said the emperor. 'Talleyrand, tell him.'

'A meeting recently took place in the Imperial Palace in Vienna between the Foreign Ministers of Russia and Austria and the British Ambassador, at which a secret treaty was agreed in principle between them. In exchange for a considerable financial subsidy from Britain, both countries will declare war on France.'

'Gold!' exclaimed Napoleon. 'Always their gold. They know that their army is no match for mine, so instead will fight to the last Austrian and Russian. Still, it means that my invasion of their rotten little island must come soon, before I am compelled to march east and deal with this nonsense. You have had word from Villeneuve?'

'I have, sire.'

'And he is back in Europe?'

'He is, sire.'

'Has he reached Brest?' asked Napoleon eagerly. 'I can be with my army in Boulogne in a matter of days.'

'He is in Cadiz, sire, and is asking for instructions,' said Decrès.

Napoleon was silent for a moment, while Talleyrand placed a well-manicured hand across his eyes.

'Cadiz?' repeated Napoleon, his voice dangerously low. 'He is meant to be breaking Admiral Ganteaume's fleet out of Brest. What is he doing in Cadiz?'

'In all fairness to him, sire, we did instruct him to return first to Spain before advancing on Brest, so as to appraise himself of the latest situation.'

'Yes, to Ferrol, from where it is but a short distance to Brest. So I ask you again, what is he doing in Cadiz?'

'It would seem to be a matter of supplies, sire,' explained Decrès. 'His fleet has suffered an outbreak of disease, so he chose to divert to Cadiz. His message was a little unclear, but he did mention the abundance of lemons, and ….'

'Lemons!' roared Napoleon. 'What have lemons got to do with anything?'

'Sire, the evidence is that in the case of the scur—'

'Enough!' said the emperor. 'I have heard quite enough of this nonsense. Send him a direct order, from me. He is to leave port immediately, giving battle if he must. Tell him that the sacrifice of a few ships is no longer important, if they are lost with glory. And send Admiral Rosily with the message, with instructions to replace Villeneuve if he refuses to obey.'

'I shall organise it directly, sire.'

*****

Days had passed since the captains' meeting on the *Victory* and still there was no sign of Villeneuve emerging from Cadiz. Clay could see the fleet as he restlessly paced his quarterdeck, searching his mind for a way to coax them into coming out. The city was built on a long peninsula cast around the inner harbour. Behind the walls and bastions on its seaward face he could see whitewashed houses beneath terracotta roofs.

Beyond them was the Franco-Spanish fleet, a forest of masts and yards, but with not a scrap of sail in sight. High above him Midshipman Russell was perched on the main topgallant yard, tallying up the numbers for his morning report.

Clay pulled out his own telescope and looked over at the masts, black against the pale blue sky. After days of patrolling, he was able to pick out individual ships from the mass of the others. The four big Spanish first rates were the easiest. Their masts rose a good twenty to thirty feet higher into the warm air. Directly behind the main dome of the cathedral he could see the masts of the *Santa Ana*, with the *Rayo* beside her. Further back was the *Principe de Asturias*, while tallest of all were the masts of the huge *Santissima Trinidad*, forest giants towering over the saplings around them.

'No change from yesterday, sir,' reported Russell from beside him. 'Thirty-three of the line and five frigates.'

Clay contemplated the flushed face of the midshipman. He must have slid down the backstay from aloft at reckless speed to have appeared so quickly.

'Thank you, Mr Russell. Mr Armstrong, kindly have the ship put about and close to within signalling distance of the *Sirius*, if you please.'

'Aye aye, sir.'

The frigate turned away from the coast of Andalusia, and headed out to sea. Clay resumed his pacing, his hands clasped behind his back, his head bowed, but inspiration still eluded him. He was not helped by the life of the ship around him. In addition to the usual watch there were several fresh distractions. Close at hand Rudgewick, the frigate's gunner, and his mate were overhauling the slide of one of the carronades, whistling noisily as they worked. Further forward Taylor and the boatswain were looking over the mizzen deadeye lanyards, deciding which needed replacing and which had another storm left in them. Across the deck Blake was working on a watercolour of Cadiz, hastily adding detail as the city receded behind them. Then came a hail from the masthead.

'Deck there! Sail ho!'

'That must be the *Sirius*,' announced Armstrong. 'Have that signal bent and ready to hoist, if you please, Mr Todd. *Griffin* to flag, enemy at anchor. Situation unchanged from yesterday.'

'Aye aye, sir.'

'I'm not sure it is the *Sirius*, sir,' said Russell, who had climbed part way up the mizzen shrouds. 'There is nothing ahead of us.'

'Where away was this sail, Dawson?' yelled the sailing master.

'Two points off the starboard quarter, sir!'

'Astern!' fumed the American, spinning around to look aft. 'Well why in all creation didn't he say?'

'Not the *Sirius*, then,' said Clay, abandoning his walk to join the American. 'What do you make of her, Dawson?'

'Trading brig, just clearing that headland up the coast, and making for Cadiz, I reckon, sir,' said the lookout. 'Going like the clappers. Her colours be white for the most part. Could be Portuguese.'

'Put the ship about once more and let us have the topgallants on her if you please,' ordered Clay. 'Plot a course to intercept her.'

'Aye aye, sir.'

'All hands! All hands to make sail!'

'Let us hope she is a Spaniard,' said Taylor, coming over to join his captain. 'A little prize money will be some compensation for such a long delay to our return home.'

'I'm just pleased I didn't send our report to an empty horizon,' said Armstrong.

With her topgallants drawing, the frigate heeled far over as she raced towards the shore. The trading brig was sailing as fast as she was able, leaving a churning wake behind her as she struggled forward. But she was also heavily laden, and the *Griffin* was closing fast.

'Portuguese colours, for sure,' reported Taylor, trying to hide his disappointment. 'A neutral, then.'

'She is hardly acting like a neutral,' scoffed Armstrong. 'Why, she appeared the moment we headed out to sea to transmit our report. I reckon she was watching us all the time, waiting until the coast was clear to slip into Cadiz. Besides, even if she is a neutral, she's still a legitimate prize if we catch her carrying warlike stores into an enemy naval base.'

'I dare say we will learn the truth of it presently, gentlemen,' said Clay. 'Kindly clear away one of the bow chasers and have a boarding party ready, Mr Armstrong.'

'Aye aye, sir.'

The coastline was coming up fast, a long stretch of sandy beach backed by dunes with a flat plain beyond it. A few miles ahead of the brig was the estuary of a large river that might provide some refuge for her. Clay made a careful assessment of the relative speeds and distances, and decided that the *Griffin* would be up to the brig at least a quarter of a mile before she would reach safety.

The master of the brig seemed to come to the same conclusion, and she came around amid a flurry of flapping sails, heading back out to sea.

'Follow her, if you please, Mr Armstrong.'

'Aye aye, sir.'

The heavy frigate was slower in the turn than her

smaller opponent, but once she had settled on her new course, she began to rapidly overhaul her. As the *Griffin* came within range the brig tried to turn back towards the shore again.

'Too late for that, my friend,' said Armstrong with satisfaction.

'Give them a gun, if you please,' ordered Clay.

The cannon banged out, raising a column of water close to the brig, and she abandoned her turn and came to a halt, hove to, waiting for the frigate's arrival. A flash of red from near the wheel caught Clay's attention. When he focused on the spot he saw an elderly man in a crimson coat, pointing towards him. There was something familiar about the way he stood and gestured. Suddenly Clay realised that he had been here before. A neutral ship, trying to evade them. The man in his red coat. Even something that Armstrong had said earlier, about signalling to an empty horizon, seemed significant. His mind cleared, and he knew with certainty how he would get Villeneuve to come out and fight.

'Mr Armstrong, heave the ship to just to windward of the chase and send the boarding party across,' he ordered. 'I want a thorough search of the cargo and that fellow in the red coat sent across.'

'Aye aye, sir.'

'Isn't he the owner of that *Fortuna* we took in the south Atlantic,' said Taylor, lowering his telescope. 'The one we replenished our fresh water from?'

'I very much hope so, George,' said Clay. 'Now, Mr Russell, kindly come here. I have a particular service that I require you to perform when he has come on board. You too, Mr Taylor.'

While Clay explained what he wanted, Preston took the *Griffin*'s launch across to the brig. A little later he hailed Clay from her deck. 'She is the *Boa Ventura* of Lisbon, sir. I am just sending her master across now with his papers.'

'Very good, Mr Preston. See you search her thoroughly.'

'Aye aye, sir.'

It didn't take long before a familiar figure appeared in the frigate's entry port. 'You and your cursed ship again!' he spluttered as he was shown on to the quarterdeck.

'Don Sorondo, what an unexpected pleasure,' said Clay, taking his visitor's hand.

'For you, perhaps, Captain,' said the Spaniard. 'After the loss of my *Fortuna* I had sincerely hoped never to set eyes on you again, yet here we are. But at least it gives me the opportunity of thanking you for the courtesy that you showed to myself and my wife. After landing in Gibraltar, the authorities allowed us to return to our home in Cadiz with the minimum of delay.'

'That is very gratifying to hear, sir. And I trust Dona Sorondo has quite recovered from her ordeal?'

'She is in good health, I thank you.'

'Good,' said Clay. 'Now, perhaps we can move on to more formal matters. Can I ask why your latest ship is masquerading as a Portuguese-registered vessel?'

'Because that is exactly what she is, Captain. Thanks to the unfortunate war between our nations, the merchant houses in Cadiz are facing ruin. So of late some of us have been working with partners across the border in Portugal in order to carry on some limited trading.'

'But you must know that a neutral flag cannot protect you, if you are found to be carrying materials that would aid Spain in war.'

'True, but we are only carrying food, as your one-armed

lieutenant will presently find,' said Sorondo. 'No guns or warlike stores.'

'Food?' queried Clay. 'If it is salt beef in casks, or ship's biscuit, that would count as contraband.'

'The *Boa Ventura* is carrying a cargo of fruit. Lemons, if you must know.'

'To treat the scurvy in your warships?'

'To accompany the fish that we Catholics are obliged to eat on our many fast days, Captain. Would you care to examine my papers? I assure you they are quite in order.'

'Thank you, sir, said Clay, accepting the documents. 'Would you excuse me while I take these below to inspect them properly?'

'Of course,' said the Spaniard.

Clay disappeared down the ladderway, turning towards his cabin at the bottom. Then he stopped and quietly made his way to the shadows under the grating, where he could hear what was said on the deck above him. Meanwhile the Spanish merchant walked around the quarterdeck, showing some interest in what he saw. 'Is this a Ramsden sextant you have, señor?'

'It is indeed, sir,' replied Armstrong. 'I find it to be most reliable.'

'It certainly looks to be better made than those obtainable in my country.'

'Mr Taylor, sir,' said Russell. 'It is almost six bells. Shall I send the usual report on the enemy fleet?'

'Can the signal be clearly observed from Cadiz?' replied Taylor.

'I believe so, sir.'

'Then carry on, Mr Russell.'

'Aye aye, sir.'

Clay heard Russell quietly giving the flag numbers to the signal rating, followed by the squeal of the halliard running through a poorly lubricated block as it was hauled aloft.

'Tell me, señor, to whom does this man signal?' asked Sorondo, after a moment. 'I can see no ships other than those in Cadiz, and my poor *Boa Ventura*, of course.'

'It's for the benefit of your lookouts in Cadiz,' explained Russell. 'To make them think we have a fleet in the offing, even though there are none of our ships within …'

'Thank you, Mr Russell,' said Taylor, cutting in. 'That will be all. Kindly return to your duties.'

'Aye aye, sir.'

'And I will trouble you not to interrogate members of my crew, Mr Sorondo,' continued Taylor. 'Kindly be silent until the captain returns.'

Clay pulled out his watch, waited five more minutes, and returned to the quarterdeck. 'These papers seem to be in order, sir,' he said. He paused for a moment's thought, the documents still in his hand. 'I am tempted to take your ship on the basis that your cargo is certainly intended for the fleet, but I also do not relish the prospect of being sued by you for wrongful seizure.' He paused a moment more, then handed back the papers with a sigh. 'Very well, Don Sorondo, you may go on your way. Kindly give my regards to your wife.'

'I shall, Captain. And thank you.'

Clay watched the *Boa Ventura* resume her course with Taylor beside him.

'Did Mr Russell and myself play our parts well, sir?' asked the first lieutenant.

'Prodigiously so,' said Clay. 'I declare there is a career for the pair of you treading the boards in Drury Lane, when the navy has no further use for you. I do hope that all our efforts are not in vain, and Admiral Villeneuve gets to hear of your little pantomime.'

'It will be the waste of a fine capture if he does not, sir. I am sure most prize courts would have ruled in our favour.'

'Probably,' said Clay. 'Consider it a sprat to catch a mackerel, George. There will be prize money galore to be earned if the enemy does come out. I am just pleased that the cargo was not more obviously warlike. How would I have been able to allow a ship full of powder and shot to pass? We had best hasten to find the *Sirius*, and make that signal in earnest this time.'

Chapter 16
Calm

The twentieth of October was a Sunday, which meant a welcome change in routine for crews throughout the Royal Navy. This applied on board the *Griffin* as much as to any other ship, even though a powerful enemy lay within an hour's sailing of her. Indeed, she was so close to Cadiz that her crew could hear the clamour of bells drifting across the calm water as the city's churches summoned the faithful to mass.

The day had started early, with the crew scrubbing and polishing their ship to a heightened level of perfection, ready for their captain's inspection. When this was done, they had looked to their own cleanliness, washing clothes and hair, before dressing in their best slops. The inspection was followed by divine service, concluded with the reading of the Articles of War. But the high point for the crew was the afternoon. Once the minimum number required to manage the ship had been posted, the rest were at leisure to do as they pleased.

Many had gathered on the forecastle to enjoy the fine weather. With the approach of autumn, the sun had lost its fierce edge, and instead was merely pleasantly warm. Most were content to sit in small groups with friends, yarning as they repaired clothes or worked on pieces of scrimshaw, but others were engaged in more purposeful activity. Both catheads were crowded with sailors sitting astride them, each man dangling a line baited with a fragment of pork fat in the hope of a fish. Above their heads a group of ship's boys were engaged in a frantic game of chase through the foremast's rigging, the shrill piping of their voices merging with the cry of gulls passing overhead.

The few literate members of the crew were in high demand, now that post from home was arriving from Gibraltar, only seventy miles away. Sedgwick's services were particularly sought after, given that he was known to have written an actual book. He was sitting in the shade of the headsails, a respectful queue of sailors before him, each one gripping a fluttering sheet of paper.

'Your missus chiefly writes about teeth, Bill,' reported the coxswain, scanning through a letter. 'Her sister's baby cut his first one at four months, which she holds to be a wonder. Meanwhile your grandfather has shed his last, and can only feed on mush and gruel. It has been that hot, the village ford has run dry and the cottage roof needs repair, but you're not to worry because the Clerk of the Cheque has let her draw some of your prize money from the *Fortuna* to fix it, which is a comfort. She ends by sending you her love, and asking when you'll be home.'

The sailor took the proffered letter back, a smile playing on his lips. 'Thankee kindly, Able,' he said. 'I'll have a little think, and maybe ask you to send sum'it back to her for me?'

'Happy to, shipmate,' said Sedgwick, moving on to the next proffered letter. 'Oh dear, this is a burdensome hand to read,' he commented turning the new letter over to see if the scrawl improved on the other side.

'What you saying, Able Sedgwick?' demanded the sailor, a burly giant from the afterguard. 'That's writ by my nipper Thomas! Burdensome hand, indeed!'

Trevan chuckled to himself as he witnessed his friend's discomfort from the safety of the lee rail. 'There be some days when I'm right glad no bugger ever taught me to read,' he commented.

'Able's tried to learn me one time, but I ain't no scholar,' said Evans. 'Could have been bleeding Dutch.'

''Tis passing strange to be getting word from my Molly so prompt,' said Trevan, touching a hand to the letters in his own pocket. 'It be grand, of course, but sad an' all. When we was in the Indies it were that far away I didn't think on her so much. But now the Falmouth packet can bring word from her so quick, I find I miss home all the more.'

'We might as well be in the fecking Indies, if them buggers don't come out, at all,' said O'Malley, nodding towards the cluster of masts over in Cadiz.

The others followed his gaze. From behind them Napoleon appeared, jumping up on to the rail between them, and closed his eyes with pleasure as Evans idly scratched his head between the ears. Then the mongoose raised his head aloft, his nose twitching.

'What you sniffing at there, Nap?' said Evans. 'Didn't I wash proper this morning?'

'That creature be more of a seaman than you'll ever make, Big Sam,' said Trevan. 'Can't you feel it? The wind's changing.'

The breeze was still light, but there was no doubt that it was steadily shifting around. The fresh Atlantic air, cooled by its long passage over so many miles, was replaced with a warmer current, flowing down from the hills of Andalusia, fragrant with juniper and thyme. Men across the forecastle began to look up as they felt the change. Above them the jib flapped lazily and the windward edge of the fore topsail began to hum.

'Can't hold this course, sir,' announced the voice of Old Amos at the wheel.

Clay and the Immortal Memory

'Come off the wind,' ordered Preston, who was officer of the watch.

The frigate settled on to her new course, heading slowly towards the coast of Spain. She would eventually have to wear around, but Preston decided to delay the moment he had to call the men from their afternoon off for as long as possible. Slowly the coast grew closer, while the men returned to their various activities. One of the sailors on the cathead cried out in triumph as he hauled up a large fish, curling and shimmering in the sunlight, and Napoleon scampered over in the hope of a share.

'Deck there!' called the lookout. 'I reckon sum'it be happening with the enemy fleet. I can see men going aloft, like.'

On the quarterdeck Preston picked up his telescope, catching the eye piece under his chin to extend it, and then used the mizzen shrouds as a convenient rest. Cadiz was much closer now, and he could clearly see the lines of topmen making their way up the shrouds and out on to the yards. A tiny strip of white appeared, followed by another one on a ship further back in the harbour.

Preston felt a thrill of excitement pass through him. 'Go and find the captain, Mr Todd,' he ordered. 'Give him my compliments and tell him that I believe the enemy fleet may be coming out.'

*****

It had taken most of the afternoon for the fleet to leave Cadiz. The light air was gusty and unreliable so close to land and some of the huge Spanish first rates had proved particularly troublesome. At one stage the mighty *Santissima Trinidad*, with her four red strakes, had blocked the entrance altogether. But they were out at sea at last, formed in a straggling line several miles long, as the sun dropped towards the western horizon.

On board the *Redoubtable* most of the officers were on deck, enjoying the evening air. Brissot and Dorre were together by the rail, discussing the prospect of action, when the ship's surgeon came across to join them. 'You think there will be a battle, Captain Dorre?' he asked, when there was a pause in the conversation.

'I damned well hope so,' said the marine officer, rubbing his hands at the prospect. 'My lads are fed up with all this training, only for the fleet to keep running away. Now they just want to get stuck in.'

'I had heard that there may not be a Royal Navy fleet in the offing at all,' said Paillard. 'Did the Spanish authorities not report as much?'

'I shouldn't trust in that nonsense, Doctor,' scoffed Dorre, pointing towards the north-west. 'If there is no English fleet about, pray to whom is that frigate signalling?'

The officers followed the line of the soldier's arm to where the *Griffin* lay halfway to the horizon, sailing on a parallel course to the fleet. A pair of blue lamps shone from high on her mizzen mast, glowing in the gathering gloom.

'Do you know, I have the strangest feeling about that ship,' said Brissot. 'I feel that I have seen it before. Do you recall the one that followed us for a day, back in the spring and then disappeared? When we first crossed the Atlantic to Martinique? I could swear that it was the same.'

'One ship looks very like another to me,' said Dorre. 'But the most important thing I want to know is if the crew will be well enough to fight?'

Paillard shrugged. 'They are over the worst of the scurvy, but many are still weak. It would certainly have been better if we could have had another few weeks in port.'

'I don't think the admiral had that much time,' said Brissot. 'The captain was saying he had to choose between coming out or being cashiered.'

'Come gentlemen, pray do not spoil a pleasant evening with such negative talk,' said Dorre, gesturing towards the crowd of ships that surrounded them. 'Look about you! Are we not a mighty fleet? What have we truly to fear, I ask you?'

'Well said, Yves,' said Brissot. 'But I would recommend that you gentlemen enjoy this weather while you may, for it will not last.'

'You think not?' asked the surgeon.

'Can you not feel the motion of the waves? The sea is too restless for these light airs. Mark my words, there is a storm coming. Not immediately perhaps, but soon. It would be best if we were further out to sea when it breaks.'

Paillard looked back towards the shore but only one distant part was visible, a rounded mass of pale rock turning to orange in the evening light. 'Tell me, Francois, what is that headland I can see over there?'

'That is Cape Trafalgar,' said Brissot. 'A strange name, is it not. Moorish in origin, I believe. I trust we will not pass it too close, for there are dangerous shoals near it.'

*****

The rain squall came out of the night, accompanied by a gusting wind that heeled the frigate over before the men at the wheel could pay her off. Clay had sensed its approach moments before it struck, from the hiss of rain on sea and the cold breath of air rushing past him. It rattled against the sails and poured down on to the deck. He was thoroughly wet long before Harte could reach him with his oilskins and sou'wester.

'Lookout there!' he yelled up into the deluge. 'Any sign of the enemy?'

'None, sir! Can't see beyond the end of the yard in this, beggin' yer pardon,' came the reply, from somewhere in the darkness.

'Damnation!' he cursed. 'I thought this was all going too easily.'

'I should stand over here, sir,' suggested Armstrong, with the calm of a man who had donned his own oilskins in good time. 'I am in the lee of the mizzen course, where it is quite sheltered.'

'A little too late for that, Jacob,' said his captain, coming to join him.

'This squall will blow over presently, sir,' said Armstrong, 'Villeneuve has been making indifferent progress so far this night. He will not have gone far.'

'That is true enough, but somewhere out there, Lord Nelson is relying on our direction to place his fleet in the best position to come at the enemy,' explained Clay, pointing vaguely towards the west.

'Will the battle be tomorrow, sir?'

'Very like. His lordship has been obliged to wait so long for this moment, I doubt if he will seek to delay matters now.'

'That is well, sir,' said the American. 'I don't like the feel of this sea, nor these rain squalls. There is a tempest on its way, or I'm a Dutchman.'

'That you most certainly are not. Ah, I believe the rain may be easing.'

Water still chattered and gurgled in the scuppers, but the rain steadily lessened and a few stars appeared overhead through a rent in the clouds. Clay strode across to the binnacle to check the frigate's heading, and then hailed the masthead once more. 'Anything in sight, Dawson?'

'Not yet, sir. That there squall lies betwixt us and them. It'll need to clear first.'

'Would you care to come below, sir,' said Harte, appearing out of the night. 'You could shift them wet togs, and I've a glass of grog and water waiting, spitting hot from the galley.'

Clay wrestled between the desire to get out of his wet clothes and his duty to remain on deck in the face of the enemy.

'It will be a while before we see them again, sir,' said Armstrong.

'Very well,' said Clay. 'Call me the instant that we do, if you please.'

'Aye aye, sir.'

Clay need not have worried, for he was towelled dry by Harte, dressed and back on deck again in good time for the hail from above.

'Deck there!' called Dawson. 'I can see the enemy, ag'in. Off the starboard beam.'

Clay and Armstrong turned their night glasses in that direction. At first Clay could only see the dark sea, restlessly shifting. Then he saw a navigation light, a yellow point high up on a mast. With that to guide him the silhouette of a big ship appeared, with more light showing from its stern lanterns. The last of the rain swept away, and the lone ship became one of many, spread across the sea.

'There they are,' breathed Clay.

'Heading west, if I am not mistaken, sir,' added Armstrong. 'They must have gone about while we were unsighted.'

'You are right, Jacob,' said Clay. 'Kindly have the ship put about to match their course, if you please.'

'Aye aye, sir.'

'All hands! All hands to wear ship!'

While the boatswain's calls summoned the watch below from out of their warm hammocks, Clay summoned the signal midshipman across. 'Mr Sweeney! How do we indicate that the enemy is standing to the westward?'

The young officer angled the night signal book towards the light spilling from the binnacle and ran a finger down the list. 'Three guns, fired in quick succession, sir.'

'Thank you. Kindly have it made please.'

'Aye aye, sir.'

Once the *Griffin* had settled on her new course the watch was dismissed below, but many loitered to gaze across the dark water at the enemy fleet, a trail of fireflies in the night. From beneath the forecastle came the rumble of three of the frigate's eighteen-pounders being run out.

'Stand clear!' called the first gun captain, and a gush of fire rushed out into the night. The boom of the other two cannon followed one another closely.

Clay turned towards the western horizon and after a few minutes was rewarded by a rolling triple flash of orange in the distance.

'*Sirius* has relayed the message, sir,' announced the midshipman. 'Shall I have the gun crews stood down, sir?'

'For now, Mr Sweeney, but we may need to repeat the signal in an hour, if the enemy continues on this course.'

'Aye aye, sir.'

Clay wondered what Nelson would be doing. The message would arrive with him quickly enough. Behind the *Sirius* was Blackwood's *Euryalus*, at the centre of the frigate screen, and beyond him would be the fleet, hastening through the night. He imagined the admiral, pale but determined, sitting at his rosewood table in a cabin filled with light. He would be pouring over the chart as he manoeuvred his ships into the perfect position. John Scott, his secretary, would be beside him, recording everything; while a midshipman stood by, ready to rush the great man's orders up to the signallers on the deck above.

'Turn!' said a voice from beside the binnacle as the hour glass ran dry of sand. A moment later eight bell strokes rang out from the belfry and the sleeping frigate came to life as the watch changed over.

The deck trembled to the thunder of rushing feet. Clay watched the younger Saleem brother racing aloft. Moments later Dawson came sliding down the backstay, droplets of water spraying out from the damp rope at the speed of his descent. Closer at hand Blake and Armstrong were a point of stillness among the bustle all around them as the American gave his replacement an update. Then with a touch of his hat towards his captain, the ship's master was gone, and as suddenly as it had begun the *Griffin* was calm once more, with a different man at every post.

'Good morning, sir,' said Blake. 'Have you been on deck all night?'

'I have indeed, John. In truth I don't believe I would be able to sleep with the enemy so close at hand and Lord Nelson relying on us to guide him.'

The young lieutenant looked across at the enemy fleet. The wind was backing towards the north west, and had dropped to a light breeze, although the sea still rose and fell, slopping against the side in a way out of keeping with the conditions. 'It seems hard to believe there will be a battle tomorrow, sir. All is so peaceful. What is our task to be?'

'Not to fight this time,' said Clay. 'We shall leave the

battle fleet to do that. But I daresay we will be called on to repeat signals and take in tow any ships that are disabled. Let us see what the morning brings. We shall not have long to wait. Meanwhile it is time to report the enemy's progress again.' He looked around to see who had replaced Midshipman Sweeney. 'Ah, Mr Todd. Good morning to you, and kindly repeat the night signal for "The enemy is standing to the westward." You will find it is three guns, fired briskly.'

'Aye aye, sir.'

This time the triple glow from the *Sirius* was less bright. Clay looked around him and realised that he could now make out the eastern horizon, a bar of black sea against a paler slate grey. He turned his attention to the enemy. Increment by increment the dark ships began to resolve themselves in the gloom. Ghostly pale sails, floating through the air. The white strakes painted on the side of a big French eighty-gunner. The high stern of a Spanish first rate, encrusted with gilded figures that gleamed in the light of the ship's three big lanterns.

The sea turned to stone grey and a blush of pink showed in the east. 'Deck there!' called Saleem. 'I am seeing sails on larboard quarter, sir.'

Clay looked around, to find that Blake had been joined by Taylor, and that he could clearly see both men's faces in the growing light.

'What do you make of them, Saleem?'

'Two ships comings towards us, sir. Two miles, maybe between them. All sails to royals is being set. Even studding sails. Very big ships, with maybe more coming behind.'

'Mr Russell!' ordered Blake. 'Up you go with a glass, and tell us what you can see.'

'Aye aye, sir.'

'Good morning, sir,' said Taylor, while they watched

the midshipman race up the shrouds. 'And congratulations. I have no doubt that will be Lord Nelson, with the weather gauge and the enemy just where he wants them.'

'Deck there!' cried the voice of Russell. 'The southern ship is definitely the *Royal Sovereign*, sir. She is a little closer. And I am reasonably certain the northern ship is *Victory*. I can see other ships astern of both of them, forming up into line of battle.'

'And the enemy is after signalling, sir!' added Saleem.

Clay looked around just as a cannon banged out across the water. A puff of dirty brown smoke rolled up from the French eighty-gunner he had noticed earlier, calling attention to a string of flags fluttering from her mizzen halliard. Beneath her long bowsprit he could see her figurehead, a huge golden centaur pawing at the air with its front hooves.

'Admiral's duster at the forepeak,' commented Blake. 'It must be Villeneuve. I wonder what the signal might be?'

As Clay watched, the enemy fleet began to turn towards the north. It was an untidy display, with some of the smaller French ships settling on their new courses while the largest Spanish ones had barely started to lumber around.

'I believe they may be trying to return to Cadiz, sir,' said Taylor. 'Although they are making a sad hash of the manoeuvre. I cannot discern any sort of sailing order.'

'Good luck with that,' scoffed Blake. 'It will be a long beat back against this wind. Nelson will catch them with ease.'

'Let us hope so, gentlemen,' said Clay. 'Kindly signal the change of course to the flagship, Mr Todd, which in all probability shall be our last duty before battle is joined. His lordship will be able to see the enemy as clearly as we can presently.'

'Aye aye, sir.'

'Mr Blake, have the ship put about, if you please, and let us rejoin the fleet. Our station is a mile to windward of the *Victory*.'

'Aye aye, sir.'

'Now, George, can you see that the men get a substantial breakfast this morning, and once they have eaten, we will clear the ship for action. We have a busy day ahead.'

Chapter 17
HMS *Victory*

'What is he doing?' fumed Lucas to his first lieutenant. 'We are milling about like a flock of sheep before a wolf! Where is our line of battle? Or our discipline?'

Dupotet had to admit that the fleet did seem disorganised. The loose formation they had fallen into during the night had been further muddled by the abrupt turn to the north at dawn. The sailing order of those squadrons that had managed to stay in formation had now been reversed. Some ships had chosen to accept the new state of affairs, while others were breaking from the line to try to regain their correct positions. The result was a battle line in a messy crescent shape with Spanish and French ships mixed together. In the centre the line was dangerously thin, composed of widely spaced single ships, while towards the ends it was two or even three ships deep. 'Perhaps he will reorder the line presently, sir,' he suggested.

'He had best be quick about it,' grumbled his captain. 'Look about you! Half our ships won't be able to fire because another is between them and the enemy, while here in the centre they can pass through us like milk through a sieve!'

Lucas glared towards the stern of Villeneuve's flagship, just ahead of the *Redoubtable*, waiting for a signal. Although the *Bucentaure* was also a two-decker, she was noticeably wider. Yet despite her size the heavily gilded stern was rolling in the swell coming from the west, her tall masts exaggerating the movement as they swayed through the air. 'These waves are going to make for difficult shooting, Camille,' he said. 'See that our best gun-layers man the larboard cannons.'

'Yes, sir.'

'And have us close to within a cable of the flagship. We at least will show that we know how to form a proper battle line. Then you can clear for action.'

Lucas turned his back on the burst of activity unleashed by his first lieutenant implementing his orders, and looked towards the west. He could feel the wind, a gentle breath on his face, cool and fresh from the open sea. Closest to him was the frigate that had been waiting for them outside Cadiz and had followed them through the night. It was beating away from him now. Behind was a grey murk on the western horizon, steadily retreating as the sun rose higher. Within it he could see ships sailing towards him, elephantine shapes in the mist. There were two distinct groups, both headed by huge three-deckers with every sail set to catch the light air. The battle line to the south he dismissed. It was on course to cut into the fleet towards the rear, perhaps a mile or more from him. Instead, he concentrated on the northern group, which was heading directly for him. 'Monsieur Pascal! Kindly bring me the best spyglass,' he ordered.

'Yes, sir.'

In the time it took the midshipman to bring the telescope across and for Lucas to focus, the head of the northern group was emerging from the vanishing mist. The lead ship had towering spires of canvas that had turned pink in the dawn light as it made slow but remorseless progress across the pale blue sea. Behind the big three-decker was a second one, almost as large, and behind that a third, the line of warships steadily growing as the light improved. Lucas felt apprehension rising from the pit of his stomach as he took in the enormous concentration of firepower that was coming towards him. The busy chatter of the gun crews taking their places on the quarterdeck hushed as they too took in the approaching enemy.

'Those Spaniards said as how there was no fleet out here,' hissed a lone voice to his neighbour. 'Just look at all those buggers'

'Hush, mate! Or the old man will hear you.'

Lucas closed his telescope, and turned from the rail to find Thibault standing behind him, holding out his sword belt. He looked over his ship as his steward settled the weapon around his waist. Above his head he could see the fighting tops crowded with all the extra sharpshooters Dorre and Brissot had trained up. In the mizzen rigging above them was the ship's armourer and his mate, reinforcing the rope slings that held the mizzen yard in place with an iron chain. Then he looked at the nearest gun crew, and the sailor who had spoken. 'Are you nervous, my friend?'

'A little, sir,' said the man.

'That is good,' said Lucas, projecting his voice so that others could hear. 'It shows that you understand what is to come. Only an idiot feels no fear on the edge of battle. This fight will be different, lads. We have spent long months training for it, and preparing a little surprise for our enemy. Do your duty, follow the lead of your officers, and all will be well.'

'Yes, sir,' said the sailor.

'A cheer for the captain!' called out someone as Lucas turned to join his first lieutenant. The cries were muted, but they gradually spread down on to the crowded main deck.

'Shall I stop their clamour, sir?' asked Dupotet.

'Certainly not,' said Lucas. 'I am pleased to hear it. Let us hope they still feel inclined to do so when this day is over.'

'Yes sir. The ship is ready for action, and we are in position a cable astern of the flagship.'

'Good,' said Lucas. 'Although in these light airs it will be some hours before the enemy is in range. Has the admiral been signalling at all?'

'Nothing since the general instruction to wear ship, sir.'

Lucas glared forward, looking along the length of his ship. He could see Villeneuve on the poop deck of the *Bucentaure*, standing apart from his staff with a telescope to his eye as he studied the approaching enemy. 'Do something,' he muttered, but the admiral seemed content just to watch and wait.

*****

'That is a mile to windward of the *Victory* as near as makes no difference, sir,' reported Armstrong, looking up from his sextant. He had used it to measure the falling angle between the waterline of the flagship and the admiral's pennant streaming out from the top of the foremast.

'Thank you,' said Clay. 'Kindly let the ship fall off until we are on a parallel course with the fleet, if you please Mr Taylor.'

'Aye aye, sir.'

The frigate swung in a broad circle, her yards hauled around until she too was heading towards the enemy. The sun was clear of the horizon, climbing up into a pale blue sky dotted with thin cloud. The *Griffin* was one of a widely spaced line of six smaller ships: four frigates, a cutter and a topsail schooner. Just to the south of them was the northernmost of the two British divisions, more than a dozen ships of the line bow to stern, all under full sail. The solid yellow lines painted along their sides were broken into a checkerboard by the open gunports, each one showing a heavy cannon pointing towards him. Through the gaps between the masts, Clay could see the second column of ships, almost as strong, with Collingwood's *Royal Sovereign* in the lead.

'Quite a sight, is it not, sir,' said Armstrong. 'I reckon there must be six hundred cannons pointing our way, and the same again on the starboard side, and that is just Lord Nelson's division. Why, this will be the greatest battle of the age, and here we are, in the guinea seats to witness it.'

'Although we may have to wait for the performance to start,' added Clay. 'At this speed it will be some time before we are in range.'

Both men looked across at Villeneuve's fleet, a straggling line several miles long, but slowly pulling itself into some sort of order.

'They seem game enough, sir,' commented the American. 'No sign of them falling away.'

'No, and his lordship's plan is not without risk. The ships will have to endure quite a few buffets without reply before they come up with the enemy.'

'A warm day for such hot work,' commented Taylor. 'And the glass is still falling.'

'Aye, we are in for heavy weather before long,' said Jacob, looking back towards the west.

'Let us take our fences as we come to them, gentlemen,' said Clay. 'We have a battle to fight first. Mr Russell, have you seen the flagship is sending a signal for you to repeat?'

'Yes, sir,' said the midshipman, who was standing next to the flag locker with three sailors assisting him.

'Can that be one signal?' queried Taylor. 'It seems long, given that all is as it should be.'

'What does it say, Mr Russell?' asked Clay.

'Just decoding it, sir,' said the harassed midshipman, leafing through his signal book. 'Some of the number groups are new to me.'

The officers watched on, while the signal ratings selected flags from the locker, ready to repeat the message for the ships further down the line. Eventually Russell looked up from his slate, a puzzled frown on his face. 'I'm certain I have it right, sir, but I'm unsure what we are to do. You see, it's not really an order.'

'Let us hear it,' said Clay.

'General signal, sir,' reported Russell. 'England expects that every man will do his duty.'

*****

On board the *Redoubtable* all that was left to do was wait. Every item not required for the battle ahead had been safely stored deep in the hold. Every weapon was where it should be and every man was at his post. Lucas knew this for certain, because he had just returned from a lengthy tour of his ship. He had seen Paillard and his assistants with their gleaming line of saws and knives down in the cockpit. Then he had peered into the magazine, with its lining of soft copper plates, where the gunner and his mate were filling extra charge bags for the battle ahead. And he had gone to every gun crew, offering a joke here and a word of encouragement there. He had looked into each face, and read every emotion from fear through indifference to calm. Now he was back on his lofty poop deck, and still he had to wait.

The enemy was coming ever closer, the line slightly curving, so that he could see a little of each bow peeping from behind the ship in front, as if they were a hand of playing cards. The *Victory* led, coming on ponderous and slow, heading directly for him. Her broad hull sat deep in the rolling swell, the sides studded with guns, her huge foremast soaring up, the yards spreading vast sails far out on either side. He had been waiting for this battle for over a year, and yet it still refused to start. He carefully assessed the range, and concluded it was too long. With a sigh he reconciled himself to waiting a little longer.

He looked around to pass the time. The gun crews beneath him were all sitting on the deck, a few talking quietly, but most silent with their thoughts. Following behind him was a smaller Spanish ship, the sixty-four-gun *San Leandro*. Beneath her bowsprit was the figure of the saint, robed in white, with a hand held aloft in blessing. A deck above him Lucas could see the much smaller figure of a chaplain as he toured the men on her forecastle, offering them absolution with a similar raised hand while swinging a smouldering censer in the other. Then a muffled roar came from somewhere to the south, and Lucas turned to see a cloud of gun smoke rolling slowly upwards in the warm air.

'One of the Spanish ships in the rear has opened fire on that other English column, sir,' reported Dupotet.

'The English are nearer there,' said Lucas, focusing his telescope on the *Royal Sovereign*. 'And I can't see that they have inflicted much damage.'

Another ship in the rear vanished in a cloud of smoke, and after an appreciable gap the sound of the broadside reached them. Splashes peppered the sea over a wide area in front of the target, some falling quite close. Encouraged by this, another ship tried its luck, and then another.

Lucas transferred his attention to the *Victory*. She was

closer now, sailing well ahead of the three-deckers behind her in her haste to reach them.

'Do you suppose she is in range yet, sir?' asked Dupotet.

'Almost,' said his captain. 'See that the crew are ready.'

Across the main deck beneath him men were picking themselves up, some stretching as if newly awakened, others adjusting the bandanas protecting their ears, or fiddling with their equipment. Brissot was busy striding along behind them. 'Stand to your guns, there!' he ordered. 'See they are at maximum elevation, and your linstocks are still lit!'

Now the crews were taking their places, crouching down and feeling for grip on the sand-covered planking. A gun captain beneath him swung fiery life into the slow match, the swinging linstock trailing smoke in a way oddly reminiscent of the Spanish chaplain.

'The guns are ready, sir,' reported his first lieutenant.

'Very good,' said Lucas, glancing back at the *Victory*. Was she in range yet? he wondered.

At that moment the *Bucentaure* just ahead erupted in fire and smoke, the hull rolling away from the force of the broadside. Lucas watched as splashes rose all around the British flagship. Most were short, but a small circle of grey appeared in her forecourse where one ball at least had found its target. 'You may open fire,' he ordered. 'On the up roll, if you please. And have the time noted in the log.'

'Yes, sir.'

The broadside came in two distinct parts. Morin, in command of the lower gundeck, gave the order to fire first, a fraction too soon for the roll of the ship to the latest wave. The effect was to push the *Redoubtable* further over, so that Brissot's guns on the main deck, firing a moment later, almost certainly went high. He felt sure they would all have missed their target, but with the smoke from the *Bucentaure* drifting down to join that from his own ship, he had no way of seeing their effect. Now more and more ships were opening fire, each one adding a fresh blanket of brown fog.

Beneath him Brissot was calling out the orders as the men reloaded the guns. 'Stop your vents!' A pause until every gun captain had done so. 'Now swab out the barrel!' Another pause. 'Fresh charge in!'

When the last gun had been run up and primed, the smoke was thinning at last, the sunlight making golden shadows as it streamed through. The *Victory* was appreciably nearer, a brief looming presence before the *Bucentaure* fired again, filling the world with smoke once more.

'Quoins in a half turn!' yelled Brissot. 'Hands up when you're ready!' A line of arms, with one missing. Then a full set, while the lieutenant waited for the next wave. 'Fire!' he bellowed, this time together with Morin, and the ship heeled back, the sound deafening. 'Stop your vents!' resumed Brissot, but his next order was lost in the sound of the *San Leandro* firing just astern.

When the *Redoubtable* fired again, Lucas felt as if he was standing on the lip of a volcano rather than at the rail of his ship, as the smoke and fire from the guns boiled out, completely masking the sea below him. Smashing broadsides followed one another all around him, filling his world, and yet still the enemy came on. He could see the *Victory* all the time now, a dark shadow, growing closer like the phantom in a nightmare. Then she was there, thrusting her way forward through the fog, heading for the gap between his ship and the *Bucentaure* ahead. Her mizzen topmast had been shot through, reduced to a splintered stump jutting up above the mizzen top. The sails on her foremast were full of rents and tears. Shreds of canvas hung down like weed. One studdingsail still drew, but the other hung in an untidy mass. Her bow was pockmarked with white gashes, and much of her head rail had been smashed away, and yet still she came on.

'Reload those guns,' yelled Brissot, 'Make haste!' But Lucas could tell that there would not be enough time before the enemy would be upon them. Nothing could stop that remorseless advance, so slow yet powered by such crushing momentum. Above his head the sharpshooters massed in the tops began firing, and a sailor at work in the *Victory*'s tattered rigging fell, turning in the air like a discarded doll as he plunged towards the deck. Little puffs of smoke from the enemy's forecastle showed where her marines were firing back.

Closer and closer came the battered ship, her side like a curtain being slowly drawn across in front of the *Redoutable,* as she headed to pass directly astern of the *Bucentaure* at point-blank range.

'She means to rake the admiral!' warned Dupotet. 'What shall we do?'

'We can do nothing to save him now,' said Lucas, his face grim. 'But we must look to ourselves, before we collide with her! Helm hard over!'

'Helm over!' repeated the men at the wheel.

Now the bow of the *Victory* began to overlap with the stern of the *Bucentaure*. She was so close that her fore yardarm caught the vangs of the French ship's gaff, tearing them free. A huge carronade on the forecastle bellowed out, followed by an endless procession of crashes as gun after gun sent its huge ball to tear a destructive path through the entire length of the French flagship.

'*Mon Dieu*!' gasped Lucas. 'They are finished, poor souls.'

Now the starboard side guns of the *Victory* began to bear on the *Redoutable* as she pushed on. Tongues of flame shot towards them and a ball struck somewhere forward with a crash like the blow from a hammer.

'Why the hell isn't this ship turning!' roared Dupotet, towards the wheel.

'We barely have steerageway, sir,' protested the helmsman.

'Sheet the headsails over,' bellowed Lucas towards the forecastle. 'We can't let her shoot us to pieces like this!'

Slowly, painfully, the French ship began to inch around. More and more of the *Victory*'s guns were starting to bear on them as she advanced further, the crashing blows helping to push the *Redoutable* into her turn. The British flagship moved clear of the *Bucentaure*, leaving her beautiful gilded stern reduced to a smoking cave, and began to match her new opponent's turn.

'Stand by, larboard side!' ordered Lucas. Brissot waved his hat in acknowledgement as the last few of his guns were run out. Up above him Lucas could see the tops packed with marksman, busy firing away. 'We have trained and planned for this moment for all these months,' he said to his first lieutenant. 'Close the range with that ship, and let us put it to the test.'

'Yes, sir.'

The ships were surrounded by the swirling cauldron of battle as the fleets came together, but for Lucas his world had narrowed until only two things existed – the *Redoutable*, and the huge first rate coming ever closer. The firepower that faced him was truly overwhelming. The side of the *Victory* seemed as broad as a sea cliff through the smoke. Flashes flickered up and down as her three decks of guns pumped ball after ball into his ship at a speed that was staggering. When they came, the

Redoutable's ponderous broadsides seemed to have no more effect than a fistful of gravel thrown by a child. Through the deck he could feel the shock of each impact as shot thudded into the hull. With a groan of splintering wood, the fore topmast toppled over, coming to rest hanging down in a ruin of broken spars and torn sails, masking the view of many of the marksmen placed in the foretop. Down on the main deck he could see that two of the eighteen-pounders were out of action. The one closest to him had been tossed over on its side like a toy. From beneath the broken red carriage protruded a pair of legs amid a dark pool.

The quarterdeck rail suddenly burst into a shower of splinters just next to one of the eight-pounders, sending a member of the gun crew tumbling to the deck. Another sat mesmerised by a jagged shard of oak sunk deep into his blood-soaked thigh.

'Monsieur Quellec,' said Lucas, turning towards the midshipman, but the Breton officer was dead, his hat knocked across the deck by the musket ball that had struck him just above the ear. 'Ah … Monsieur Pascal, then, perhaps you would be good enough to have these men taken down to the surgeon.'

Pascal was transfixed by his fallen friend, so swiftly had been his end.

'Come on, lad,' said Lucas, placing an arm around his shoulders. 'You can do no more for him. We will honour him when we can, but for now there are other shipmates who need your help.'

'Yes, sir,' said the youngster, wiping his sleeve across his eyes and turning to the afterguard. 'You two! Over here with me.'

'Monsieur Dupotet,' said Lucas returning to the battle.

'It is time, my friend. We cannot long endure this punishment. Bring us alongside, if you please.'

'Yes, sir.'

*****

Dorre had positioned himself high above his captain's head, in the mizzen top. It was a square platform five metres wide and four long, built around the mast and currently crammed with men, all busily firing away. Laid out beneath them was their own ship, lying parallel with the *Victory*. Between them was a canyon of water perhaps fifty metres wide, choked with flame and smoke as the rival ships battered each other across it. The range was gradually dropping as the *Redoubtable* moved closer, which was as well, because from his eyrie it was clear that the British ship was winning the artillery duel with ease.

Things were not going as smoothly as he had hoped. When he had sat down with Brissot all those months ago the task of subduing an opponent with small-arms fire had seemed much more straightforward, and the training sessions they had held in the calm waters of Toulon and then Port Royal harbours had done little to dent his confidence. But actual battle was proving considerably harder.

For one thing, the *Victory* was a much bigger ship than the *Redoutable*, with fighting tops proportionately higher. This gave the red-coated marines stationed in them a distinct advantage as they fired down on his own men. He had already lost a dozen of his marksmen to their withering fire, and he was only just starting to gain the upper hand over them. Then there was all the smoke that hung between the two ships, obscuring his men's view of the enemy's upper deck, reducing them to firing blind most of the time.

A resounding crash came from somewhere beneath him, and the whole mast shook so badly that the man next to Dorre almost dropped his ramrod. Dorre recognised him as Guillemard, the soldier from the 16th Regiment whose shooting had so impressed him back in Toulon. 'Steady there, Private,' he said. 'If the mast is still standing, it can't be too bad.'

'Yes, sir,' said the soldier, resuming his loading, his eyes wide with fear.

Dorre leant out over the side of the platform to inspect the damage. A big chunk had been knocked out of the mast, leaving a white splintered wound the size of a water melon. 'Nothing to worry about, lads,' he lied. 'Just a glancing blow.' Then he pointed across at the *Victory*'s mizzen top, where two red-coated figures had appeared, aiming back across at him. 'There's your mark, lads!'

A volley of shots rang out around him, and one of the marines ducked back into cover, leaving his companion slumped over the side of the platform.

'Good shooting!' enthused Dorre. 'There can't be many left up there. Start concentrating on clearing their upper deck.'

'Yes sir.'

The ships grew even closer, the blast of the guns sending wafts of hot smoke swirling up from below and shaking the damaged mast alarmingly.

A figure made his way across to stand beside him, leaning close to be heard over the thunder of battle. 'I reckon our grenades might reach them now, sir,' he yelled.

Dorre looked down and saw the man was right. 'Quite correct, Sergeant,' he shouted back. 'Signal to the maintop to start throwing them.'

The officer he had put in charge of the maintop raised

his hat in acknowledgement, and then waved forward some of his men. As Dorre watched, a cluster of dark spheres arced through the air, each one trailing a thin line of smoke behind it. Some burst before they reached the target. Several more fell short, vanishing into the maelstrom between the hulls, but one burst flush on top of the barricade of hammocks that lined the side to protect those on board, and more fell down on to the packed deck of the *Victory*.

Then his sergeant grabbed at his arm. 'Look, sir!' the man urged. 'Down there! It's him! It must be!'

Dorre followed where he pointed. The smoke had swirled clear for a moment to show two officers pacing side by side on the enemy's quarterdeck. One was very much taller than his neighbour, who was slightly built. The smaller man was dressed in a coat with several glittering orders pinned to the front. He also had only one arm. 'Guillemard!' yelled Dorre. 'Have you finished reloading?'

'I have, sir,' replied the soldier, sliding his piece up to his shoulder. He settled on the target, took a moment to steady himself, and pulled the trigger.

Chapter 18
The Immortal Memory

Hardy could scarcely believe he had achieved such a perfect rake on the *Bucentaure*. During the *Victory*'s final approach, her sails and rigging had been reduced to rags by the storm of fire converging on her from all sides. Then her mizzen topmast had been shot through, giving her an unnatural, unbalanced feel. Finally, a lucky shot had bowled its way down the entire length of the big first rate, missing everyone but reducing her wheel to a splintered mass. Now he was forced to steer using an officer to bellow instructions through the grating at his feet, to be relayed via a succession of men down to a team in the gunroom hauling the rudder across with relieving tackles. Yet despite all this, the broad, glittering stern of the French flagship had appeared through the smoke just beside his ship, her rail lined with a mix of horrified marines and officers, to receive a point-blank broadside from the double-shotted guns of the *Victory*.

'Oh, bravo!' enthused Nelson, as the last gun banged out. 'You have delivered a blow that no ship could recover from, Tom. Kindly note the time, Mr Scott.'

'Yes, my lord,' said the secretary, who was busy recording all that passed.

'Which opponent would you have us tackle next, my lord?' asked Hardy, indicating the various options. Ahead of them was another French eighty-gunner, waiting for the flagship to sail clear before firing, while off to one side lay the

Redoutable, turning slowly to bring her guns to bear. 'I should caution that our wounded masts may not endure much more punishment.'

'I care not,' declared Nelson. 'It does not signify which we run on board. Take your choice.'

'Mr Pasco! A point to starboard, if you please,' ordered Hardy. 'Bring us down on that French seventy-four off the starboard bow.'

'Aye aye, sir,' said the lieutenant, pointing his speaking trumpet towards the grating.

From beneath their feet came the sound of the gun crews moving across to man the starboard cannon as the ponderous flagship began to bear down on a new opponent. Ahead of them the French eighty-gunner vanished behind a wall of smoke. Moments later spouts of water erupted all around the *Victory* and there was a series of crashes from the bow. Hardy looked up anxiously as a fresh cascade of debris fell from overhead.

Now the *Victory*'s guns were firing as swiftly as their well-drilled crews could manage, and the whole ship began to vibrate to the almost constant roar of the cannons. From out of the clouds of smoke loomed the *Redoubtable*, dark and silent, before erupting into fire. More heavy blows thundered into the *Victory*'s hull, greeted by a chorus of cries from the wounded.

As the ships grew closer, Hardy paused for a moment, listening carefully. He was a veteran of many sea fights, but something about this one seemed different. A musket ball smacked into the planking at his feet, leaving a scar, followed by another. One of the sailors manning the starboard carronades dropped his rammer clattering to the deck, clutching his arm. A marine further along the side fell in a heap to the deck.

'That Frenchman seems to have a damned lot of sharpshooters, your lordship,' he reported.

'What of it?' queried Nelson. 'They will hardly answer against your great guns.'

'But it does grow hot on deck, and you are rather prominent, my lord. Might you remove some of your military orders to the safe keeping of Mr Scott?'

'And let the men think that I am frit?' replied the admiral. 'I would sooner die with honour than live with such shame, Tom.'

'May I at least insist we walk a little, my lord?' said Hardy. 'It may serve to unsettle their aim.'

The two men began to pace the deck, side by side, as if out for a leisurely stroll in a London park, while battle raged all around them. They barely missed a step when a shot from the *Redoutable* crashed through the ship's side, reducing John Scott in an instant from a man to a barely recognisable mess. Nelson paused for a moment beside his body, before indicating to one of the midshipmen that he should pick up the notebook and pencil that lay beside his secretary's remains. Then grenades began to rain down as the French ship came alongside, rumbling and hissing as they rolled across the deck. Many were put out by gun crews using the water from their swab buckets, but a few burst, creating fresh carnage.

But it was the French small-arms fire that was truly doing the damage. The remorseless rain of bullets had grown more intense as the ships had closed. The crack of musketry had become all pervasive and the upper deck of the *Victory*, so crowded when the battle started, was noticeably thinner of men as they were struck down and carried below to the surgeon. With a cry, one of the signal midshipmen was hit, his slate sliding from his grasp to rattle across the deck. Lieutenant Pasco was killed next, struck by two bullets in quick succession at his post above the grating. Then, as Hardy reached the end of the stretch of deck he had been pacing with Nelson, he realised that the admiral was no longer beside him.

'Oh, my word!' he exclaimed, turning back to see what had happened.

Nelson had sunk to his knees, as if in prayer, his face racked with pain and his left hand supporting him on the deck. From beneath the glittering epaulette on one shoulder a dark stain was growing. Hardy was just in time to prevent him collapsing as his arm gave way.

'They have done for me at last, Hardy,' gasped Nelson. 'My backbone is shot through.'

The captain looked desperately around and saw a bulky figure in a red coat. 'Sergeant Secker!' he roared. 'You two over there as well! Come and take his lordship down to the surgeon. At once!'

'My handkerchief!' cried Nelson as the men gently picked him up. 'It is in my coat pocket. Cover my face so the men are not discouraged.'

Hardy pulled it out and shook it open. 'I will come to you as soon as I am able,' he promised.

'Not before your duty is done, Tom,' said the admiral, his face fierce. 'When the battle is won there will be time enough for such things.'

'Until then, my lord,' said Hardy, and he placed the handkerchief over his friend's face, as much to conceal the tears in his own eyes. Then he rose to his feet, and returned to the fury of the battle that still raged all around him. Over the continuing roar of the cannons, he heard the clear sound of a trumpet, calling urgently. He hurried across to the ship's side, stepping over the fallen that littered the deck to join the few survivors manning it.

Below him lay the *Redoutable*, the remains of her fore

topsail hopelessly entangled with the wreck of the Victory's fore studdingsails. Her side was battered and scarred with the pounding she had received, and to Hardy's eye she sat lower in the water than she should. Between the two hulls lay a canyon of fire and smoke, where the guns of his own ship continued to fire, without reply from their opponent. He was about to congratulate himself on this, when a port lid on the lower deck of the French ship beneath him banged shut. Then another did, further forward, and another. 'Curious,' he muttered. 'Why would they be securing guns in the heat of battle?'

He looked down into the well of her main deck, searching for an explanation, and noticed sailors making their way up the ladderways. Many stumbled with weariness, their naked torsos grey with powder smoke. They stepped across their fallen comrades littering the deck towards the rows of arms chests that lay open along the centreline of the ship.

'The firing from the tops has stopped, thank Christ, sir,' commented the marine beside him. 'Maybe they're about to surrender?'

'I don't think their captain looks beat yet,' said Hardy, pointing to where Lucas was waving his sword and bellowing something to those in the mizzen top above him. Lines of men with muskets slung across their shoulders began making their way down the tattered remains of the shrouds. 'By Jove!' he exclaimed, as it came to him. 'I believe they mean to board us, the rogues!' He spun from the side and searched the quarterdeck for any surviving officers. Among the fallen stood the slight figure of a midshipman, his hands clasped behind his back, trying not to look at the horror that surrounded him. 'Mr Ogilvie!'

'Yes sir?' said the youngster.

'Make haste and go below! I need the gun crews on

deck. Summon all hands to repel boarders!'

'Aye aye, sir.'

'Pray God they come in time,' said Hardy, eyeing the teeming masses of Frenchmen gathering along the gangway beneath him and comparing them to the few exhausted survivors left on the *Victory*'s upper deck. In his mind he heard the voice of his friend who lay somewhere beneath his feet. 'Time is everything, gentlemen,' he had said to the assembled captains in the great cabin a few weeks ago. 'Five minutes may make the difference between victory and defeat.'

'Five minutes!' he roared, drawing his sword. 'Keep those bastards back for five minutes and we shall win the day!'

*****

'What is the delay?' fumed Lucas. 'Captain Dorre? Lieutenant Brissot? When are you going to board their flagship?'

'It's not so straightforward as we had planned, sir,' explained the marine officer.

'Their side is so much higher than ours, and both ships have a tumblehome that makes the gap even wider,' supplemented Brissot. 'Some of the men tried to jump across, but after the first few fell between the hulls, the others are fearful.'

Lucas made his way to the side, shouldering through the jostling mass of armed sailors to peer across the gap, two metres of smoke-filled chasm at sea level, but appreciably further at the height of the gangway. He gestured forwards to where the anchors of the two ships were interlocked together. 'What about boarding at the bow?'

'The enemy have a prodigiously big carronade mounted

on their forecastle,' explained Dorre. 'With one blast of canister it killed most of those trying to cross. I have sent my sergeant with some of our best marksmen to try and kill the crew. Perhaps we might try something when it is out of action.'

'We need some sort of bridge,' said Lucas. 'Like those Romans had.'

'The main yard!' cried Brissot, gesturing to where it jutted out over the deck of the *Victory* like the arm of a crane. 'It is certainly big enough and we have only to lower it down.'

'Do it now!' ordered Lucas. 'And find any other spars that may have survived. We must get across! And quickly.'

'Yes, sir.'

Sailors scrambled aloft to cast off the huge main yard, and soon it was making its jerky way downwards, leaving folds of tattered mainsail crushed beneath it. Lucas pulled his father's watch from his pocket and saw the minutes passing by. 'Come on!' he urged. 'Faster!'

It finally dropped into place, a steep ramp that rocked and grated as the two hulls rolled in the swell, and the first of the boarders began to make their uncertain way across it. Clustered at the far end were the marines and sailors who still survived on the *Victory*'s upper deck, being marshalled by a big figure in a captain's uniform. Muskets began to bang out, and the leading two French sailors fell between the hulls, but the rest pressed on. They had barely reached the far side when the swirling smoke behind the *Redoubtable* grew dark.

Lucas turned to see the enormous presence of another Royal Navy three-decker filling his world as it moved across his stern. The rest of the British line had arrived, and the five minutes that lay between victory and defeat were up. Lucas had barely begun to register the enormity of what was about to happen when the newly arrived *Temeraire* opened fire.

Clay and the Immortal Memory

A gale of shot poured across the deck of the French ship, ploughing into the massed sailors waiting to board the *Victory*, leaving furrows of dead and wounded among the dazed survivors. Choking gun smoke, thick as fog, rolled across the stricken ship. From just behind Lucas the mizzen mast let out a crack like a gunshot. It slowly leant over, then, gathering speed like an avalanche, it came tumbling down. He crouched low as the debris poured from above. A heavy block trailing a line of rope struck him on the shoulder, knocking him to the deck, where he lay stunned.

It was Brissot who found him, at the head of a party of axe-wielding sailors as they hacked at the last few shrouds that held the wrecked mast lying across the ship. He helped Lucas to his feet and pulled his flattened hat from beneath a shattered yard. 'What orders, sir?' he asked.

Lucas looked around his devastated ship. The *Victory* was still on one side, her rail filling with men as they arrived from below. Some of them fired muskets down on to the *Redoubtable*, while others got her upper deck guns back into action. One fired as he looked, sending a blast of canister through the boarders clinging to the mainyard. The crowd of survivors beat a hasty retreat back to their ship. Off his quarter was the *Temeraire*, slowly turning to come along his disengaged side. Beyond, more British ships could be vaguely seen in the smoke, each one battling with an opponent.

Lucas turned to his young rescuer. 'Get Dorre to shoot down those men,' he ordered, gesturing towards the *Victory* with the crumpled hat.

'He is dead, sir,' said the lieutenant, his face bleak. He indicated his own arm, spattered with blood. 'He was just beside me, and then …'

'What of the first lieutenant?'

'He went below with the carpenter, sir,' said Brissot. 'We have two metres of water in the hold, with more coming in all the time.'

Lucas looked at the younger man, taking in his red and weary eyes, the beautifully tailored coat his uncle had bought him filthy and torn. 'It's not over!' he said, grabbing Brissot's arm and then wincing at the pain in his shoulder. 'More of our fleet will be arriving from the south all the time. I'll look after the upper deck. You take every sailor you can find, and get some of our starboard guns in action against that ship.'

Brissot followed where he pointed. The *Temeraire* had made her turn and was closing in towards them. All along her side the triple row of cannons were being run out as their crews completed reloading them. 'Right,' he said. He reached for the whistle hanging around his neck, only to find it had vanished in all the chaos. Instead, he inserted two grimy fingers into his mouth and let out a piercing blast. 'Gun crews! To me!' he yelled, waving his hat and stumbling back towards the main ladderway.

Sailors followed him, leaving the many dead and wounded behind, relieved to be escaping the growing carnage on the exposed upper deck. But when Brissot arrived on the lower deck he found he only had enough survivors to get eight of the big thirty-six-pounders into action. The guns on the side facing their new opponent had yet to fire, so at least they were still loaded. He quickly organised his crews.

'Monsieur Pascal,' he said to the midshipman who had followed him below. 'Instruct the ship's boys to bring up fresh charges.'

'Yes, sir.'

'The rest of you, up ports!'

A line of squares appeared in the side, revealing a brief

expanse of sea, dangerously close to the bottom rim of the gunports, and then a wall of yellow and black as the *Temeraire* ranged alongside. So close were the ships that Brissot could make out the face of a sailor, staring back at him through a port directly opposite. 'Run up,' he said, and the line of guns trundled forwards to bang against the ship's side. 'Ready!' He waited until every gun captain had his glowing linstock poised over a touch hole. A little water slopped in through the port nearest to him, splashing across the deck, while outside the *Temeraire* drifted on, the sailor replaced by a passing series of square vignettes. 'Fire!'

The broadside was a mean version of the ones the ship had been firing earlier. The thunder of sound was quickly lost across the abandoned deck, the recoil of the guns barely heeling the waterlogged hull in response, but it still created enough smoke to blanket the target. As the men swabbed out the barrels, Brissot looked around for the ship's boys he had allocated to each one. 'Come on! Bring up fresh charges, there!' he yelled.

'There aren't any, sir,' reported Pascal from the ladderway that led down towards the hold. 'Leastways no dry ones. The gunner says the magazine's awash.'

'How are we meant to fight with damp powder …' began a voice, but he was cut off by the colossal roar as the *Temeraire* fired again. She was so close alongside that Brissot felt the heat from the gun flashes as a scorching wind blasting in through the ports. Every shot struck home. The thunder of cannon balls bursting through the ship's side was like a rapid tattoo played with giant hammers. Each shot howled and crashed its way across the deck, destroying all in its path, many unleashing whirling splinters of wood. One scoured its way along the barrel of a gun, sending molten fragments flying through the crew crouching around it. Moments later came a shuddering crash from above. The ship rolled and shook under the blow, and more water poured in over the sills of the open ports.

Once the gale of fire had swept through, Brissot stood looking at the carnage around him. The upper half of the gundeck was cloaked by a thin haze of smoke. Beneath this the stunned survivors stood among the sobbing wounded and motionless dead who littered the space around the guns. From somewhere above came the sound of a volley of musketry. 'Pascal, take charge here,' he ordered. 'See these men are taken down to the surgeon, and secure the guns. And close those port lids, before we founder. I must report to the captain and see what is happening on deck.'

'Yes, sir.'

Brissot ran up the aft ladderway, the sound of fighting growing as he went. He emerged on to the quarterdeck to find chaos. Both remaining masts were down, leaving mounds of shattered spars and heaped canvas and rope blanketing the ship. On both sides a three-decker towered over them. The side of the *Temeraire* was lined with red-coated marines, busily picking off remaining members of the crew as they emerged from under the wreckage. Astern another newly arrived British ship was passing, this time a seventy-four. Mercifully she was not firing into the stricken *Redoutable*, presumably for fear of hitting the other two ships.

Brissot picked his way through the wreckage, ducking as musket bullets whined passed him, to where the captain was sitting on a quarterdeck cannon, having a gash in his arm bandaged by a sailor.

'What word from the guns, Lieutenant?' Lucas shouted, over the crackle of musket fire.

'We could only fire them once, sir. There are no dry charges to be had, and the water is up to the sills.'

'While up here we have lost all our masts and most of our remaining men,' said Lucas, waving towards the destruction around him with his good arm. '*Tant pis!* The old girl fought bravely, but we can do no more, Francois. It is over. We must surrender.'

Brissot could only nod at this, his eyes blinking.

Lucas indicated the tattered tricolour that hung limply from the stump of the mizzen mast, the white part grey with smoke, the red fly torn and shredded. 'Haul it down,' he ordered.

*****

It took the *Victory* some time to disentangle herself from the defeated *Redoutable.* Even when the fallen wreckage of the French ship's masts was cleared away, their anchors were still hooked together. As the foundering seventy-four sank lower in the water, she seemed intent on pulling the British flagship down after her, the thick iron of her best bower groaning as it slowly bent under the colossal strain. Eventually the battered *Victory* pulled free, ready to seek new victims. But the battle had moved on. The centre of Villeneuve's fleet had been defeated, with only badly damaged French and Spanish prizes rolling in the swell, their prize crews trying to get them underway. And the *Victory* herself was hardly able to make rapid progress. She had lost most of her mizzen mast and her main and foremasts were so badly damaged that Hardy dared not risk more than minimal sail. Her fight with the stubborn *Redoutable* had wounded her in other ways too. A stream of water spouting from her side bore witness to how her crew had to work to combat the flooding within.

The *Victory* lumbered on, but the fight was always ahead of her, and the only enemies she encountered were more prizes, littering the sea. It was late afternoon and the sun was dropping towards the ominous clouds that were building on the western horizon, when Hardy concluded that his ship could do no more. He left his post at last, tired and aching from having been on his feet since long before dawn. Pausing only to order the galley relit to provide a hot meal for his crew, he made his way down through his ship, smiling and offering encouragement to the gun crews as he passed them on each level.

The orlop deck was just beneath the waterline. It was a low, dimly lit space at the best of times, but now it resembled a scene from hell. At its heart was the cockpit, the only brightly lit part, where William Beatty, the ship's surgeon, worked in his blood-sodden clothes on yet another patient. His operating table was made from sea chests lashed together under a canvas cover slick with gore. Radiating from this central point were the wounded, laid out in ranks that covered most of the deck, while further forward were the dead, stacked like timber. Hardy picked his way forward, stepping over the sprawling legs and arms with care, his tall frame doubled over beneath the low deck beams.

'Did we win, sir?' asked a marine, grabbing at his coat sleeve as he passed. His head was swathed in a bandage, so that only one bright eye was visible.

'We did, Private. Most handsomely, I declare, although the fight still goes on.'

'Thank you, sir. A proper tonic, that is,' said the soldier, sinking back down again.

'I come for word of his lordship, Doctor,' said Hardy,

arriving eventually at the entrance to the cockpit.

'A moment, I pray, sir,' said Beatty in his Irish brogue. 'I must part this poor man from his foot first, and then I shall take you to him.' He leant over the sailor, whose head was supported by one of his assistants, his face racked with pain. 'Jacobs, get another tot of grog down you. That's it. Now we must gag you with this strap for the preservation of your tongue.'

'Will it take long?' gasped the patient.

'Not above five minutes, less if you can lie still, and then you'll be free of that sadly crushed leg. 'Tis the only way, to be sure.'

'All right, Doctor. I'm ready.'

'Clap on to him, men,' ordered Beatty, tightening the torniquet around the sailor's thigh.

Hardy chose to look away from the struggling sailor, as his body arched against the pain of the first cut, but his ears were not so easily spared. It was the grating of saw on bone that most disturbed him. He sighed with relief when Beatty completed the final suture and appeared at his elbow, pulling off his apron and wiping his hands on a cloth. 'How will that poor soul fair, Doctor?' he asked.

'Jacobs will do tolerably well, if there is no corruption,' said the Irishman. 'His is the eleventh amputation I have performed this day, and the other ten are all yet with us.' He indicated a large basket where Jacob's foot had joined those of the previous patients, legs for the most part, mixed with the occasional arm.

'And what is the butcher's bill?'

The surgeon pulled a stained slip of paper from his coat pocket. 'Fifty-six dead so far and a hundred and fifteen wounded, although at least six of those will not recover, perhaps more. An unusually high proportion of marines, I note, sir.'

'And what of his lordship? Does he yet live?'

'He does at present, but he is one of my six, sir,' said Beatty. 'Indeed, it is near miraculous he has clung to life as long as he has.'

'No!' exclaimed Hardy. 'That cannot be! Surely, he was only hit in the shoulder?'

'The left shoulder, but the trajectory of the bullet was near vertical, sir. It missed his heart and the greater blood vessels by a whisker, passed through his lung and severed his spine, where it still resides. No person can long survive such a dreadful wound. I have made him comfortable in the purser's cot over yonder.'

Beatty led the way through the rows of wounded to the cabin. Lines of soft yellow light shone from between the slats on the door. He pushed it open, and stepped to one side to let his captain go through first.

Nelson lay on the cot. He had been stripped naked and wrapped in a sheet, with his face, pale from loss of blood, propped up against the bulkhead on pillows. Were it not for a thin trickle of red by the corner of his mouth, he might have been peacefully sleeping. The warmth of the crowded orlop was added to by the oil lamp that swung from a beam overhead, which his steward did his best to combat by fanning him with his hat.

'How does he fare?' asked Hardy.

'He's hot, sir, and perishing thirsty,' replied the servant. 'He was awake just now an' asking for you.'

Nelson's eyes fluttered open as they approached, and he extended a hand towards the *Victory*'s commander. 'Hardy, my friend, how goes the battle?' he whispered. 'How goes the day with us?'

Clay and the Immortal Memory

The captain knelt down beside him, his bulk dwarfing the thin figure on the cot, and took the proffered hand. 'Very well, my lord. We have twelve or fourteen of the enemy's ships in our possession.'

Nelson nodded at this, the ghost of a smile playing on his lips. The trickle grew in strength and Beatty leant forward to wipe it away.

'That is good,' continued the admiral, 'but I had bargained for twenty.'

'If you have taught me anything in all our years together, my lord, it is never to be content with less than a full measure,' smiled Hardy, although his heart was breaking. 'The battle goes on in a desultory fashion, so I cannot say exactly how many will finally be taken. But I am sure the victory will be a complete one. Their van may escape us, but few others will.'

The hand gave his a feeble squeeze and the eyes closed once more. 'That is good,' he muttered. 'Thank God, I have done my duty.'

He lay silent for a moment, and other sounds intruded into the room. The roll and creak of the hull as the *Victory* sailed on. The dry hiss of the lamp, the distant clank of the pumps and the low moan of the wounded just beyond the door. Then the eyes opened once more, full of concern. 'Anchor, Hardy,' he croaked, 'before that storm is upon us.'

'I have made the preparations to do so, my lord, although our best bower was sadly bent out of true by that damned Frenchman.'

But the concern on Nelson's face remained. 'Don't throw me overboard, when I am gone, I pray you,' he whispered.

Hardy looked towards Beatty for help.

'His lordship has been speaking of his desire to be buried on land, sir,' said the surgeon. 'I thought that if you were to furnish me with a cask to act as a sarcophagus, and we were to fill it with sufficient ardent spirits, I daresay we could see his body home.'

'Then we will certainly not bury you at sea, my lord,' promised the captain, and Nelson closed his eyes again.

Minutes dragged by. Beatty bent over his patient and pressed two fingers to his neck, feeling for a pulse. 'Very feeble, sir,' he commented.

Nelson stirred once more, muttering something, and they bent close to hear. 'I am a dead man, Hardy,' he breathed. 'It will be over with me soon.'

Hardy turned away to dash the tears from his eyes and missed what Nelson said next.

'I believe he asked you to kiss him, sir,' offered Beatty.

Hardy shuffled a little closer, kissed his friend on the forehead, and never spoke with him again.

Chapter 19
Storm

The crew of the *Griffin* found the battle a strange, confused affair that they experienced as spectators rather than as participants, as if they were servants left outside a house, listening to a lively ball taking place within. They were ordered to keep station on the *Victory*, but she had vanished into a rolling storm of smoke and fire. Thanks to the almost windless conditions the fog spread ever wider as ship after ship in the long British line joined the fight.

With the approach of evening, the wind began to strengthen, settling into the south-west and sweeping away the smoke. Now the men of the *Griffin* fell silent at the view before them. The sea was covered in badly damaged ships, many with broken or missing masts, so that it was hard to pick Royal Navy survivors from their French and Spanish prizes. Some were still locked together with their opponents, like wrestlers too exhausted to break hold. Others drifted free, slowly turning among the flotsam of broken spars and torn sails that covered the surface of the water. One captured French seventy-four was sending a twisting column of black smoke up into the sky from a fire that burned unchecked on her deck. Close at hand was the *Victory*, her smoke-stained side a colander of shot holes. She had heaved to, rocking in the waves, to allow her crew to work on repairing her shredded rigging.

Clay was first to break the silence. 'My God! What carnage is this? Look at the poor old *Royal Sovereign*.' He pointed towards Collingwood's flagship, strangely unbalanced with only her foremast and bowsprit left standing.

'But it is a victory, sir,' said Preston. 'I count eighteen prizes. That will make it greater even than the Nile. And the battle goes on. See? Away to the north. Some of our ships are chasing their van.'

'A victory, but at what cost?' queried Clay.

'Is that the coast of Spain?' asked Taylor, pointing ahead at a blue line on the horizon.

'We must have drifted during the battle, sir,' commented Armstrong. 'That will be the push of the wind and the swell that has been running all day.'

Clay looked behind him, to where the horizon was growing dark with cloud. 'And we are in for heavy weather soon. Many of these ships will struggle to get clear. We will be required to take some of them in tow, I make no doubt.'

'Shall I get the boatswain to rouse out a suitable cable, sir?' suggested Taylor.

'If you please. Also secure the guns and have the galley relit,' ordered Clay. 'The men must be famished.

'Aye aye, sir.'

'Boat putting out from the *Victory*, sir,' reported Russell. 'It looks to be heading our way.'

Clay watched the launch come nearer. A single officer was seated in the stern sheets next to the coxswain. 'Heave to, if you please, Mr Armstrong.'

'Aye aye, sir.'

His visitor proved to be a lieutenant, his clothes grimed with gun smoke and what looked suspiciously like blood on one shoe. 'Captain Clay?' he asked. 'My name is Hills, third lieutenant of the *Victory*, sir. Apologies for my appearance, but the ship is still cleared for action.'

'No matter, Mr Hills. I am very pleased to make your acquaintance. Let me congratulate you on your role in this great victory.'

'Thank you, sir,' said Hills, his face grim. 'Captain Hardy is sending me across to the *Royal Sovereign* with a message that is not appropriate for a signal. But he asked me to come here first, knowing that you were a particular acquaintance of Lord Nelson.'

Clay felt cold grip him. 'What message?' he asked.

'I have melancholy tidings to relate, sir. His lordship was struck down during the battle, and has since succumbed to his injuries. I am to inform Admiral Collingwood that he is in command of the fleet. Captain Hardy wanted me to pass on his condolences, and to assure you that his lordship clung to life long enough to learn of his victory, and in consequence died content.'

Clay stared at the officer. 'Nelson dead?' he queried, slowly absorbing the news. 'How can that be?' He thought about the times that his career had crossed with that of the great man, first in the Mediterranean, then in the Baltic, and more recently here. The supportive letter Nelson had written to the court martial when he had lost his previous ship. Then he remembered his final meeting with him, and Nelson's quiet certainty about his future. 'How the deuce did he know?' he muttered.

'Sir?'

'Nothing, Lieutenant. Pray pass on my thanks to Captain Hardy for his kindness.'

'I will, sir,' said Hills. 'The captain also thought that you might be able to assist the *Redoubtable*. She is in quite a deplorable state, little above a hulk, and only has a small prize crew on board furnished by the *Temeraire*.'

'Very well. Be good enough to point her out to me, after which you had best make haste to reach the *Royal Sovereign*. There is much for the admiral to do before the weather closes in.'

'The *Redoubtable* is the dismasted prize over there, sir. She fought most gallantly, against prodigious odds. It was from her that the shot came that killed the admiral.'

*****

Blake's climb out of the *Griffin*'s longboat and up the side of the *Redoubtable* proved easier than he had expected. Her hull had sunk so low in the water that the waves were slapping against her closed lower gunports, and although many of the ladder rungs fixed to her side had been destroyed, jagged shot holes made convenient holds for his feet and hands.

He stepped down on to her deck and into a living nightmare.

'Thank God you have come,' said a thin, harassed-looking naval lieutenant, hastening across and grasping his hand. 'I am truly at my wits' end. I'm Wallace, of the *Temeraire*.'

'John Blake, second of the *Griffin*,' said the new arrival, taking in the scene around him. In every direction was utter destruction. None of the *Redoubtable*'s masts had survived the action, leaving only splintered columns to mark where they had once stood, which meant the upper deck was curiously flooded with light. The planking was scarred and battered, heavily stained with blood, and awash with debris. The shattered hull of a ship's boat, torn in two, lay heaped among a nest of broken spars and cut rigging in front of him. Overturned guns, broken fragments of rail, jagged splinters of wood, discarded weapons and equipment were everywhere. And there were bodies, dozens upon dozens of bodies, staring glassily back at him, all strangely animated as the hull rolled in the swell. They were perhaps the lucky ones, to judge from the pitiful cries of the wounded coming up through the gratings from the deck below. He wrenched his attention back to the man in front of him. 'What steps have you taken so far to secure the ship, Mr Wallace?' he asked.

'I have done what I can,' said the officer, running a hand through his hair, 'but the *Temeraire* went into battle a hundred under complement, and with so many opponents still to fight the captain would only sanction twenty sailors and a dozen marines for my prize crew. I have moved the living and wounded, of which there are a multitude, below decks, guarded by my marines; and my men have cut free the wreckage of the masts. But the ship has no serviceable rudder left, no binnacle, no boats and will surely founder soon, unless we are driven on to the coast of Spain first. I ask you, sir. What more am I to do?'

'Is the French captain still on board?' said Blake. 'Perhaps we could ask him to order some of the prisoners to help us?'

Wallace shook his head. 'I sent him on board the *Temeraire*, together with all the other wounded officers. There were a couple of lieutenants among the prisoners. Shall I have them found?'

'Not yet. Let me first report back to my captain.'

The *Griffin* was hove to, close by the stricken *Redoubtable*, but the wind had picked up considerably in the time that Blake had been on board, and he had to yell at the top of his voice to be heard. The dark clouds in the south west had advanced over the horizon, stained blood red where they masked the setting sun. Silver threads of lightening flickered and stabbed among them.

'You had best stay on board, Mr Blake,' bellowed Clay through his speaking trumpet. 'I will send a dozen hands across to you, along with Mr Corbett to assist their surgeon in tending to the wounded. Then we must get you under tow. You are still drifting towards the shore.'

'Aye aye, sir.'

While Blake was waiting for the new arrivals, he and Wallace climbed up to the open poop deck at the stern from where they could look over the *Redoubtable*, and discuss how to save her. All around them ships were preparing for the approaching storm, in whatever way they could. Thin spars, bending and flexing in the strengthening wind, were being hauled upright and lashed to the stumps of masts to allow a little sail to be carried. On more fortunate ships that had retained their masts, men worked aloft, fishing damaged yards and splicing severed rigging.

Blake pointed towards a nearby captured Spanish ship having a jury mizzen mast set up. 'Might we be able to attempt something similar, when the extra men promised by Captain Clay arrive?'

'We might, if a single spar had survived the battle,' said Wallace. 'All those stored on the skid beams were destroyed when the main mast fell.'

'Can we anchor if we are forced to?'

'I'm afraid not,' reported Wallace. 'All the larboard ones were ripped off by the *Victory*, while the starboard cathead hasn't survived the battle.'

Well, it could be a deal worse,' said Blake. 'At least we haven't taken fire like that poor fellow.' He pointed to the prize that Clay had seen earlier, which continued to burn. The column of black smoke had swollen in size, and they could see flames licking across her hull, fanned by the rising wind. One of her remaining masts was a flaming crucifix against the dark clouds filling the western sky, and sailors were pouring down her sides into boats sent across from nearby ships. They pulled clear, rowing frantically, full to the gunnels, the fire behind them growing all the time.

Then the fire reached her magazine.

Blake must have been a full mile away when she erupted like a volcano, black arms of smoke punching outwards in every direction. Blasted fragments of timber and debris soared through the air, splashing down all around her. He felt the shock wave in his chest as it reached him, along with the roar of the explosion. A dark mushroom rose high above her, and was quickly torn away by the wind. Then there was nothing but madly rocking boats amid a field of debris to show where the ship had once been.

'Poor bastards,' exclaimed Wallace. 'How many do you suppose were still on board?'

'Most of the wounded, I imagine,' said Blake, shaking his head. 'Come, let us see that we don't share their fate. Here come the men my captain promised.'

Wallace looked to where the sailors from the *Griffin* were swarming over the side, carrying bundles of dressings and several leather cases of surgical equipment. They were followed rather more slowly by Richard Corbett, one hand clutching his hat against the tug of the wind. 'Let us get her under tow first, Mr Blake. Then we can see about saving the ship.'

*****

The *Griffin* was hove to in the late evening light, her backed topsail rippling in the strengthening wind. Off to one side the coast of Spain had grown from a faint line on the horizon to a distant view of scrub covered hills and cliffs, with angry lines of surf breaking at their feet. Behind the frigate lay the *Redoubtable*, rolling freely in the swell without any sails to hold her steady, each rush of movement accompanied by a collective cry from her wounded.

'Where is that damned cable?' Clay demanded. 'The sooner we can get some way on that poor ship, the better.'

'Just coming across now, sir,' said Taylor, who was leaning out over the stern rail.

Clay came to join his first lieutenant. Beneath him was the longboat, pitching and surging in the swell, while one of the frigate's huge anchor cables was slowly passed down to them through a stern gun port. Some of the boat crew were busy bailing out the water that slopped freely over the sides, while the others pulled the stubborn rope into the boat. Up on the forecastle of the French prize Clay could see Blake surrounded by the party of men from the *Griffin*, anxiously waiting for it. Further back more sailors were lightening the ship. He watched as a body was heaved over the rail, thumping heavily against the side as it fell.

'The cable is secure, sir,' yelled Preston, from the longboat.

'Carry on!' ordered Taylor, through his speaking trumpet. 'Make sure that you only pay the cable out as swiftly as the boat progresses, Mr Hutchinson!'

'Aye aye, sir,' replied the unseen boatswain, from the deck below. 'Keep it steady, there!'

Slowly the longboat pulled across towards the *Redoubtable*, rocking violently in the waves, a thick snake trailing behind it. At one stage Clay held his breath as it disappeared from view behind a passing wave, but then the boat pulled through, still heading for the French prize, the bow two oarsmen now bailing furiously. Clay watched as two of Blake's men clambered down among the shattered remains of the seventy-four's head rails to lower a rope towards the sea. Even without his telescope he would have been able to recognised the hulking Evans, and Trevan's blond pigtail blowing in the wind.

'Pay out more scope, Mr Hutchinson!' yelled Taylor, as the cable began to rise dripping from the waves.

'Aye aye, sir,' replied the boatswain.

Now the longboat had arrived beneath the broken bowsprit of the *Redoubtable*, rising and falling to the rhythm of the waves. The line dangling down from above led to a group clustered in the middle of the boat. Then they broke apart and Clay saw Preston waving to those above him. Evans and Trevan heaved on the rope, which now had the end of the thick hawse bent to it. More sailors scrambled down to help them, and the stiff cable slowly rose up on to the beakhead. Clay let out a sigh as the heavy rope wormed its way on board the French ship.

While they waited for the towing cable to be made fast in the *Redoubtable*, Clay looked around at the rest of the prizes. Some were limping along under what fragments of sail they could bear, trying to claw their way out to sea, others were under tow. A British seventy-four that had escaped the battle with only the loss of her main topmast passed up wind of the *Griffin*, towing a big Spanish eighty-gunner behind her. As Clay watched them, a gust of wind laid the British ship over, sending waves crashing high up the side of the prize. The curve of the tow rope became a solid bar as the strain came on and for a moment he felt sure it must part. Then the seventy-four let the wind spill from its fore topsail, the Spanish hulk surged forward, and the moment of danger passed. But the same gust of wind was now hurtling down towards him, ripping white foam from the wave crests as it came, ready to drive the *Griffin* down to leeward much faster than the mast-less *Redoubtable*. If that happened, the frigate would tear the cable out of the French ship long before Blake could possibly have made it fast.

'Mr Armstrong! Let fly the sheets!' roared Clay. 'Mr Taylor, let out as much cable as you are able! Do it now!'

A moment of frenzied activity, in which Clay thanked his stars he had experienced officers and crew, and then the gust hit the *Griffin*. Her released topsails volleyed and cracked overhead, a counterpoint to the mad shriek of the wind through her rigging. Even without the pressure of the sails, the frigate still heeled over, and Clay could feel her being driven down to leeward. The cable between the ships rose dripping out of the water, despite the speed it was roaring out of the gunport, sending up a cloud of hemp fragments. And then the gust had gone, speeding over the waves towards the looming bulk of Cape Trafalgar, only eight miles away.

'That was close,' he breathed. 'I'll have that topsail backed once more, Mr Armstrong,' ordered Clay. 'Resume paying out that cable, Mr Taylor.'

'Aye aye, sir.'

Now it was growing dark as the boiling wall of cloud in the west masked the sun, and Clay pulled his coat a little closer against the wind. 'What can be keeping Mr Blake?' he muttered. 'We shall both be on the rocks presently if we don't get underway.' He stared towards the *Redoubtable*, rolling even more extravagantly than before as the rising waves crashed against her sides, driving her remorselessly towards the land. Then something white appeared on her forecastle and was waved furiously in their direction.

'Make all fast to the brace bits, Mr Hutchinson!' bellowed Taylor.

'Aye aye, sir.'

'Longboat is lashed down and secure, sir,' reported Preston.

'Good, let us get underway,' said Clay. 'An extra pair of helmsmen on the wheel, if you please, Mr Taylor. She will want to fly up into the wind with that huge dead weight dragging behind. And we will need to start slow and build up speed, else that cable will part for sure.'

'Aye aye, sir. I'll get the topsails reefed,' said Taylor. He looked to the west, almost black as night beneath the boiling clouds. Streaks of falling rain could be seen among the flickering lightning. 'We will struggle to make much progress against this storm, but if we can at least haul her off to the south we will have more sea room.'

'Let us make it so, George,' said Clay. 'I do believe we are in for a busy night.'

*****

The few unharmed members of the *Redoubtable*'s crew had been housed in the manger at the bow end of the lower deck, which meant they were treated to the full effect as the colossal strain came on the tow cable made fast to the fore bits above their heads.

The volley of groans and creaks that shook the hull brought Lieutenant Dupotet from out of the dark place into which he had sunk. He was resting with his back to one of the solid vertical beams, and could feel the wood as it vibrated. He looked up, ignoring the other able-bodied survivors lying around him in the gloom, and watched the grating above his head. It was trembling so much that even the pair of marine sentries posted on the deck above exchanged troubled glances. Then the shaking lessened and the roll of the hull became a little easier.

'That's better, sir,' said Tournier, the boatswain, who was beside him. 'The old girl is underway at last.'

'Old girl?' queried Dupotet. 'Old Girl? Don't you understand? It's not our ship any more, you fool!' He pointed towards the red-coated figures. 'It is theirs now, and a fine addition it will make to their Royal bloody Navy. Why the hell did Lucas surrender?'

'We couldn't fight on, sir,' said the boatswain, to nods from those around him. 'You were down in the hold with the carpenter at the time, but we were finished. No charges for the guns, no masts standing, and a dirty big three-decker or each side shooting us like fish in a bucket.'

'So much for Dorre and Brissot's great plan,' scoffed the first lieutenant. 'Where are that brilliant pair, by the way?'

'Captain Dorre was killed on the main deck earlier, sir,' said Tournier. 'But the lieutenant is still alive. Last I saw of him he was helping the doctor with the wounded.'

'Of course he would be,' muttered Dupotet. 'Ever the man of the people.'

'Do you think we should be helping too, sir?' said a voice. 'There are hundreds. The lower deck is covered in them.'

'Listen to me,' said Dupotet. 'For good or ill, we have surrendered. That means the running of the ship isn't our concern anymore. The English wanted to capture it so much. Now they can deal with the problems.'

There were uneasy glances around the space, but no one said anything. From beyond the flimsy canvas partition that separated them from the rest of the deck came the continued sound of the wounded. Someone whimpering from close at hand. A chorus of others, all pleading for water. Another voice, loud with delirium, calling out a woman's name over and over. And further off the choked scream of some unfortunate being operated on.

Brissot appeared around the end of the screen, his beautiful coat tattered and stained with blood, his face pale and drawn. 'The English want to speak with the person in charge of the crew, sir,' he explained. 'I said I would come and find you.'

'Strategist, surgeon and now errand boy for the enemy,' said Dupotet, rising to his feet. 'Are there no end to your talents, Monsieur Brissot? Well, you had best lead me to them.'

The lower deck beyond the partition was a scene of horror. The port lids were closed and bolted, where they had not been smashed off, leaving only a few swaying lamps and a little evening light shining in through shot holes to illuminate the space. Discarded equipment and shattered fragments of wood lay in heaps across the deck. Between them every inch of planking was occupied by the wounded, save a thin corridor kept clear down the middle of the deck. Some, the lucky ones, were able to sit up against the sides of the ship, with stained bandages tied around a minor wound. But most lay prostrate on the deck, either waiting for attention or lying insensible after the trauma of amputation with only swathes of darkly stained cloth to mark where their missing limb had been.

A small man in a leather apron with steel-rimmed glasses was bending over one patient who had lost both his legs below the knee. Then he stood back up. '*Ici*,' he called across to a pair of lightly wounded assistants. 'He is dead. *Mort*. You understand?' He pointed to where two gunports had been beaten into a single jagged hole by gunfire. 'Over the side with him. *Dans l'eau, oui*? But keep his bandages. *Les pansement, oui*? We shall have need of them yet.'

The two men stripped the corpse of its sodden bandages and carried it away to the hole in the side. The body proved difficult to manoeuvre through it, but eventually there was the sound of a splash.

'This way, sir,' said Brissot, threading his way through the wounded. 'But have a care. A round shot has damaged the ladderway.'

'Who is that man?' queried Dupotet as he followed his colleague. 'The one with the glasses.'

'He is the surgeon from the frigate that has us under tow, sir. He is helping Monsieur Paillard, which is just as well. There are over two hundred wounded to tend to.'

'One less now,' muttered the first lieutenant.

On the deck above they were stopped by another pair of marines blocking their way with crossed muskets, bayonets fixed.

'Let them through, Private,' ordered a young naval officer with sandy hair and pale blue eyes. 'Gentlemen, my name is Lieutenant Blake, from his majesty's ship *Griffin*, here to assist Mr Wallace and his prize crew,' he explained. 'My French is quite indifferent, so I trust we can speak in English? Or shall I pass the word for one of my men to translate?'

'I speak good English, Monsieur,' said Brissot. 'When I was young, we often had American visitors to our house. My father was anxious to learn how they had succeeded in freeing themselves from the rule of a king.'

'I can also speak it,' said Dupotet. 'And I am the superior officer. What can I do for you, Monsieur Blake?'

'Gentlemen, a very ugly looking storm is coming, and you must be aware that this ship is in a perilous state to receive it. Dismasted, repeatedly holed below the waterline, and on a lee shore. My ship is attempting to tow her to safety, but the situation is very bleak.'

'What is it that you need from us?' asked Brissot.

'Your carpenter survived the battle, did he not?' said Blake. 'Your boatswain also. They could work to repair some of the holes in the hull, while the rest of your men could man the pumps.'

'*Non*!' said Dupotet. 'Out of the question! None of my men will be used in this way.'

'But sir …' protested his colleague.

'Silence, Monsieur Brissot,' ordered the first lieutenant. 'I am in command.'

'Actually, Lieutenant Wallace is in command,' corrected Blake. 'And pray consider what you are saying. How will all those wounded men on the lower deck fare if the ship should founder?'

'Do you have anything else to discuss, Monsieur?' asked Dupotet. 'Or is this interview at an end?'

'Sir! Your attitude renders me quite speechless … ' began the Englishman.

'Excellent, that will save me from having to refuse any more of your requests,' said Dupotet. 'You will receive no aid from my men. The *Redoubtable* is your responsibility now. Good day to you.'

*****

An hour later and the full fury of the storm was upon them. Across the fleet sailors of all nationalities, exhausted from a day of fighting, found themselves in a fresh battle. The wind picked up to a howling frenzy, roaring out of the night and seemingly determined to sweep everyone, whether victors or vanquished, on to the hard coast of Spain. All around the *Griffin* the waves were surging mountains of slate, while overhead lightning split the night.

Clay stood hunched in his oilskins, his legs well apart on the bucking deck as a fresh cascade of water broke over the side and washed across it. He could feel that the lithe frigate was doing her best to ride the waves, but just as she rose to the next one, she was pulled back by the leash of tow rope held by the dead hand of the *Redoubtable.* A flash of movement caught his eye, and he watched as a sailor came sliding down the mainmast backstay, his clothes thrashing in the wind.

The man came running across the deck to report. 'That French flagship what the *Victory* raked away down yonder is sending up distress signals, sir,' he reported in a steady shout over the violence of the storm. 'I think she has dragged her anchor.'

'Where away, Pickford?' he asked, in a matching bellow.

'To the north, sir. She be mighty close to the rocks, an' all.'

'There is nothing we can do in this,' said Clay. 'We have enough to occupy us with our own prize. Return to your post, and pray use the shrouds to come down next time. The backstay is too hazardous in this gale.'

'Aye aye, sir,' replied the lookout, touching his forehead and making his way across the deck.

He was quickly replaced by another figure in full oilskins. 'Two foot in the well, sir,' reported Taylor, leaning close to be heard over the shrieking of the mizzen shrouds. 'I've got a party at work on the larboard pump to keep it under control, and Mr Preston is going around the guns double-breeching them.'

Before Clay could reply another wave crashed into the frigate's windward side and a fresh deluge broke across the deck. Both men instinctively clung on to the rail as the wave swept onwards.

'We may need to take in another reef, sir,' continued Taylor, clutching the brim of his sou'wester as he peered aloft. 'I'm amazed that nothing has carried away.'

'Not yet, George,' yelled Clay. 'We are barely making any progress as it is. This wind blows us down to leeward as quickly as we can claw back against it.'

The two men turned to watch the reason for the *Griffin*'s miserable progress. The cable was stretched into a black bar angling down to leeward, vanishing and reappearing as it sawed through the huge waves. At its far end was a low, dark shape, rolling like a whale among a welter of white water.

'Hell must be a lot like the inside of that poor ship,' said Armstrong, coming across to join them.

'Is it me, or does she seem to be riding even lower, sir?' commented Taylor.

Clay looked for comparison towards some of the other damaged ships. Just to windward was another hulk, this one with a little sail set on the stump of her lower foremast. She was being bodily hauled through the storm by an undamaged Royal Navy seventy-four. 'You're right. Look at that French prize over there, the *Fougueux*. She carries her lower ports much higher,' he observed.

As they turned to watch, the *Fougueux* buried her bow into a huge wave. A curtain of white arced over her forecastle and she came to an abrupt halt. For a moment the tow rope became visible as a spray of white water was squeezed out of the fibres by the colossal strain. Then it parted with a bang like a gunshot, audible even over the storm. The British ship surged forwards through the water, and the stricken prize was swept away towards the coast.

'God help those poor souls,' muttered Clay to himself.

'Shall we try and send a boat across, sir?' shouted Taylor. 'See if we can take anyone off?'

Clay shook his head. 'Look at this sea. No open boat could survive in these waves.'

Taylor looked back at the *Redoubtable*. 'Then how do we get our people off if she should break free, or founder, sir?'

'In truth I don't know, George. Pray God that she does neither, and somehow survives the night.'

*****

Down on the lower deck of the *Redoubtable*, a ring of space had been created around the cracked base of the main mast by sliding the worst of the wounded aside. It was here that the ship's pumps were situated. Most had been destroyed in the battle, leaving only one in action, the handle clanging around and around, drawing water up from the well at the foot of the mast and sending it away over the side. The line of sailors from the *Griffin* turning the pump handle had the grim determination of desperate men.

It was difficult work. The rising storm was making the deck roll and pitch beneath them with such violence that even experienced seamen were struggling to keep their footing. Waves thundered against the ship's sides, the noise deafening, each fresh impact accompanied by jets of water shooting in through the many shot holes that still remained un-plugged. Despite this, the lower deck was uncomfortably hot, thanks to the huge numbers of French prisoners confined there. As the men toiled away their bare torsos glistened in the light of the wildly swinging lamp hanging from the beam above them.

'Holy Mary!' gasped O'Malley. 'Are we after pumping the whole of the fecking Atlantic from out of the hold?'

'Near enough, Sean,' said Trevan. 'There be sieves as leak less than this barky. That Grunter from the old *Temeraire* be after fothering a sail to go over the side, but it'll never answer with this sea running.'

'Just keep pumping,' growled Evans, whose place was directly over the grating. 'The bleeding orlop's awash now.'

Trevan shifted his position a little, until he could peer down to the deck below. Light flickered off the surface of water that had risen from out of the hold, and was running freely across the planking. 'Aye, pick up the pace lads,' he agreed.

Further forward Brissot was also looking at the water. He and the boatswain had levered up the hatch in the middle of the deck that led down to the orlop.

'She is settling, sir,' he reported to Dupotet. 'By the stern, from the feel of the deck. There is a little water in the passage way, but it will be much worse further aft.'

The first lieutenant looked up, and came across to the square hole in the deck. 'Interesting,' he murmured. 'That must be the corridor to the light room for the magazine.'

'Yes, monsieur,' confirmed Tournier. 'As well as the sail room and the carpenter's stores.'

'Carpenter's stores?' repeated Dupotet.

'Are you thinking we might use them to help patch the ship, sir?' asked Brissot.

'I was thinking more about his tools,' said the first lieutenant, looking towards the grating. 'No sign of those two sentries. Put the cover back on loosely after me. I won't be long.'

'But sir …' began Brissot, but Dupotet had gone,

dropping down into the corridor beneath them, and wading out of sight.

'What do we do, sir?' hissed the boatswain.

'Best do as he asked,' said Brissot, pulling the hatch back into place. 'He is in command.'

The two men waited, trying to look nonchalant. After what seemed an age, there was a knock on the underside of the hatch and Tournier gently pushed it to one side.

The face of Dupotet appeared in the opening and he began handing tools up from below. 'Hammers, some nice sharp chisels, and best of all these.' A pair of axes joined the rest of the hoard. 'Hide them all under the bowsprit, Tournier. Give me hand, Francois.'

Brissot helped the first lieutenant to clamber up. His clothes were soaked but there was no denying the look of triumph on his face.

'It was difficult down there,' he explained. 'Most of the lanterns had been doused and the water is surging every time the hull rolls. I lost my footing a few times, but at least we have some weapons.'

'To do what with, sir?' queried Brissot.

Dupotet glanced upwards towards the two marine guards and lowered his voice. 'To help us to recapture our ship, should the opportunity present itself.'

'But that is madness, sir,' exclaimed Tournier. 'Even if we were to succeed, the frigate towing us would simply cut us adrift. With this gale blowing, and no masts, we will be wrecked on the coast for certain. That is if we don't sink first.'

'Tournier is right, sir,' said Brissot. 'We are not fighting the English any more. We are fighting the storm. Besides, we struck our colours and that surrender was accepted. It would be completely dishonourable to set on the prize crew.'

'What does the emperor care about such niceties?' snorted Dupotet. 'You think we should just tamely accept surrender to the English? Even collaborate with them?'

'If it saves the lives of our men, sir,' said Brissot.

'If the ship survives, Lieutenant, she will be repaired and join the ranks of our enemies,' said Dupotet. 'It is our duty to France to do our best to prevent that.'

'But it will just be suicide, sir!' protested Tournier.

'I for one am not afraid of dying for my country,' continued the first lieutenant.

'And what of the wounded?' said Brissot. 'Must they be sacrificed too?'

'I might have known you would use them to hide behind,' spat Dupotet. He turned his back on his fellow lieutenant and appealed to the others. 'Who is there among you who is still willing to serve France?'

Most of the crew avoided his gaze. 'Ain't we done enough?' commented one voice.

'We can't fight muskets and pistols with hammers and chisels, sir,' urged Brissot. 'Even if it was the right thing to do.'

'Kindly do not interfere, Lieutenant,' said Dupotet. 'I know my duty, even if you do not.'

A tense few minutes passed. From beyond the skin of the ship came the sound of the storm as it beat itself in fury against the *Redoubtable*, the timbers around them groaning and creaking with every fresh roll of the deck. From closer at hand came the high-pitched yell of one of the ship's boys, pleading with the surgeon. It was almost a relief when the sound became choked and indistinct, presumably as a gag was inserted in his mouth.

All of them were listening so intently that most of them did not notice the sound that was missing.

Brissot rose to his feet. 'I can't hear the pump turning,' he declared.

'That's not good, sir,' added the boatswain. 'With the water already knee-deep in the orlop.'

Sailors got up all around Brissot, exchanging looks of concern and someone pulled the canvas partition aside. Through the grating overhead came a warning cry from one of the marine guards, but Brissot and Tournier carried on, advancing towards the group of men stood around the pump. 'Why have you stopped?' he asked in English.

'Because we're fecking wasted,' said O'Malley, who was sat on the grating, his chest heaving.

'*Pardon*?' queried the Frenchman. 'Your accent is strange for me. What is this "fetching waste"?'

'We're blown. Gasping. In need of a bleeding breather,' supplemented Evans.

'Oh, I see,' said Brissot. 'But surely, you will be relieved soon?'

'By who?' queried Trevan. 'Them Lobsters be guarding the hatchways, and the others be patching up this hull as is shipping water faster than we can clear it.'

'Might help if you buggers lent a hand,' growled Evans. 'Don't you want to bleeding live? The sea don't care where you're from. She'll swallow a Frog as soon as a Jack, just for spite.'

'What did he say, sir?' asked Tournier, and Brissot translated the gist of it.

'They are right, sir,' said the boatswain. 'I would sooner help than sit around waiting to drown, as would most of the men.'

There was the sound of booted feet running on the deck above, and Blake appeared, coming down the ladderway with a pistol in his hand and a file of marines behind him. 'Stand back there!' he ordered. 'What is going on, and why have you left the manger, Monsieur?'

'I came to investigate why the pumping had stopped, Lieutenant,' said Brissot. 'These men were explaining how they have no relief.'

'That is correct, but I cannot see how that is your concern. Your first lieutenant made his views on the matter very clear.'

Brissot looked at the Englishman, noting his red-rimmed, tired eyes. 'I do not agree with him,' he said. 'Nor do most of the men. If you will accept my word as a gentleman that I will attempt no rising against you, I am prepared to undertake the manning of this pump. I am sure you can find better uses to put these men too.'

'You have no idea,' said Blake, a grim smile flickering across his face.

'As your giant sailor there put it, the sea doesn't care who it takes, Lieutenant,' said Brissot, holding out his hand.

'I gratefully accept your offer,' said Blake, returning his pistol to his coat pocket and taking the Frenchman's hand. 'You men, go and report to Mr Wallace on the quarterdeck for orders. And corporal, your sentries can return to their posts.'

'Aye aye, sir.'

Brissot turned to the boatswain. 'Tournier, kindly fetch some of the hands. Allocate eight to this pump, with another eight in reserve. They are to change places each half hour, and not to stop until I tell them to. And if Monsieur Dupotet tries to interfere, tell him I am relieving him of command.'

'Yes, sir,' said the boatswain, heading back towards the manger.

'We will soon have this pump working, Lieutenant,'

said Brissot. 'In return, may I ask you a favour? None of my men have been fed since the morning before the battle. They will work all the better with food inside them.'

'Nor have I eaten, or any of my men,' said Blake. 'And while the ship is in grave peril, I have no time for such matters.'

'I understand,' said the Frenchman. 'But our cook has survived the battle. I was thinking that if he was given access to the galley, he might be able to produce something for us all. The wounded, at the very least, should be fed.'

'I will put your request to Lieutenant Wallace, who I am certain will gratefully accept,' said Blake. 'And you have my thanks for your cooperation in the matter of the pump. Ah, here come your men now.'

Brissot turned to see a line of sailors picking their way through the wounded with Tournier at their head. He saw that the boatswain's face was troubled.

Once the pump was back in action Brissot turned to Tournier. 'What is the matter?' he asked. 'Did Monsieur Dupotet cause any trouble?'

'He's gone,' whispered Tournier. 'It must have happened when those two marines guarding the grating went off to get help. I reckon he has climbed up out on to the main deck. Goodness only knows what he is up to.'

Chapter 20
Le Redoubtable

Brissot was trying to think where the first lieutenant might have gone, when a portly man with a drooping moustache appeared before him. 'You sent for me, sir?'

'I did,' agreed the officer. 'If you were returned to the galley, do you believe you could produce some food? For us as well as the English?'

The cook considered this for a moment, his plump hand rasping against the thick stubble on his chin. 'Even if I could find dry firewood, it is impossible to light the galley in this storm, sir. But there may be enough cold provisions left unspoilt,' he conceded.

'What do you need?'

'My assistant, Jules,' said the cook, indicating one of the men waiting to take his turn at the pump. 'And Thibault with his keys. The captain's pantry will have better food.'

'Collect them together, and meet me at the foot of the ladderway,' ordered Brissot.

'Yes, sir.'

A less threatening group than the collection of three cooks and stewards was hard to imagine, but Brissot's party was still met with levelled muskets as they came up the steps and on to the main deck.

'Halt right there!' barked the corporal in charge of the marine guard.

'These are the men that I agreed with Lieutenant Blake

would have access to the galley,' explained Brissot. 'They are to feed us all.'

'Looks like they've been a-feasting already,' said one of the marines to his mate, pointing with his musket towards the nearest rotund stomach.

'Quiet there!' barked the corporal. 'You lot stay put, while I go and ask Mr Blake.'

Brissot listened to the storm, seemingly much nearer now his head was above the level of the main deck. The pitching of the ship made it hard to keep his footing on the steps. Rain thundered down on the quarterdeck above his head. A wave crashed against the bow with a low boom, sending water cascading over the forecastle to pour down in a curtain on to the planking below. He thought of his men struggling to clear all this with their single pump.

The corporal returned, his scarlet tunic soaked from his brief visit to the quarterdeck. 'All right, off you go,' he ordered. 'Just see my lads get the first of the scoff.'

'Very well,' said Brissot, waving the cooks forward towards the galley at the front of the ship.

They tried to stay in the shelter of the starboard gangway, but the roll of the hull sent them reeling out into the pouring rain, so that they arrived soaking wet beneath the forecastle. A few lamps still hung here, swinging wildly and sending splinters of light playing across overturned guns, discarded equipment and slumped bodies that had yet to be pitched over the side. At the area's heart was the solid block of the galley stove, dark and cold, its chimney torn aside by a passing round shot.

'Can you prepare any food?' asked Brissot.

'I shall need more light and fewer bodies,' said the cook, entering his wrecked galley by stepping over a dead sailor lying across the threshold. 'To work, my friends. First we must make this area a little cleaner.'

Brissot helped them drag the body of the sailor aside, and stepped back as the cooks got to work. The bow fell into another trough and crashed into the face of the following wave. Moments later water flooded through a gap torn in the forward bulkhead that should have separated the forecastle from the open beakhead beyond. It lapped over the deck, pulling at the dead bodies strewn across it like a tide on a beach. He could see the gap, wide as a door, the edges jagged against the grey sky outside, the first hint of the approach of dawn. When the water had passed, he advanced to see if he could block up the hole. As he was examining the torn wood, he heard a solid thud.

It was barely audible over the shriek of the wind, and he was going to ignore the sound when it was repeated. Intrigued, he ducked through the gap, just as a flash of lightning seared across the sky, and for an instant night was day. He saw the wild, tumbling landscape of huge mountains and valleys of sea, frozen into stillness. He saw the *Griffin*, struggling on through the gale with close-reefed topsails, the cable connecting them as straight as a rod, leading to the fore bits on the open forecastle above him. And he saw the figure of Dupotet, sitting astride the stump of the bowsprit, caught mid-swing as he struck at the white gash he had already made in the side of the towing cable.

'No!' yelled Brissot, stepping forward, but the first lieutenant could either not hear over the storm, or ignored him. The axe swung again, and the next thud was lost in a loud bang as the tow rope parted.

*****

Black, howling night lay all about the *Griffin* as she struggled through the mountainous waves surrounding her. Most of her crew were on deck, manning the sheets and tackles, closely watching Armstrong and Taylor. The two veteran officers were using all their skill to coax their ship and the leaden mass she towed away from the rocky coast of Spain filling the horizon to leeward.

On her quarterdeck Clay clung to the mizzen shrouds and tried to steady his night glass against the force of the wind. In the distance he could just make out the dark shape of one of the prizes, rolling wildly among the waves and throwing white water high into the night as she was driven remorselessly towards the shore. Closer to him, among the shoals that lay at the foot of Cape Trafalgar, a new obstruction had appeared. The *Fougueux*, the two-decker that he had seen break free from her tow earlier, lay on her side, the swollen curve of her coppered hull gleaming through the rain as lightning crackled across the sky above her. In that moment of brilliance Clay picked out a few tiny figures clinging on. Then a huge wave surged over her, and when the lightning flashed again they had vanished.

'Can we not make better progress, Mr Taylor?' he shouted, closing the telescope, and struggling across to join the first lieutenant. 'Yonder cape draws a might too close for my liking.'

The older man pointed to where the topsail yards were bent like drawn bows by the force of the wind. 'She is at the limit of what sail she can bear, sir,' he yelled back. 'Should anything carry away, we shall be in irons in an instant. Then that hulk will drag us on to the rocks.'

Clay and his officers looked across to the *Redoubtable*, a dark mass veiled by the rain, and watched as a wave broke high over her bow. The riding bits by the main mast let out an audible groan as the strain came on the towing cable and Clay held his breath, wondering if the rope would hold. Then the frigate forged on, pulling the French ship out of the trough, and another little crisis passed.

'She is settling by the stern, I fancy, sir,' said Armstrong, his usual periwig replaced by an enormous sou'wester secured with tapes beneath his chin. 'Why, she rides lower in the water than we do, for all her having an extra deck and no weight of masts.'

'Dawn soon,' commented Taylor. 'Pray God the wind will ease with the coming of day.'

Another crack of silver broke across the boiling clouds, illuminating the *Redoubtable.* In among the broken headrails that lay like an untidy nest around the stump of her bowsprit Clay thought he saw movement, but almost before it registered darkness returned. The *Griffin* laboured up to the crest of the next wave, heeling over as the wind hit her. At the moment of maximum strain there was a dull crack from astern, and the frigate shot forward.

'What the blazes …' began Armstrong.

'The cable must have parted!' exclaimed Taylor. 'Oh, those poor souls.'

Without steady forward pressure, the *Redoubtable* had been transformed into an inert mass, adrift among the waves, a plaything for the storm. Her bow sank down out of sight behind a mountain of dark water, seemingly never to rise again. Then the wave struck with a booming crash, and she was wrenched around until she was broadside on to the pounding sea. First it rolled her far over at an impossible angle, and then released her to ponderously right herself, just in time for the next crashing blow.

'We must help them,' declared Clay.

'But how, sir?' queried Taylor. 'We can't possibly get another cable across in this storm, and they will be swept on to the rocks presently.'

'Then we must get as many of her crew off as we are able,' said his captain. 'Haul that cable back on board and put the ship about. I am not condemning Blake and the others to drown without raising a finger to help them.'

'Aye aye, sir.'

Armstrong handled the tricky business of tacking the *Griffin* through the teeth of the howling gale and Taylor went below to help the boatswain secure what remained of the towing cable. This left Clay to watch the stricken *Redoubtable*. She was resisting stubbornly to the last, rolling to and fro, tossing a mane of white spray from her upper deck as she did so. He made an estimate of how quickly she was drifting down to leeward, and looked across to the shore, much nearer now. The cape loomed up darkly against the grey of the sky, waves sending spray far up the cliffs. He could see that the wrecked prize at its feet had broken apart. So close had they drifted that in the next flash of lightning he could even read *Fougueux* painted in an arc of white letters across her shattered stern. One hour at most, he decided, before the *Redoutable* would share her fate.

'The cable is on board, and the rear port is secure, sir,' said Taylor. 'Mr Hutchinson is stowing it away.'

'Good, now we must plan for the rescue. We shall need men posted along the larboard gangway with coils of line, ready to haul survivors from the water. Have Mr Preston organise them. And pass the word for my coxswain, if you please.'

'Aye aye, sir.'

'Mr Armstrong, now the ship is put about, I want you to close with the *Redoubtable*,' ordered Clay. 'I want the ship hove to a cable to leeward of her.'

'To *leeward*, sir,' queried the American. 'You want us between that hulk and the shore?'

'Precisely so, Mr Armstrong. Kindly attend to it now. Time is not our friend.'

'Aye aye, sir.'

Next Sedgwick appeared, knuckling his forehead, swaying on the heaving deck. 'You wanted me, sir?'

'I want to know if there are enough men who can swim on board to man the longboat? Strong swimmers, like you, and all volunteers.'

The coxswain considered this for a moment. 'I can only think of a bare dozen, sir, but if I asks around I daresay I might be able to scratch together a crew. But you can't be thinking of launching a boat in this here storm, can you? Begging your pardon.'

'See how that French ship lies,' said Clay, pointing across to the stricken prize. 'She is like the breakwater of a harbour. There will be some shelter in her lee. Enough for a well-handled boat to survive for a while. I won't order any man to attempt it, but I would take it as a kindness if you would try. Mr Blake and our shipmates are on there, along with the prize crew from the *Temeraire* and a deal of Frenchmen.'

Sedgwick took a final look at the mountainous waves, and briefly nodded his head. 'I can't be leaving Trevan and Evans to drown in this, and even O'Malley deserves saving, sir. I best be seeing about that boat crew.'

*****

The moment the tow rope was cut the motion of the *Redoubtable* changed. First her bow sank down into the valley between two waves, her battered hull groaning in protest. The men manning the pump heard the water on the flooded orlop deck as it surged forward, bursting upwards through the hatch covers in a series of powerful geysers. Then a wave thundered into her, slewing her around and rolling her far over. Sailors across the ship lost their footing as the deck angle approached that of a roof. On the lower gundeck there was a collective wail from the wounded as they found themselves in motion, tumbling and sliding over the planking to collect in a drift against the side.

In the forecastle the sudden heel of the deck caught Brissot unawares, sending him rolling across the deck. Then, as the ship began to right itself, he clambered to his feet, bruised, winded but otherwise unharmed. He picked up a discarded handspike from the deck and began to make his way back towards the opening on to the beakhead as the hull rolled back up again. He could see the opening thanks to the dawn outside, although the storm seemed as fierce as ever. But no sooner was the deck level, than the next wave struck, rolling the poor *Redoubtable* over once more. This time he was ready for it, clinging to the fore bits while his world tilted over.

Brissot waited for the deck to level, and took his chance to dash out on to the beakhead. The full power of the storm struck him as he emerged. He was blinded with spray driven into his face by the wind. When he had dashed the water from his eyes, he was shocked by how low the *Redoubtable* was riding. Just beneath him was the boiling sea, while the crests of the waves towered above him. Dupotet seemed to be exalting in the madness he had unleashed. His wet clothes thrashed around him, his hair streamed in the wind, but he laughed with glee as he clung to the rope gammoning holding the broken bowsprit in place.

'What have you done?' yelled Brissot, gesturing

towards the looming black cliffs of the cape, terribly close now. The deep thunder of the surf was so loud it could be heard over the fury of the storm.

'I have restored our ship's pride,' the first lieutenant shouted back. 'Where is the honour in meekly surrendering?' He gestured towards the broken stern of the *Fougueux* as it appeared between two waves. 'That will be our fate. Dying in glory for France, and taking our enemies with us!'

Before Brissot could answer, the ship rolled over once more. Water broke over them both as they clung on, and through the deluge he heard the renewed cries of the wounded behind him. As the big ship ponderously righted itself, he realised that Dupotet was still shouting to him.

'Come and join me, Francois, my friend! Let us bury our differences at the end and die as comrades! Come, there is room here beside me! We can witness our beloved ship's final moments together!'

'No, you madman!' he replied. 'Can't you hear the misery you have inflicted on those poor souls?'

'They will be at peace soon enough,' yelled Dupotet. 'Nothing can save us now!'

Brissot felt white-hot rage close around his heart. He gripped the handspike with its heavy steel tip and looked out to sea for the next wave, a mountain of dark water looming high above them. Beyond it he could see the reefed topsails of a frigate, and he wondered why they were coming in so close to the shore. Then the moment he was waiting for arrived.

With a boom the wave struck the side of the *Redoubtable*, rolling her over once more, and water came boiling up from below them. Brissot flung himself across the beakhead at Dupotet, the handspike swinging in an arc above his head and down on the arm with which the first lieutenant was holding on. With a cry Dupotet let go, just as the ship's roll reached its steepest. He slid across the tilting platform, clawing at the splintered head rails around him with one hand, the arm Brissot had struck broken and useless. Brissot dropped his weapon and clung to the gammoning in his place as water burst over him, washing his feet away and sucking him downwards like a mountain torrent. For a moment he hung there, unable to breathe, and then he felt the ship start to right itself. The wave rolled by, leaving him manically holding on, alone on a beakhead washed clean of any sign of Dupotet. He saw the struggling figure of the first lieutenant in the water being swept away from him, and heard a faint cry. He expected to feel pity, or perhaps remorse, but instead he felt relieved. A wave broke over the man; when it passed, Dupotet had vanished.

'Lieutenant!' called the voice of Blake from the forecastle above him. 'What the bloody hell are you doing out there? Do you want to be washed off? Get back inside and help round up as many of your men as possible. They are to come to the main deck. The *Griffin* is going to try and take them off.'

Brissot released his grip and staggered back into the forecastle, coughing and retching. He reached the entrance to the galley, where the cooks were picking themselves up from the deck.

'Are you all right, sir?' asked Lucas's steward, eyeing him strangely. 'Only we heard a deal of shouting earlier.'

'I'm fine, Thibault. But I need you all to stop what you're doing and follow me. We have to get off this ship before it founders.'

'But, where will we …'

'No time for that! Just come!' snapped Brissot.

He led them out on to a main deck that was crowded with figures, with more scrambling up from below. Many were the walking wounded, others the unharmed prisoners that he had left manning the pumps. It had stopped raining and the motion of the ship was becoming less wild as she settled. He looked down through the fore hatch and realised that the water had risen from the orlop to flood the lower deck too. Through the grating came cries for help. Looking down from the quarterdeck was a line of marines backed by Royal Navy sailors. Lieutenant Wallace stood among them, his coat tails flying in the wind. Off to leeward, between the ship and the coast, was the frigate he had seen earlier.

'Monsieur Brissot, I need you to translate for me,' said Blake, appearing behind him.

'Of course.'

But the Englishman paused for a moment, scanning the crowd of French faces. 'Where is your first lieutenant?'

'He was washed overboard, sir,' said Brissot, repeating the words he had prepared in his mind for this moment. 'We heard the cable starting to break, and went to investigate, but we arrived too late.'

'Poor man,' said Blake. 'But I doubt you could have saved the cable. It will have been under intolerable strain as the ship flooded. Now, I need you to tell these men to find anything that will float among the wreckage to help them get across to the *Griffin*, and to be swift about it. As soon as they have something, they are to go up on to the lee gangway and take to the sea.'

'Most of my men cannot swim,' protested the Frenchman.

'Nor can mine. Tell them to use what they find to keep their heads above water and kick steadily with their legs towards the *Griffin*. Steadily, mind. They have a way to go.'

'What of the wounded?' said Brissot. 'Surely you

cannot mean to leave them?'

In answer Blake pointed towards the shore, terribly close now. 'There is no choice. It will be a miracle if we can save the able-bodied. Any wounded who cannot reach this deck unaided will never be able to swim to safety.'

*****

The *Griffin* was hove to in the storm, pitching among the waves like a restive stallion, the wind shrieking through her rigging, and making the few scraps of canvas she was showing flap thunderously. Just to windward of her was the hulk of the *Redoubtable*, so low that her main deck was almost level with the water. With little hull above the surface exposed to the waves she was rolling much less, but now when they struck, they broke freely over her, forcing those gathered along her lee rail to cling on.

'Twenty minutes, Sedgwick,' yelled Clay down into the longboat. 'Tell Mr Blake not a moment more. After that, any that haven't reached us shall have to shift for themselves.'

The coxswain waved a hand in acknowledgement, and set out towards the stricken ship, the men pulling hard into the teeth of the wind. As Clay had predicted, sea on the leeward side of the *Redoubtable* was calmer, the mountainous waves replaced by shorter ones, but they were still enough to send the longboat soaring and plunging among them, with water slopping over the side. The boat had only gone thirty yards before the two forward oarsmen had stopped rowing and were frantically bailing instead.

'Pray God I am not sending fresh men to drown,' said Clay, leaning close to be heard by Taylor, who was beside him. The roar of the storm was competing with the crash of waves on the coast behind them, backlit by the light of dawn, and growing ever louder as they were driven down towards it. From further out to sea rose a thin line of golden sparks, followed by a burst of red against the low clouds.

'Another prize in distress, sir,' said Taylor. 'I fear this storm may prove more costly than the battle.'

'Perhaps so,' said Clay, watching the longboat's uncertain progress. It was halfway across, and entering slightly calmer water. 'Come on, Blake,' he urged. 'Surely you can see the boat can take no more than a dozen.'

This conclusion seemed to have occurred to those on board, and as the next wave broke across the upper deck of the *Redoubtable* a few hardy souls jumped down over the side, each one clinging to a piece of planking or a fragment of wood. Clay watched as they struck out towards him amid the waves. A larger cluster of men appeared, heaving a grating between them. As the ship rolled its lee rail close to the surface they launched their improvised raft, and jumped after it.

'Stand by, Mr Preston,' roared Taylor, towards the parties of men grouped along the frigate's side and trailing lines down into the water to haul survivors on board.

'They need to take the plunge,' fumed Clay. 'She is settling fast.'

Another wave crashed into the seventy-four, and this time her punch-drunk roll was accompanied by a series of muffled bangs from deep within her. When she came back upright, her stern was beneath the surface.

'Not long now,' commented Taylor, waving to those on board, urging them to jump.

Now the first signs of panic started. The marines were discarding their muskets and tearing off their equipment. More and more sailors were taking to the water, filling the sea with points of thrashing white. Many were making for the longboat, but Sedgwick ignored their desperate arms, heading for the *Redoubtable* instead. Clay watched those swimming towards him. Some were kicking steadily, harbouring their strength. But most were blinded by panic, splashing, and crying for help. One man only reached half way before exhaustion overtook him. Clay watched as he feebly stirred his legs, his head slumped over his piece of wood, wet hair masking his face. He was lifted high by a wave, and then rolled deep into a trough. When the piece of wood reappeared, the sailor had vanished.

Clay gripped the rail in frustration, and turned to his first lieutenant. 'Get the launch in the water,' he ordered. 'We must try and help some of the swimmers.'

Taylor started in surprise, looked at the sea and then at the steel in his captain's eyes, noticing that both were the same shade of grey. 'Aye aye, sir.'

Another wave thundered into the *Redoubtable*, heaving her over once more, and this time she did not roll back. Her lee rail sunk below the surface, and with a collective wail, most of those left on board took to the water, many simply slithering down the angled deck.

From further forward there came shouts of encouragement as the first survivor was pulled up the side. The man collapsed to his hands and knees, retching on the deck. The longboat had finally reached the *Redoubtable* and Clay could see the crew dragging people out of the water. One looked to be the slight figure of Richard Corbett, the frigate's surgeon, another the bulky Evans. But there were far more waving hands around the boat than could possibly fit on board, and as he watched, it turned back towards the frigate, leaving most behind.

Closer at hand the launch was swooping among the

waves, scooping up exhausted swimmers. As he watched, two men pulled an unconscious sailor on to the thwart, only to release him back into the water as they realised he was dead. Meanwhile more and more sailors were being hauled on board as they arrived alongside.

'Sir!' said Taylor, pulling at his sleeve and pointing towards the shore behind him.

Clay looked around. The splintered wreck of the *Fougueux* seemed close enough to touch, the air above it white with spray, the crash of the waves deafening. 'Five more minutes, Mr Taylor.'

The longboat came alongside, releasing a tide of survivors to scramble on to the frigate. Trevan came over the rail, his blond pigtail a dripping cord down his back, and then paused to help an unknown French officer join him.

Clay looked down into the boat. 'Where is Mr Blake, Sedgwick?' he yelled.

'Just returning for him, sir,' he replied. 'Him and the bloke from the *Temeraire* wanted to be last off.'

'Be swift!' urged Clay.

As Clay watched on, the officer Trevan had helped on board joined him at the rail. 'Lieutenant Brissot, sir,' said the man in reasonable English, lifting a hand towards a hat that had long since disappeared. 'Third lieutenant on the *Redoutable*. I must witness the end of my ship.'

'Of course, Lieutenant,' said Clay, looking at the man's torn coat, one sleeve of which was missing.

'My uncle would be disappointed,' said Brissot. 'But I would rather wear my uniform, while my ship yet lives.'

'I believe I understand, Monsieur,' said Clay.

More and more survivors were coming on board, some rescued by the launch, others having made their own way across. One of these was O'Malley, who arrived like a drowned rat, too exhausted even to swear. But Clay had eyes only for the longboat as it lifted to one huge wave and vanished behind the next, making its way across once more.

Suddenly there was a collective cry as the launch, already half full of water and overburdened with survivors, was neatly flipped over by a wave and sent crashing against the frigate's side. In an instant the water was full of struggling bodies, clinging to oars or the upturned hull.

'Lines here, men!' yelled Preston. 'Get them out of the water!'

'Sir!' pleaded Taylor at his elbow. 'We are almost in the surf!'

'We must go,' agreed Clay, looking around at the wild coast that filled his world. 'Have the sheets manned. The moment the last of the launch crew are on board, let us beat out to sea. We can recover the longboat closer to the prize.'

Taylor's orders were barely audible, so loud was the roar of the waves. But the frigate's crew knew the danger the ship was in, and worked like demons to get her underway, even though the last of the launch crew were still clinging to the ship's side. No one chose to look back to mark the dozens of struggling figures they had left behind in the water.

The *Griffin*'s progress was desperately slow as she battled against a storm that still had her in its grip. With extra helmsmen at the wheel, and her boatswain minutely supervising her headsails, every inch of progress forward seemed to be accompanied by an inch of drift towards the suck of the wild coast to leeward

Clay left sailing the frigate to Taylor and Armstrong once more, and returned his attention to the longboat as it arrived next to the *Redoubtable*. The last few survivors scrambled over the side and Sedgwick turned towards him, pausing for a moment to assess matters. Then the boat set off on a course to intercept the *Griffin*. But the moment the boat left the lee of the prize's stern, it was exposed to the full fury of the storm. Now the waves all around were truly mountainous. Clay could see Sedgwick half-standing at the tiller, somehow balancing in the pitching boat, as he tried to chart a way ahead. Up, up it rose, oars clawing at the slope of water. Then down into a deep trough from which it would surely never emerge. But it appeared again in a welter of spray, the survivors on board bailing furiously among the straining oarsmen, and the ascent of the next summit began.

Time after time the longboat rose to the crest of a wave only to vanish from view once more. Clay held his breath each time until it appeared again, always a little nearer. Eventually it was close enough for him to recognise Blake amid those in the boat, desperately bailing with the others as they plunged out of sight again.

'Stand by to heave to, Mr Taylor,' he ordered. 'We shall do so when the longboat reappears. Mr Preston, have your men ready to haul the crew on board. Pray abandon the boat, we have no time to recover it.'

'Aye aye, sir.'

The last wave swept on, heading for the shore, but nothing appeared from behind it. Clay scanned the water in disbelief, but the longboat seemed to have been swallowed whole. Then he saw a struggling figure waving towards the frigate.

'Bear down on that man, Mr Taylor,' he said, a feeling of dread washing over him. He tried to search the area with his telescope, but it was shaking too much in his hand. As the frigate beat its way closer, a little more detail became visible.

The waving man was one of the longboat crew, holding on to a floating oar with his other hand. Then two more figures appeared in the sea, one undoubtedly Sedgwick, swimming on his back and towing someone in a uniform coat. Clay saw the flash of gold from an epaulet, and relief flooded over him that both men had survived. Then he realised this officer had dark hair, while Blake's was fair.

Clay spent as long as he could searching for survivors, but only those three were picked up.

'Lieutenant Wallace of the *Temeraire*, sir,' said the officer, when he was brought on board.

'Welcome, Lieutenant,' said Clay, his face drawn and pale. 'Can you tell me what happened to Mr Blake?'

'I … I don't know, sir,' said Wallace. 'That coxswain of yours did a fine job. It's a miracle we survived as long as we did, but that last wave came right down upon us like a ton of lead. It drove us under in an instant. I scarce know how I survived myself.'

'Anything to add, Sedgwick?' asked Clay.

'Not really, sir. I done my best, diving for survivors, and managed to collar Mr Wallace here, but I didn't see no sign of Mr Blake, for which I'm truly sorry.'

'Thank you, Sedgwick, for all your efforts this day,' said Clay, his smile forced. 'Pray go below, both of you, and get warm. Mr Taylor, get the frigate underway and off this wretched shore.'

'Aye aye, sir. I'm sorry about John.'

'Thank you, George.'

Clay returned to the rail, partly to conceal his tears from the others, and stared out to sea, remembering the young lieutenant he had first met an age ago on the *Titan*. Next to him stood the French lieutenant in the torn coat. Clay followed where he was looking, and saw what appeared to be a reef, with surf breaking against it. Then he realised that it was all that was left above the surface of the *Redoutable*. Another wave thundered over it, and when it had passed there was nothing left. The Frenchman raised his hand in salute and after a moment Clay did the same, in a last farewell to his friend.

Epilogue

An autumn gale had buffeted the port for much of the night, but by morning it had blown itself out, leaving a blustery wind that stirred an unpleasant swell in the sheltered waters of Boulogne harbour. The massed lines of invasion barges were still there, knocking and fretting against each other, but the blocks of patient infantrymen had gone.

The *Armée de l'Angleterre* was no more. It had been renamed *La Grande Armée*, and for the last week its members had been packing up their camps around the Channel ports. Now they were marching through Germany towards the distant Danube and war with Austria.

Admiral Bruix stood on the same spot as over a year ago, when a similar gale had prevented him demonstrating his craft to Napoleon. He looked out into the Channel, as if searching for the promised fleet that would now never come.

'What shall we do with all these boats, sir?' asked his flag lieutenant.

Bruix shrugged his shoulders. 'For now, they remain here, until they rot at their moorings. The navy has failed the emperor, and he is not a patient man. He has turned his back on the sea, and will make war in the way that he knows best. I fear that it is a terrible mistake.'

'You do not think our army can beat the Austrians, sir?'

'Oh I am sure that they can, and the Russians after that, and the Prussians next year. But eventually our victories will come to an end. Then we will look back and remember this day as the one on which we lost the war.'

'Why, sir?'

The admiral pointed towards the faint line on the horizon that was the coast of Britain. 'Because it is the day on which we gave control of the sea to the English,' he said. 'Now they won't fear us any more, for we can never reach them. And because they control the sea, in time they will gather all the world's trade to themselves. How will France win against such unbridled wealth and power, Lieutenant?'

The End

Note from the author

My novels are a blend of fact and fiction. *Clay and the Immortal Memory* is more factual than most of my work, partly because it follows a historic campaign, but also because many of the events are so remarkable that they need little embellishment from me. These notes are for the benefit of readers who would like to understand where the boundary lies between the truth with the made up.

Alexander Clay, the *Griffin* and her crew are fictional, as are the ships and crews of the *Utrecht*, *Fortuna* and *Boa Ventura*. All other ships are historic. The preparations made for a French invasion at the start of the novel are accurate: thousands of craft were assembled under Admiral Bruix in the way I describe, and the bulk of the French army were encamped in the Pas-de-Calais area for the two years prior to Trafalgar. Napoleon did visit Boulogne in June 1804 to witness a rehearsal of an embarkation in poor weather. The difference to my Prologue is that he insisted that the demonstration go ahead, against naval advice, and two hundred soldiers were subsequently drowned.

Regency Madras was broadly as I have described. The 1804 China Fleet did survive an attack by a French squadron commanded by the Comte de Linois. Lord Bentinck, a noted cricket enthusiast, had recently been appointed governor, and the behaviour of Major Kirkpatrick, the Company Resident in Hyderabad, was the scandal of the day. Black Town did exist, although the adventures of the *Griffin*'s sailors there are my invention. The *Griffin*'s return journey to Europe is fictional, although the trick used to evade the French frigate squadron is loosely based on one in Lord Cochrane's autobiography.

The *Redoutable* was a French 74 in the Mediterranean Fleet, commanded by Captain Jean Lucas. Apart from him, the officers and crew mentioned in my novel are all fictional. Lucas was an exceptional commander who retrained his crew to focus on the use of small-arms fire and boarding to counter the superiority of the Royal Navy in seamanship and naval gunnery. These tactics proved highly effective in the pell-mell battle that was Trafalgar, and most naval historians believe that without the timely intervention of the *Temeraire* he might well have successfully boarded the *Victory*. I am conscious that in transferring credit for this innovation to my own fictional character, Lieutenant Francois Brissot, I do Lucas a disservice, for which I apologise. When I decided to include Trafalgar in my novel, I saw that the battle would be best explained from the French point of view, and I chose the *Redoutable* as my vehicle to do this. No offence was intended to the actual crew of the *Redoubtable* or their descendants.

The one historic event that the *Redoubtable* did not take part in was the recapture of Diamond Rock off Martinique. I have substituted the French 74 *Berwick* with the *Redoutable*, and made Lucas the senior officer. In reality it was the captain of the *Pluton* who was in command of this operation. The story of the Royal Navy's occupation of Diamond Rock, a basalt column rising out of the sea, and its subsequent conversion into HMS *Diamond Rock*, is a remarkable one, which I do not have the space to describe here. Suffice to say that the details in my book are correct, once more demonstrating how fact is so often stranger than fiction.

The broad arc of the Trafalgar campaign shown in my novel is correct. Napoleon's 1805 plan for a simultaneous breakout of French and Spanish fleets to rendezvous at Martinique is accurate, as was the failure of the Brest fleet to escape. Nelson's subsequent pursuit of Villeneuve to the West Indies is also correct. For reasons of plot complexity, I have simplified the detail of both fleets' return to Europe, removing events that are not germane to the story. Villeneuve went first to Ferrol before moving to Cadiz, where he had an inconclusive action with a Royal Navy squadron under the command of Rear Admiral Sir Robert Calder. Nelson sent most of his ships to help Collingwood's blockade of Cadiz and briefly returned to Britain between 18 August and 13 September 1805, before returning to take command of the fleet assembling to oppose Villeneuve.

One aspect of the Trafalgar campaign that is often overlooked is the different state of disease control in the two fleets. Scurvy was a debilitating disease that killed an estimated two million sailors during the age of sail. From 1795 onwards, thanks firstly to the work of James Lind, and more importantly Sir Gilbert Blane, the Royal Navy had implemented a daily dose of lemon or lime juice. This virtually banished scurvy at a stroke. For various reasons, the French and Spanish navies failed to adopt similar measures, and in consequence were severely hampered during lengthy naval campaigns, such as that leading up to Trafalgar. After only six months at sea, many of Villeneuve's ships had over two hundred cases each, with one Spanish ship having over three hundred. This undoubtedly limited Villeneuve's scope for action, and the residual effects of the disease almost certainly contributed to the fighting performance of his ships at Trafalgar.

Much has been written about the Battle of Trafalgar. The various accounts may disagree on points of detail, but all acknowledge the ferocity of an action fought at such close ranges by ships equipped with such destructive weapons. The *Victory*'s opening broadside, for example, which stern-raked the *Bucentaure,* has been estimated to have inflicted almost four hundred casualties and dismounted twenty of her eighty cannon.

No Franco-Spanish ship fought as heroically as the *Redoutable*, which found herself engaging both the 100-gun *Victory* and the 98-gun *Temeraire*, not surrendering before most of her crew had been killed, and the ship entirely dismasted. For this part of the book, I have largely left the unadorned events to speak for themselves.

Nelson was fatally wounded by a French marksman firing from the mizzen rigging of the *Redoutable.* The bullet hit him on the top of his left shoulder, passed through his chest, narrowly missing his heart, and lodged in his spine. Such a wound was untreatable in that period. He remained conscious until 4.30 pm, just long enough to learn of the scale of his victory, before he died. Again, I have done little to fictionalise this event, wherever possible using the individuals present speaking their reported words.

Nelson's death, at the moment of his greatest triumph, elevated him to Olympian status in Regency Britain. His funeral, held in January 1806, was a huge affair, attracting a similar outpouring of emotion to that which accompanied the death of the late Princess Diana. The phrase 'Immortal Memory,' used in the title of this book, comes from that time. Like all great men, Nelson was a mix of both virtue and vice. He was undoubtedly highly courageous, very charismatic and a brilliant admiral who understood how to win in the age of sail. But he was also vain (it was his love of his military orders that made him easy to target), pompous, often prone to self-doubt, and his treatment of his first wife can only be described as cruel. We tend to expect our heroes to be flawless in every aspect, a measure that they inevitably fail to match.

I have tried, with a certain amount of artistic licence, to be true to the spirit of the man at the time of his death. Some of the dialogue I use comes from attributed quotes or from Nelson's letters at the time. He did have a strong premonition that he would die at Trafalgar, which he shared with several witnesses before the battle, and which I include in his last meeting with Clay. It is also true that he had a phobia about being buried at sea, and made Hardy promise to see him buried on land. William Beatty, the *Victory*'s surgeon, did have his body placed in a cask full of brandy, in which it was subsequently transported back to Britain. The body was then transferred into a coffin. Rumours that members of the *Victory*'s crew subsequently drank the brandy have never been proved.

After the battle there was considerable interest in identifying the individual who had fired the fatal shot. For the romantic novelist Alexandre Dumas, it was fired by the Count de Sainte-Ermine, masquerading as a sailor called René. More prosaically, the view among Royal Navy sailors who were present was that the identity of the soldier would never be known, because he almost certainly died during the battle – a likely proposition given the exceptional number of fatalities suffered by the crew of the *Redoutable*. In 1826 the memoirs of Robert Guillemard, a retired sergeant, were published in France. Among various other spectacular claims was that the author had killed Nelson. Regrettably, the book was later exposed as the work of Alexandre Lardier, a minor naval clerk, who had invented the whole thing. In the absence of a better candidate, I have chosen to include Guillemard in my novel.

Some accounts of the Battle of Trafalgar end with the death of Nelson, but in many ways the story was just beginning. The ominous swell that most participants had detected before the battle was indeed caused by an approaching storm that struck within hours of the last guns falling silent. Most of the ships, whether prizes or victors, were badly damaged and those sailors who had survived were exhausted from a day of hard fighting. Worse still, they were on a dangerous lee shore. The storm proved to be of unprecedented ferocity and blew for the next three days and nights.

Far more men were killed and many more ships were lost in the storm that followed Trafalgar than in the battle itself. Many, like the *Fougueux* and the *Bucentaure*, were wrecked when towing cables parted or anchors dragged, and they were driven ashore. Others were scuttled as too badly damaged to save. The giant *Santisima Trinidad* foundered when her exhausted crew at the pumps no longer had the strength left to keep the rising water at bay. Although attempts were made to take off their crews, the mountainous seas and awful weather made this exceedingly difficult, and many on board, especially the wounded, perished with their ships. Of the eighteen prizes captured by the Royal Navy in the battle, only four were subsequently brought safely into Gibraltar. The *Redoutable* was not among them.

After her surrender she was in a shocking state, with less than a hundred of her almost six hundred and fifty crew unharmed. A prize crew was put on board by the *Temeraire* and she was taken in tow by the British 74 *Swiftsure.* She survived the night, but the following day began to sink by the stern. The *Swiftsure* launched her boats, but only managed to rescue fifty of those on board before the *Redoutable* vanished beneath the waves.

The wounded Captain Lucas was received with great courtesy in Britain, and was subsequently returned to France, where he was given a new ship to command. He took part in the Battle of the Basque Roads, where he once again found himself fighting against considerable odds, although this time he managed to save his ship from capture by the Royal Navy. He retired from the French navy after the fall of Napoleon, and died in Brest in 1819.

Books by Philip K Allan

The Alexander Clay Series

The Captain's Nephew

A Sloop of War

On the Lee Shore

A Man of No Country

The Distant Ocean

The Turn of the Tide

In Northern Seas

Larcum Mudge

Upon the Malabar Coast

Clay and the Immortal Memory

World War 2

Sea of Wolves

The Wolves in Winter

About the Author

Philip K Allan comes from Hertfordshire in the United Kingdom where he lives with his wife and two daughters. He has an excellent knowledge of the 18th century navy. He studied it as part of his history degree at London University, which awoke a lifelong passion for the period. A longstanding member of the Society for Nautical Research, he also writes for the US Naval Institute's magazine *Naval History*.

He is author of the Alexander Clay series of naval fiction. The first book in the series, *The Captain's Nephew*, was published in January 2018, and immediately went into the Amazon top 100 bestseller list for Sea Adventures. The sequel, *A Sloop of War*, was similarly well received, winning the Discovered Diamonds Book of the Month Award. He has now published twelve novels, including two set in the Second World War.

If you want to find out more about him or his books, the links below may be helpful.

Website: www.philipkallan.com

Facebook & Twitter: @philipkallan

Instagram: @philipkallanauthor

About the Cover

The cover artwork for this book was commissioned from the talented marine artist Colin M Baxter. If you would like to acquire a signed reproduction of this picture or to see any of his other work, please contact Colin direct.

Colin M Baxter Marine Artist

Telephone: +44 (0)2392 525014

Email: colinmbaxter@hotmail.co.uk

Website: www.colinmbaxter.co.uk

Printed in Great Britain
by Amazon

29593833R00219